Time Shall Reap

Time Shall Reap

by

Doris Davidson

BIRLINN

This edition published in 2007 by
Birlinn Limited
West Newington House
10 Newington Road
Edinburgh EH9 1QS

www.birlinn.co.uk

ISBN13: 978 1 84158 598 7
ISBN10: 1 84158 598 X

Originally published in 1993 by HarperCollins *Publishers*

British Library Cataloguing-In-Publication Data
A Catalogue record for this book is available from the British Library

Typeset by Initial Typesetting Services, Edinburgh
Printed and bound by Creative Print and Design, Wales

To Doreen, who read this book chapter by chapter as it came off my typewriter in its original, raw state, and who read each revision with the same enthusiasm. She once remarked that it would be the happiest day in her life when she saw it in print . . . well, here it is!

My thanks also go to my daughter, Sheila, for her continued encouragement, and to Amy for the sustained interest she has shown in my writing.

Part One

Chapter One

November 1914

It was 'black as the Earl o' Hell's waistcoat' – a favourite expression of her father's which had conjured up terrifying images in her mind when she was younger, for it had been easy to imagine him on friendly terms with the devil – even the steadily-deepening snow reflected the darkness of the sky above. Elspeth Gray pulled her shawl up to cover her nose. She had been breathing through her mouth and the wool for some time, but facing the way she was now thick flakes were going up her nostrils and down the back of her throat, making it difficult to breathe at all. She should have listened to her mistress and set out before the storm was so bad, for she could see nothing in this raging blizzard, and she should have reached home long before this.

She concentrated all her strength on putting one foot past the other, but her seventeen-year-old brain was awash with morbid speculations. The dykes must be completely covered by now; what if she'd gone off the road altogether and was wandering round in circles? If she collapsed from exhaustion her body wouldn't be found until dawn, and maybe not even then, for it could be buried under a foot of snow. Nobody would see her until the thaw came, and by that time she would be frozen solid, her blood turned to ice.

Panic rising in her tight chest, she plodded on with her eyes closed and a prayer in her heart. *Dear God, please let me see the lights in the cottar houses soon.* She did not have much faith in the power of prayer and waited for only a short time before lifting her eyelids, but, miraculously, in the brief second before she was forced to lower them again, she saw a faint glow in the vast blackness. It was the very first time one of her prayers had been answered, but God must have known it was the most desperate she had ever put up, and she would never complain again about having to go to church every Sunday.

But why was there only one light? There were four cottages provided for the married farm servants at Mains of Denseat, built in a little row at right angles to the road. Shielding her eyes with one hand, she peered steadily ahead, and was dismayed to see that the glimmer of light was closer now, swaying from side to side. It wasn't a house at all, it was somebody carrying a storm lantern. At first, she felt bitterly disillusioned that God could dash her hopes so callously, then her heart began to thump with fear of this unseen man, but in the next instant she chided herself for being silly. Whoever he was, she should be glad that she wasn't the only person in Auchlonie to be out in the storm.

Relieved, she bent her head and took a deep breath before making another effort to carry on, but glanced up cautiously every few seconds. The gap between her and the bearer of the lantern was narrowing slowly, and when she judged that she was within hearing distance, she called out, 'Excuse me, can you tell me . . . ?' Her words seemed to be blown away as soon as they left her mouth, and she broke off with the intention of trying again in a minute or so, but

4

the lantern was held up, and a deep, startled voice exclaimed, 'God Almighty! Elspeth Gray! What in God's name took you out on a night like this?'

Unable to see his face, she had no idea who he was, but he knew her name and she responded to his concern. 'I'm coming home from my work, but I think I'm lost.'

'You're past your house, I can tell you that, but I'll see you back.' Her elbow was fixed in a vice-like grip, and she was turned round and propelled along at such speed that she stumbled and would have fallen if the man had not put his arm round her to steady her as she held her side and gasped for breath. 'I'm sorry, Elspeth. I was going some fast for a wee slip o' a thing like you.' The wind abating suddenly, he lowered his voice. 'I've seen you wi' your mother an' father in the kirk, that's how I ken't who you were. I'm John Forrest, in case you were wondering.'

Now she understood. 'I've seen you in the kirk, and all,' she said, shyly, her heart beating madly, and not just from exertion. She could have added that she had often dreamed about him at night, like all the other single females in the district – and maybe some who were not single – for he was a handsome young man, but she hadn't seen him in the kirk for some time and wondered if he had been away.

Without the force of the wind at their backs, they walked on at an easier pace, but John kept his arm around her, and in only a few minutes, he said, 'Here's your house, lass.'

She looked round somewhat sadly, and could just make out, in the flickering glow from the lantern, the low wooden gate poking through the snow like the first tips of the daffodils in spring.

'You haven't much to say for yourself, have you, Elspeth?'

She knew that he was teasing her, and searched desperately for some means of keeping him with her for a little longer, but she lacked the experience to make a light-hearted reply. 'Will you not come in for a heat at the fire?' she said, at last, in desperation. 'You've a good bit to go yet, and you must be soaking.' The invitation was apologetic, for she was apprehensive of his reaction to such unmaidenly behaviour. It wasn't seemly for a young girl to ask a man to her house unless he had declared serious intentions, and they had only just met properly for the first time. Would he be disgusted?

But John Forrest showed no disgust, and scrabbled with his hands until he could find the latch, pushing the virgin snow into a wall behind the gate as he opened it. Striding to put her boots in his footprints on the path, she wondered what her mother would say about her taking a young man home with her. Thank goodness her father wouldn't be in, for he would show his anger, no matter who was there.

A pot of soup was on the hob, the fire was glowing in the range, but otherwise the kitchen was in darkness, and there was no sign of her mother. Elspeth pumped up the Tilley lamp on the table and lit it with a taper, then turned round to face the tall stranger, for he was a stranger to her, though she knew that half the girls in the village had set their caps at him at one time or other. As far as she knew, though, he had never shown interest in any of them, for all the pairings in and around the village of Auchlonie were discussed in the workroom, and his name had never once been coupled with anybody else's.

6

Having blown out his lantern, he set it on the table and turned to heat his hands at the fire, but, sensing that she was looking at him, he swivelled round and raised his eyebrows, waiting for her to speak.

'Sit you down,' she whispered, pointing to her father's wide high-backed chair.

He looked ruefully at his dripping clothes, reluctant to sit in case he soiled the cushions.

'You could take off your coat for a while.' Perplexed as to where her mother could be, she scarcely dared to look at him as she said it. It was bad enough bringing him in with her in the first place, but it was a thousand times worse when the house was empty.

Taking off his lugged bonnet and his long greatcoat, he spread them over the fender in front of the fire then straightened up, and because she had not known he was a soldier, the stretch of bare knees between his kilt and his long socks came as a surprise to her. 'I'll help you off wi' your boots, lass,' he said, pushing her gently into her mother's chair.

He knelt on the floor to lift her sodden skirts before he untied her laces, and she had to brace herself against the back of the chair when he pulled off her boots and set them inside the fender. Then, taking one of her stockinged feet in his hands, he massaged it until her numb toes tingled and she wiggled them to let him know that the feeling had come back to them. She had a strong urge to stroke his dark bowed head, or to bury her face in his dark curls, and was shocked at herself for even thinking such things.

He kept hold of her second ankle, looking up now with his serious brown eyes, so serious that she dropped hers in some confusion.

7

'How old are you, Elspeth? I'm twenty.'

'I'm going on eighteen.' She was not long seventeen, but what were a few months back and fore? 'I work for Miss Fraser, the dressmaker.'

'I used to work for my father, but I was just an ordinary farm-servant like the rest, and . . . here, you're shivering, lass.'

'I'm fine,' she said, firmly, knowing that her trembling was not a result of the cold. She had never been so close to any man other than her father, and it was the nearness of John Forrest's muscular body and the manly smell of him that was making the butterflies flutter in her stomach and the shivers race up and down her spine.

'I wanted to see a bit of the world,' he continued, 'not just this wee corner of Aberdeenshire, and I was all set to go to Canada last year, but my father refused to sign the papers. I meant to go next February, as soon as I was twenty-one and could sign for myself, but the war started, and I was in the Terriers, so . . .'

'The terriers?'

'The Territorials of the Gordon Highlanders, and I'll not be able to go till we lick the Huns. We've been training in Perth since the beginning of August but we're being sent to France when I go back.'

A tight band squeezed Elspeth's chest. Was she to lose him so soon, the first man who had ever put an arm round her and made her feel like a woman? 'Will your mother not be wondering where you've got to?' she murmured.

This made him laugh. 'She knows I can look after myself. It was her that sent me to the Mains to ask if they'd sell her some eggs, for her hens have gone off laying, but they'd none to spare. That was at dinnertime, and the storm was just starting when I got there, so they made me wait to see if it eased a bit. Well, I waited for hours but there was no sign of it stopping, but the cook wouldn't let me come away till she gave me something to eat.'

'Your mother'll be worried about you if you've been away that long. You'd have been better to come right back.'

'Och, she'll guess what's happened, and she's not the kind to try to smother me wi' mother love. She wasn't against me going to Canada, for she said I'd be better to try my wings a bit, but my father wants me to carry on Blairton after him, me being the only son.'

'I can't understand why you wanted to leave when your life was planned out for you.'

John pulled a face. 'I wanted to plan my own life, and I'm determined to go some day. I want some excitement before I'm too old to enjoy it, and besides, it would be a good thing to learn how the farmers over there manage their land. If things don't work out, I can always come back.'

'I've heard stories about men going to Canada and not finding any work. They've no money to pay their fares home, and they end up down and out.'

His laugh was hearty. 'Folk are aye ready to tell stories, whether they're true or not. Can you see me ending up down and out?'

Shuddering, she switched her mind away from the awful picture he had evoked. 'I wonder where my mother can be?'

'She's maybe in wi' one o' your neighbours.' John stroked her ankle idly, making her draw in her breath as her pulse raced and his eyes danced with impish devilment. 'Are you feared at being here on your own with me?'

'Oh, no!' She was feared he would leave if he thought she was so childish. 'It's not like her, she's aye here.'

'Has a lad ever kissed you, Elspeth Gray?'

The suddenness, and directness, of the question startled her, but she answered honestly. 'I've never been out wi' a lad.' What could she say if he asked if he could kiss her? Worse, what would she do if he kissed her without asking?

'Your mouth's just waiting to be kissed,' he said, softly. 'Like a flower ready to bloom.'

When his fingers brushed her lips, she turned away, not knowing how to cope with the emotions he had aroused, and only then saw the paper propped up against the glass of the grandfather clock. As she jumped to her feet, she knocked John off balance and laughed as he sprawled on the rag rug.

Unfolding the note, she read it aloud. '"Dear Eppie",' she began, then stopped to explain. 'That's what my mother calls me. "I got word this morning that your Auntie Janet is ill again, so I am away to catch the ten to two train to Aberdeen and I will try to come home tomorrow. See your father gets some broth when he comes in at nine, and steep the meal all night for his porridge in the morning, for he does not like lumps in it. Your loving mother."' Elspeth laid the sheet of paper on the table. 'My Auntie Janet's aye got something wrong wi' her.'

'Your father's not to be in till nine?' The words came thoughtfully from the floor. 'That's near two hours yet.'

Elspeth's heartbeats quickened even more, but she tried to postpone his departure in case she was reading more into his remark than he intended. 'Will you have a cup o' tea to heat you up before you take the road again?'

'I'm needing no tea to heat me up, as well you ken.' His lips were smiling, but his eyes seemed to be boring right into her soul as he took her hand and pulled her down beside him.

Carried away by the wonderful feelings within her, she said nothing as he removed the pins from her hair, and when the long wavy tresses cascaded to her waist in ripples, he touched them reverently and breathed, 'It's as soft as silk. Spun gold silk.'

She held her face up quite naturally, but, as she savoured her first kiss, gentle and tender, his lips suddenly became demanding. 'You're so bonnie, Elspeth,' he groaned, 'enough to set a man's body on fire.'

Her own body had also been set on fire, and she responded passionately, but he drew away from her suddenly. 'Oh, it's more than I can bear, lass.'

Certain that her heart would burst from her ribcage in her frustration, she pulled his head down and kissed him with an abandonment which astonished them both.

'Oh, God! Elspeth, Elspeth.'

His husky, throbbing voice stilled any doubts she may have had as his hands fumbled with the buttons on her blouse and bodice, and shafts of sheer, shivering delight sped swiftly downwards when his icy fingers uncovered her skin. Silently, she willed him to keep fondling her, quite unaware that her body was telling him exactly how she felt.

When his hands moved urgently lower, she murmured, weakly, 'No, John,' but his mouth stopped her feeble protest and she gave herself up to her turbulent emotions,

11

until, when she thought that her heart must explode altogether, there came an ecstasy she had never imagined – wilder, more satisfying than anything that had gone before. Wilder even than the storm outside.

Elspeth had often felt cheated when, just at the crucial moment, the writers of the cheap novelettes she read put a row of asterisks instead of describing what was taking place, but now she understood. There were no words to describe to anyone who had never experienced it the unadulterated bliss of being served by a man.

As if doused by cold water, her thoughts came to an abrupt halt. Served? As the bull at Denseat served the cows? No, no! It wasn't the same at all! She loved John, and he loved her, for a man didn't do. . . that to a girl if he didn't love her. A coldness in her nether regions made her realise that her clothing was in shameful disarray, and she sat up, most embarrassed, to cover herself.

John's eyes were studying her from under his dark lashes, and he gave a soft laugh. 'You're a funny wee thing, do you ken that, Elspeth?'

Alarmed, she asked, 'What d'you mean?' Surely he wasn't comparing her with some other girl?

'There's nothing wrong wi' me seeing you like that.'

She couldn't think of anything to say which wouldn't sound prudish or childish, and wriggled out of his encircling arm, fastening her buttons as he sat up with a sigh.

'Aye, maybe you're right, for I've done more than I should already.'

She was relieved when he turned away and glanced round the room – he would find nothing wanting though he compared this homely kitchen with the one at Blairton

12

– but she was glad when his eyes came to rest on the tall grandfather, standing sentry at the side of the fire. 'That's a fine clock.'

This pleased her even more. It was the pride of the Gray household, and looked magnificently beautiful tonight, she thought, the Spanish mahogany reflecting the glowing coals in the range. 'My father bought it as a wedding present for my mother at a sale in Findhavon House when Lord Hay died, and he got their initials engraved on the pendulum. He must have been real romantic when he was young, though it's hard to believe when you look at him now.'

Jumping up, she opened the door in the long case to show him the brass disc, and he hoisted himself round on to his knees to make out the letters as they swung from side to side. 'GG – EW. That would be George Gray and . . . ?'

'Elizabeth Watt, that was my mother's single name.'

'Aye, right enough, that was real romantic.' He glanced idly up at the clock face. 'My God! It's half after eight.'

Clambering to his feet, he lifted his steaming bonnet and coat from the fenderstool and put them on, then held a lighted taper to the wick in the lantern. 'Your father would have a fit if he came in and found me here,' he laughed, walking to the door.

Standing with him in the tiny porch, Elspeth wished that he didn't have to go, but his last kiss made her heart sing with joy again, and she went inside happily to pin up her hair and to wash before her father came home. In the cold, corrugated iron lean – to which her mother referred to as the 'back kitchen' – it had been erected a few years previously so that a sink with running water could be installed – her blood cooled down quickly, and she was sitting by the fire again, outwardly calm but inwardly reliving every moment of her time with John, when she heard her father at the porch and stood up to ladle out his soup, her hands trembling.

Geordie Gray removed the snow from his boots by thumping his feet on the stone step before coming into the room, a huge white figure. Taking off his coat and bonnet, he looked around him, his eyes widening when he saw that his wife was not there. 'Where's your mother?'

'She'd to go to Aberdeen.' Elspeth pointed to the note still lying on the table, accompanied now by the large steaming bowl.

He grunted when he read it. 'Janet would have your mother running after her though it was only a sore head she'd got. She's aye been the same.'

He said nothing else until he finished his broth. 'Well, lass, how did you fare coming home? I'd a bit o' a struggle, just the wee bit I'd to come.'

Elspeth thought it would be best to tell him at least part of the truth. 'I went past our house without seeing it, and I'd have been lost if I hadna met John Forrest. He made sure I got back here.'

Geordie's brows shot down, his piercing blue eyes full of suspicion as he said sharply, 'And since when did you ken John Forrest? You've never let on that you ken't him before.'

'I didna, but he told me who he was.'

'You should ken better than speak to a man you've never been introduced to.'

Her heart sinking, Elspeth tried to defend herself. 'I thought I was lost . . . I thought I'd perish in the snow if I'd to keep on wandering about . . .'

14

'Perish? Havers! You've two sturdy legs, so what made you think you would perish?'

'I was getting awful tired, and when I saw the lantern, I just asked if . . .'

'You spoke when you didna ken who the man was?'

'I . . . I didna think, Father, I was that worried.'

'So I've raised a weakling,' Geordie growled. 'A lassie that can't even find her way home without asking a strange man to help her.'

'John Forrest's not a strange man.'

'He was a strange man to you . . . or so you said.' He eyed her with renewed suspicion.

'I didna ken him, truly I didna.'

'If I ever find out you've been lying to me, Elspeth, I'll leather your backside till you'll not be able to sit down for a week.'

Flustered, she turned away and concentrated on breaking up the coals with the heavy poker, so that the guilty scarlet of her cheeks could be attributed to the heat, and when she looked round again, her father had lifted the big family bible from the dresser and taken it over to the table. When he bent his head to read his daily passage, she took the opportunity to study him. Nearing fifty, he had the erect bearing of a far younger man; his white hair – she couldn't remember it being anything else so he must have turned white when he was quite young – was wiry and unruly; his lined face and rough hands were weatherbeaten from years of working out of doors.

At ten o'clock, Geordie stood up. 'It's time we were housed up, so get to your bed now. I'll bank the fire wi' dross before I come up.'

She rose obediently. 'Goodnight, Father, and I'm sorry for making you angry.'

He nodded gravely. 'Aye, and you'd best ask God to forgive you, and all.'

Climbing the narrow stairs, Elspeth wondered what he would have said if she had told him everything, for, as far as she was concerned, her father's wrath was even worse than God's.

Chapter Two

At five o'clock the following morning, Elspeth was awakened by the sound of Geordie Gray clearing snow from the door before he set off for the farm, but she lay on for nearly another hour, remembering how she had dreamt of John Forrest's kisses, of his gentle caresses, of his growing passion . . . and hers. At last, ashamed of her dreams and of her own part in what had happened the night before, she flung back the blankets and got out of bed. The bedroom was ice-cold, so she did not linger over dressing, and went down to cook the porridge for her father. The coarse oatmeal was soft after soaking in the pot all night, so he would have no complaints about lumps when he returned for breakfast at half past seven.

Having to stir the grey mass until it came to the boil, she gave herself up to daydreams. Would John want to court her? If only he would, it would be all she would ever want, and she was practically certain that he loved her. Not that he had said it, but he hadn't needed to. What he had done was proof enough for her. She did not know how long he would be at home, but surely it would be long enough to let them get to know each other properly, to avow their love, to make plans for the future. She could just imagine herself keeping their little house clean and tidy, laundering his clothes, cooking for him . . . making porridge as she waited for him to come down to kiss her good morning after a heavenly night of passion. He would take her in his arms for so long that she would forget what she was supposed to be doing, and it would be John who noticed that the pot was boiling . . . the pot! The lovely pretence evaporated in a flash as she jerked the fiercely bubbling pot off the fire and laid it on the hob. Thank goodness she had noticed it in time; her father would go mad if his breakfast had the least taste of singeing.

The kettle also having come to the boil, she took it into the back kitchen and gave herself a wash. Then she filled it again and put it on the hob, moving the porridge pot farther away from the heat, for it only needed to be kept warm now. At last she was ready to set off for work, a little earlier than usual in case there were drifts. It was still dark, but her father had cleared a passage from the porch to the gate, and much of the snow had been blown off the road into the fields overnight, and what was left was crisp now and easy to walk on.

Early as Elspeth was, Nettie Duffus and Kirsty Tough were in the little anteroom behind the workroom when she arrived, hanging their heavy coats and shawls on the hooks provided by their employer, Miss Fraser.

'What a storm last night.' Kirsty lived just along from the shop and couldn't really have known how bad it was.

'How did you manage home, Elspeth?' Nettie asked.

'It took me a long time,' Elspeth admitted, 'and I'd went right past our house without seeing it. I thought I was lost, but I met John Forrest and he saw me home.' As she had hoped, the other two girls pricked up their ears at this, and wee Kirsty, only fourteen, listened with open curiosity when Nettie, a year older, plied Elspeth with questions. 'John Forrest? What's he like? What did he say? Did he ask to see you again?'

Elspeth blushed. 'He's awful nice, and I asked him in.'

Kirsty's large brown eyes widened, and Nettie's breath was so taken away that it was a few seconds before she said, 'What did your mother say about that?'

'She wasna there, and my father wasna back from seeing to the beasts.' Elspeth savoured their shocked wonder to the utmost.

Nettie was first to recover. 'Elspeth Gray! You were never in the house wi' him on your own? Did anything happen?'

Fortunately for Elspeth, Miss Fraser put her head round the door at that moment. 'Stop chattering, girls. It's turned half past seven and there's work waiting to be done.'

In the workroom, three box-topped treadle sewing machines stood against one wall, and two long benches in the centre of the floor. Elspeth was now trusted with some cutting, she and Nettie carried out all the machining, while Kirsty, as well as basting for them, had been learning how to sew buttonholes and invisible hems. Grace Fraser herself added braid or frogging to the heavier costumes after they were assembled. She was a strict taskmistress, but her young assistants accepted any reprimands from her in the same way as they accepted the low wages and long hours – with gratitude for being taught their trade by such an excellent needlewoman. Only when their employer was closeted with a material salesman, or a valued customer, did the girls talk in whispers, discussing the plots of the cheap

19

love stories Nettie got from her older sister, or turning over the gossip of the area.

As soon as she could, Nettie returned to the attack. 'I'm near sure somebody tell't me John Forrest was in the Gordons, but maybe it wasna him. Did anything happen, Elspeth?'

'He's home on embroc . . . embarkation leave, for he's being sent to France, and he's going to Canada when the war's finished.'

Nettie was obviously disappointed. If he was intending to go away, there was little chance of him allowing himself to become serious about Elspeth or anyone else, but that didn't mean that he hadn't tried something when he was presented with such an opportunity. 'Did he not even kiss you?'

Flushing deeply, Elspeth kept her head down.

'Aye, I can see he did.' Nettie was triumphant. 'You wouldna have went all hot and bothered like that if he hadna.'

'All right, then, he did kiss me, and . . .'

'Was it like it was in the *Awakening of Emma*?' Nettie interrupted eagerly, referring to a romance they had all read recently. 'Did you get shivers up your back and the shakes in your legs?'

'Aye, and my stomach was going round and round and all, but . . .' Elspeth broke off, then said, earnestly, 'Oh, I can't describe it, it was that exciting, but I think he loves me . . . and I ken I love him.'

Young Kirsty, who had been drinking everything in, shocked them suddenly by saying, 'Did he seduce you, Elspeth, and take you against your will?'

Nettie gasped, and Elspeth's cheeks flamed guiltily but

Miss Fraser's appearance saved her from having to reply.

'Your face is as red as a beetroot, Elspeth. What's wrong with you?'

'I've been coughing a bit, Miss Fraser.' She was conscious of the suppressed mirth of the other two girls, but they had their heads down, seemingly engrossed in their work.

It was almost an hour before Nettie had the chance to press Elspeth for an answer to Kirsty's question. 'Well, did he?'

Elspeth didn't pretend not to know what Nettie meant. 'No, he didna,' she said, trying to sound as indignant as she could.

'Was you disappointed?'

'Och, Nettie, that kind o' thing just happens in stories.'

'It doesna just happen in stories. Our Aggie said she'd to fight her Chae off the very first time she went out wi' him.' Nettie's eyes danced as she added, 'She must have stopped fighting him off damn quick, though.'

Knowing that Nettie's sister, married three months before, was already six months pregnant, they dissolved into fits of muffled laughter. They had learned the facts of life early, from what they heard passing between the women of the village, and from watching the animals on the farms.

At mid-day, they sat round the fireguard in the anteroom to sup the hot soup they carried with them in flagons which had been left sitting at the fire. Conversation at this time was rather limited, however, because Miss Fraser sat with them. 'You got home all right last night, then, Elspeth?'

'Yes, Miss Fraser.' Elspeth kicked Nettie's foot under the chair in retaliation for an elbowed nudge.

21

'That's good. I was quite worried about you having to walk so far in that dreadful blizzard, and I was glad that your brother came for you, Nettie, not that you'd so far to go. Of course, you're only a door or two along, Kirsty,' Miss Fraser went on, to show that there was no favouritism, 'so I suppose you got home safely, as well?'

Kirsty, always tongue-tied when their mistress spoke to her, nodded her head so vigorously that her soft, dark hair escaped from its restraining ribbon and the woman tutted impatiently. 'You can't see with that mop over your eyes, get Nettie to tie it back properly for you.'

Only the clatter of the sewing machines and the thump of the goose iron broke the silence of the afternoon, and Elspeth allowed herself to return to the daydream of a torrid romance with John Forrest; a romance which, if it ever did transpire – there was her father to reckon with – would be short-lived if he carried out his plan to emigrate after the war.

At six o'clock, the girls put the lids on the machines and swept up the threads and clippings that littered the floor, so it was almost twenty past before they went outside, where the darkness of the village street was illuminated somewhat eerily by a scattering of gas lamps. The two younger girls walked off in the opposite direction, and Elspeth turned to make her way home alone, thankful that it wasn't snowing. It was still very windy, however, and, bending her head against the biting cold which stung her cheeks, she jumped nervously when a voice spoke close beside her.

'Are you not going to speak to me?'

'Oh! Hello, John.' She had been afraid that he might think she was a trollop, as her father described any woman with loose morals, and was pleased that he still wanted to see her. She was also glad that the dim light hid her blushes.

He tucked her arm through his when they left street and gas lamps behind, and they made their laboured way along the ice-rutted road towards the Denseat cottar houses. She felt rather uncomfortable that he had said nothing more, but guessed, quite correctly, that he was just as embarrassed as she was, and was relieved when he stopped walking and turned towards her. 'There's a dance in the Masonic Hall tomorrow night . . . eh . . . would you like to come wi' me?'

'My father wouldna let me.' She could foresee the trouble there would be if she as much as mentioned it.

'I'll wait outside when you get home till you let me ken what he says. You're old enough to go dancing.'

She was old enough, she thought sadly, but John didn't understand how strict her father was, and he wouldn't approve of dancing, she was sure. When she went into the house, she found that Geordie wasn't yet home – she hadn't been able to think clearly about that – but her mother was sitting by the fire, cutting off the tail of one of his flannel shirts to make a new collar. 'Mother, would Father let me go to the dance tomorrow night? John Forrest's asked me to go wi' him.'

Lizzie Gray was taken aback by the request, and the name of her daughter's intended escort completely disconcerted her. 'John Forrest? How do you ken him?'

'He's waiting outside for me to tell him.'

'He's not standing out there in the cold?' Lizzie's kind heart forced her to add, 'You'd best ask him in.' Bundling up the mutilated shirt and pushing it behind the cushion at her back, she turned in time to greet the young man who was standing shyly just inside the door. 'Now, what's this about a dance?'

Holding his cap in both hands, John pleaded, 'Can Elspeth come wi' me to the Masonic Hall the morrow night, please?'

Lizzie had no idea how Elspeth came to be on such friendly terms with John Forrest, but he came of a respected family and they were obviously very attracted to each other, so her sense of romance overrode her anxiety for her daughter. 'You'll see she gets home safe?'

'Oh, aye. She'll come to no harm wi' me, I promise you.'

'She'd better not.' Lizzie smiled to take the sting out of the words. 'I'll get your father to agree, Elspeth.'

The girl's anxious face cleared. 'He kens John helped me to get home last night, for the storm was that bad I was lost.' She conveniently overlooked Geordie's reaction to John's good deed.

'Is that right?' This information astonished Lizzie even more, but she turned gratefully to the boy. 'It was awful good o' you, John, and I'd like you to come to supper one night, for I'm sure Elspeth's father would like to thank you as well . . . that is, if you want to come?'

'I'll be pleased to come, pleased and honoured.'

His manners impressed and warmed Lizzie. 'You'd best come on Saturday, then, when Geordie's not so late in finishing.'

'Thank you, I'll look forward to that, but I'll have to get home now. Goodnight, Mistress Gray.'

'Goodnight, John, and thank you again for taking care o' Elspeth last night.'

The boy and girl looked at each other, a fresh awareness springing up between them at the memory of just how well he had taken care of her the previous evening. In the porch, he gripped her hand briefly before walking rather jauntily down the cleared path and disappearing into the darkness, leaving Elspeth wishing that he had at least kissed her.

'I hope Father lets me go,' she said, when she went inside. 'He aye says dancing's the "devil's instrument for loose living".'

Lizzie shook her head in mock disapproval of her daughter's imitation of Geordie's gruff voice and scowling face. 'He didn't aye think that, lass.' Putting her hand up to the bun at the nape of her neck, she tucked in some stray wisps of hair, still almost as golden as Elspeth's. 'But tell me, how did you come to meet John Forrest last night?'

Omitting the incident on the hearthrug, Elspeth told her, then remembered the reason for her mother's absence. 'How's Auntie Janet?'

'She's a good bit better. She's never been right since her second miscarriage, and that's coming up for nineteen year ago.' Lizzie pursed her mouth suddenly. 'Mind you, I have my doubts sometimes about her bad turns. I wouldna put it past Janet to put it on a bit.'

'It's Uncle Harry I'm sorry for.' Remembering her aunt's sour, pinched face, Elspeth couldn't help wondering what Harry Bain had ever seen in her. 'He's had to put up wi' an awful lot.'

Lizzie retrieved Geordie's shirt from its hiding place, and laid the dismembered tail over the frayed collar. 'She doesna realise how lucky she is, for he does near every blessed thing for her.'

'I hope Father doesna put his foot down about me going to the dance.' Elspeth's mind had returned to John Forrest's invitation, the most exciting thing that had happened to her in her whole life – apart from. . . but she dared not think of that now. 'He was angry at me for speaking to John when I'd never been introduced to him.'

'I'll make him see sense.' Lizzie's scissors were busy again. 'You're seventeen, and he's kept you a bairn long enough. It's time you got out to enjoy yourself.' She was not quite as confident as she sounded, because Geordie was an immovable force once he made his mind up about anything, but surely he wouldn't stop his daughter from being friends with the son of the most influential farmer in the area.

She said nothing about it to her husband when he came in, but answered his questions about her sister then sat back until he had finished his supper. She knew that he did not like her to talk to him while he was eating, and she did not mean to jeopardise her daughter's chances of going to the dance by aggravating him.

When Geordie pushed his plate away and rose to get the bible, Elspeth decided that it might be better if she went to bed, so that her parents could discuss the situation in private. Lizzie cleared the table and washed the dishes, to give her husband time to read his passage, then sat down at the opposite side of the fire, trying to work out the best way to go about her mission. She was thankful, therefore, when he remarked, 'Did Elspeth tell you she let young Forrest see her home last night?'

'Aye, she did. It's a good thing she met him.'

There was a short silence before he said, thoughtfully, 'I wasna that happy about it, she'd no business to be speaking to somebody she didna ken.'

'She kens who the Forrests are,' Lizzie pointed out, 'and John's a real nice laddie.'

'He's going to France in a wee while, I believe?' Geordie had made a few discreet enquiries of his fellow workers and had been relieved to learn this. It meant that nothing could come of any liaison between the boy and Elspeth.

'He met her outside her work tonight,' Lizzie said, a trifle uncertainly, 'and he's asked her to the dance the morrow. Now, don't you go and spoil it for her,' she burst out, as her husband scowled. 'She's not your little bairn any longer, and she needs to get out. I've said she could.'

'So you've got it all cut and dried?' Geordie observed, sarcastically. 'A man's not the master in his own home these days, it seems.'

'Och, Geordie,' Lizzie coaxed, encouraged that he had not lost his temper, 'you can't keep her at home all her life. Like I said, John Forrest's a real nice laddie, and you'll be able to judge for yourself on Saturday, for I've asked him to come for his supper.' She hesitated, then went on, 'Can I tell her you'll let her go to the dance, then?'

'If I say no,' he sighed, 'I'll likely have two weeping women on my hands, so I'd better say yes. I suppose it's time I let her off the leash, but tell her she'll have to be home by midnight.'

Smiling broadly, Lizzie rose to her feet. 'I'll go up and tell her right now, and I'll not bother coming down again.'

When her mother came into her room, Elspeth could tell that the battle had been won, but she was disappointed

27

when she heard the condition which had been set. She knew that the dances in the village usually went on until one o'clock or later, but she also knew that it would be very foolish to disagree with her father – he might change his mind about letting her go.

Guessing shrewdly what was going through the girl's mind, Lizzie murmured, 'Midnight's late enough, lass, especially when you've your work to go to the next day. Goodnight now, and don't lie wakened all night thinking about it, for you'll not want John Forrest to see you looking washed out.'

'Goodnight, Mother, and thank you.'

Elspeth was far too excited to sleep and lay awake for some time thinking about John and wishing that it was time to go to the dance.

Chapter Three

'What'll I wear the night, Mother, seeing I haven't got a frock?' Helping her mother to clear the breakfast table, Elspeth could think of only one thing.

'Och, your Sunday blouse and skirt'll do fine. I'll give them a run over wi' the iron, and you can buy a bonnie bit of ribbon for your hair when you're at the workroom the day. I'm sure he'll not worry what you're wearing, any road. Hurry now, or you'll be late for your work.'

The dressmaker's shop was very busy that Thursday. Several of the village girls wanted quick alterations done to what they were wearing that night, and wives from the farming community called to have their children's clothes let out or let down – even taken up and taken in, if they'd been handed down from older brothers or sisters – so Elspeth had no time to think.

During their half-hour break in the middle of the day, Miss Fraser having gone out, she asked Nettie and Kirsty to help her choose a piece of ribbon. They were excited, too, at the prospect of her rendezvous with John Forrest, but were inclined to pick colours they liked themselves – pinks and reds – which did nothing for her. Finally, after some rummaging in a box of remnants she had found at the back of a shelf, Kirsty produced a length of beautiful, deep blue satin ribbon. 'It's the same colour as your eyes, Elspeth,' she exclaimed, proud at having solved the problem.

Nettie took it from her and held it up to Elspeth's face. 'It's the exact same,' she pronounced, sighing enviously as she rolled it up again.

When their mistress returned, Elspeth asked her how much the ribbon cost, explaining that she wanted it to make a bow for her hair because she was going to her first dance.

'Your first dance?' The magic words conjured up a memory of a far-distant evening for Grace Fraser, and a servants' ball in Gordon Castle where she had once been a sewing-maid. She would never forget the thrill of it, but the young footman who had set her pulse racing when he kissed her, had been lost to the Boers just after the turn of the century and no other man she had ever met had measured up to what she remembered of him.

Sighing soulfully, she gathered her thoughts together. 'This ribbon's a remnant, and you can have it for nothing since it's your first dance.' Waving aside the girl's profuse thanks, she went on, 'I'll make it up for you. It'll not take long, but there's a real knack to it, you know.' With a few stitches strategically placed, she soon produced a professional floppy bow. 'It'll fix on with a hairpin, but see what it looks like in the mirror.'

The effect delighted Elspeth. The ribbon made her hair seem more golden and her eyes a deeper blue, and John must surely fall in love with her tonight, if he hadn't already done so. She could hardly bear to wait until half past seven.

30

Having run all the way home after the shop closed, Elspeth was so breathless that Lizzie shook her head in wry amusement. 'I won't have time for any supper,' the girl told her, 'for I want to wash my hair and have a sponge down.' She carried kettles of boiling water through to the back kitchen and when she had finished, she towelled her head vigorously and dried it at the fire. Then she gave her hair one hundred strokes with her brush and ran upstairs to change.

She was ready early, the wide blue ribbon pinned daintily at the back of her head, her shining hair bearing evidence of the attention bestowed on it. Regarding the bright eyes glowing with happiness, Lizzie had to swallow the lump which had come up in her throat – her daughter was too young and vulnerable to be going out with a young man. Her fears were stifled when she opened the door to John, his curls plastered down with water and his head held stiffly in embarrassment. Although he was wearing the uniform of a soldier, he was still only a boy, she reflected, and there was no need to worry about them.

'Good evening, Mistress Gray.' His mouth lifted nervously at the corners, but his eyes were seeking Elspeth's.

Smiling shyly, she said, 'I've to be home by midnight.'

'That's fine wi' me.' He would have agreed to anything as he held up her coat.

'Put your shawl round your head, Eppie.'

Elspeth did as her mother told her, taking care not to crush the cherished bow, and once they were outside, John drew her arm through his. 'I'm sorry we'll have to come away so early,' she remarked ruefully. 'I hope it doesna spoil things for you.'

31

'I'll be happy having a few hours with you.' He pulled her round and kissed her with lips icy from the frost, then hurried her on towards the village.

The dance was well under way when they entered the Masonic Hall, two fiddles and an accordion making the rafters echo with the lively strains of an eightsome reel. Open-mouthed, Elspeth looked at the whirling, skirling figures in the centre of the circles, and her face fell in the next minute when she saw the intricate pattern the participants in each set were weaving through each other.

'Oh, John, I don't know the steps for any o' the dances,' she whispered, somewhat tearfully. Not having given a thought to this before, she turned stricken eyes to him, expecting him to be angry, and was quite put out to find him laughing at her.

'I haven't done much dancing myself, so we'll pick it up together. We'd best take off our coats first, though, before we start.' Leading her into a side room to hang up their outdoor garments, he made her sit down while he removed her boots and helped her to fasten on the strapped shoes she had been carrying in a bag, and when she stood up he said, 'Your ribbon matches the blue of your eyes.'

Pleased that he had noticed, she felt more at ease, and when they entered the main hall again, she was relieved to see that most of the girls were wearing skirts and blouses too. She was thankful that her mother had been a laundry maid during her days in service, and had set the ruffles at the neck of her blouse with the goffering iron, for it looked as good as new, which was more than could be said for some of the others.

John was not the only soldier, she discovered. Several kilts were flaring out as the young men swung their partners round over-enthusiastically, the girls screeching with delight, or perhaps with the fear of being swung off their feet altogether? When the music stopped and changed to a more sedate rhythm, she placed her hand trustingly in John's and they moved on to the slippery floor to try their steps in a Scottish waltz.

'It's just one two three, one two three,' he told her.

A few of the girls simpered at John coyly, and Elspeth felt a surge of pride at being his partner, and, with his guidance, she soon stopped having to count in her head. She had a pang of jealousy when he took Tibby Leslie as his second partner for the Dashing White Sergeant, though the girl was the daughter of one of Blairton's men, but Tibby kept them right until they learned what to do, and Elspeth enjoyed this dance as much as the waltz. The workings of the Strip the Willow took her more time to fathom, and her arm was chafed from rubbing against the men's rough jackets as they whirled her round, but it was good fun.

During the interval, John led her over to the long trestle tables where refreshments were being served – porter for the men and home-made lemonade for the ladies – and she accepted a tall glass thankfully, after the exertion of the past ten minutes. As they stood, John was approached by several young Gordon Highlanders, and, during the ensuing talk, Elspeth gathered that he was as proud of her as she was of him.

One gangling boy with spindly legs which weren't enhanced by the kilt, gave him a playful poke in the ribs. 'I see you've got yourself a lass, John?'

He grinned. 'Looks like it, Donald.'

A second youth, with prominent teeth and a long, thin nose, said, 'You fair ken how to pick 'em.'

John slipped his arm round Elspeth's shoulders. 'Oh, aye, Willie, only the best's good enough for me.'

Elspeth, pleased at what he was saying, felt ill at ease at being the centre of their discussion, and looked away when the third soldier glanced at her questioningly. 'I havena seen you here before?'

'This is Elspeth Gray, Alex. Her father's grieve at Mains o' Denseat.'

'Big Geordie Gray?' Donald remarked. 'I heard he kept his lassie under lock and key.'

John grinned wickedly. 'I must have the key then, lads, and I'm real pleased he saved her for me.'

'Oh, aye?' Willie exchanged knowing glances with the other two soldiers. 'It's serious, is it, John?'

Thumping John on the back, Donald said, 'When's the wedding, lad? We'll be looking for an invite.'

The butt of their teasing joined in the laughter for a few minutes, then led the girl over to the chairs which were placed around the room. 'I'm sorry about that, Elspeth, but we're all leaving on Sunday forenoon for France, and we're not looking forward to it. It was just a bit o' fun for them, for you're the first lass I've asked out.'

'It's all right, John.' Although it had embarrassed her, she had enjoyed the banter as much as any of them, and knew there had been nothing spiteful in their remarks. What had pleased her most was hearing John openly declaring that she was his lass, leaving her in no doubt that he loved her.

He hesitated, nervously studying his nails. 'Mind, they're right about it being serious. I never met a lass like you before, Elspeth, and I'm real sorry for what I did on Tuesday. I hope you didna think I was just a coarse beast?'

As she shook her head in denial, he blurted out, 'No, I'm not sorry! I couldna help myself, for I was wanting you more than I ever wanted anything in my whole life, and you're as good as my wife now, so we'll need to make it legal as soon as we can.' Tilting her head up with his hand, he raised his eyebrows. 'What do you say?'

Her eyes were shining, but she could not find the words to say what she felt, and he gave a short laugh as the band struck up again. 'I have to ken, lass, and we can't speak here. We'll have to go into the passage.'

She felt bewildered as he led her through the dancers, but as soon as they were in the corridor, he said, earnestly, 'I've been thinking, you see, and I've no notion now for leaving Blairton when the war's over. I love you, Elspeth, and I want to wed you when I come home the next time, and we'll settle down here when I'm back for good. Tell me you feel the same.'

'Oh, aye, John,' she breathed, her throat constricted with love, but there were other things to consider. 'What'll your folk say?'

'They'll have to like it or lump it. I'll not change my mind, for you're the only lass I'll ever want. I'll speak to your father on Saturday, and he'll surely not refuse when he sees how much we love each other. You do love me, Elspeth?'

'Oh, aye, John. I love you wi' my whole heart.'

About to kiss her, he drew back as someone came out of the hall. 'We'd best go back to the dancing for we'll get no peace here, an' we've the rest o' our lives in front o' us.'

The remainder of the evening was a pleasant blur to Elspeth, and the hectic reels and strathspeys left neither of them any breath to talk, but mindful of Geordie's stipulation, they left the hall at twenty minutes to twelve and made their way towards her home, laughingly recalling their first, rather awkward, attempts at dancing.

They were more than halfway to their destination before John touched again on the subject of their future. 'I'm sure my father'll let us have one of his cottar houses. There's one been sitting empty since Bobby Brough went to bide wi' his son in Dundee, for the new man's single and bides in the bothy. I could maybe get the key before Saturday, and you could be cleaning the place out and getting it ready for me coming back. You're not saying anything, Elspeth, do you not like the idea?'

'You havena given me much chance to speak, and besides, I can hardly take it in, it's happened that quick.'

'We've the storm to thank for that, and fate must have meant for us to meet. I'm a great believer in fate.'

'So's my father,' Elspeth remarked. 'He aye says what's in front of you'll never go by you . . . oh!'

Her little exclamation went unnoticed by John, who went on eagerly, 'That's what I mean, so he'll understand.'

'No, John, he won't.' Elspeth hated to disillusion him, but she could not let him carry on thinking that her father would agree to their marriage. 'He'll say I'm not old enough to be any man's wife.'

'I'm quite prepared to wait for you, maybe another year? Would he agree then, do you think?'

'Oh, John, I don't know.' Elspeth couldn't stop the tears which spilled out suddenly. 'I don't want to wait at all . . . I love you and I want to marry you . . . but . . . I can't go against my father.'

He pulled her to him then. 'I'm not asking you to go against him, Elspeth. I'll wait for as long as it takes. He can't hold out for ever.'

'He could, you don't know what he's like.'

She had lifted her face to speak, and suddenly his arms tightened round her, his lips came down hard on hers, and she could taste the salt of her tears in her mouth, and was ashamed that John must taste them, too. He didn't seem to care, for, in spite of the cold, he kept on kissing her for a long time. When he stopped, he said, his voice thick, 'I don't think I can wait, Elspeth, do you know that? I love you too much. I'll ask him on Saturday, and if he says no, I'm taking you away with me. My mother'll look after you till I come back.'

Her tears, stopped for a while, began to flow again as he declared the depth of his love. 'He'll try to stop you,' she sobbed. 'He might even hit you.'

John gave a derisive snort. 'He'd come off worst, then, for I've been trained to fight, but I'm sure it'll never come to that. He's a sensible man and he'll give in when he sees we're determined. Stop crying, my darling, everything's going to work out. Now we'd better get on, for I don't want to anger him by taking you home late.'

She believed his assurances, and began to feel happier. It would be all right. Everything would be all right. John would see to it. They hurried now, saying nothing else, and when they reached the little wooden gate he pulled her against him once more. 'I just remembered, Elspeth. My father has to go to Aberdeen tomorrow for the day, and my mother's going with him to do some shopping. They'll not be home till suppertime, so . . .' He paused briefly, then went on, 'so the house'll be empty. If you come there instead of going to work, nobody would know and we could . . .' He kissed her again before she could answer, such a kiss that robbed her of all sense.

'I'll be there,' she murmured, as soon as she could.

Elspeth stood for a few minutes after he walked away, trying to compose herself before going in, though she knew that both her mother and father would be in bed. She didn't know what to think, it had all happened so quickly – too quickly? – and John had made his plans without worrying about their parents. But, after all, it wasn't important what anybody said. They loved each other, and that was all that mattered, so she would marry him as soon as it was possible, even if she had to go against her father's wishes, and he against his. She had been certain from that very first night by the fire that she wanted to spend the rest of her life with him, and nothing would stop her.

Shivering a little, she went inside. Mrs John Forrest! The thought warmed her whole body as she crept up the stairs. He had said earlier that they were as good as man and wife already, and after tomorrow . . . Tomorrow? Oh God! What had she done?

Chapter Four

Elspeth had convinced herself after she went to bed that what she had promised to do was quite excusable under the circumstances. She loved John, and he would be leaving on Sunday forenoon after having spent Saturday evening at her house, so today was the only chance they would have to be alone again. She felt no guilt as she dressed in the morning, and went downstairs without a care in the world.

From six o'clock until seven she chattered on about the dance. 'All the lads that were in the Terriers wi' John tormented him about me, for I'm the first lass he's ever taken out, and they said he must be serious and he didna argue wi' them. You don't think we're too young, do you, Mother? John's near twenty-one and I'll be eighteen on my next birthday.'

'Lassie, lassie!' Lizzie Gray shook her head and looked at her daughter's flushed face. 'I should never have made your father let you go to that dance. Your head's got filled wi' romantic notions, an' the laddie can't be serious when he's only been out wi' you the once.'

'He is so, an' he's full o' romantic notions, and all, the same as Father was when you were courting.' Here Elspeth glanced meaningfully at the grandfather clock. 'He says he'll have to run Blairton one day, but we'll get one o' their cottar houses for a start. Bobby Brough's has been empty since he retired and went to Dundee, and . . .'

'Whisht, whisht! You hardly ken the lad, forbye him being a farmer's son and you just a grieve's lassie.'

'I ken I love him and he loves me.'

Lizzie sighed with exasperation. She would be the buffer between Elspeth and Geordie, she could see that, for they were both as stubborn as the very devil. 'Look at the time,' she said, sharply. 'You should be away.'

Only now did Elspeth's stomach start to churn, but she put on her coat and shawl and set off as if she were going to work as usual. When she came to the village, she turned off the street before she came to the workroom, to avoid the risk of meeting Nettie or Kirsty, and took the back road to reach the Blairton track, thankful that it was too dark for anyone to see her. It was over two miles from there to the farm, and her legs had turned to jelly before she went round the gable end of the large granite house. With her hand raised to knock on the back door, she had an attack of conscience. It was not too late to turn back, she thought. She could still go to the workroom and say she had been sick but she was feeling better now. Miss Fraser would be glad to see her, for there was a lot of work in hand.

Before Elspeth could move away, however, the door opened and John pulled her inside. 'I wasn't sure if you'd come,' he told her, and she knew that he was as nervous as she was, which made her feel much better. 'I heard your feet coming round the side of the house,' he went on, to explain how he had known she was there.

He took her into a large, airy room, where varying sizes of copper pans hung from hooks along one wall. A long, scrubbed table stood underneath, with a huge jar of flour and a smaller jar of salt at one end, and a few brown and yellow mixing bowls at the other – where Mrs Forrest did her baking, presumably. On another wall there were shelves holding milk churns and metal measuring cups – Blairton had a dairy herd as well as producing crops – several fish kettles of varying sizes and china tureens, also of varying sizes. On each side of the window on the third wall there stood a wooden dresser, laden with dishes of all kinds – dinner and tea services, both bone china and earthenware. The fourth wall was almost entirely taken up by an immense range, where a cheery fire was crackling up the chimney.

Realizing that it was rude to stand looking like this, Elspeth turned round. 'I'm sorry,' she began, but John laughed. 'Have you seen all you want?'

'I don't know what you must think of me,' she protested.

He came close to her then. 'You ken what I think of you. Take off your coat, and we'll have a cup of tea before . . .' His voice tailed off, and he turned to the range, his face as scarlet as Elspeth's own when it came to her what he was meaning. In a few moments, they were sitting at the table with cups and saucers in front of them, too embarrassed to look at each other. She took up her cup and put both hands round it, glad of the heat on her icy fingers, but after a little time she began to drink it, and the familiarity of the action eased her feelings of shame at what she knew would happen later.

'Are you sorry you came?' John asked, suddenly.

41

She faced him then, and could not feel sorry she had come. Not trusting herself to speak, she just shook her head, and John took her empty cup from her and laid it down. 'I don't want you to do anything you'd rather not,' he told her, looking at her so earnestly that she had to gulp. 'I thought last night it was a good idea, but now I'm not so sure.'

Neither of them spoke for some time, then he stood up. 'The fire's lit in the parlour. We'd be more comfortable sitting there than on the hard chairs here.' He took her hand and led her through to a darker room, the light from the tall window somewhat obscured by heavy velvet curtains. A long couch was placed quite near the front of the fire, and two armchairs, upholstered in what looked to Elspeth like tapestry, stood one on either side of the fender. Afraid to create a wrong impression by sitting on the couch, she sat on the edge of one of the chairs and was pleased when John sat down on the other. At least he did not mean to rush her into anything.

Having felt so impolite at being inquisitive in the kitchen, she kept her eyes on the leaping flames, waiting for the boy to say something, but was a little disappointed at first when he asked her about her work with Miss Fraser. While she told him something about the things she did, she realized that he was interested, that he wanted to find out more about her everyday life, and she ended up by giving him little thumbnail sketches of the customers who came into the workroom. They were soon laughing together about the foibles of some of the women he knew, then he began to tell her a little of the more humorous side of his training under canvas in Perth, which had them laughing even more.

Then came a short lull, into which John said, 'It's been like we're really man and wife, hasn't it, just sitting speaking together?'

'My father and mother don't speak as much as we've been doing,' she smiled, 'not that I've seen, anyway, though maybe they do when they go to bed.'

She hadn't thought when they came out, but her last few words caused John's eyes to darken, and he stood up and came across to pull her to her feet. 'Oh, Elspeth,' he moaned, as he crushed her in his arms, 'I love you so much.'

Their kisses made their passion grow quickly, so quickly that Elspeth was hardly aware of being edged down on the couch, and even when John's hands practically ripped open her buttons she did nothing to stop him. She wanted him to take her, she needed him to take her, she rose to meet him when he entered her. It was over far too quickly for both of them, but this time she left her clothes undone, her skirts pushed to the side. She felt no shame, it was the most natural thing in the world.

They lay for some time, kissing, stroking, murmuring words of love and meaning them, until desire was roused again. The second time took much longer than the first – John explored every inch of her body with tender, yet insistent, fingers, and made her do the same to him, then his mouth took over from his hands, nibbling and nuzzling until she was almost begging him to stop before it was too late. He did stop in time and just lay on her for a while, and she could feel his hardness against her stomach, but when he sensed that she had cooled off a little, he began to move gently against her then guided her hand down to let her feel how big he had grown. At last, he went inside her, slowly bringing her to the same point as himself before he made the telling, urgent strokes that ended in an explosive, wild satisfaction for each of them. Then he lay back, breathing quickly for a few minutes until he recovered.

Elspeth's heart gradually slowed down, but it still ached with love for him, and she knew that not even her father would stop her from marrying this man. After a few minutes, she realized that John's eyes were closed and took the opportunity to study the dear face so close to her own. He still had the chubby cheeks of a schoolboy, although he would be twenty-one in less than three months, but there was a shading of dark on his chin and upper lip. His brow was smooth, ending in finely arched eyebrows, and his eyelashes, lying against his cheekbones now, were long and curling.

His eyes jerked open, as dark and as velvety as the coat of a mole. 'I'm hungry,' he observed.

The mundane words after her own more aesthetic thoughts made her laugh. 'Just like a man, the belly has always to come first.'

He gave a long, luxurious sigh. 'Don't expect too much of me, Elspeth. Twice is enough for a while, but we've plenty of time yet.' He sat up and set her clothing to rights, then said, 'My mother left some cold meat for me, but there's always more than enough, and there's some bread-and-butter pudding left from yesterday.'

He stood up and stretched himself. 'I didn't know I'd feel so tired, but by God it was worth it.' He whipped round, his kilt flaring up, to put some coal on the fire, and Elspeth turned away quickly. It felt wrong to look at his bare backside, though she had already found out that he wore no drawers.

They went back to the kitchen, where she was astonished to find that it was almost twelve o'clock; she must have been with John for nearly four hours. As they ate, she said, 'When will your mother and father be coming home?'

'I don't know exactly, but not before five, I'd say.'

'I'd better leave long before that.'

'How long did it take you to walk here?'

'Over an hour, I think.'

'And you usually get home from your work . . . when?'

'After half past six, sometimes a wee bit earlier.'

'Stay till just before five, then. I don't want to let you go, and it'll be safe enough.' He could see that she was afraid, and added, 'I promise, Elspeth.'

His persuasion made her put her fears to the back of her mind. It was so nice to be sitting at the table like an old married couple, and they had quite a long time yet to be together. After having a cup of tea, they cleared the table, washed and dried the dishes they had used, then John showed her round the house. Downstairs, in addition to the parlour and the kitchen, there was a small room which John told her his father escaped to when his mother was on the warpath, also a large bedroom. Upstairs, there were three more bedrooms, each one larger than both bedrooms together in the cottar house, John looking at her with his eyebrows raised when they went into the last one. 'This is mine,' he grinned. 'Would you like to try the bed for size?'

For some inexplicable reason, she felt a trifle angry. 'I hope you don't think that's all I came here for.'

45

'Don't get your feathers ruffled. We both knew what would happen when you came here, didn't we? But I don't think any the worse of you for that. In fact, it's made me love you even more, if that was possible. Anyway, it's too cold up here, we'd be better in the parlour.'

Knowing that she was feeling guilty now, he made light conversation for over an hour, simply holding her hand as they sat together on the couch, and the tension inside her eased slowly. He was really a decent lad and had done nothing that she hadn't wanted him to do, and she was starting to want him to do it again. Snuggling up to him, involuntarily giving him the signal that she was ready to make love once more, she gave a small, breathy sigh when he enfolded her in his arms.

'Oh, God, Elspeth, I'll never forget this day. No matter how bad things are when we get over to France . . . and I've heard some stories that have put the fear of death in me . . . but I'll be able to take comfort from thinking of you. That'll keep me going.'

Time meant nothing now to either of them. The passing of the hours, marked by the chimes of the grandfather clock in the corner – as John had told her, not nearly as beautiful as the one in the cottar house – went unheeded as their passions were spent and raised and spent again. It was as if they were in world of their own, a world of unending paradise in which nothing mattered except proving their love to each other.

They were still recovering from the most perfect of all their unions when John's whole body stiffened. 'Listen!' he urged, but before Elspeth could hear anything, he had sprung to his feet. 'It's the trap! My God! They're back already!'

In the ensuing scramble to make herself decent, Elspeth had no chance to think, but John darted through to the kitchen to retrieve her coat and shawl, which had been left over one of the chairs. 'They're still gathering up all my mother's parcels,' he told her, 'so you'll get away before they come in.'

He pulled her towards another door, explaining, 'I'll let you out at the front, so they'll not see you. What time will I come for supper the morrow night?'

Still scarcely able to think, she said, 'Seven?'

He gave her a hasty kiss as he pushed her outside. 'I'll see you at seven, then. Oh, Elspeth, I'm sorry about this.'

While she ran down the rough farm track, her coat and shawl held in her hand and her hair streaming out behind her, Elspeth's head and heart were pounding, her throat constricted with the fear of being found out. With every step she took, she expected to hear a shout from behind, a shout which would mean that John's father had seen her, but she reached the back road in safety, and once she judged that she was out of sight, she sank down on the grass verge to get her breath back, and promptly burst into tears.

When the heat of her panic subsided, she realized that she was sitting on the snow and was actually shivering with cold as well as fear. Standing up, she drew on her coat and threw her shawl over her head, wondering if she had the strength to walk home. Home? How could she face her mother in a state like this? Tears came again, and she leaned back against the dyke wishing that she was dead.

Giving herself up to abandoned weeping for some time, she calmed down at last and was able to think properly.

The darkness had just been gathering when she ran out of the house, so it couldn't have been four o'clock, but the sky was black now, so it must be wearing on for five, and she couldn't go home until at least half past six. Even walking slowly, she would be too early and there was nowhere else she could go. Wait! She had noticed, on her way up the farm track, that there was a small shed a little to the left. If it wasn't locked, she could go inside and at least set her hair to rights as best she could.

Her legs were still shaking when she turned into the track to Blairton again, and she felt like a criminal as she crept into the unlocked shed, but feeling round with her hands, she found a large crate to sit on. Her hair proved quite a problem, for not only could she see nothing, she had no brush or comb with her to tame it, and half her pins were missing. Holding those that were left tightly in her hand in case they fell and were lost to her, too, she ran the fingers of her free hand through and through her long tresses until they felt smooth. It took her several attempts to fix all her hair with the few hairpins she had, but at last she felt reasonably satisfied and started on her journey home.

As she walked towards the village, it occurred to her that, even if she went in too early, she could tell her mother that she hadn't felt well, and that Miss Fraser had let her go before six. The lie was no worse than pretending she was going to work that morning when she had really been going to see John. Her dragging pace quickened, but her heart was still heavy at the thought of her own depravity. She had told lies, she had spent a whole day in the arms of her lover, she had fled from discovery by his parents. Even one of these sins would be enough to have God's wrath down on her, and for all of them, He might strike her dead with no warning.

She carried on fearfully, waiting for the end, and when she came to the main road, she could hardly believe that she was still alive. Turning right, she made for the cottar houses, her spirits a little higher.

Glancing at the clock when she went into the kitchen, she saw that it was exactly half past six, so there was no need for another lie . . . except to tell her mother that she wasn't hungry and that she had a sore head, neither of which were really lies, because she couldn't have eaten a thing and her head was thumping like a steam mill.

Lizzie, as her daughter had known she would, ordered her to bed immediately and promised to take up a hot 'pig' for her in a few minutes.

So ended the most wonderful, the most nerve-wracking, day of Elspeth Gray's young life.

Chapter Five

After having agonized for half the night over the awful things she had done, Elspeth had spent the other half telling herself that they weren't so awful. She and John were as good as married and they had only done what would be perfectly lawful in a short time when the minister had actually made them husband and wife. The only bad aspect of it had been the secrecy which had resulted in her ignominious flight from Blairton. In years to come, however, they would be able to laugh about that, would even regale their grandchildren with the hilarious story of how Grandfather and Grandmother were almost caught out.

She felt much happier when she rose on Saturday morning, but when she went into the workroom, her face, white from lack of sleep, made Miss Fraser tell her that she should have taken another day off. 'No, I'm fine now,' Elspeth assured her, with a broad smile to prove it.

Nettie and Kirsty, of course, were waiting to hear about the dance on Thursday night, and were glad when their mistress left the room. They were much more receptive than Lizzie had been and were soon laughing at Elspeth's account of her efforts to master the different dances, but when she went on to describe the dresses and blouses the other girls had been wearing, Nettie said, impatiently, 'Are you any further on wi' John Forrest, that's what I want to ken?'

'He wants to wed me,' Elspeth said, but the doubt on her friends' faces made her add, 'He's going to ask my father the night when he comes for his supper.'

'But you've only been out wi' him once, so will your father agree to you getting wed?'

'He'll likely say we should court a while first, but John's set on us getting married next time he's home.'

The two younger girls exchanged glances, and Elspeth could tell that they didn't believe a word of what she was saying. She was tempted to tell them what had happened the day before, but it was too sweet, and too dangerous, to make public. 'It's true! He did ask me, honest he did.'

When they still looked sceptical, she started refilling the spool of her machine. 'Just wait, then you'll see.'

Miss Fraser's return put a stop to any further discussion on the subject, but Elspeth didn't really care what the other two girls thought. They would have to believe her on Monday, for it would be all cut and dried by then.

She rushed home after the shop closed and insisted on laying the table. Taking out the best damask cloth, used only on very special occasions – the last had been her paternal grandmother's funeral six months previously – she smoothed it out then set four places with the equally rarely used willow pattern dinner service and silver cutlery. Lizzie, stirring a small pan at the side of the fire, sniffed but said nothing.

Geordie came in at half past six, stamping his feet to get his circulation going again, then went over to the fire to take off his boots. It was his custom to sit all evening in his thick wheeling wool socks, matted and discoloured on the soles, but Elspeth said, tentatively, 'Could you please leave your boots on, Father, seeing there'll be company?'

'As though I didna ken.' But he sat back with his boots still on his feet. 'Fine company indeed – the great John Forrest himself. I'll need to wash my face as well, I suppose.'

When everything was ready, Elspeth sat down nervously on a high chair and fidgeted so much that Lizzie said, 'Settle yourself, Eppie. He'll not come any quicker for you hodging about like that. What time did you tell him?'

'Seven o'clock.'

'Well, it wants fifteen minutes yet. Have patience.'

The big black kettle spat out suddenly, and the girl jumped up to unhook it from the swey. She laid it on the hob at the side and settled back in her seat, looking at the clock as its steady tick measured out the silence, although she had grown up loving this majestic member of the family and knew every beautiful inch of it. The wheatsheaf painted at the top of the face meant that the house would never be short of food, her mother had once told her, and the dial itself was marked out in black Roman numerals. Inside their circumference were two smaller circles, the top one showing the seconds passing, and the bottom one giving the date of the month. When she was a child, Elspeth had always been allowed to push that tiny hand forward to the correct date if there had been a month with less than thirty-one days.

A small smile crossed her face as she recalled how she used to climb up on a chair when she was a little girl, to peep through the glass panel at the side of the clock. She had watched with awe as the little toothed wheels and cogs clicked round, and marvelled, even now, at the intricate machinery which kept her 'grandfather' alive. Her father made a ritual of the winding, taking the crank-shaped key from behind the ornamental scrolls on top of the long case and inserting it first into the hole at the left side of the dial. He turned it slowly until the weight controlling the chiming mechanism was cranked to the top, then transferred it to the right-hand hole and the second weight rose. Thus the working of all the hands was ensured for the next seven days.

Elspeth's eyes shifted now to the small pillars, one at each side of the face, which shone from many years of polishing – her mother used only the best beeswax polish on the clock – and reflected the brass feet on which they stood. The mahogany case itself glowed a deep red in the light from the fire and the Tilley lamp.

Eight minutes still to wait. She rose and went over to the dresser, which stood between the door from the porch and the door through to the back kitchen, its overmantel broken up by shelves and niches which displayed the ornaments Lizzie had amassed over the years. Some had been gifts, some had been picked up at the sales held when houses had to be given up due to the death of the occupants, and some had even been bought in shops in Aberdeen, for Lizzie was a great collector of knick-knacks.

Looking at a little woolly lamb made of bone china, Elspeth admired again the perfectly sculpted curly head and body, and the sweetness of the face. Next sat a very delicate Chinese teapot, another of her favourites, an unusual grey in colour with hand-painted oriental flowers, and a wicker-work handle arched over the top. Then came the huge bible, leather bound with two brass clasps, wherein the births, marriages and deaths in the Gray family had been recorded for over a hundred years. She flipped over the pages filled with faded spidery writing to look at the last three entries – the deaths of her paternal grandfather and grandmother and her own birth. A thrill shot through her as she thought that her marriage would be next.

When the clock boomed seven times, Geordie took his silver watch from his waistcoat pocket, the chain and fob jingling on his chest. 'Dead on,' he remarked, as he did every day at some point, although his daughter was never sure whether it was the watch or the clock he was checking. Her restless legs took her over to the window, where spotless white lace was almost hidden by thick, deep red curtains. In front of the window, a tall round table held a healthy aspidistra in an earthenware flowerpot. Automatically poking her finger into the soil to check if it needed water and finding that it didn't, she went back to sit at the fireside, where the high mantelshelf held more ornaments and two tall brass candlesticks.

Elspeth was thankful that she had persuaded her mother to remove Geordie's flannel linder and drawers from the string under the shelf where they usually hung to air, ready for him to change into if he had an unexpected soaking. The girl had wanted to set the supper in the best room – the green plush chairs and sofa would give a better impression – but Lizzie had said, 'He'll have to take us the way we are.'

Glancing round, Elspeth felt satisfied with the kitchen, after all. It was more friendly than the other room, and they would all feel more at ease, including John. What was keeping him? She had said seven, and it was after ten past now. Had something happened to him; had his parents found out what had gone on in their absence; or had he never intended coming at all?

Her stomach turned over at this last thought, and she pushed it hastily away from her.

Time dragged past while she counted the seconds ticking away and laid one finger on her knee each time she came to sixty. She had reached eighteen minutes when she became aware of her mother's eyes on her and stopped.

At half past, Geordie lumbered to his feet, his hoary eyebrows lowering. 'I'm waiting no longer, the lad'll not be coming after this time. We should have ken't better than ask a farmer's son to eat in a cottar house.' He stamped through to the back door to go to the outside privy, and Lizzie took a thick, flannel cloth from its hook at the mantelpiece and removed the large tureen from the oven at the side of the fire. The macaroni and cheese was meant as a special treat, but each mouthful tasted like sawdust to the disappointed women. Geordie, on the other hand, seemed to be enjoying his, finishing his plateful quickly and asking for a second helping. He was the only one to have any of the apple pie – made from their own apples, stored in a barrel – and Lizzie brewed some tea while he was eating it.

By the time the dishes were washed and everything had been tidied away, it was almost nine o'clock, and Elspeth could bear her mother's silent sympathy no longer. 'I've a bit o' a sore head again, so I'll just go to my bed now.'

Catching his wife's cautioning eye, Geordie closed his mouth on his intended condemnation of the young man, and Lizzie said, 'Goodnight, Eppie.' She knew that no words of comfort would help her daughter.

Waiting until the door closed, Geordie grunted, 'John Forrest's got a lot to answer for.'

Lizzie glanced at him anxiously. 'Oh, Geordie, you'll not say anything to him if you see him, will you?'

'Why not, woman? He's insulted our hospitality, as well as giving the lassie a sore heart. Let him try to excuse himself for that, if he can.'

His wife felt sick thinking of what he might say if he met the boy while this anger was still on him. 'Something must have kept him – a sick beast, or the like.'

'There's other men at Blairton that could see to that, dammit! No, he'd changed his mind about coming, that's what it is. Well, he'll never be asked back to this house, and I'll not have Elspeth seeing him again.'

'But she really likes him, Geordie.' Romantic Lizzie could excuse the boy blindly. 'Will you not wait till we see if he apologizes to her for not coming?'

'He'll likely never come near her again. You ken fine the sons o' the gentry are just after one thing from a lassie, and our Elspeth would never have let him touch her. He'll have found somebody else to oblige him by this time, the filthy swine that he is.'

Dangerously, Lizzie took the last word. 'No, you're wrong, Geordie. He's a decent laddie, in spite o' what you think, and I'm sure there's a good explanation for him not coming. He's not the kind to hurt a lassie without reason.'

56

Chapter Six

Meg Forrest took off her tight-fitting hat with relief. Her head had been sore enough without having to wear it, but she'd had to keep up an appearance in the kirk. Blairton was the largest farm for over twenty miles round Auchlonie, and the Forrests were respected by villagers, farmers and farm servants alike, and she couldn't have let it be seen that she was upset. Anyway, John wasn't the only one who had drunk himself stupid yesterday forenoon, and five other mothers must be feeling the same. Knowing the boys as she did, Meg guessed that their drinking had been a means of forgetting what lay in front of them, but it had been an awful affront when Sam Coull and his brother had taken her son home after the hotel bar closed at half past two. She had been so angry that she had told the hotel-keeper what she thought of him for giving them drink at all.

'They're bona fide travellers, being members of His Majesty's Services,' Sam had excused himself, 'so I couldn't refuse them.'

'Bona fide nothing!' she had ranted. 'They're still just bairns.'

The two men had taken John up to his bed, and he had slept for almost eighteen hours, though his head hadn't been properly clear when he left to catch the train to Aberdeen.

Her husband gave a sudden grunt beside her as he opened his front stud and pulled his shirt over his head, moving his chin from side to side to ease his chafed neck. He sat down on the bed to remove his Sunday boots, then stood up and held on to the knob of the bed to pull off his trousers. Normally, Meg would have reprimanded him for not opening his buttons first, but this wasn't a normal day and he looked so vulnerable in his semmit and drawers, his dark curly hair all tousled, that she couldn't say anything.

He looked up at her sadly. 'If only I'd signed that form to let him go to Canada, he'd not be on his road to France this day.'

It was the first time that Meg had heard her husband admit he had been wrong, and it made her realize how upset he was. 'You did what you thought was best for him,' she consoled.

'I did what I thought was best for me.' John Forrest senior – known to all by the name of his farm as was the custom in these parts – had slipped on his old shirt and trousers and rose to lift his tweed jacket off the peg on the back of the bedroom door. 'I wanted him to learn the running o' the place so he could take over Blairton from me some day, but maybe I worked him some hard.'

'I never heard him complaining.'

'No, but he could hardly wait to get away to Canada.'

'He was looking for excitement, that's all.' Meg fastened her skirt buttons. 'But he'll have had more than his fill o' excitement by the time this war's finished, and I'm sure he'll not want to leave again, so maybe it's a blessing in disguise.'

His worried expression eased. 'Aye, lass, I'm being daft. He'll settle down when he comes back from the war.'

When he comes back, Meg thought – if he comes back would be more like it. How many of the six young men would come back? And if they weren't killed or maimed in some way, would they be content to return to the farms, where the only excitement was when a cow calved or a horse foaled? Or would they roam the world, seeking other causes to fight, other injustices to put right, once they'd got the taste for it?

Blairton made for the door. 'I'll have a walk to the farthest park to see if Donaldson's sorted the paling yet, but I should be back for my dinner.'

Listening to his tacketty boots clattering down the stairs, she wondered how long the war would last, and what the outcome would be. Would the Huns be victorious and the Kaiser sit in Buckingham Palace one day? She could even put up with that, if John came back to her all in one piece.

The constant clicketty-clack was annoying John. There was something he had to think about and the noise wouldn't let him concentrate – not that his brain was in a fit state to concentrate, anyway, it was too fuzzy. He had drunk far too much yesterday – he couldn't even remember going home – and his head had still been pounding when he left Blairton this morning. The other lads had been as bad, of course. None of them had said a word when they boarded the train, and they were all sleeping now, lying back with their mouths open. If he could just remember what it was that was niggling at the back of his mind, he could sleep, too. He hadn't wanted to go drinking with them, he could remember that, but they'd laughed at him and teased him about . . . being tied to the apron strings already? Whose apron strings, and why hadn't he wanted to go with them? He had always been ready for a drink before.

Still puzzling, he closed his eyes again, but he couldn't relax. It was awful to have lost almost a whole day and not to know . . . there was something he should have done that he hadn't been able to. Somewhere he should have gone last night. Somebody he should have seen . . . Elspeth! Oh, Christ! Jerking up, he felt as sick as he had done yesterday. He had been invited for supper and he hadn't gone! What would she be thinking of him? After all that had happened between them on Friday, he had let her down as if she meant nothing to him. She would think he was tired of her. She would believe he had cast her aside because he'd had enough of her. He would never have enough of her; he loved her so much that his heart was aching unbearably because he had hurt her.

He wished now that he had told his mother about Elspeth. He had meant to tell her before he went to the Grays' house, but that had been knocked on the head by his getting drunk. If she had known about the invitation, she would have sent somebody to apologize to the Grays for him not being able to go, but as it was, they would have been left waiting, and Geordie would likely never let him set foot inside the house again. He would have to write to her, to let her know that he did love her, and that he couldn't help what had happened.

Couldn't help it? He should have had the sense to stick to his guns and not let himself be talked into going to the Boar's Head with his friends. He'd been a weakling, and he despised himself, as Elspeth would despise him when she found out why he had never appeared. He would have to do something to make it up to her, for he couldn't bear the thought of losing her.

As soon as Geordie set off on his Sunday afternoon walk, his wife took out her knitting – she had to wait until he went out because he disapproved of even this harmless occupation on the Sabbath. Elspeth pretended to read, but could not concentrate for worrying. John hadn't been in church, but Blairton had seemed normal enough, and Mrs Forrest – her cloche hat, just like Queen Mary's, fitting closely on her head – had smiled to the Grays when she went out. She couldn't have known that her son had been invited to the cottar house for supper, otherwise she would have told them why he hadn't gone.

Her hands going like shuttles, Lizzie glanced across at her daughter with a rush of tenderness and wished that she could do something to soothe the girl's wounded feelings, she looked so miserable. 'He maybe had a cold.'

Elspeth shook her head. 'A cold wouldn't have kept him away.' John had said he was leaving in the forenoon, she thought, mournfully, so he would be gone now and he hadn't even come to say goodbye.

When Geordie returned, Lizzie put a small kebbock of home-made cheese on the table, and some of the oatcakes she baked every Friday, but, as on the previous evening, he was the only one with an appetite, and was quite oblivious to the fact that his wife and daughter hardly ate a thing.

Elspeth, who generally chattered on during the long Sunday evenings, sat morosely looking into the fire for over

61

an hour, and when her father at last noticed her silence, he cursed John Forrest for hurting her. The uncomfortable situation lasted until just after eight o'clock, then Elspeth stood up. 'I think I'll go to my bed, for I'm . . .' Putting her hand to her mouth to stifle a sob, she ran out.

Geordie was about to vow vengeance on the young man, but one look at his wife's face – her lips compressed, her eyes daring him to swear – made him tone down his words. 'I'll tell him what I think o' him the next time I see him, the . . . scoundrel that he is.'

Lizzie gave him time to simmer down, then said, softly, 'Leave it be, Geordie. If the laddie's as decent as I think he is, he'll write and let her ken why he didna come last night, and if he's not . . . well, she'll just have to get over him, for she'd be better off without him.'

Making her way cautiously along the icy road on Monday morning, Elspeth was dreading being questioned by Nettie and Kirsty about Saturday night, but when she entered the back room of the dressmaker's shop, her puffed eyes told them that she had been weeping and they remained sympathetically silent. She knew they were thinking that John hadn't asked her father about courting her, or that her father had refused his permission, and it was best to leave it at that.

About eleven o'clock, Mrs Taylor, wife of the cattleman at Upper Mains, came in with a skirt to be let out, and was full of what she'd just heard. 'Donald Stewart's mother was telling me he got blazing drunk in the Boar's Head on Saturday morning. Mind you, there was other five besides him that had to be taken home helpless – Alex Paterson,

Willie Anderson, Dougal McLeod, John Forrest and Davie . . . mercy on us! What's wrong wi' the lassie?'

Elspeth had let out a low moan, and was hanging on to the bench, her face chalk-white, her eyes like saucers. 'I think I've got a touch o' the flu,' she whispered.

Grace Fraser looked quite concerned, peering at her over the top of her steel-rimmed spectacles. 'Yes, you don't look at all well, Elspeth. You'd better go home.'

In a daze, Elspeth went to get her coat, feeling worse than ever when she heard Mrs Taylor saying, 'They'd to leave wi' the first train on Sunday, and God kens when they'll come back, if they ever come back at all.'

As she stumbled unseeing along the road, the girl tried to come to terms with what she had just learned. John had got drunk – that was why he hadn't come to supper on Saturday – and she'd been worrying herself sick in case he was ill. She was trembling with hurt at his thoughtlessness, with anxiety for his future well-being, with annoyance at herself for having reacted so badly in front of Mrs Taylor and Miss Fraser. And Nettie Duffus and Kirsty Tough would be laughing at her for believing him when he said he loved her. But he did love her, and now be was gone, and she didn't know when, or if, he would come back. And nothing would ever be the same again.

Lizzie was taken aback when Elspeth dragged herself into the kitchen. 'Eppie! What ails you, lass?'

Her mother's concern made the girl burst into tears. 'It's John! He went to the Boar's Head on Saturday morning wi' some of the other lads, and they . . .' She couldn't go on.

'What is it? What happened? Was he in a fight?'

'Oh, no. He got drunk and had to be taken home!'

'Is that all?' Lizzie couldn't help laughing.

Elspeth was put out by her mother's insensitivity. 'I don't know if I'll ever see him again, and you ask me, "Is that all?"'

'Eppie, lass, it's not as bad as that. He'll write to you, and he'll be back on leave – maybe in just a few month.'

'Just a few month?' It was an eternity to a girl in love.

'It'll soon pass, Eppie, and don't blame him too much. Like your father, I've aye been against strong drink, but I can excuse the laddie for trying to drown his troubles at such a time. It was daft, but he's young, and he'll be home in no time. You've had too much excitement lately, that's why you're so easy upset, and you'd feel better if you took a lie down for awhile. Wait, I'll make a drop tea for you first.'

When Geordie came home in the middle of the day, his wife explained the situation to him, doing her best to make him keep his voice down when she saw that he was about to explode over the boy's thoughtlessness. 'Eppie's up in her bed, and she's miserable enough already without listening to you going on.'

'Aye, and it's all young Forrest's blame.' Geordie did keep his voice low so that the girl would not hear. 'He's near a man, but he's still a bairn, getting drunk without a care in the world.'

'Bairns don't get drunk,' Lizzie said, caustically, 'and he wasn't the only one. I'm not denying they were all fools to do what they did, but they're on their way to France now and God knows what lies in store for them. They were only trying to forget about it for a wee while.'

'Aye, well.' Geordie fell silent for a moment, then asked, 'Is she terrible upset?'

'What else would she be? He broke his promise to her and went away without saying goodbye, and she doesna ken if she'll ever see him again.'

Although he had always been a strict father, Geordie Gray loved his only child more than even Lizzie could guess. 'I suppose I'd best go up and say something to her?'

'As long as it's nothing against John Forrest,' Lizzie warned.

Ever since she came to bed, Elspeth had wondered if this was God's way of showing his displeasure at what she had done. Had He set the Devil out to make John turn from the straight and narrow path so that he wouldn't be fit to come to supper at her house? Had Lucifer himself urged the other boys to make John go drinking with them? It must have been something like that, for surely John wouldn't have got drunk willingly, knowing that he was to be seeing her in the evening. It must be her that God was punishing, and she wished that she had never gone to Blairton . . . no, she didn't wish that. At least she had all the hours of bliss with John to remember until he came back.

At dinnertime, she heard her father coming in, and prayed that he would not come upstairs – she couldn't face him just yet – but in a few minutes he walked in, looking very ill at ease. Standing at the foot of her bed, he murmured, rather awkwardly, 'The war'll be over by Christmas – the Gordons'll make short work o' Kaiser Bill and his Huns.'

Looking at her sympathetically, he turned and went back

to the kitchen, leaving Elspeth considering what he had said. She had heard other folk in the village saying the same thing, now that she came to think of it, and Christmas was less than five weeks away. John would be home . . . and they would be married . . . and everything would be all right.

Chapter Seven

The hostilities were not over by Christmas – only an English festival and an ordinary working day in Auchlonie, even the bairns waited until the last night of each year to hang up their stockings. Nettie and Kirsty had commiserated with Elspeth when she went back to work the day after learning what John had done, but had forgotten about it in the anticipation of Hogmanay, and she felt that no one understood her misery at being denied the opportunity to say goodbye to him and to wish him luck.

She was unable to enter into the spirit of the festivities to bid farewell to 1914 and to welcome in a new, hopefully better, year, although the neighbours 'first-footed' the Grays with the traditional gifts of shortbread or lumps of coal, taking their own whisky bottles in with them because they knew that Geordie never had any spirits in the house. Her New Year's Day off was like another Sunday to her, apart from not having to go to church.

In the workroom next day, Nettie told the other two what had happened at her house after the clock had struck midnight on Hogmanay. 'Everybody was singing, and Johnny Low was that drunk by the time he got to us, he was going round kissing all the lassies.'

'Did he kiss you?' little Kirsty asked eagerly.

'He tried, and I wouldna have said no if he'd been sober.' Nettie's laugh was rueful – Johnny Low was quite handsome in a rough sort of way. 'I can't stand the smell o' drink on a lad, and that's a fact.'

Elspeth reflected sadly that she would have let John kiss her supposing he had hardly been able to stand, but he hadn't given her the chance that Saturday in November.

On January 3rd, having had to unpick the lining of a costume jacket because she had inserted a right sleeve into a left armhole in her distraction, Elspeth was doubly dispirited and wondered why her mother seemed so excited. 'A letter come for you second post, Eppie,' Lizzie burst out.

Her dejection falling away like magic, the girl picked up the buff-coloured envelope addressed in a flowing hand to Miss Elspeth Gray, The Cottar Houses, Mains of Denseat, Auchlonie, Aberdeenshire, Scotland, with 'Army Post Service' stamped at the side. Her fingers trembled as she feverishly tore it open and Lizzie watched with amusement as her daughter skimmed over the page, then went back to the start and read it again out loud, her face wreathed in smiles.

My Dear Elspeth,

I am very sorry for not coming to supper that night, it feels like years ago. I suppose you had heard that I got drunk that forenoon, and I am really ashamed of it. I should not have let the other lads talk me into going drinking. I was still not right

68

sober when it was time to catch the train on Sunday morning, and I did not have time to come to see you anyway. I could not manage to write to you before we sailed, but I often thought about you. Please forgive me for leaving you waiting, it must have been terrible for you, not knowing. Remember, you are my whole life and I promise to wed you when I get home next time. Thinking about that is what keeps me going in this awful place. Once again, I am very sorry for what I did, but I *will* make it up to you some day soon. Yours forever,

John

P.S. I love you

This written avowal of his love made Elspeth's brimming eyes spill over, and Lizzie's sniff sounded suspiciously as if she were on the verge of weeping, too, but she said, brusquely, 'Stop your nonsense, lass, or you'll make yourself ill.'

Nettie and Kirsty, however, joined in her rejoicing as soon as she had the opportunity to tell them, the letter being shown proudly and inspected with great interest.

'Oh, I'm right happy for you,' Nettie burst out. 'I didna believe you before, for I thought you was just making it up to make us jealous.'

'It's that romantic,' sighed young Kirsty. 'And it's really real, not a story. You're awful lucky, Elspeth.'

'I ken,' Elspeth said, blissfully.

At suppertime, when Geordie was told that John had sent a letter of apology, he muttered, 'Saying he's sorry doesna excuse him for keeping you waiting like that, and he's not worth bothering wi'. Thank God you didna ken him long enough to get fond o' him.'

Knowing that it had been love at first sight for both boy and girl, Lizzie's heart sank as she saw her husband's tightly-gripped, disapproving mouth. Even if Forrest of Blairton agreed to let his son marry, Geordie Gray would definitely not let Elspeth be the bride.

The letter became crumpled and barely legible over the next few weeks with the girl reading it so often, but Lizzie shook her head each evening to show that no second one had come, her own heart as sore as her daughter's, perhaps even sorer, because she foresaw more heartache in store for Elspeth when Geordie forbade the marriage.

'It's weeks since we'd a letter from John.' Meg Forrest voiced the thought for the first time, though it had been uppermost in her mind for ages. Her husband had no patience with worrying women, but he must surely understand what their son's silence was doing to her. If she had only known, he was as concerned as she was, but thought it unmanly to admit it. To reassure her, he said, 'The Huns'll not stop fighting to give our John time to write home.'

His sarcasm was wasted. 'I keep praying he's safe,' Meg murmured. 'Are you not worried for him?'

His Adam's apple rose and fell as he swallowed. 'Aye, lass, I am worried for him, but I try not to think about it. We can do nothing except wait for word.'

'Aye.' Meg laid her hand on his sleeve to let him know that she understood what he felt, and when he went out, she washed up the breakfast things and put the kettle back on in case Willie Mavor had something for her.

Twenty minutes passed before she saw the postman cycling up the dirt road, whistling as he always did, so she masked a pot of tea for him. She was not superstitious as a rule, but as she opened the door, she crossed her fingers that there would be a letter from France today.

Willie knew how anxious Meg must be to hear from her son, and handed her the envelope as soon as he went inside. 'It's been a while since your John wrote,' he remarked, sitting down at the table and helping himself to a home-baked scone. 'It's a worrying time, especially for the mothers, for they seem to take it harder than their men.'

'Aye.' Although Meg knew that he was waiting for her to open the letter so that he could pass the news on, she wanted to be on her own when she read it; she might give way and weep, and she couldn't let Willie have that to pass on.

At last, the postman pushed away his cup and stood up. 'I hope young John hasna been in the heart o' the fighting.'

'I hope no'.' She felt guilty at not satisfying the man's curiosity, but closed the door and hurried over to pick up the letter, fatter than the only other one John had sent.

'Dear Mother.' The words danced on the page and she had to rise to get her spectacles. She had been having trouble reading anything other than fairly large print for some time now, and had seen the optician on his last monthly visit to Auchlonie. It was only a week since she had collected the glasses he had prescribed and she still forgot to put them on before she started to read anything.

71

Dear Mother,

I am sorry you have had to wait so long for this letter, but we do not have much peace to sit down and write, as you can imagine. We are back off the line just now, so I want to tell you something I meant to tell you that last Saturday but I was in no state. I took Geordie Gray's daughter to the Masonic Hall dance when I was on leave, and to cut a long story short, we love each other and I am going to wed her when I come back. I don't want to go to Canada now, so I am sure Father will be pleased. When I was in their house, I saw a grandfather clock with Geordie and Lizzie's initials engraved on the pendulum. It was the most romantic thing I had ever seen, so I've written to a clockmaker I saw in Perth, asking him to make one exactly the same, but with Elspeth's initials and mine. It will be delivered to Blairton, but it's for Elspeth. I can hardly wait to see her face on our wedding day when I give it to her. I hope you and Father are both keeping well, your devoted son,

John

Meg sighed as she laid the letter down. She was happy that he had found a lass – the Grays were a decent family, and he could do a lot worse – and that he was intending to settle down at Blairton after the war, but it must be terrible out there in France. One of his friends had been reported killed in action already, and another one was missing.

'Dear God,' she prayed, 'please don't let my son be taken from me for good. I'll be happy to share him with

Elspeth Gray or any other girl if he comes through the war safely.'

Rising to carry on with her housework, Meg's mind kept going over what John had written. She knew the lassie by sight, a pretty wee thing sitting with her parents in the kirk, but she couldn't be more than sixteen or seventeen, if she was that. It wasn't likely that Geordie Gray knew about her attachment to John, so it would be best not to say anything about it to him or Lizzie.

When Blairton read the letter, he smiled. 'I was feared he had no interest in lassies, and I'm pleased he's not like that, for a man needs a wife.'

'Elspeth looks a sober enough creature,' Meg observed, 'and I'm sure Geordie Gray'll not be against the match, though he'll likely want them to wait a year or so, for she's still a bit young.'

'She'll not be so young by the time this war's finished.' He looked serious. 'It's going to be a long, hard struggle, for we'll have our work cut out to beat the Huns.'

'As long as our John doesna get killed.'

'Don't let your mind dwell on that.' He sat for a few more minutes, then said, 'Stop worrying, Meg, everything'll come out all right. Elspeth Gray's put Canada out of his head, thank goodness, and though I'd hoped he'd pick a farmer's daughter for a wife, she comes of good enough stock. I'll have no objection to him marrying her when the time comes, and maybe they'll have sons to carry on Blairton, like I've aye wanted. Now, is my dinner ready?'

Towards the end of January, Elspeth became numbly aware that her actions on the night of the storm in

73

November and on the day she had spent at Blairton could not be kept secret much longer, but she was afraid to consult Doctor McLean in case he told her parents. Her mother would be angry, there was no doubt about that, for she'd be worried about what folk would say, but once she got over the shock she would shield her daughter as much as she could and see her through her time. It was what her father would do that made Elspeth shiver with fear. He could be cruel and unforgiving, and would likely throw her out into the street like the heroines in Nettie's sister's novelettes. She was desperately miserable, recalling the disgust of the local women when the dairymaid at Denseat had to leave in disgrace some months before. 'Easy meat for anything in breeks,' they had sneered, and it would be unbearable to have them saying things like that about her. Each morning, she forced herself to go to work, but could show no interest in anything, not even in the chit-chat that went on when Miss Fraser was out.

She could think of nothing but her own dilemma, a dilemma she knew was all of her own making, and the only thought she could dredge up to comfort herself was that John would surely be home in time to wed her before the baby was born.

Chapter Eight

Feeling quite out-of-sorts this February morning, Meg Forrest put it down to another sleepless night worrying about John, topped by Willie Mavor delivering only a bill from a cattle-feed company in Aberdeen. She couldn't rid her body of the sense of being weighted down, as if her limbs were made of lead, and poured herself a cup of tea at half past eight to see if that would revive her.

She was still trying to summon up enough energy to go and feed the hens when someone rang the front door bell, and her heart turned over – all the usual callers knew to come round the back. It was young Davie McIntyre, in his telegraph boy's uniform, which didn't altogether surprise her – this was what her body had been preparing her for. When she stretched out to take the yellow envelope, the boy held on to it, murmuring uncomfortably, 'I'd best get your man. I saw him in the near park.'

Meg was ice-cold when she returned to the kitchen. She knew, without having to read it, what the telegram would say. Hearing her husband's heavy feet echoing rapidly on the stones in the yard, she turned to face him when he came running in, red-faced and breathless, and was surprised to see that the envelope in his hand was still unopened. Had he, too, known what it would contain? He did not even look at her as he ripped the side off and extracted the message inside, but one quick glance made his face blanch as though a bucket of whitewash had been thrown over it.

'Oh, God,' he groaned, 'I was feared this is what it was. John was killed in action on the tenth.' Staggering like a newly-blinded man, he collapsed on to the nearest chair and buried his face in his hands, so unaccustomed to showing such a private emotion as grief that it came from him in eerie, wailing moans.

Meg picked up the small sheet of paper which had fluttered to the floor, and studied the strips of words on it to make sure that he had read them all, but there was nothing other than the bald statement of John's death. The blood-curdling sounds still emanating from her husband made her move to grip his shoulder, and he flung one arm out to encircle her waist. 'Oh, Meg,' he muttered, brokenly, 'it's me should be comforting you. I'm a poor kind o' man letting go like this, but . . . I . . . I can't help it. I'm . . . sorry, I'm sorry.'

'It's best you let it out,' she soothed, stroking his head. 'It's only natural.' Her own eyes were dry, for she had steeled herself not to give way to her sorrow. That could come later, when she was alone.

'I was aye . . . feared for this,' he went on, 'though I tried not to let you see. There's been a weight on my heart since the very day he went to France.'

'Aye, I know,' she murmured, for she had felt the same.

'When he told us about him and Geordie Gray's lassie, I was that pleased. I was sure there would be grandsons to

76

carry on Blairton when me and John was both away, but
. . .' His lined face crumpled again. 'Oh, Meg,' he sobbed,
'has God forsaken us?'

She had wondered that, too, but hastened to console
him. 'God didn't take John, it was the Huns, and we're not
the only ones to lose a son. There'll be a lot o' sore hearts
before this war comes to an end.' She looked down at his
tear-stained face compassionately. 'Would you like a drop
whisky to settle you?'

In answer to his mute nod, Meg took the bottle of
Johnnie Walker and a small glass out of the press. She
couldn't get over how steady her hands were as she poured
out the spirits – after the shock she had just received, she
would have expected to be more affected, but she felt
nothing except a heavy numbness. She was not surprised
when her man downed the dram in one gulp, but took the
glass from him and refilled it. This time, he sipped slowly,
and gradually his colour came back and the hiccupping
sobs grew less harsh.

He pushed the empty glass from him, shaking his head
when she held up the bottle with her eyebrows raised.
'Even if I drank the lot, I'd not feel better.'

But she knew that what he had drunk had helped him to
regain his composure, for his breathing was easier, his eyes
calmer. After a few minutes, he wiped his face with his
handkerchief then blew his nose loudly. 'I'm sorry, lass, but
it come on me that quick. I'm over it now, and I'd best get
back to what I was doing.'

She did feel a pang of resentment that he did not want
to be with her in their time of trouble, but, when he
reached the door, he turned with his hand on the knob.

'I've got to keep working, lass,' he said, sheepishly apologetic, 'to take my mind off it.'

Left alone, she sat recalling little things about John. He'd been such a bonnie bairn, even when he was new-born, his dark thatch of curly hair so like his father's. When he got up to any childish pranks, he had only to look up at her with his big brown eyes and she couldn't chastise him, but he hadn't been spoiled, though he was an only child. He had been a good bairn, always laughing and . . . Her thoughts wavered. She would never see the mischievous twinkle in his eyes again, nor the way his nose crinkled just before a great burst of mirth came out. Oh, God, why?

Meg succumbed to her grief then, sobbing for the bairn who used to be, for the young man whose life had been cut so drastically short. During all the anxious hours she had spent at John's bedside when he was small, seeing him through measles, scarlet fever, whooping cough, she had never imagined, not even in her wildest nightmares, that he would be taken from her in a war.

When her tears stopped, and she could think rationally, she remembered that she would have to let her brother know about John. She had never been that close to Tam – he was so much older than she was – but he was all the family she had, and Blairton himself had no brothers or sisters.

After the letter was written, she laid it on the dresser to be given to Willie Mavor the following morning to post for her, and sat down at the table again. Little incidents in her son's short life kept coming back to her, things that only a mother would remember: his first day at school, when she had watched him set off on his chubby little legs to walk the two miles with some of the cottar bairns; his first bicycle, when he'd fallen off and skinned his knees so many times that she'd thought he would never learn to ride it; his fourteen-year-old pride in his first pair of long trousers, which had been ripped when he'd fallen coming home from church on the first day he'd worn them; disagreements with his father as he was growing up and the last big argument when Blairton had stopped him from going to Canada.

She had been sitting in the gloaming for some time before she realized how dark it was and rose to light the oil lamp. She had wanted Blairton to install gas, but he had said it would cost too much because they were so far from the village. It came to her then that her husband had not come back for any dinner, and that she hadn't had anything to eat herself since early morning, so she stood up, wearily, to prepare a meal. Life had to go on – a semblance of life, at any rate. It was not until she had put some Kerr's Pinks in a basin that the appalling thought occurred to her. What about that poor lassie, Elspeth Gray? She wouldn't have heard the tragic news yet, but it wouldn't take long to filter through the grapevine of the close farming community, and it was up to Meg to break it to her first. She would have to write to Elspeth, too, and one of the men could cycle to the village tonight to post it, so that she would get it first thing in the morning.

Meg laid the basin in the sink and sat down again. Her hand was unsteady as she dipped the pen in the crystal inkstand and started to write. 'Dear Miss Gray . . .'

Lizzie regarded her daughter anxiously. 'I think you must be sickening for something, Eppie, you've been looking that poorly. Take a day in your bed to shake it off, or go and ask the doctor for a bottle o' something.'

'I'm fine, Mother.' Elspeth reflected sadly that no bottle could cure her ailment, and she couldn't risk seeing the doctor. Listlessly, she struggled into her coat. It was cold, and still dark at seven in the mornings, although most of the February snow had disappeared except from the sides of the dykes, where it was 'lying waiting for more', as the country folk said.

A cruel north wind was blowing, and she shivered as she let down the latch of the gate. She had walked only a few steps along the road when a dark figure loomed up ahead of her and it flashed across her mind – could it be . . . ? – but before the hope had properly taken shape, she realized that this man was too short, too fat, and her disappointment almost choked her. She blinked as a powerful torch shone in her face.

'Oh, it's yourself, Elspeth,' boomed a hearty, familiar voice.

'Aye, Postie.' She was about to pass when Willie Mavor thrust a slim envelope into her hand. 'It's for you, lass.'

'Oh, thank you, Postie.' Not worrying that it might make her late for work, she ran back inside to read the long-awaited letter, but found that it wasn't John's writing, after all, and the address at the top was Blairton Farm. Could Mrs Forrest have found out what she and John had done?

Dear Miss Gray,
This is a very difficult letter to write, but I felt it was up to me to let you know. John wrote and told me that he intended to wed you when he came home, but we got

a telegram this morning saying that he has been killed in action, just a week short of his 21st birthday.

Elspeth's sharp moan of despair made Lizzie run through from the back kitchen, drying her hands on her flowery overall. 'I thought you were away . . .' she began, then saw her daughter's stricken face. 'What is it, Eppie?'

The girl, still reading, ignored her.

I am sure you loved him as much as me, and I would be pleased if you could come to Blairton as soon as it is convenient for you, so we can speak about him and help each other to get over it. Your sincere friend,

Margaret Forrest

Her sorrow too great even for tears, Elspeth handed the single page to Lizzie, who read the first paragraph then said, 'Oh, my poor lamb!' Gathering her daughter into her arms, she rocked her as she had done when she was a child seeking comfort for a scraped knee.

When Elspeth's trembling lessened, she stepped back. 'I'm going to have John's bairn.' It was as if that were nothing compared with what she had just learned, and she carried on in spite of her mother's involuntary gasp. 'And he never ken't anything about it.'

'So that's it. I never thought . . . how far on are you?'

'Near three month.' Even in her present state, Elspeth knew that things would be much worse for her if she told of the day she had spent at Blairton Farm. 'It was the night he took me home in the storm and we were just ourselves two in the kitchen . . . oh, Mother, we couldna help it.'

Lizzie wrestled with conflicting emotions: guilt at having left the house empty that day; outrage that they had done such a thing in her kitchen; anger at the boy for taking advantage of an innocent girl; sorrow over his death; concern for her ewe lamb. Motherly compassion won the day. 'This is a bonnie kettle o' fish, I must say, and we'll need to keep it from your father.'

Indeed, Lizzie was terrified of what might happen if Geordie learned of this tragic turn of events. He would do anything rather than be shamed by his daughter in front of the whole community, and he had a temper that could whip up into white-hot fury, as she had seen once or twice during their married life, although he had never vented his spleen directly at her. 'We'll have to work out something to tell him so you can get away,' she went on, 'so we'd best have a cup o' tea.'

A hint of a smile crossed Elspeth's agonized face. Tea, her mother's cure for everything, would not extinguish the new life growing inside her, and, in any case, she didn't want it extinguished. It was John's child, as much as hers.

They sipped the strong brew in silence until Lizzie laid her cup down with a satisfied thump. 'I'll say Janet's got a good job for you in Aberdeen, and you'll have to go before he notices anything. I'll write and ask if she'll take you in, and she'll not be hard on you when she kens the poor laddie's been killed.'

Elspeth doubted that. Her mother's sister was sharp-tongued and narrow-minded, and was strong in condemnation of any girl who had an illegitimate child. What did she know about love?

'It's the only thing I can think on,' Lizzie added.

Elspeth nodded sadly. Her aunt would sneer and make life difficult, especially after the bairn was born, for she had no children of her own and had no time for other people's. But where else could she go?

Lizzie stood up. 'You'd best go back to your bed, for you'll not feel like working the day.' She made up her mind to wait until suppertime before she said anything to Geordie; that would give her time to plan how to tell him.

While her mother went about her daily chores, anxiously trying to think of ways to shield her daughter, Elspeth lay weeping upstairs. John was dead! The child she was carrying would be born with no name, and such a stigma would go with him – or her – to the grave. She did not mind so much about herself, for it was her own actions that had brought her to this, but a poor innocent babe . . . ? There couldn't be a God, or if there was, He wasn't a good God as she had always been taught to believe. She had often heard the minister saying, in that boring way he had, 'God is Love,' so how could such a God punish John and her in this dreadful manner when all they had done was to love each other?

Puzzling this out, she remembered the lies she had told, the clandestine meeting at Blairton, the hours of loving madly . . . though the minister, and her father, would call it fornication. But both telling lies and fornicating were sins, and she would have to suffer for them.

When Lizzie went upstairs, half an hour before Geordie was due home for his dinner, she found Elspeth asleep, exhausted from crying, by the look of her, poor lassie. Well, there was no need to tell her father that she was here, not yet. Suppertime would come soon enough. She had made his favourite tattie soup for his dinner, and arrowroot for his pudding, so that should keep him in a good mood for the afternoon, and if she ran to the village after he'd gone back to the farm, she could get a bowl of potted head for his supper, and give him curds for a pudding. Surely that would sweeten him for what she had to tell him.

As he usually did, he came in just after twelve, and ranted on about something the farmer had said to annoy him, but Lizzie was too preoccupied to take it in. Ferguson of Denseat was always roaring at somebody, but he was a good enough master, for all that. The tattie soup did make her husband simmer down, and by the time he had finished his pudding, he was calmer. His half hour over, he went out without a word, which was not unusual, for he was not a man to waste his breath needlessly.

Lizzie poured another cup of tea for herself. She had not realized how keyed up she was, but she sagged now in relief that he had noticed nothing. Having washed up the dishes, she went upstairs to see if Elspeth wanted anything to eat, but she was still sleeping. It was the best thing for her, the mother thought, and sat down to write to Janet. She would post it when she went to the butcher in the village.

Elspeth was awake by the time she got back, but Lizzie made her stay in bed. 'It's best I tell your father when there's just the two of us there.' Never having deceived her husband before, she was afraid that she would not be able to carry it off if her daughter was looking on.

As soon as Geordie came home in the evening, he looked surprised that his wife was alone. 'Eppie's surely late in coming home the night?'

84

Having had all day to work it out, Lizzie was ready with her story. 'She got two letters this morning, and she was awful upset, so I made her bide at home and go to her bed.'

'What kind o' news upset the lassie like that?'

'Mrs Forrest wrote to tell her young John's been killed.'

'Oh.' Geordie was obviously shaken. 'I'm sorry to hear that, but Eppie didna ken him well enough to be that upset, surely?'

She couldn't have known him much better, Lizzie mused, wryly, but said, 'She liked him an awful lot.'

'Ach! She's young and there'll be other lads.' Geordie callously glossed over Elspeth's heartbreak. 'It's Blairton I'm sorry for. He'd his heart set on young John taking over from him some day. It makes you wonder if there's a God at all, letting things like that happen.'

This shocked his wife more than anything he could have said, for Geordie had always been a religious man, too religious at times, for he could not see past the teachings of the scriptures. He looked perplexed suddenly. 'But I thought you said there were two letters for her?'

'The other one was from Janet. She'd heard o' a sewing job in a big house in Aberdeen, and asked about it for Eppie, and she's to start on Monday week, wi' a lot more pay than she gets from Grace Fraser. It's a blessing, really, coming at this time, for a change o' job'll take her mind off the laddie's death.' Amazed by her ability to distort the truth like this, Lizzie was thankful that Geordie didn't question what she had told him. She would likely have broken down under pressure.

But his face had darkened. 'What right has your Janet to arrange a job for my daughter?' he demanded. 'Elspeth can just write and tell her she's not taking it, for she's far better here where I can see she comes to no harm.'

'Janet'll look after her,' Lizzie murmured.

'Janet can't even look after herself without having you running at her tail every time she snaps her fingers.'

'She can't help being delicate . . .'

'There's nothing delicate about Janet! If Harry Bain had put his foot down from the start and made her be a proper wife instead o' a self-styled invalid, she'd have been a better woman the day.'

'She was never very strong,' Lizzie ventured, 'and if Harry doesna mind, it's nothing to do wi' us.'

'It is when she starts poking her nose into our lives,' Geordie thundered.

Beginning to fear that she was fighting a lost cause, Lizzie made one last stand. 'She was only doing it for Elspeth's sake. It's a grand job, by all accounts, and a lot more money, so you surely wouldna begrudge the lassie a chance to better herself? She'll never get any further wi' Grace Fraser, but think on the opportunities she'll have in the town. This big house would just be a start, and she could maybe end up working for the nobility.'

'And you think the nobility's better than us, do you? Some o' them's that perverted, they think about nothing but whoring wi' their servants and throwing them out on the streets if they fall wi' a bairn.'

'They're not all like that,' Lizzie began, then jumped as Geordie thumped his fist on the table. 'I've said no, woman!' he roared. 'Now, am I to get my supper?'

Giving up for the moment, but determined that the matter was not over yet, Lizzie rose to serve him the potted head and vegetables. He was an obstinate, cantankerous devil, but she could be just as obstinate when she liked, as he would find out when he had finished eating. She had never gone against him before, but there was always a first time.

By the time his pudding plate was empty, he seemed to have cooled down, but she waited until she had cleared up and he had read his passage from the bible before she sat down and said, as scornfully as she could with her insides quaking, 'I aye thought a father was supposed to love his children.'

His head jerked up. 'And who says I don't?'

'It doesn't look like it when you're stopping her taking a job she wants.'

His eyes widened. 'Elspeth wants the job?'

'She wants to get away from Auchlonie.' Lizzie could see that she had made him think. 'She wants to get away from everything that reminds her on John Forrest.'

'Och, John Forrest.' Geordie spat in the fire to show his contempt.

'She did love him, Geordie, though she didna ken him long. She's heart-broken, and you surely don't want to cause her any more misery?'

'No,' he said, slowly, 'I wouldna want to do that.'

'Well then.' Lizzie's body relaxed a little, her heart slowed down.

Geordie didn't speak for a few minutes, obviously mulling over what she had said, then he muttered, his voice flat, 'I suppose I'll have to let her go. She likely will get over young Forrest quicker in the town, but I'm going to miss her, for she's never been away before. Still, it's time

87

she saw a bit o' life, and Aberdeen's not the other side o' the world, so she'll be able to come home on her days off.'

No, Lizzie thought, fiercely, she'll never be able to come home again, and Geordie wouldn't want to see her if he knew the whole story.

On Friday night, the second after the delivery of the telegram, Meg Forrest slept soundly the whole night through, and rose on Saturday morning feeling much better. She had exhausted her tears and, although she would never completely get over the loss of her son, she could now accept it.

In the middle of the forenoon, the clattering of horses' hooves in the yard made her wonder who could be calling, and she was quite surprised to see the carrier at the door when she answered the loud knock. She was expecting no parcels.

'I've a grandfather clock here for you, Mistress Forrest.'

'Oh!' She tried to hide her agitation. 'Oh, aye.'

Eck Ewen eyed her inquisitively. 'I thought you'd one already, but maybe I was mistaken.'

'No, you werena mistaken.' Meg left it at that.

Eck, recognizing the finality of her tone, asked no further. 'It come up from Perth on the train this morning, so I loaded it on and came right here. Is Blairton about, or some o' your men to give me a hand?'

'They're ploughing behind the byre.' Meg went inside, reproaching herself for having forgotten about the clock, but when the men guided it carefully through the door, she instructed them to put it in the parlour, the only place there was room for it, and after the men left, she took a good look at it. It was much more impressive than the one in the farmhouse, which had been here before she came as a bride, and it struck her, with a plummeting of her heart, that it would never be used as a wedding gift from John to his bride now.

However, it had been meant for Elspeth Gray, so she would have to be told about it when she accepted the invitation to come to Blairton. Where would she keep it, though? There was less room in the cottar house than there was here.

Elspeth went back to work on the day after she received Mrs Forrest's letter – excusing her absence by pleading an upset stomach and saying that she would be leaving at the end of next week because she had found a better job in Aberdeen.

'That's very sudden, but if it's to benefit you, I'll not stand in your way.' Grace Fraser had grown quite fond of the girl during the three years she had employed her, and was sorry to be losing her. To cover her sentimentality, she said, 'Did you hear young John Forrest had been killed? They say his mother's taking it very badly.' She was appalled to see the girl's face blanching – she hadn't connected Elspeth's leaving with the boy's death until now.

Elspeth took a deep breath. 'Aye, I did hear. Poor woman.' She wished that she could accept the 'poor woman's' invitation and go to Blairton to tell her about the coming child, but it was better not to. Mrs Forrest would only think the worst of her and be disgusted.

The sad news having gone round, Nettie and Kirsty felt awkward with Elspeth. When Mrs Taylor told them about

John the day before, Kirsty had said, 'It's like it was a story,' and Nettie had snapped, 'It's a lot sadder, any road.'

Elspeth was ready with her answer when Nettie asked what kind of job she'd got. 'It's a sewing maid in a big house in the town that my Aunt Janet got for me. I'm working a week's notice, and I'll be leaving here next Saturday.'

This didn't satisfy Nettie, so she asked bluntly 'Is it because John Forrest was killed you're going away?'

'Aye, that's it.' Elspeth grasped the excuse eagerly; it would save them suspecting the real reason for her leaving.

Next morning, a letter came from Janet, agreeing to take Elspeth, but saying it was a disgrace that a woman in poor health had to bear the brunt of the girl's sins. Having known what her sister's reaction would be, Lizzie burned the letter without showing it to her daughter.

All the following week, Elspeth marvelled that she could behave so normally after the terrible calamity which had befallen her. It would have been bad enough to be expecting a bairn if John had still been alive, even if he hadn't come home in time to wed her and avert a scandal; not to have his support at all would be unbearable, but she was going to have to bear it, whatever happened.

On Saturday night, Nettie and Kirsty presented Elspeth with a small, cheap brooch, almost breaking down the reserve she had built up, and Grace Fraser added to her discomposure by saying, as she was going out, 'Just a minute, Elspeth. I wish you the best of luck in the future, and please take this in case things don't work out for you.' She held out an envelope and closed the door before the overcome girl had time to thank her.

The pound note which Elspeth found when she opened it was the final straw, and she gave way to her tears. They were all so kind, it made her half regret allowing, encouraging, John Forrest to make love to her that night by the fire, and that day in Blairton farmhouse, but she wanted to have his child, the proof of his love, and was prepared to do anything in order to keep it.

Later that evening, Lizzie helped her to pack a Gladstone bag, then said, in some embarrassment, 'Here, this'll maybe help you a bit. I don't suppose Janet'll give you any money, seeing she'll have to keep you.' She pressed two sovereigns into her daughter's hand. 'No arguments now – you'll likely need them.'

Elspeth spent her last night in Auchlonie thinking sadly of John Forrest, whom she would never see again, and worrying about what was to become of her in the big city.

Chapter Nine

Geordie Gray lifted Elspeth's bag. 'I'll walk wi' you to the station, and you'd best take a tram when you get to the town, for it's a fair bit to be humping this.'

Elspeth gripped her mother's hand. They had no idea when they would ever see each other again, but they couldn't let their emotion overcome them in front of the man, who was quite ignorant of the poignancy of the parting.

Father and daughter walked to the village in silence, meeting no one on this quiet Sunday afternoon, and, as they passed the road to Blairton, Elspeth regretted not having gone to see Mrs Forrest. Maybe she wouldn't have condemned, maybe she would have been glad to have a grandchild as a remembrance of John . . . but it was too late now. When they reached the little station, Geordie cleared his throat of a sudden obstruction. 'Mind and do what your Auntie Janet tells you, for she can be a real besom when she likes.'

'I'll mind, Father.' Her voice was a trifle unsteady. He wouldn't be so considerate if he knew that she was three months gone with child.

When the train came, she took the bag from him and entered a carriage, her last glimpse of him showing him gazing rather forlornly after the train as it steamed away from the little platform. Sighing heavily, she put her bag up on the rack and sat down facing the only other occupant. She felt all choked up, knowing that she could never return to Auchlonie, for she couldn't leave her bairn with Janet, not even for a day, and her father must never know about it.

'It's not quite so cold the day.' The woman facing the engine gave her a friendly smile. 'I've been to Portkillie to see my sister, an' it's aye cold up there on the coast. Was that your father seeing you off?'

Reluctant to start a conversation, Elspeth nodded, but the woman was not be thwarted of a chat. 'You'll be going to Aberdeen to work? There's no need for you to look so upset, for you'll get used to the town, and if you've got good lodgings you'll soon be laughing at yourself for worrying.'

She was a pleasant, rather plump woman, a few years younger than Lizzie, Elspeth thought, taking stock of her. Her bright bird's eyes were kind and sympathetic, her plain navy coat and hat gave her a stamp of respectability, and it should be safe to tell her the story that Lizzie had concocted. 'My mother's sister found me a place in Aberdeen, and I'm to be biding wi' her.'

'Oh, that's good . . . what's your name, lassie? I aye think it's more friendly if you ken folks' names.'

'It's Elspeth. Elspeth Gray.'

'Well, Elspeth, I'm Helen Watson. I was saying I'd been to see my sister, her man's the auctioneer at Portkillie and he'd to be away for a while to a big sale in Glasgow, so she asked me up there for company.'

'That had been a fine change for you.' Elspeth couldn't help warming to her travelling companion.

'I fair enjoyed myself. We went to Elgin one day to the shops, then had a while in Cooper Park, and yesterday, we'd a walk along the seafront at Portkillie. I love the sea and the boats, being born in Peterhead, but it's funny, I never think o' going to the harbour or the beach in Aberdeen. What kind o' work have you got?'

Elspeth's mind had been wandering, worrying about living with her aunt, but the sudden question broke into her thoughts. 'Oh . . . I'm to be a sewing-maid. I worked for the dressmaker in Auchlonie, you see.'

Fortunately, the woman asked no more questions, and when the train drew into the terminus, she gathered up her belongings while Elspeth took her bag from the rack. On the platform, Mrs Watson said, 'Have you far to go to your auntie's?'

'She bides in Rosemount Viaduct, and I've to take a tram.'

'I'll walk you up to Union Street, then, and show you where to get it.' Becoming aware of the girl's increasing distress, she said, 'Is something wrong? I ken a troubled face when I see it. Look, what about me buying you a cup o' tea and you can tell your Auntie Helen all about it?'

It was meant to cheer the girl, but it broke down the fragile barrier, and when they sat down in the small cafe, Elspeth sobbed out her story. Mrs Watson raised her eyebrows once or twice although she said nothing, but when the girl came to a hiccupping end, she said, 'And you think the whole world's against you? You're not the first to get landed in the family way, though it's a great shame your lad was killed, but I'm sure your auntie'll look after you.'

94

'You don't know Janet,' Elspeth muttered, faintly, then, ashamed of confiding in a complete stranger, she added, 'No, I'm being stupid. I suppose I'll be fine there.'

Eyeing her earnestly, Mrs Watson said, 'Well, Elspeth, if you're not wanting to go, I'd be happy to look after you. We've a spare room since our Donald went away to the war.'

'Thank you very much, but I'd better go to my auntie's.'

'I see you've been brought up to do what your mother tells you, but sometimes a mother doesna really see what's best for her bairn, so if your auntie makes things bad for you, just you come to me. I bide on the middle floor of the middle house in Quarry Street. Will you mind that?'

Elspeth nodded bleakly and the woman said, briskly, 'Come on, then, and I'll see you to your tram.'

After going up a long flight of steps, they emerged breathlessly on Union Street, where green and cream tram-cars were gliding along the rails, their metal antennae extending skywards to connect with the overhead electric cables. Coming to a red tramway stop, Mrs Watson announced, 'We'll wait here.'

In a few minutes, she said, 'Ah, here's the number five and my number four's just behind it. Cheerio, now, lass, and mind what I tell't you.'

'Yes. Thank you. The middle floor of the middle house in Quarry Street,' Elspeth said, as she boarded the vehicle.

Mrs Watson was a very nice woman, she reflected, as she sat down, and it was good to know that she had a refuge if things got too bad for her, but . . . she would have to put up with her auntie.

When Janet Bain opened the door in answer to Elspeth's timid knock, her face was even more forbidding than the girl remembered. 'So you've come? A fine thing this, when a decent woman has to save her sister's face, or more like it, her niece's face. If it was up to me, you'd have stewed in your own juice, for why should I take on a girl that's gone against God's commandments?'

Luckily for Elspeth, her uncle appeared behind his wife. 'Come in, Elspeth,' he said, kindly, taking her bag. 'You'll be tired after your journey.'

'A wee bit,' she admitted.

'Not too tired to make up your bed, I hope,' Janet sniffed, as they went inside. 'My back's been bothering me for days, and I wasn't able to do it for you.'

'Oh, it's all right, I'll manage to do it myself.' Elspeth knew that things were not going to be all right. It was not going to be easy to live with this woman, whose antagonism screamed from every pore of her long, thin face.

'I'll take you through to your room,' Harry remarked, 'and I'll give you a hand to make up your bed the time Janet's dishing up the supper.' Ignoring his wife's gasp of indignation at being made to do something herself, he led the way into a room off the tiny lobby. It was only slightly larger than Elspeth's bedroom at home, but the long window let in far more light than the skylight she was used to.

As her uncle helped her with the sheets and blankets, she observed, 'I think you're accustomed to making beds.'

'I'm accustomed to doing most jobs in this house,' he smiled. 'Not that there's anything really wrong with Janet, but it makes my life easier if I do things and say nothing. You'll have gathered she didn't want you here, and I'd a hard job making her agree, so you'd be best to keep your tongue between your teeth, and all.'

Knowing that in her uncle she had a staunch ally, Elspeth just nodded, and he went on, 'Maybe it would be a good thing if you took a wee job for as long as you're fit, so you wouldn't have to be in the house with her all day, for she'd have you working harder than any mistress.'

'Will she not be angry if I take a job?'

'She was going on about how much it would take to feed you, so you could tell her you wanted to pay for your keep. That might make her happier about things.'

'Aye, that's right.' Elspeth felt a little happier herself. She had not thought about taking a job, but it would be good to have a little money of her own.

'You could go to Collie's in the morning. They keep a register of domestic employment . . .' He looked at her anxiously. 'You wouldn't object to being a servant, would you? It's the easiest way to get a job.'

'I wouldn't object, as long as Auntie Janet doesn't.'

'She'll not object if you're giving her money.' As he fitted his side of the counterpane, he said, looking very serious, 'I'm sorry you're in trouble, Elspeth, and I maybe won't always be able to smooth things between her and you, but remember, I'll always be on your side, no matter what it looks like.'

'Thank you, Uncle Harry.'

'Your lad was killed, I believe.'

'Aye.' A lump rose in her throat. 'He would have wed me when he came home, but . . .'

'Aye, that was a tragedy.'

When they returned to the kitchen, Janet was sitting with her hand on her heart. 'I took a bad turn just now, but I've set most of the table. You'll manage to dish up, Elspeth?'

'I'll do it,' Harry put in, before the girl could say anything, and as he filled the three plates he said to his wife, 'Elspeth's to be looking for a job the morrow. She doesn't want to be a burden on us, she wants to pay for her keep, as long as she's able to work, that is.'

His wife looked surprised, but not displeased. 'You're not very far on by the look of you?'

'Just three month.'

'So you could work for . . . four months yet, maybe more?'

Harry Bain frowned. 'It depends what kind o' work she gets. She couldn't do anything heavy if she was getting near her time.'

The thin mouth was drawn in. 'She's a strong girl, and we'll need every penny we can get if she starts eating for two. And she'll need to remember we'll be feeding her and the child after it's born, though how Lizzie expects me to manage with an infant in the house . . .'

'Elspeth can start working again after it's born,' Harry interrupted, 'and a new-born bairn doesn't need much looking after.'

'It'll not stay new-born,' his wife snapped, 'and I'm not fit to be . . .'

'We'll sort things out when it comes to it,' Harry said, hastily.

Supper was eaten to the accompaniment of Janet's solitary voice listing her illnesses and ailments, Elspeth having to turn her head away to avoid laughing aloud when her uncle winked to her to let her know that most of them were in his wife's own mind. Her uncle was fun to be with, but she couldn't see herself living in this house for long after the bairn was born. She would have to find a live-in job where they would not mind her taking it with her, but, as Harry had said, she could sort that out when the time came.

After seeing his daughter off on the train, Geordie Gray walked back home thoughtfully. When he went into the cottar house, he eased himself into his chair without saying a word, apparently deep in thought, and Lizzie waited a few minutes before she asked, 'Did Eppie get away all right?'

Her husband roused himself. 'Aye, but she didna look all that happy about the grand new job she's going to.'

Lizzie held her breath. Surely unobservant Geordie hadn't guessed? 'She'd been upset at leaving home for the first time,' she ventured, but the dark scowl on his face told her that he had seen through her lame excuse, and her stomach lurched as she waited for him to speak again.

'You've been keeping something from me, woman.'

Alarmed by the accusation, she straightened the table-cover to hide her confusion. 'What d'you mean, Geordie?'

'You ken what I mean! She's been looking poorly for weeks, and I can recognize the signs as good as the next body, though it took me a while. She's got herself in trouble, that's what it is. Isn't it?' he demanded fiercely.

Lizzie's heart slowed with fear. 'Aye,' she admitted, 'and the poor laddie was killed, as fine you ken.'

'It was John Forrest, then?' His voice was heavily sarcastic. 'Are you sure she hadn't been served by other men and all?'

'No, no, Eppie would never have done that, and what chance had she, wi' you never letting her out to enjoy herself?'

His face was turkey red now, a thick cord beating at his neck. 'She must have been enjoying herself wi' him long before she let on she ken't him, the sleekit besom!'

'She wasna. It was just once, when he took her home the night o' the terrible storm. She took him in and there was nobody here, for I was at Janet's.'

His frown deepened to a grotesque grimace, his eyes looked at her wildly as he sprang to his feet. 'You mean to tell me their fornicating took place under my roof, and you ken't about it?'

Lizzie shrank back as his hand came up menacingly. 'I didna ken, Geordie, not till she told me she was having his bairn. I'd no idea that . . .' She began to sob.

'That he'd served her?' Another, more comforting thought struck him. 'He must have forced himself on her, for she couldna have been willing.'

But Lizzie couldn't allow him to think ill of the dead boy. 'She loved him, Geordie, so I don't think he . . .'

'She said she didna ken him before, so that story'll not hold water. He must have forced her, for she couldna have been in love wi' him as quick as that.'

Hesitating for only a second, Lizzie burst out, 'We fell in love quick ourselves, Geordie, mind? That was what annoyed our Janet, for she thought you'd want her.'

Thrown out of his stride, Geordie growled, 'I never

100

wanted her, and she wed Harry Bain within a month o' our wedding.'

'That was just spite, for she aye had her eye on you.'

'You're trying to make me forget what I was saying, but it'll not work. Elspeth would never have let that lad take his way wi' her the very first time they met, surely?'

Lizzie thought sadly that he had forgotten what it was to be young and have feelings that were difficult to suppress. 'They maybe couldna help theirselves.'

'She'd been asking for it, the bloody little whore!' he burst out, before Lizzie's scandalized face, her tears stopped with shock, made him curb his language. 'She's a disgrace to this house, and she'll never set foot in it again.' He looked without pity at his wife and roared, 'Do you hear me?'

'Would you turn your back on your only bairn?'

'I wish I'd never sired her, and if you hadna been so soft wi' her, this would never have happened.' Having fixed the blame squarely on his wife now, he sat down again, obviously searching for some other grievance to lay at her feet. Knowing that his silence did not mean that the awful confrontation was over, she waited fearfully for his next venomous outburst, but when he did speak, a touch of sadness had crept into his voice. 'You should have given me other bairns. She wouldna have been spoiled if she'd had brothers or sisters, but once was enough for you, though I've often wondered how you got rid o' the seed I planted in you.'

'I never did anything. I wanted other bairns as much as you, Geordie.' Lizzie began to weep again. She felt like reminding him how ill she had been after Elspeth's birth, but he didn't want to understand, and he was deliberately forgetting that the doctor had said she could never have another child. He was beside himself with anger at his daughter, and it would be a waste of time arguing with him.

He grunted suddenly, but he had lost the urge to wound her further. 'I'm sure my seed was fertile.' He paused for a moment. 'But mind this. You're not to write to her, and you'll burn her letters without reading them.'

Nodding helplessly, she saw that his train of thought had changed, and knew that he wasn't finished yet.

'What's Janet to say when she finds out about this, after getting a job for her . . . ?' Breaking off, he eyed her with deep suspicion. 'Or was that a pack o' lies, and all?'

Lizzie's heart sank even farther. He would go mad altogether when he learned of her scheming, but she couldn't go on like this; she would be found out eventually. 'Come on, woman, I'm waiting!' he thundered, his fingers drumming on the arm of his chair. 'Did Janet get a job for her or no'? It doesna sound like Janet to me!'

'I couldna think on anything else to get Eppie away before you noticed. No, Janet didna get her a job, but I wrote and tell't her about the bairn, and she wrote back that she'd take Eppie in.' Lizzie braced herself for the next explosion, cowering away from him when he bounded over to her. 'I ken't you'd be angry at Eppie, and I just . . .'

'Angry?' he screamed, his open hand taking her across the cheek. 'I'd have thrown the little bitch out . . . like I should throw you out for the lies you've tell't me! Never did I think my own wife would turn against me!'

'I haven't turned against you, Geordie, I was just trying

to save Eppie. I could never have stood by and watched you putting her out of the house with nowhere to go, and her to be having a bairn. If you had, I wouldna have waited for you to throw me out, I'd have gone wi' her.'

'You'd have left me?'

She could see that this had shaken him. 'Aye, I'd have left you, for I couldna have bidden wi' a man who put his only child out in her time of trouble, and that's why I got her away.'

He stood motionless for some time, then turned and sank down in his chair again, his body sagging like an empty sack. Although he had been strict with her, his daughter had been the light of his life, his everything, and what she had done was as though she had stabbed him in the back. He would have to shut her out of his mind now. At last, he let out a low moan. 'Oh, God! The deceit that's been going on under my very nose.' Looking at his wife piteously, he suddenly straightened, his expression hardening once again. 'Ha! She'll get her punishment yet, for your Janet'll make her wish she hadna been so free wi' her favours. But don't you forget what I said! You burn any letters she sends . . . without reading them!'

He stood up, lifted the bible from the dresser then sat down at the table, and Lizzie leaned back trembling, but thankful that she had only suffered a slap on the face. She deserved more for telling him lies, and she was glad that it was she who had been at the receiving end and not Elspeth. A great sadness came over her then. He had washed his hands of their daughter, and clearly regarded this chapter of their lives closed.

Chapter Ten

Coming off the tramcar at the end of Union Terrace, as her uncle had instructed her, Elspeth crossed the two sets of rails cautiously, afraid of being electrocuted if she stood on them, and gave a gasp when a man walking alongside her placed his foot right across the metal, making him turn to her in surprise. 'I thought you'd get killed if you stood on them,' she blurted out, embarrassed at drawing attention to herself.

He laughed loudly. 'You'll only get electrocuted if you put one foot on the rail and the other one on the overhead wires to complete the circuit.' Smiling broadly, he walked on ahead of her.

She looked up at the cables and realized that he had been teasing her, for they were too high to be touched with anybody's foot. He must have thought her very ignorant. Going along Union Street, she kept her eyes open for the shop called Collie's, which Uncle Harry had told her was at the opposite side. She spotted it at last, and made her way over the rails a little more confidently this time. A delicious smell of coffee wafted out of the large store – nothing like the shop at home, where ever-obliging Sandy Moir, genial in his shirt sleeves and big white apron, stood behind his counter and produced whatever his customers wanted, be it a packet of safety pins or a gallon of paraffin; a jug of syrup or a poke of sweets; a bag of flour or a packet of starch. But the counters and glass cases here stretched farther than she could see from the door, and trim girls in neat black dresses were serving customers who could have passed for the gentry from the big house just outside Auchlonie. Elspeth was sure that it couldn't be the right place, but it said Andrew Collie & Sons over the windows, so she plucked up courage and went in.

One of the men assistants was feeding dark brown beans into a grinding machine. She hadn't known that coffee came from beans – her mother had only occasionally bought small tins of Bantam as a special treat – and while she stood there, fascinated, she was approached by a smiling, middle-aged man in a smart dark suit and spotless white shirt. 'Can I help you, Madam?'

'Oh! I'm looking for the register – the register for jobs in service. Is this the right place?' She felt like an intruder in the elite establishment and fully expected him to ask her to leave at once, but he smiled graciously. 'Go straight through, Madam, and up the steps at the far end.'

'Thank you very much.' Elspeth was about to add 'sir' but stopped, fearing that she might make a fool of herself for the second time that morning.

She walked past a display of crusty loaves, tempting buns and cakes, counters and shelves filled with whiskies and exotic chocolates, and came to an area selling different grades of flour, oatmeal, rice and other cereals. She was afraid to stop – any hesitancy on her part might bring one of the men whose job seemed to be directing people. After the wines, teas and dairy produce, she came to a flight of six wide steps, at the top of which was a frosted glass door marked, 'DOMESTIC REGISTRY.' She tapped lightly on one of the glass panels and opened the door timidly.

A rather elegant woman looked up from her desk and smiled. 'Good morning, Miss . . . ?' Her voice was soft and friendly.

'Gray. Elspeth Gray. I'm looking for a place.'

Accustomed to dealing with country girls, the woman knew what she meant. 'What type of work? General? Laundry?'

'Whatever there is, I've never been in service before. You see, I worked for the dressmaker at home, but I'm willing to take anything you've got.'

'Do you live in Aberdeen now?'

'Yes, in Rosemount Viaduct with my auntie and uncle.'

'How old are you, Elspeth?'

'I'll be eighteen on my birthday.'

All the information duly recorded, the woman riffled through the pages of her large ledger. 'This might be suitable – a doctor's wife in King's Gate is asking for someone to cook and sew, and who is willing to look after two young children.'

'I could manage that fine.' Elspeth couldn't believe that it was so easy to find work in Aberdeen. Before Uncle Harry had told her about this place, she had pictured herself having to trudge from house to house asking.

The woman finished writing and held out a card. 'There's the address. I can't guarantee that Mrs Robb will engage you, of course, and if not, come back to me and I'll look for something else for you.'

'Thank you,' Elspeth murmured, then added, hesitantly, 'I'm sorry, but I don't know where King's Gate is.'

'No, it's my fault, I should have told you. A number three tram will take you, ask the conductor to put you off at the top of Fountainhall Road. If you turn left, you'll be on King's Gate, and the doctor's house is not far up on the left hand side.'

Elspeth walked back through the shop, too preoccupied to pay attention to its treasures, and stood uncertainly in the sunshine outside, wondering if the doctor's wife would be anything like Mrs McLean at home. She was an old dragon, and never kept any of her maids for long. Still, it would be a job, if she got it, and beggars couldn't be choosers.

Mrs Robb turned out to be a young woman of perhaps twenty-five, with wavy fair hair and dancing blue eyes which regarded Elspeth approvingly as she took her inside. 'I don't have to ask if you can cook – all country girls can cook – and I see from the card that you worked with a dressmaker before, so the sewing will be easy for you, and the children are really no problem. The hours are from eight in the morning until eight at night, meals provided, with a half day off every week and a Sunday once a fortnight.'

Elspeth smiled nervously. 'If you think I'm suitable, I can start as soon as you like, Mrs Robb.'

'I've no maid at the minute, so . . . is tomorrow too soon?'

'No, that would be fine.'

'Right! I'll see you at eight o'clock, then. Don't look so worried, I'm sure you'll manage very well. I will supply

107

your aprons, and I don't insist on a cap as long as your hair is clean and tidy.'

Mrs Robb opened the front door for her, then asked, 'Do you know how to get home from here?'

'I'll have to take the tram back to Union Street, and . . .'

'I saw on the card that you live in Rosemount Viaduct?'

'Yes, with my auntie and uncle.'

'Well, there's a much quicker way to get there. You came here on the number three tram? That route is called the Queen's Cross Circular, and it goes into town again via Rosemount Viaduct. Get on at the same stop where you came off, and no doubt you will know your aunt's house when you come to it. Goodbye, Elspeth, and I won't mind if you're a little late in arriving on your first morning, but once you find out how long you take to get here, I'll expect you at eight o'clock sharp every day.'

'Thank you, Mrs Robb.' Elspeth's head was reeling as she walked to the tram stop, but she liked the look of her new employer. Mrs Robb was a real lady, very slim and stylishly dressed, but her manner was friendly and cheery, and the work didn't sound too hard.

Janet Bain's face tightened when her niece burst in. 'Must you be so noisy?'

'I've got a job, Auntie Janet.' Elspeth's excitement was too great to be squashed by the cool reception. 'I'm to be working for a doctor's wife, and Mrs Robb's really nice, and I'm to be cooking and mending and looking after her two bairns, and she's going to supply my aprons. She said I won't need a cap, as long as my hair's neat and tidy.'

'Really, Elspeth, your chattering has given me a head-ache. You'll have to remember I'm not strong.'

'Oh, I'm sorry Auntie Janet.' A little deflated, Elspeth kept quiet for a short time, until her high spirits could be held in check no longer.

'The Robbs bide in King's Gate and I've to start at eight the morrow morning. I'll finish at eight, and I've a half day off once a week, and a Sunday off once a fortnight, and . . .' She broke off as the woman's hands jerked up to her head. 'I'm sorry, Auntie Janet, I forgot you'd a sore head. Will I make you a cup of tea?'

'A cup of tea might help if you would only stop speaking.'

The hint of a whine in her aunt's voice irritated the girl, but she said nothing until the tea had been made and drunk. 'Is your head better now?' she asked, knowing quite well that the headache, if it existed at all, was not nearly as bad as the woman was making out.

'Not much. Maybe . . . sometimes your Uncle Harry rubs the back of my neck for me . . . ?'

The words were more an order than a hinted request, and Elspeth jumped to her feet at once, thinking, as she laid her hands on the scrawny neck, that she wouldn't mind strangling her aunt. After a few minutes, however, the woman said, 'At least you've got fine, strong fingers. You're even better than Harry.'

The compliment, if it was a compliment, did not please the girl, because she knew what it meant. From now on she would be expected to carry out the massaging whenever her aunt wanted it. Going to the sink at the window, she washed her hands, but before she could ask where to find a towel, Janet said, 'As long as your hands are wet, you'd be as well paring some potatoes for the supper – Harry doesn't have time to come home in the middle of the day

– and when you've done that, you could sweep the stairs and . . .'

Apart from making two poached eggs on toast at half past twelve, Elspeth's day was taken up with doing the chores Harry Bain normally did, but she did not complain. As from tomorrow, she would be out of the house all day, and would be getting paid for the jobs she did. When her uncle appeared at ten past six, she told him her good news, keeping her voice low in deference to her 'delicate' aunt, and he seemed to be as pleased for her as she was herself.

Janet, of course, had to spoil it. 'Did you tell the doctor's wife . . . does she know the condition you're in?'

Having almost forgotten her condition, Elspeth felt her heart plunge. 'No, I didna tell her.'

'Hmm.' The thin lips were compressed, the hard eyes grew even more like steel. 'I just hope you don't see much of the doctor, then, for a medical man would notice quick.'

Elspeth's eyes sent a desperate appeal to her uncle, who leaned across the table and patted her hand. 'If they do find out, you can explain, lass. They'll not think so badly of you when they know your lad was killed.'

Janet bridled. 'Humph! Folk are not all like you, thinking the best of everybody.'

'And thank God they're not all like you,' he retorted, 'thinking the worst.'

'Oh!' she moaned, suddenly. 'I've got that terrible pain in my heart again.'

Rising to help her into an armchair, Harry winked at Elspeth, who did not feel any better for knowing the 'heart attack' was put on. She did not want to cause trouble between her uncle and aunt, but how could she avoid it when Harry took her side against his wife's?

For the rest of the evening, she sat in silence, wondering if she should tell Mrs Robb the truth in the morning, but when Janet went down to the lavatory on the half landing, Harry said, as if he knew what she had been thinking, 'Don't say anything to your Mrs Robb. Just make sure you do your work the best you can, and by the time you've to leave, she'll think that much of you, she'll understand what you're going through and why you didn't tell her at first.'

Remembering Mrs Robb's friendly manner and her modern dress, Elspeth felt better. Her employer would have a different outlook on life from her aunt, and would surely not condemn her for what had happened.

Next morning, Elspeth, too excited to be hungry, supped her porridge to save hurting Harry's feelings, and set off for King's Gate, where Mrs Robb explained that she did some Red Cross work every day. 'That's why I need someone to look after the children. The doctor's out at all hours, of course, and meals have often to be kept hot for him. My last girl married a soldier, and went off to live with his parents in Huntly, so I'm glad you turned up when you did.'

While she was speaking, she had shown Elspeth the kitchen and the sitting room and now opened another door off the large square hall. 'This is the dining room, which isn't used very often these days. The children will take their meals in the kitchen with you to save work, and Alex, my husband, usually takes his on a tray in the sitting room. I'm like a bird, I peck at whatever's available wherever and whenever I find time, so you won't have to worry about setting or serving meals in here.'

The girl was relieved. 'That's good, it was the setting and serving I was worried about, not the cooking.'

Mrs Robb pointed through the window. 'The children play in the garden there if it's fine, and if it's wet, they're supposed to play in the nursery upstairs. They like to spend a lot of time in the kitchen, though, but don't let them pester you. They're really quite good, and they'll do what you tell them – most of the time, anyway.' She laughed as they came out into the hall, and indicated one of two doors at the far end. 'The surgery – my cleaner attends to that – and patients come in by the side door there, so you won't see them. Mrs Balneaves does the washing and ironing as well as all the heavy cleaning, so she'll give you whatever needs mending. That and the cooking, and looking after the children, should keep you fully occupied.'

Mrs Robb smiled at Elspeth's bewilderment. 'You'll soon get into the swing of things. You'll be mostly on your own, as I go out a lot, and Mrs Balneaves is only here in the mornings and isn't one to spend time talking.'

'I'll do my best, Mrs Robb.'

'I'm sure you will. Now, I've left a note in the kitchen of the meals I'd like you to cook today, and I'll send Alexander and Laura down to you shortly, so you can get to know them.'

The grandfather clock had been in the farmhouse for two weeks before Meg Forrest cycled to Auchlonie and called at the dressmaker's shop. Grace Fraser gave her a welcoming smile; it was seldom that any of the farmers' wives asked her to do anything for them – they usually patronized the tailors or dressmakers in Aberdeen. 'Good morning, Mrs Forrest, I was very sorry to hear about your son. It must have been a dreadful shock for you and your husband.'

Meg just nodded, for she couldn't trust herself to speak about John's death yet. 'I hope you don't mind, but I was only wanting a word wi' Elspeth Gray.'

Putting two and two together, Miss Fraser came up with an answer which verified her previous suspicions about her ex-employee's hasty departure. Poor girl. John Forrest must have been the father, but the secret was safe with her. 'I'm sorry, Mrs Forrest, but Elspeth left last Saturday for a better job in Aberdeen.'

'Oh.' Meg had never considered this possibility. 'It was just . . . would you have her address?'

'No, I don't, but she might write to Nettie or Kirsty once she settles in; she was very friendly with them. Her mother would be able to tell you, though.'

'Aye, thank you.' Meg did not want to go to Lizzie, in case the woman hadn't known about her daughter and John, so she stood for a few minutes on the pavement outside, wondering how to trace Elspeth, who must feel as heartbroken as she did herself. Should she come back next week in case Nettie got a letter . . . or should she wait and see if Elspeth took up the invitation to the farmhouse on one of her days off? Aye, it would be best to wait, for the lassie might not want anybody to know how far things had gone between her and John. The poor thing had likely been too upset about his death to come to Blairton before she went to Aberdeen, but they could have helped each other to get over the shock. Becoming aware of the curious glances of two passing women, Meg walked on to Sandy Moir's shop to buy some sugar.

'Here's a letter from your sister in Aberdeen.' The postman smiled as he handed it over. 'I hope she's keeping better.'

Lizzie returned his smile. 'Our Janet enjoys her bad health, it's what keeps her going.'

In the kitchen, she opened the envelope, thinking ruefully that Janet was likely complaining already about Elspeth, so the long tale of woe about the extra work the girl was causing came as no surprise, though she suspected that Harry would be doing most of it. After scanning the second page – full of details of Janet's aches and pains, imaginary or otherwise – she dropped both of them into the fire. There was no sense in letting Geordie see it, for he would just start ranting on about Elspeth again.

She did wonder how her daughter was, for Janet had said nothing about that, but surely Elspeth would write herself . . . unless she wasn't keeping well. With a great effort, Lizzie concealed her agitation from her husband at suppertime. But she spent a restless night and was relieved when the postman knocked again the following morning. It would surely be a letter from her daughter this time.

Willie Mavor's grin spread all over his face. 'A letter from Aberdeen two days running, Lizzie. It's likely Elspeth telling you about her grand new job.'

Lizzie's hand trembled slightly as she accepted it and she prayed that he wouldn't notice. 'Aye, that's her writing.' She closed the door on his curiosity, remembering that Geordie had said to burn Elspeth's letters without reading them, but she had to find out how she was.

The letter did a lot to relieve her mind. Elspeth said that she was keeping very well, and that she had got a job as a maid with a doctor's wife. What could be more respectable than that? Lizzie thought, glad that the girl would be out of Janet's way most of the time. And she would be able to pay for her keep, so that should make her aunt happier, but . . . she wouldn't be able to work for very long, and it was what would happen when the child was born that worried Lizzie. However, she had disobeyed Geordie by just reading the letter, so she had better not risk answering it, and even more important, she had better burn it right now.

Chapter Eleven

The novelty of her job kept Elspeth from being homesick, and she went home every night so tired that she was glad to tumble into bed. This, of course, also had the welcome result that she had little contact with her aunt except on her half days and every second Sunday. At those times, she was careful not to say too much about her life at King's Gate, merely satisfying Janet's curiosity about what the house looked like inside, and what kind of people the doctor and his wife were. She never told her about the Robb children, though she had grown very fond of them. Laura, at two, was an affectionate little thing, pulling at Elspeth's skirts a dozen times a day, but Alexander, two years older, was more serious though he had an appealing, gurgling giggle when he was amused by anything.

Pleased with her new maid, Ann Robb nevertheless soon became rather worried about her. 'Elspeth never talks about her parents,' she remarked to her husband one day. 'I'm sure something awful must have happened to her.'

Alex Robb glanced fondly at his wife. 'She probably feels ashamed of her parents now she works in the city.'

'She's not a girl like that,' Ann said, doggedly, still firmly convinced that there was a hidden tragedy in the girl's life.

As week succeeded week, Elspeth had to tighten her stays to conceal the tell-tale bulge, and she was well advanced in her pregnancy when Mrs Robb approached her. 'Sit down, Elspeth, I want to talk to you.'

'Yes, Mrs Robb?' She sat down somewhat awkwardly, and very apprehensively, because her employer's face was so serious.

'My husband and I have both noticed that you have put on some weight, and we believe . . . are you expecting a baby, Elspeth? You had better tell me the truth.' Elspeth's expression told her that her suspicions were correct, and her voice became gentle. 'How far on are you, my dear?'

'Eight month.' The girl fought to keep back her tears. 'I was over three month gone before I started here.'

'Why didn't you tell me?'

'I couldn't tell you, I was feared you wouldn't give me the job, and I wanted to save enough to see me over my time.' Gulping, she added, 'I'm sorry, Mrs Robb, I didn't mean to annoy you, and I'll leave now, if you want.'

'I'm not annoyed, my dear, and we don't really want you to leave, but it's not good for you to be working so hard so late in your pregnancy . . . and it's not good for the baby, either. You should have time to rest, and to prepare a layette for its arrival. Do you understand?'

'Oh . . . I didn't think about that.' The realization of what the baby clothes would cost made the tears spill over. 'Mrs Robb, what am I going to do? I'll never be able to buy the gowns an' hippens it'll need.'

'What about the father? He should be made to help, you know – you didn't do this by yourself.'

'He was killed in France in February. He didn't know

117

about this, but he was going to wed me the next time he came home, and now . . .' She burst into wild sobs.

Ann Robb took her hand. 'Oh, my dear girl, it must be terrible for you, but wouldn't your parents stand by you?'

'Mother was feared my father would find out, for he's a strict man and very religious, so she tell't him her sister had got me a fine job in the town, and I had to come and bide wi' my Auntie Janet.'

'Oh, I'd forgotten that. So you do have someone to look after you? I was afraid you were just in lodgings.'

Thinking sadly that she would probably be better if she were just in lodgings, Elspeth said, 'Yes, I've somebody to look after me, though Janet's not very strong.'

After looking pensive for some moments, Ann Robb suddenly brightened. 'Elspeth, I've been thinking. I'll give you my children's baby clothes, they're quite presentable, but the napkins, or hippens, as you call them, were so worn after two babies we used them as floor-cloths. You can have the pram, though. Alex was just saying the other day that we'd have to get rid of it now Laura's got a go-car.'

'Oh, Mrs Robb, I don't know how to thank you.'

'I'll look out the clothes tonight and you can take them home with you tomorrow, that will definitely be your last day here, but it's considered unlucky to get the pram before the baby. An old wives' tale, but. . .' Ann Robb shrugged sheepishly for believing the superstition. 'If your uncle doesn't object, he can collect it when it's required.'

Janet Bain scowled when she learned that Elspeth was to stop work the following day. 'So you'll be amongst my feet all the time? Well, just don't think you'll be allowed to sit about and do nothing, for I'm not able to run after you and do all the housework as well.'

Harry opened his mouth as if he were about to tell his wife there was nothing wrong with her, but, thinking better of it, he turned to Elspeth. 'Your Mrs Robb must be a real good woman to give you her children's old clothes.'

'Aye, she's awful good. She wasn't angry with me for not telling her before, though she'd every right to be.'

'You can tell her I'll collect the pram as soon as your baby's born. My, that's going to save you a lot, for prams are real dear.'

Janet sniffed. 'It's nothing to her, a doctor's wife.'

'It's a lot to Elspeth, any road,' Harry stated, glaring at his wife.

'Oh aye, you'll stick up for her, though she's just a little trollop.'

'I'm not a trollop,' Elspeth shouted. 'I was only ever wi' John Forrest and we loved each other.'

'A trollop,' Janet repeated, adding in disgust, 'with no respect for her betters.'

Paying no attention to Harry's warning hand on her arm, Elspeth yelled, 'Betters? And since when were you any better than me?'

The thin mouth curled down. 'For one thing, I never let any man touch me, not even Harry till after he wed me.' With that, she flounced out and stamped down to the lavatory.

Harry looked sorrowfully at Elspeth. 'Oh, lassie, you shouldn't have got on her wrong side.'

'She shouldn't have said I was a trollop,' Elspeth said, heatedly, 'and what man would have wanted to touch her any road? She's nothing but a . . .' She stopped in confusion, remembering that he was the woman's husband.

But he was smiling wryly. 'She wasn't as bad as that when she was young, though it was sometimes a case of me asking her permission first before I . . . and she hasn't let me near her for . . .' He, too, halted, then, after a moment, he said, 'Try to put up with her, lass, for you'll come off worst if you don't. Get away to your bed now, before she comes back. She'll have cooled down by the morning.'

Next day, as Elspeth got ready to go to King's Gate for the last time, Janet spoke not one word to her and gave no sign of having cooled down, and the girl began to regret her impetuous remarks. Laura and Alexander Robb kept her from brooding, however, though she had a little weep when she told them that she was leaving that night and would not be coming back. Alexander was too much of the little man to show his sorrow, but Laura's tears mingled with Elspeth's as they hugged each other at the children's bedtime.

At five to eight, when Elspeth was making sure that she had left everything in proper order, Mrs Robb came into the kitchen carrying a large parcel. 'Here are the baby clothes. They were all clean when they were laid away, but perhaps you had better wash and iron them before you use them. Things get musty when they haven't been used for a while.'

'Thank you, Mrs Robb, I'll do that.'

'Here are your month's wages, and something extra as holiday pay. Look after yourself, my dear, and remember, I'd like to see your baby after it's born.'

Too emotional to say any more, Elspeth lifted her coat and went out, but on her way to the tram stop she opened the envelope she had been given and burst into tears when she saw the extra five pound note. It was almost four months' wages, so Mrs Robb had given her a gift, not just a little something to make up for the holidays she had never had.

Elspeth's days were even harder now than at King's Gate, for Janet Bain made sure that she never had time to sit down, and carped constantly that things were not being done properly, but the girl was afraid to rouse her aunt's anger again. The weight of the baby inside her made her easily tired, and she felt embarrassed at being so cumbersome, but she was determined not to break down and give Janet something else to sneer at. Only when she was in bed did she let the tears flow, tears of sorrow for John Forrest, of pity for herself, of dread of her life once the baby arrived, for she couldn't see Janet taking kindly to it. Night after night, she cried herself to sleep, until her nerves were in tatters and her face grew wan and drawn above the huge, swollen mass of her belly.

She realized herself that things could not go on like that, and, knowing that it would not take much to ignite the power keg, bit her lip until she drew blood when her aunt went on and on at her. Janet had the sense not to go too far in front of her husband, so Harry was not aware of what the girl was suffering, although he did notice that she looked ill. Not having any experience of how women looked during pregnancy – Janet's two miscarriages had both been at three months – he put Elspeth's gaunt looks down to her condition and hoped that the infant would not be long in coming.

The inevitable explosion between the two women occurred late one afternoon in August, days before Elspeth believed her confinement to be due. She had been feeling off colour all morning, and was taking twice as long to do things as she normally did. Janet watched her closely for some time, then said, sarcastically, 'You couldn't go any slower, could you? A snail could work faster than that.'

A red flash burst inside Elspeth's head. 'I'm going as fast as I can,' she spat out, 'as you would understand if you had even a spark of humanity in you.'

Janet's head jerked up. 'How dare you speak to me like that, you little slut!'

'I'm not a slut!' the girl screamed. 'I'm a red-blooded woman, something you've never been! You're just a dried-up old maid . . . you couldn't love anybody if you tried, for you don't know what love is!'

Janet, in spite of her alleged sore back, leapt to her feet and struck the girl full in the stomach. 'You bitch! You speak about love, when you're just a whore?'

Doubled up with pain, Elspeth lashed out with her foot, although she was not near enough to do much damage. 'I'm not a whore, but at least a whore's got feelings, and you're so . . . so wooden, you . . .'

Hopping on one leg, her other smarting from the light blow it had received, Janet screeched, 'If Geordie Gray heard what you're saying to me, he'd kill you, you . . . ungrateful bitch! I've a good mind to write and tell him you're in the family way, and let him see what kind of a girl his precious daughter is.'

'Write then! I don't care what you do, for my father can't touch me now.'

'Your mother's turned her back on you, any road! She never answered any of your letters, did she? And she's never come to see how you are.'

This taunt, instead of deflating the girl as Janet had hoped, only served to enrage her further, because she had been extremely hurt that her letters to her mother had gone unanswered. 'I wouldn't put it past you to have written to my father already, and he'll have forbidden my mother to write to me.'

Janet bridled. 'You can think what you like! I'm a good God-fearing woman and . . .'

Common sense having deserted her altogether, Elspeth retorted, 'More like God's feared at you, for you've just got a stone where your heart should be. You've had me working for you from morn to night when you could see I wasna fit, and it's a wonder to me your man didna leave you years ago. You're no proper wife to him, and havena been for a long time, according to what he told me.' Her hand flew up as if to still her runaway tongue.

The woman's chest was heaving now, her mouth opening and closing like a stranded fish, but, in a moment, her eyes glittered dangerously. 'So that's the kind of thing you and him speak about? It's maybe all you think about, but I'm above the sins of the flesh. You're a filthy-minded harlot, and you'll get out of my house this minute! I never want to see you again . . . or your bastard, either!'

Holding her head high now, Elspeth marched through to her room, her fury keeping her from crying. It did not take her long to throw her few belongings into the old Gladstone bag, and she slammed the door behind her as she went out, drawing on her coat as she lumbered down the stairs. Once on the pavement, she went as fast as she could to get away from the terrible woman who was her aunt . . . had been her aunt, for she did not regard her as such any longer, and it was not until she was halfway along Union Terrace that she realized that she was home-less now.

Slowing down, she felt the tears coming to the surface and, rather than have anyone see her weeping in the street, she went down the steps into the gardens which ran along the railway line, for there were seats there, where she could think what to do. She needed her mother, more than she had ever done in her life, but she could never go home again. Collapsing on to a bench, she let her tears out in harsh strangled sobs, ignoring the increasing discomfort in her belly, presuming it was the result of Janet hitting her. A few old men, taking advantage of the sunshine to have a stroll, eyed her with some concern, but she was not aware of them and they did not stop.

At last, the cramp grew so bad that she realized she was in labour, and her tears stopped with the shock. She couldn't sit here . . . she couldn't let her baby be born out in the open like a tinker's. She tried to think where she could go, but her brain would not function properly. John Forrest had no right to get himself killed. He should have come back to her and they would have been married and he would have looked after her . . . but he couldn't help being killed. Oh, God, what was she to do? She didn't know anyone in Aberdeen except Janet and Harry Bain, and she wouldn't go back there though she was dying on her feet, which was exactly what she would be if she couldn't find somewhere else to go.

When the answer came, she wondered why she had forgotten for so long. The woman she'd met on the train – Mrs Watson! The middle floor of the middle house in Quarry Street! She would be made welcome there, for she'd been told to go if she was in trouble, and she couldn't be in deeper trouble than she was now.

Heaving herself to her feet, Elspeth made her ungainly way up the steps again, having to stop every now and then to wait for the wash of pain to subside. She had no idea where Quarry Street was, but she had a vague recollection that Mrs Watson had said she took the number four tram, and the conductor would be able to tell her where to get off.

She was so dishevelled and so obviously in labour that the conductor looked anxious when she asked him to tell her when they came to Quarry Street. 'We only go as far as Bayview Road, and you've a good bit to walk after that.'

She didn't care how far she had to walk, as long as she reached Mrs Watson before it was too late. 'You'll tell me where to get off?'

'You've to go right to the terminus.'

She held her bag tightly against her stomach, gripping herself in to stop the pain, but her mind was easier. She was on her way to a friend, someone who would make sure she was all right . . . that her baby was all right.

When they came to the terminus, the conductor helped her off, and pointed up the street. 'Carry right on and when you come to a lane, turn in and go along past the quarry, and you'll see Quarry Street in front of you. You can't miss it, it's just one big block of tenements.'

'Thank you,' Elspeth murmured, then cringed as another pain struck her.

'Will you be all right?'

'I'll . . . be . . . fine,' she gasped, waddling forward, for she could feel the baby slipping farther down and wanted to get there as quickly as she could.

Having to stop every few minutes, it took her some time to reach the lane, and she turned off the main road thankfully. There was no sign of the block of tenements the conductor had spoken about, however, and she was so tired, both physically and emotionally, that she sank down on the grassy bank, sure that she could go no farther. After about five minutes, she had the presence of mind to move behind a tree out of sight of anyone who might chance to walk along the lane, and her last conscious thought was that Janet Bain would be sorry when she learned that her niece had died in a lonely lane all by herself.

It was dusk when she wakened, chilled and frightened at finding herself in such an eerie spot. Where was she and why was she here? A familiar sensation beginning in the pit of her stomach brought the awful memories back, and she picked up her bag and struggled to her feet. The spasms she'd had before must have just been the first stage of her labour, and she must find Mrs Watson before the final stage began.

Carrying on in the direction she had been going, she passed one or two small cottages then saw the dark outline of a large building standing on its own some way ahead. It must the block of tenements, it must. She crossed a small wooden bridge over a burn, and found a path going off the lane to the right, appearing to lead straight to the tenement block. Her goal so near, she stumbled on until she came to the front of the building, where she saw three doors. Making for the middle one, she glanced up to see how many storeys there were, and was glad that there were only three, for it meant that she would only have to go up one flight of stairs.

Dragging herself painfully up each step, she leaned against the door on the half landing – the lavatory, likely – until she got her breath back, then went up the next set and peered at the two nameplates. The first said 'Murdoch' but her heart lifted when she saw 'Watson' on the other, and she rapped loudly on one of the panels.

It seemed an eternity to her before the door was eased gently open, then flung wide when the woman recognized her. 'Oh, my God! It's the lassie on the train. Elspeth, isn't it? You look worn out, come in, for any sake.'

Mrs Watson ushered the girl into a little lobby, then asked, 'What's happened?'

Elspeth did not try to explain anything, stating, baldly, 'I'd a row wi' my auntie and she put me out.'

'And you so far on? That wasna very Christian o' her, but never mind, you're safe here. But I shouldna be keeping you standing, come ben to the kitchen.'

The room was even smaller than the kitchen of the cottar house. A man was sitting in an old leather armchair reading a newspaper, but he rose stiffly at their entrance, and Elspeth saw that he was stockily built and not much taller than his wife. His mousey hair was combed straight back off his brow, and his ruddy face was smiling a greeting to her.

'This is Elspeth, Jimmy, an' she's going to be biding in our Donald's room.'

'Oh, aye?' Jimmy Watson inclined his head towards the girl then sat down to continue reading, and Elspeth was amazed at his lack of curiosity. Her father would have wanted to know all the whys and wherefores before he permitted a stranger to lodge in his home.

'Ben here, Elspeth.' Helen Watson led her through the tiny hall into an equally tiny room containing only a single bed with a white Alhambra bedspread, a tall chest of drawers with a cheval mirror on top and a low basket chair. It wasn't all that different from her own room at home, Elspeth thought, but she'd had a marble-topped wash-stand with a floral basin and ewer on it. This place wasn't even big enough for that.

'Hang your things up in the press.' Mrs Watson indicated a cupboard door between the foot of the bed and the window wall. 'I'll clear a couple o' drawers in the kist once we've had a cuppie tea.'

'I minded you said to come to you if I . . . I hope it's all right me turning up like this?'

'I'm pleased you did. You shouldna be wandering about the town in your state.' She gave Elspeth a searching look and added, 'I some think you're about ready to drop the bairn. Have you had any pains?'

'Some, but not that bad, and I'm not sure if they were labour pains at all. They've stopped now.'

'It sometimes takes a while. That had been just a warning, likely, to get you prepared for it. You maybe havena noticed yet, but I'm expecting, and all.' She gave a light chuckle. 'You must have given me the smit that day on the train. I thought it was the change, but I wasna feeling very great, so I went to see a doctor, and I'm over seven month now.'

Elspeth clapped her hands with glee. 'If you're that far on already, you'd been expecting before you ever met me.'

They both laughed, then Helen said, 'It's not laughing, really. I'm over forty, and what'll my Donald think?'

'Are you not pleased about it?'

'I'm delighted, and so's Jimmy. It's just . . . we're maybe a bit old to . . . no, a bairn'll keep us young, eh? Now, I'll leave you to hang up your things, but come ben for a cuppie when you're ready.'

Elspeth smiled to herself as Mrs Watson went out – another woman with the teapot always at hand, it made her feel less strange. In fact, she was much easier in her mind now about everything. Opening her holdall, she unfolded her skirts and blouses and hung them in the cupboard along with her coat, but left her underclothes and the small parcel of baby things in the bag until the drawers were made ready for her.

Mrs Watson, meantime, had filled the kettle at the sink under the window, and lit the gas ring on the cooker, talking all the time to her husband. 'It's the lassie I met on the train when I was coming back from Portkillie, mind, I tell't you about her? The poor thing's in the family way, but the laddie that fathered the bairn was killed in the war. She was supposed to be biding wi' her auntie, and I tell't her to come to me if they didna get on, seeing our Donald's room's sitting empty. Well, they've had a row and the woman's put her out, and she'd no place else to go, and she minded what I'd said, so she came here.'

Jimmy nodded agreeably. He was an easy-going man and quite accustomed to his wife's impulsive actions. 'She's only a bairn herself,' she went on, 'and she needs somebody to be a mother to her, poor thing.'

Jimmy scratched his head. 'Aye, you'll look after her well enough, but are you fit for the extra work?'

'Ach, I'm as strong as a horse, and she'll not be that much bother, for I some think her bairn's started its journey. Once she's on her feet again, she can give me a hand in the house, though I wouldna want to work her too hard, for she's only a young lassie.'

'Well, it's up to you.'

While she set a wooden tray on to the chenille table cover and laid a dainty embroidered traycloth over it, Mrs Watson conjectured aloud about the row Elspeth had had with her aunt, her husband paying no heed to her ramblings, and only Elspeth's appearance put a stop to them. 'You'll have a cuppie the now, Elspeth, but have you had any supper yet?'

'I'm not hungry.'

'You have to eat, lassie. Jimmy'll pare some tatties, and there's a bittie boiled ham left.'

'I don't want to be a bother to anybody.'

Jimmy stood up. 'It's no bother, Elspeth. I'm a dab hand at boiling tatties.'

'That's about all he can do,' his wife laughed, and sat down to winkle Elspeth's story out of her.

Once she began, the girl spilled out everything from the time she had gone to Rosemount Viaduct, making Mrs Watson wax loudly in condemnation of Janet Bain's heartlessness, and even Jimmy tutted in the background as he set a pan on to boil. When Elspeth had eaten, and it had all been discussed outside in, the woman said, 'Well, it's all past, and best forgotten about. I'm sure you're ready for your bed, so I'll clear the drawers in the morning, but, mind, if anything starts to happen, come right ben here and tell me, though it's the middle of the night.'

A few minutes later, Elspeth lay down in bed, feeling safe at last. The pains had not started again, but when they did, Mrs Watson would look after her. She wished that she could let her uncle know that she was all right, for Harry had been good to her, but she didn't want Janet to know. It would do the woman good to be kept wondering what had happened to her, though the old hag probably didn't care.

It was just as well that events had taken the turn they had, the girl reflected. Janet would have been worse than ever when the baby arrived, and life would have been even more intolerable, but at Quarry Street she could bring her child up the way she wanted, with no one to interfere. She was so tired that it never crossed her mind to wonder what would happen when the little money she had left ran out.

In the high bed in the kitchen recess, the Watsons were trying to decide – or, rather, Helen was trying to decide – how to explain her to their neighbours. 'I'll say she's a cousin o' yours, Jimmy, in from the country.'

He looked dubious. 'But they'll see she's . . .'

'We'll need to make an excuse for her being in the family way, to save any scandal, but something'll come to me. We'll just have to take it as it comes.'

'Imphmm,' agreed her husband, drowsily.

Chapter Twelve

Next morning, Elspeth went through to the kitchen looking most astonished. 'I slept like a log,' she informed Mrs Watson, 'and I havena had any more pains.'

The woman smiled. 'Aye, well, it's been a false labour. That often happens. It could be days yet before it starts in earnest. Sit you down there, and have some porridge. Jimmy's in the lavvy the now, and he'll be going to his work in a minute or so and then we'll get peace to speak things over.'

Sitting down at the set place, Elspeth said, 'What does your man work at?'

'He's on the crusher at the quarry. That's the machine that breaks up all the bits o' granite that's no use for anything else, and makes them into chuckles for paths in folks's gardens. It's a messy job, and his clothes are grey wi' dust when he comes home, but . . . och, well, it's a good enough job, and it's steady.'

Having heard the last part of his wife's remarks as he came in, Jimmy took his jacket off the hook at the back of the door and observed, 'This block o' tenements belongs to the quarry, you ken.'

'Rubislaw Quarry,' Helen said, over her shoulder. 'A lot o' famous buildings is made wi' Rubislaw granite, but I think Marischal College here's the bonniest in the world. Near all the houses in the town's built wi' granite, that's why it's ken't far and wide as the Granite City.'

'The folk in Quarry Street are a grand lot.' Jimmy seemed to be prouder of his workmates than of the edifices created from the stone they quarried.

'It's a bit like biding in a village, though,' put in his wife. 'Everybody kens everybody else's business, and they're just as narrow-minded as the folk in your Auchlonie, I'll be bound, so we'll need to make up a story about you to stop their tongues wagging, but we'll wait till Jimmy's away.'

'I'm just going.' He smiled at Elspeth on his way to the door. 'I see you havena started yet, but maybe it'll all be past before I come home at night.' Giving a nod to his wife, he went out.

Mrs Watson poured out a cup of tea for Elspeth, refilled her own then said, 'Now, we'll have to sort things out. Have you seen a doctor yet?'

'No, I was feared the doctor would tell my mother.'

'So you'll not ken when you're really due?'

'Oh, aye, for I was only wi' John . . . once.' The day they had spent together was too shameful to think about, and in any case, the conception could easily have taken place that night at the fireside. 'In the second week o' November.'

According to Mrs Watson's reckoning, Elspeth's baby was due about the middle of August, any time now, and her own at the beginning of November, and they made their preparations for their coming infants in the warm summer afternoons – the girl was too conscious of her bulk to go out – talking 'twenty to the dozen' as Jimmy would have teased them if he had heard them.

Elspeth told her landlady about her life in Auchlonie and Mrs Watson recalled the days of her youth in Peterhead, where her father had been a trawlerman, often away but free with his money when he was at home. 'There was three o' us – me and Rosie and Danny. Poor Danny.'

Elspeth was curious. 'Did something happen to him?'

'He got tired o' the trawling, and he come home one day and tell't Mother he was going to Canada.'

The girl's heart turned over sickeningly. 'My John was wanting to go to Canada, but his father wouldna sign the papers. I bet he wishes he had, now, for John would have been at the other side o' the world when the war started, and he'd never have been killed.' Her eyes swam with moisture at the thought of her dead lover.

'If he'd went to Canada, you'd never have ken't him.'

'No, that's right, I didna think. Well, I'm glad he never went.' Elspeth paused. 'Did Danny go?'

Helen Watson smiled sadly. 'Aye did he, and he wrote every week for a while, and said he was getting on fine, but the letters dwindled away and stopped.'

'Did you never find out why he stopped writing?'

'The last we heard, he was out o' job, but about six month after that, my mother got word from a mission in Toronto that he'd died in their place. They said he was a vagrant immigrant, and they'd found her address in his pocket.' Helen gave her eyes a furtive wipe. 'Poor Danny, he must have been down and out at the finish.'

Recalling that John had said he would never be down and out, Elspeth blinked her eyes and tried to hide her distress, but Helen had noticed and deftly changed to a cheerier topic.

When Elspeth laundered the baby clothes, she marvelled at the convenience of the gas iron. The flat iron at home had to be heated on a trivet at the fire, and her mother had spat on it to see if it was hot enough. If it was, the spit formed into a ball and rolled off, then the iron had to be run over an old piece of cloth to clean it, but it cooled very quickly, and had to be put back on the trivet every few minutes. Mrs Watson tested hers by touching the base plate gingerly with a licked finger. It didn't have to be cleaned, and kept its heat for as long as she wanted.

When Jimmy came home just after six one evening, he said, 'I could hear the two o' you from the bottom o' the stair. Your tongues would clip cloots.'

'Away wi' you.' Helen smiled. 'We was just having a quiet conversation, putting the world to rights, like.'

Elspeth was amazed at the teasing that went on between them. There was never a dull moment, even when they played cards in the evenings. The Watsons had to teach her the rules, for her father had never allowed playing cards in the house, but she had learned quickly, and often beat them at Snap, Rummy and Strip-Jock-Naked. She was still not very good at Whist, because Jimmy played two hands, which totally confused her.

'I ken some folk would think we're heathens,' Mrs Watson remarked on the Sunday, 'but there's nothing bad about playing cards on the Sabbath, as long as we're not gambling. Playing for money would be a real sin.'

On Monday, a letter arrived from Donald. 'He never writes much,' his mother said, after she'd read the single page, 'but at least it shows me he's still alive and thinking about me. You ken, Elspeth, maybe you should write to

135

your mother and give her your new address. She'll be wondering where you are, and she'll be worried about you.'

'She never answered the letters I wrote when I went to Janet's first,' the girl said, pouting a little.

'Maybe she was still a bit mad at you for landing in trouble, but she'll have cooled down by this time.'

'Maybe she will.' Elspeth had not thought of this before, and sat down in the afternoon with a pen and paper.

'It's from Elspeth,' Willie Mavor remarked as he handed a letter to Lizzie. 'It's a good while since you heard from her, isn't it?'

'She likely hasna had time to write,' Lizzie replied, rather frostily.

Her patent unwillingness to talk about it did not stop the postman. 'That's the young generation for you. The minute they're away, they forget about their mothers and fathers, but when they're in trouble it's us they turn to again.'

'Aye.' Lizzie edged the door shut a fraction.

'I mind when our . . .'

'I'm sorry, Willie,' she burst out, desperate to be rid of him, for he was worse than an old woman with his gossip, 'I'm terrible busy the day.'

He did not take offence. 'That's all right, Lizzie. I'll hear about Elspeth another time.'

Closing the door properly, she went across to her chair at the fire and opened the envelope warily, her eyebrows lifting when she saw the address. Elspeth had surely left Janet's house, but Quarry Street? Who did she know there?

Dear Mother,

I met Mrs Watson on the train when I was coming to Aberdeen, and she managed to get out of me why I was so upset. I told her I was to be biding with my auntie and she said if we didn't get on to come to her. I suppose you know Janet and me had a fight, and she put me out, so I came to Quarry Street, and Mrs Watson let me have her son's room. He is in the Gordons.

Lizzie took a deep, shuddering breath. Why had Elspeth fallen out with Janet, and why was she living with absolute strangers? And townsfolk had different morals from country folk – no morals at all, some of them. She bent her head to the letter again.

I am very happy and the Watsons have promised to look after me when my time comes, which should have been past by now. They are very good folk, and he works at Rubislaw Quarry.

Your loving daughter,
Elspeth

Lizzie's heart was racing with anger at Elspeth for taking matters into her own hands. Janet was maybe difficult to get on with, but she'd been brought up as a good Christian and she would never have put Elspeth out, not with her so near her time, not unless she had done something awful. The girl had gone off the rails altogether and didn't deserve a mother's love. Why should she worry about her, Lizzie thought, crumpling up letter and envelope

137

furiously and flinging them into the heart of the fire, then watching with satisfaction as the paper curled and blackened. She had been afraid to answer the other two letters the girl had sent in case Geordie found out, but she wouldn't dream of answering this, and she would burn any more that came without reading them. Elspeth had chosen to go her own way, well, let her see how she would get on. Geordie had been right all along. She was no daughter of theirs any longer.

***

Elspeth had been worrying all night again, and approached Mrs Watson in the morning. 'I can't expect you and your man to keep me for nothing . . .'

'It's all right, lassie,' Helen smiled. 'Me and Jimmy's been speaking about it, and we can easy keep you till . . .'

'I've got some money,' Elspeth protested. 'I paid my board to Janet out o' my wages, but I'd to buy the hippens out o' what my mother and Miss Fraser gave me. My last mistress, Mrs Robb the doctor's wife, gave me enough gowns and vests and jackets to do for a while, and she's promised me her old pram if somebody goes for it when I need it. So I've still got the five pounds I got from her when I left. That should see me through for a good while.'

'Keep it for a rainy day,' Jimmy said, draining his cup.

His wife smiled. 'Aye, you never ken when you might need it. You're away then, Jimmy? I'll tell her what we were saying last night.' She turned to the girl again when the door closed. 'We're willing to feed you till after the bairn's born and . . .'

'Oh, but I couldna take charity. My mother aye said . . .'

'It's not charity, it's what any decent folk would do for a lassie in trouble, and once you're on your feet, and fit enough, you can take a job and you can start paying for your keep. Just think about it and you'll see it's the best way.'

So overcome by the Watsons' kindness, it did not occur to Elspeth to wonder what would happen to her child if she went out to work. It was enough for her that she would not have to worry about money, and that she would have something in hand for any emergencies that could arise in the future.

She had received no reply to the letter she had sent to her mother to let her know where she was living now, and when she mentioned it, later in the day, Mrs Watson tried to excuse Lizzie. 'Your auntie's likely told them you're not there any longer, and your father's maybe that angry at you for fighting wi' her he'll not let your mother write.'

Elspeth was practically sure that Janet would have told her father everything, including the fact that she was pregnant, so he probably *had* forbidden her mother to write, but she would send one more letter, just in case the first one had got lost. She still thought nostalgically about her parents at times, but life in Quarry Street was so free compared with what it had been in her own home and at Rosemount Viaduct that she was quite content where she was.

On his way back for breakfast, Geordie had almost reached his own gate when he saw Willie Mavor coming, and waited to see if there were any letters for him.

'Fine morning, Geordie,' the postman observed, as he handed over an envelope, then added, 'It's to Lizzie from Aberdeen . . . Elspeth, I think.'

Receiving no reply, Willie swung his leg over the cross-bar of his bicycle again to carry on with his round, and Geordie stuffed the envelope into his pocket with trembling hands. When he went inside, Lizzie said, 'I thought I heard the postie's voice. Was there any letters?'

'He was just passing the time o' day wi' me,' her husband said, gruffly.

Having wondered if Elspeth had written again, Lizzie let out her breath as she went through to the back kitchen. She wanted to know how her daughter was – her initial anger at the girl's last letter had passed – but she was glad that there hadn't been one today, for Willie Mavor would have given it to Geordie. She wished that she hadn't destroyed the other one, for she couldn't remember the address, and she meant to answer the next one, to let Elspeth know she still cared about her.

As soon as his wife had turned her back, Geordie took out the envelope and dropped it in the fire. He would have liked to find out if his daughter was keeping well, but he didn't want the ache in his heart starting up again. It was best this way.

When another week had gone past, Elspeth grew very agitated. 'It should have been by this time,' she said one afternoon. 'There must be something wrong.'

'Don't fret, lass,' Mrs Watson comforted her, 'first bairns are often late, and as long as you're still feeling the bairn moving about inside you, there's nothing wrong.' She was sorry for her lodger, and wished that she could help, but it was into September and she was feeling burdened down herself, with her own time only six weeks off.

When the girl's labour finally began, the first sharp pain shooting through her lower abdomen about fifteen minutes after she went to bed, she ran through to the kitchen as soon as it had passed. 'I think I'm started, Mrs Watson.'

Jimmy, in the act of taking off his trousers, hastily pulled them up, and Helen turned round from washing her face at the sink, her hair, only faintly shot with grey and free of any hairpins, almost reaching her waist. 'How many pains have you had?'

'Just the one, but it was real bad.'

Elspeth's eyes were fixed beseechingly on the other woman, who said, gently, 'It'll maybe be hours yet before it's born, so it's too early to get the midwife. I'll make us a pot o' tea, an' we'll just sit a while.'

Elspeth sat down, and Jimmy pulled his shirt back over his head, resigning himself to a long wait. He would have to fetch the midwife when the time came, so he'd have to forget about sleep for one night.

They were still drinking the tea when the girl doubled over again, her mouth twisted with agony. 'That's less than ten minutes between them,' the older woman remarked. 'Maybe you'd best go now, Jimmy.'

The man nodded and lifted his shoes off the fenderstool.

'Finish your cup o' tea first, Mr Watson,' Elspeth whispered. 'What's a minute or two back an' fore?'

After the man went out, his wife said, 'Have another cup o' tea to settle your nerves, Elspeth.'

The white-faced girl accepted the cup gratefully. 'Did you have a bad time when Donald was born?'

'It wasna very good,' Mrs Watson laughed. 'It aye seems bad at the time, but you forget about it quick.'

Elspeth smiled wanly. 'How long was it wi' you?'

'Och, that's nothing to go by.' Helen did not want to frighten the girl by telling her about the seventeen sweating hours it had taken to bring Donald into the world. 'Every woman's different, and when it's past, you'll be wondering what all the fuss was about.'

'Aye, I suppose so, but I'm real scared.'

'There's nothing to be scared o', it's the most natural thing in the world. Even Queen Mary had to go through the very same. Oh, is that another one?'

By the time Jimmy returned, Elspeth's pains were strong and quick, but he shook his head at his wife when she looked up from wiping the girl's brow. 'The midwife wasna in. Her man said she was at another confinement.'

Elspeth let out a low moan, whether from the pain or the disappointment, Helen couldn't tell, but she said, briskly, 'Well, I'll manage myself. I ken what has to be done so you go back to your bed, lass, and Jimmy, you'd best go and lie down on the couch in the parlour, out o' the road. You need your sleep, or you'll not be fit for your work the morrow, and I'll likely be trotting out and in here for water.'

'I could easy boil the water for you,' Jimmy offered.

'No, no, I'll manage.' She allowed the girl to drag herself past before whispering to her husband, 'If I need you, I'll waken you, for God kens what's in front o' her.'

'Aye, it's best to be prepared.' Jimmy shook his head again and went through to the best room.

Elspeth knew she was dying. Nobody could suffer like this and come through alive. Any second now, she would find herself being welcomed by St Peter at the Gates of Heaven . . . no, he wouldn't welcome her, because . . . the reason eluded her, but it was there, somewhere in her fuddled brain. With her eyes tightly closed, she prayed to be released from these unbearable dragging pains that were ripping her whole body apart.

'Elspeth.'

She wouldn't answer. Why couldn't she die in peace?

'Come on, lass. You must keep pushing.'

Her body responded to the insistent order in spite of her. Pushing . . . pushing down. Pushing as hard as she was able.

'That's it, Elspeth. Now, just one more, that's all.'

Just one more? If it would end this purgatory, she would force herself to try. 'Yaagh!!' Who was crying out like a beast in mortal agony? 'Yaagh!!'

With excruciating speed, all her innards forced their way out of her and it was over. She was floating like a feather . . . up and up in blessed freedom. Death was a great relief after the heavy burden, whatever it was, that had weighed her down for so long. It would be sheer tranquillity now, for all eternity.

But . . . a hand was rubbing her tender belly, she realized, with some irritation – an urgent hand, making the pain return, if not quite as bad as before. She had thought she was done with it. Must she suffer more?

'I'm sorry, Elspeth, lass, but it'll be a lot worse for you if I don't get the afterbirth off you.'

Afterbirth? Once, years ago, she had seen a calf being born, and her father had told her that the horrible bloody bag of waste which came out of the cow behind the calf was called the afterbirth – or placenta. She couldn't have just given birth, surely? It would explain the pains and the aching void in her insides, but it couldn't be possible, and she didn't want to think about it – not with her father fresh in her mind.

Something slipped out from between her legs, guided down by the disembodied, firm, pressing hand, and at last there was no more pain.

'Good lassie.'

It was a familiar voice, but she was too exhausted to make any effort to place it. She had to die, to get away from the shame she had brought on her father and mother. Shame? Now she remembered. That was why she would be turned away from the gates of Heaven. After the sin she had committed, she would be sent to Hell, to be burned in the everlasting flames. She fought now against the consuming lassitude. She didn't want to die. She didn't want to go to Hell. She longed for her mother's comforting arms, but it wasn't Lizzie's voice that had talked her through the terrible ordeal. It was one she had known and trusted . . . but whose?

'Elspeth. Come on, lassie. You've got a bonnie, bonnie son. Open your eyes and look at him.'

The intruding voice was gentle, but she had no desire to see the cause of her disgrace and agony.

'Look at him, the wee angel. Thick dark hair, and all.'

Thankful that she wasn't being allowed to die, she forced her eyes open and saw a plump, smiling woman, her eyebrows raised in entreaty, holding something out. Mrs Watson. It came back to her now. This wasn't just any woman. This was Mrs Watson, her landlady, her friend, her saviour.

'Take your son, Elspeth, and feel his sturdy little body.' Mrs Watson placed the bundle on the bed, making sure that the new mother had taken a firm grip of it.

An unexpected tenderness surging up inside her made the girl look down on the tiny face, the eyes tightly screwed up and the rosebud mouth opening and closing like a new-born kitten. But it was no kitten. This small scrap of humanity had made its painful way out of her body, had been the cause of all the suffering she had endured. 'A son, did you say?' Her voice was weak, but she could feel herself drawing back from the yawning pit, the dark mouth she had so nearly allowed to swallow her.

'Aye, lassie, he's perfect, and we did it ourselves two.' There was great pride in Mrs Watson's voice as she lifted the tightly-wrapped infant out of his mother's arms. 'It's all past, and you'll be on your feet again before you ken. You'll feel tired the now, and it's little wonder, for you'd a hard time.'

'Aye, I'm awful tired.' Elspeth closed her eyes again, but her heart was lighter – a thousand times lighter – for Mrs Watson always knew what to do.

When she learned that the midwife couldn't come, Elspeth had panicked, imagining that the child would keep growing inside her until she burst, or until they both perished. It was all over now, though, and it was God's blessing that she'd had this kind, caring woman to look after her. It was lucky that she had met Mrs Watson on the train to Aberdeen that day, but maybe that had been arranged by God as well, and He hadn't forsaken her, as she had feared in her darkest moments. She had someone to advise her, whatever else she might have to face – whatever else she and her son might have to face. This comforting thought was gradually edged out of her mind by a dread of the unknown future – the punishment which had yet to come for what she had already done – and she drifted into an uneasy sleep.

Several times during the course of the past few hours, Mrs Watson had been on the point of rousing her husband, but something always held her back, and even when Elspeth lapsed into semi-consciousness she struggled to bring her out of it and made her keep pushing. At last, with the one final effort that she'd been asked for, Elspeth screamed like a banshee, but the woman was able to separate the infant from its mother and cut and tie the umbilical cord. Then she turned to the girl again to guide out the afterbirth.

When she had held the swaddled child out to the girl and urged her to hold it, Mrs Watson had been afraid that Elspeth was slipping into a coma, and getting no response, her heart had almost stopped. She had persisted, however, and after another moment of suspense, Elspeth's eyes had fluttered open, though she had seemed bewildered when the infant was placed in her arms. Then her face had been slowly transformed by a radiant smile as she realized that she was holding her son and everything was over. She relinquished him in seconds, and Mrs Watson laid him in the blanket-lined drawer she had made ready.

After doing everything she could, she took one last glance at the sleeping girl before she left the room, smiling a little as she realized that Jimmy had slept through noises that would have awakened the dead, then walked unsteadily through to the kitchen. She was ready for a cup of tea, and nobody could deny that she deserved it.

Chapter Thirteen

The bairn would be born by this time, Lizzie Gray reflected, and even if Elspeth hadn't written again, she should realize her mother would want to know how the confinement had gone. Her first grandchild, and she would never know if it was a boy or a girl. She couldn't even speak about it to Geordie, for he was a changed man these days, bitter and unforgiving, and his daughter's name never crossed his lips.

She had thought, after learning that Elspeth and Janet had fallen out, that her sister would write or come to tell her what had happened, for she thrived on making trouble and wouldn't be able to resist letting Geordie know whatever it was that Elspeth had done to annoy her. She had never forgiven him for choosing her sister instead of her.

It came as no surprise to Lizzie, therefore, when the Bains turned up one Sunday, and Janet started on Geordie as soon as she came in. 'A fine man you are,' she sneered, 'letting your daughter make herself free with any man that came to the house.'

He kept his temper. 'I ken't nothing about it.'

'Pleading ignorance doesn't excuse anything, Geordie.'

'The lad took advantage o' her in an empty house,' he

said, excusing Elspeth as much as himself, 'but he'd have wed her if he hadna been killed.'

'So he said,' Janet taunted, shaking off her husband's warning hand on her arm. 'Easy for him to make promises like that when he was away on the battlefield. He'd never have put a ring on her finger, not a farmer's son out for a quick thrill wi' an untouched lassie.' She had slipped into her natural tongue without noticing. 'Of course, Elspeth should have ken't better than let him have what he wanted, but maybe she'd wanted it as much as him.'

'Janet!' Harry Bain tried to stem her flow, but his wife was never in the habit of paying any attention to him. She had taken her own way all their married life.

She was glorying in the effect her words were having on the tall, white-haired man standing in front of her with his head bowed. 'It was Lizzie that arranged for her to come to me, so your name wouldna be shamed in Auchlonie.'

'It was good o' you to take her in,' Geordie mumbled.

'Aye, it was good o' me.' Janet's voice was heavy with sarcasm. 'But Miss High and Mighty Elspeth Gray didna condescend to accept my hospitality for long.'

Lizzie shuddered at the sight of her husband's face now. 'What's that you say?' he thundered, his eyes standing out of their sockets, his face almost purple. 'Is she not biding wi' you still?'

'I couldna have her in my house any longer. You should have heard the things she said to me, the names she called me. I'd to tell her to leave, and I was that upset I've been in my bed ever since. But I had to come and let you ken the kind o' besom she is, Geordie, so I forced myself out of my sick bed and got Harry to take me here.'

Not caring one whit about Janet Bain's ills, Geordie snapped, 'Where in God's name did she go, then?'

'I wouldna ken the answer to that,' Janet said, sharply. 'Has she not been in touch wi' you?'

'I didna want to hear from her.' Geordie's eyes swivelled suspiciously to his wife. 'Did she write to you?'

'No, Geordie, there's been no letter. I'd have tell't you if anything had come.' Lizzie's blood ran cold as she voiced the barefaced lie, uttered in sheer desperation.

Her husband's eyebrows were practically meeting in the middle now. 'She'll have to fend for herself, wherever she is, for I finished wi' her the day she left this house.'

Harry Bain made himself be heard then. 'If you ask me, you were a bit too hard on her, Geordie. She was only a bairn herself, and if she loved the laddie . . .'

Janet's glare halted him in his bid to champion Elspeth. 'She was old enough to ken what she was doing, any road,' she spat out. 'You can't get away from that, Geordie Gray, and old enough to take her own road – shouting at me like it was me that was in the wrong.'

'Well,' Geordie said firmly, 'that's an end o' it. I'm sorry you were put to so much trouble, Janet, but she's a wicked lassie, an' I want to hear no more about her.'

Satisfied that she had wounded him enough, Janet started on her favourite subject – discussing her ill health – and when she said it was time they left, Geordie offered, rather ungraciously, to walk with them to the station.

'I'm sorry for you, Lizzie,' Janet remarked, her gleeful expression belying the sentiment. 'Bringing a bairn into the world and having her be as thankless as Elspeth's been.'

She followed Geordie out with a smirk on her thin, sour

face, but Harry Bain hung back. 'I'm sure she'll be all right, Lizzie, don't worry. The row was Janet's fault, for she couldn't stop sneering, but Elspeth's a sensible lassie, and she's able to fend for herself.' Giving her shoulder a brief squeeze, he went out.

She felt a warmth in her heart for him. Janet didn't deserve such a good husband, doing everything for her without complaining. He must really love her, Lizzie thought, in some astonishment, and he was a considerate, gentle man, who would have shielded Elspeth from her aunt's tempers if only she had knuckled down. Oh, God! What had happened to her? Was she still with that folk she'd gone to, or had they put her out, and all? Was she lying dead somewhere, after losing her life in the struggle to give birth? No! No! No! Her letter had said she was happy, and that the folk were very kind, so there was no need for her mother to worry . . . though she wished she knew.

Lizzie gave a sigh which made the lamp on the table flicker. She should never have made the girl go to Janet's, for she should have known there would be trouble. Her sister had never been able to hold her tongue, and neither, it appeared now, could Elspeth, though she had been docile enough when she was at home. But Geordie would be more against her than ever now, with Janet rubbing salt into his wounds.

Elspeth named her baby John – it was the only way to prove to the world that she had truly loved John Forrest. Her recovery was slow and poor, and the Watsons worried about her lack of spirit. Jimmy had collected the pram on the evening after the birth, explaining who he was and why

150

Elspeth was living at Quarry Street, and Mrs Robb had asked to be kept informed about the girl's well-being, so he paid another visit, a week later, to tell her that the girl was still very feeble. Ann was so upset that she told her husband to call on their ex-maid the next day.

'I'm Doctor Robb,' he informed Helen Watson when she answered his knock. 'I've come to see Elspeth.'

'Oh . . . aye . . . come in, Doctor.' She was flustered by the unexpected visit, but led him through to the small room where the pale-faced girl lay sleeping. 'She hardly takes notice o' anything, and I've whiles to force her even to feed the bairn, let alone feed herself.'

He stepped forward and said, with forced cheerfulness, 'Hello, there, Elspeth. Why aren't you up and about yet?'

Her eyes flew open in alarm as she struggled to raise her head, her lank hair flopping over her face. 'Doctor Robb! Mrs Watson didn't tell me she'd sent for you . . . I can't afford . . . I'm sorry if your journey's been wasted.'

'No nonsense. I'll inspect the young man first.' Lifting the infant out of the pram, he felt the arms and legs, then ran his hand over the crown of the head. 'His fontanelle's all right you've produced a fine healthy specimen. I'd say he weighed . . . have you got a set of scales, Mrs Watson?'

'Aye, just a minute and I'll get them.'

She returned from the kitchen in a few seconds, carrying a small spring balance. 'I use it for weighing berries when I'm making jam,' she explained, as she handed it over.

Making a sling from a towel, Doctor Robb placed the baby inside and slipped the hook of the balance through the knot.

'Eight pounds, three ounces,' he said, as he held the bundle up to the light, then gave it to Mrs Watson and turned to the bed. 'Now, what about you?' He prodded Elspeth's flat stomach, looked under her eyelids then took her pulse. 'You'll be pleased to know that you're not about to waste away, young woman.' He laughed and winked to Mrs Watson. 'It's just a touch of bloodlessness and fatigue. He's a big, hefty lad, you know. I'll write out a prescription for an iron tonic, and I suggest that you stop feeding the baby yourself. It's sapping your strength when you need every ounce of it to help you back on your feet. He'll do fine on Glaxo or Allenbury's.'

'But that's dear stuff, isn't it, and I . . .'

'We'll manage,' Mrs Watson butted in, 'I'll buy a tin when I get your tonic at Davidson and Kay's this afternoon.'

The black bag was snapped shut. 'Just one more thing. Your breasts will become full and sore when you stop feeding, but Mrs Watson can probably tell you what to do about that.'

Helen nodded. 'I think I've still got the binder I'd to wear when I weaned Donald.'

Elspeth was blushing at his casual reference to the taboo subject of a woman's breasts, and he laughed at her confusion. 'You'll be as fit as a fiddle in a few days, I promise.'

'But what about paying you, doctor?'

'Don't insult me by talking about paying. I'm here as an interested party – a friend. I couldn't allow you to make yourself ill.'

'Oh, Doctor Robb, thank you very much.'

'No thanks are necessary. By the way, my wife would like to see you and your offspring as soon as you're able to walk down the hill, but remember – take it easy when you're coming back up.' He turned to the woman hovering in the

152

doorway. 'I see you're pregnant, too. I hope you're looking after yourself properly?'

'Oh, aye, I'm fine, and it's not my first. My Donald's
near nineteen now. He's in the Gordons.'

'You're not so young this time, so don't hesitate to send
for me . . . unless you'd prefer your own doctor to attend
you?'

'I haven't got a doctor. I went to one a while back, and
it was him that said I was expecting, but I didna ken him
from Adam, nor him me.'

'Remember what I've said, then. Good morning.' Alex
Robb breezed out, leaving the two women looking at each
other.

'You've got yourself a private physician by the looks o' it,
Elspeth, and me, as well.' Mrs Watson had been impressed
by the man's efficiency.

'He said to go and see Mrs Robb at King's Gate when
I'm able to walk down the hill. What did he mean? What
hill?'

'Oh, I'd forgot you've never been out since you came
here. You ken the bit tarred road in front o' our tenement?
Well, if you'd went right on, you'd have seen it's just a
rough track after that, but it goes on to King's Gate.'

'Is that the country road I've seen from my window? Wi'
the dykes at each side?'

'Aye, that's it, for there's no houses at this end o' it, but
at the other end there's a lot o' big houses – there's
solicitors and accountants and bankers . . . and doctors. So
you'll not have that far to go, but it's a steep hill, and that's
why he said to take it easy. Still, once I get your tonic,
you'll be jumping about like a two-year-old.'

The doctor's visit itself was a tonic to the girl, and with the help of the iron mixture, and the dried milk, she was up in three days, rather shaky, but determined to improve. In another week, she was perfectly fit, and doing the shopping and most of the housework for her landlady, who was easily tired now. 'I just can't think what's come over me, for I was never like this wi' Donald,' she grumbled.

'It's like Doctor Robb said, you're not so young now.'

Helen grinned, ruefully. 'I suppose that's it.'

But she continued to feel exhausted, and complained of vague pains, until Elspeth decided to ask Dr Robb to call. She knew that Mrs Watson would object, and made the excuse that she would have to go the shop near the quarry for salt. It was a tiny shop, but the only shop in the vicinity, and she had been there several times since her baby had been born, but she had no intention of going there now. Leaving the infant asleep in the pram, she ran in the opposite direction, up on to King's Gate and all the way down the hill. Neither the doctor nor his wife was at home, but she left a message with their maid, then hurried back to Quarry Street.

Pale and perspiring, Mrs Watson said, 'Oh, I'm right pleased you're back. I feel kind o' queer and I've got terrible pains.'

Elspeth confessed breathlessly. 'I've been to the doctor's and the maid said she'll tell him when he comes back.'

'Oh, you shouldna have done that. He'll maybe think I'm making a fuss for nothing.'

'He'll not think it's a fuss.' Elspeth wrung out a cloth in tepid water to sponge her landlady's face, told her that she should be in bed, then filled a stone hot water bottle and slipped it under the blankets before she lumbered in.

'Aye, that's better,' Mrs Watson gasped, then her face contorted again. 'You ken, Elspeth, it's just like labour pains, but the bairn's not due for another month.'

'Och, you've maybe miscounted.'

'No, no, I'm certain sure.' She lay back against the pillows wearily, while Elspeth anxiously wondered if she should risk going for the midwife.

At each of the woman's spasms, the girl glanced at the wag-at-the-wa' clock, and soon realized that the pains were coming every three minutes. She prayed that the doctor wouldn't be long, for she couldn't leave Mrs Watson now.

She had boiled several pans of water on the stove, and had them sitting at the side of the fire, before Alex Robb arrived. Wasting no time in talk, he took off his jacket and rolled up his shirt sleeves, and, as he washed his hands in the near-boiling water Elspeth had made ready in a basin, he asked her, 'Have you such a thing as a rubber sheet?'

It had been used at the time of her own accouchement, so she knew where it was. 'It's in the lobby press.'

Handing it to him, she remembered that she hadn't checked on John for some time. Poor little mite, he'd been neglected in all this commotion. When she looked in the pram, her son was still sleeping peacefully, but she decided to make up his bottle now, in case there was no time later. When it was ready, she left it sitting in a small saucepan of water by the fire then went to the bedside.

While she carried out Alex Robb's terse instructions, she shut her ears to the harrowing moans and screams coming from the woman, and would have ignored her own child's crying if the doctor hadn't waved her away. 'Attend to your baby!'

She sat down with her infant on her knee, his tiny mouth fixing hungrily round the teat of the bottle, but in a moment Alex Robb turned round. 'It's a girl, but I'm afraid it's been dead for some weeks,' he said sadly, then bent to his task again.

Elspeth was shocked. Poor Mrs Watson, to go through all that for nothing. Replacing her son in the pram, she put the kettle on to boil again in order to have a cup of tea ready for the doctor when he had washed his hands, and hot tears pricked her eyes as it crossed her mind that she was doing what her mother would have done in the circumstances.

'There's no need for the birth to be registered,' the man observed, as he crossed to the sink after making a bundle of everything to be disposed. 'The foetus had not developed far enough. Now, Mrs Watson may be very distressed, so you will have to be careful what you say to her.'

'Is she all right?'

'She has had a very bad time, so it's good that she's got you here to look after her.'

'She did the same for me.'

When he left, after refusing the tea she offered, Elspeth approached the bed, but her landlady was asleep, and looked so white that the girl decided it would be best to leave her until she woke. Changing the bed could wait.

Little John was ready for his next feed before the faint voice said, 'Elspeth?'

She carried the infant to the bed. 'Would you like a cup of tea now, Mrs Watson?'

'I'm thinking you could call me Helen now, for we've been through an awful lot together, me and you. Give me the bairn, for I'll need to feed it.' To Elspeth's horror, she opened the buttons on her nightdress then held out her arms.

'But . . . but . . .' the girl stuttered, remembering that the doctor had told her to be careful what she said. Obviously the woman didn't remember that her child had been dead, and she couldn't upset her now. 'You're maybe not fit to be feeding him yet. I can give him a bottle.'

'Give him a bottle? When my breasts are full o' milk?'

Very reluctantly, Elspeth handed her baby over, and felt a great tightness in her chest when the woman guided his mouth to her nipple. It wouldn't do him any harm, she assured herself. It was like in the old days, when women who couldn't suckle their infants had wet-nurses to do it for them. And surely, by tomorrow, when Helen was back to normal again, she would remember everything.

The kitchen bed had been changed and everything was in place by the time Jimmy came home, but he was alarmed to see his wife in bed. 'What's wrong, lass?'

'Nothing's wrong. We've got another son. He come early.'

Elspeth's horrified gasp made him look at her in surprise, and when she shook her head vigorously at him, he knew that something was not right. Before he turned away from his wife, however, he took her hand. 'How are you, Helen?'

'I'm fine, though I maybe wouldna be, if it hadna been for Doctor Robb.'

'Thank God he was here, then.' Jimmy straightened up, and when Elspeth motioned to him, he followed her into the lobby. 'Is there something I should ken?' he demanded. 'Is Helen worse than she's letting on?'

'Oh, Jimmy,' Elspeth gulped, 'I'm sure she's lost her senses. Her baby was dead-born, a little girl, but when she wakened up, she saw John and she thought he was hers. She even made me let her feed him, and the doctor said I'd to watch what I said to her, for she'd had a hard time . . . oh, God, what'll I do?'

A frown on his lined face, Jimmy drew in his lips. 'Oh, my poor Helen. She was built up on having a wee bairn of her own again . . . could you not just play along wi' her for a while, Elspeth? Just till she comes to herself?'

'I . . . I suppose so.' Elspeth's feet trailed as she returned to the kitchen. She would 'play along' for a wee while, but she couldn't let it run on too long.

Chapter Fourteen

The following morning, when Helen asked to hold baby John to let Elspeth get on with the washing, the girl was quite pleased, but she kept looking across to the bed to make sure that her landlady was not over-tiring herself. Almost an hour later, when she came in from hanging the sheets out to dry in the back green and saw that the woman was suckling the infant again, she couldn't stop herself shouting, 'Helen! What do you think you're doing?'

'I'm just feeding my dear lambie. What's the sense in having to buy Glaxo when I've plenty milk?'

'But . . . but the doctor tell't me to bind you.'

'I took it off. Stop fussing, lass, my milk's good.'

Remembering how expensive the tins of Glaxo were, and how quickly they went down, Elspeth said nothing more. Breast milk was far better for a baby anyway, she told herself, trying to still the tremor of fear that ran through her. So Helen was allowed to keep feeding baby John, Jimmy's brows coming down the first time he saw her at it. 'I some think you shouldna be doing that, lass,' he told his wife, who just laughed. 'Donald thrived on my milk.'

Elspeth grew more and more dismayed because she was never allowed to do anything for her son except wash his clothes and napkins, so when she remembered the invitation to King's Gate, she wondered if the doctor's wife could advise her on how to deal with her landlady. 'I think I'll take John out in the pram for a wee while,' she said, one afternoon. 'I could go and let Mrs Robb see him.'

The woman in the bed smiled. 'I think you're as proud o' him as me.'

'Aye,' the girl said, slowly, 'I am proud o' him.'

When the maid showed Elspeth in, Ann Robb fussed for a few minutes over the chubby woollen bundle, then said, 'I'm sorry I have to rush, because I'm due at a meeting at three, but I'd love to see you and your son again.'

Walking back up the hill, Elspeth knew that she had lost the opportunity of finding out how to surmount her problem. Mrs Robb would never understand how she could let it run on, when she should have corrected Helen from the first time she suspected what was happening. She had stood up to Janet Bain, but this was different. Janet was a wicked, vile-minded woman, and Helen was a friend, a friend whose mind had been turned by the loss of a longed-for child. She wasn't wicked, she was to be pitied, and shielded until she could face reality again.

In a little over two weeks, Helen was bustling around the small flat, cheery as ever, but Elspeth was troubled about the wisdom of staying on in Quarry Street when the woman had taken possession of her child. Determined to make a stand at last, she broached the subject one rainy afternoon. 'I think I should look for other lodgings, Helen. We're crowded now, wi' the pram, and all. I could take a live-in job, somewhere they wouldn't object to John.'

Helen looked aghast. 'What's John got to do wi' it?'

160

'Well, he's . . . I thought . . .' Elspeth was floundering now, and felt that it was still too soon to confront her landlady with the brutal truth.

Looking at her with some pity, Helen said, 'I ken you think the world o' him, but he's my little man, so you should just take a day job, and you'd be able to see him when you come home every night. Besides, I'm not wanting to lose you.'

Longing to say that he wasn't *her* little man, Elspeth could not bring herself to upset the woman who had befriended her in her hour of need. Instead, she said, 'I'll need to start paying for my keep, then. I've nothing left now except the money you'll not let me touch, and I can't expect you to go on paying for everything.'

'You've worked for your keep, lass. I wouldna have managed after John was born without you looking after me, and the house . . . and Jimmy.'

Elspeth felt a moment's panic. Helen really did believe that she had given birth to John. How could she have forgotten the tiny blue infant that had come out of her womb . . . lifeless? But maybe it was her way of getting over her tragedy. Maybe she would accept it come time and realize that John didn't belong to her . . . she must realize. 'You're back on your feet now, though,' the girl said, gently, 'and you don't need me to look after you.'

'I can see you're determined to get a job, and maybe it's just as well. There's not much room for the two of us in this kitchen all day.'

Elspeth sighed, but made one last attempt to claim her son. 'Would you be prepared to look after John when I'm out working?'

'Who else would look after him?'

'Will Jimmy not mind?'

'Why should he mind?' Helen lifted the baby out of the pram. 'You're Jimmy's bairn and all, aren't you, my pet?'

This final proof of what Helen believed made Elspeth feel like seizing her child and running off with him, but she realized that it might be better to have a word with Jimmy first. He would surely be willing to reason with his wife.

When he came in at teatime, Helen told him that Elspeth was thinking of going out to work, at which he scratched his head in wonderment. 'It's funny you should speak the day about getting a job, lassie, for one o' the lads was saying this morning that his auntie's in charge o' the cafe in the Market, and she can't get lassies the now – they're all making munitions.'

'It's more wages,' Helen conceded, 'but they work long hours and Elspeth wouldna want that.'

'I wasna saying she should make munitions.' Jimmy rolled his eyes to the ceiling. 'I was meaning she might get a job as a waitress, and that's a step up from being in service, I would think.' He glanced at Elspeth triumphantly.

A little frown creased her forehead. 'I don't know the first thing about waitressing, though.'

'You'd manage fine. Go down to the cafe the morrow and ask for . . .' His face fell. 'Och, I never thought to ask what her name was.'

'Och, you, you're useless,' Helen chided him, fondly. 'Just ask for the lady in charge, Elspeth, and tell her it was her nephew said she was needing waitresses. You might as well try – there's no harm in asking.' She brought the discussion to an end by rising to put the baby back in his pram, and starting to clear the table.

When Helen went to the lavatory, Elspeth seized her chance. 'Jimmy,' she began, rather apprehensively, 'do you think it's a good thing for me to leave John wi' Helen? She still thinks John's hers, and the longer it goes on, the harder it'll be for her to give him up to me.'

'I was feared for this,' he said, sadly. 'Some women can't face losing a bairn. I've heard o' some that go off their heads altogether and steal another woman's out o' a pram . . . I suppose that's just what Helen's done, when you come to think about it. John's a substitute for the poor wee thing that didna live. She needed comfort, and she's got it from him, but she's aye been a strong woman, and I'm sure she'll get her wits back in another week or two.'

'I hope so.'

'Just keep going along wi' her, Elspeth, for she's been through a real bad time.'

'Aye, so she has.' Elspeth felt annoyed at herself for mentioning it. She should be glad that Helen was so fond of John, for it meant that she would have no worries about leaving the woman to look after him.

When Elspeth returned from her mission the following day, she was babbling with excitement. 'I've to start at seven the morrow morning. Miss Mackay was pleased I went, and she says I'm just the kind o' girl she was looking for.'

Helen nodded approvingly. 'Aye, you're neat and clean, and you've a bonnie face. That would be important in a cafe.'

'We've to wear black dresses, and white aprons and caps, and they supply them but we've to launder them, and the

163

early shift's seven to three, and the late shift's three to eleven.' Elspeth stopped, breathlessly.

'Hold on, my brain's spinning.' Helen, holding baby John on her knee, was rocking him gently as the girl prattled.

'You'll not mind me working shifts? It'll be near midnight before I get home if I'm on late.'

'No, no, lassie, it makes no difference to me.'

'They've some busy spells, when the fish market porters come in for breakfasts or dinners, but in between there's sailors off the boats, and soldiers passing through, and country women waiting for a train.'

Helen burst out laughing. 'I suppose I'll get a report every day about the goings on at the People's Cafe.'

'Och, you,' Elspeth smiled. 'You're making fun o' me.'

The clock in the steeple had struck six before Meg Forrest got away from the committee meeting in the kirk vestry. Wheeling her bicycle down the stony path, she felt irritated that Mrs Black, the minister's wife, hadn't been firm enough to get them to make up their minds about the Harvest Festival. If old Mrs Proctor, the banker's wife, had been there, she'd have had it organized in record time, but she had sent her apologies.

Meg shivered as she reached the road. The vestry had been cold, but she would be warm enough by the time she got home, for she'd have to hurry. As she pedalled round the corner into the High Street, two girls came out of Miss Fraser's workshop, a little ahead, the small one shouting, 'Cheerio, Nettie,' as she disappeared into a low cottage.

The other girl looked round, startled, when Meg

dismounted beside her. 'Oh it's you, Mrs Blairt . . . Mrs Forrest. What a fear you gave me.'

Meg smiled at the confusion over her name. 'You're Nettie Duffus, aren't you? Have you ever heard from Elspeth Gray since she went to the town?'

'No, she's never wrote, and she's never been to see us. I think she'll not want to come back, for it would remind her about John For . . . oh!' Nettie's face turned scarlet.

'It's all right, Nettie,' Meg assured her. 'I ken't about her and John, and I've something to tell her. I don't want to ask her folk for her address, though, in case she never tell't them about my John.'

'I don't think Lizzie kens where she is, any road. I asked her myself last week, for I thought I'd like to write and see how Elspeth was getting on, and she looked at me real funny. I think there must have been a row about Elspeth going to Aberdeen.'

Meg was disappointed. The new grandfather clock in her parlour would have to remain where it was, though Blairton would not be pleased, for he moaned every day about having to squeeze past it before he could get a seat.

Helen Watson had been correct in supposing that she would get a daily report about the cafe. Elspeth came home full of it the very first afternoon, her worry about John forgotten for the time being. 'D'you ken this, Helen?' she said, after she had exhausted everything else. 'We've to serve from one side and take the dirty dishes from the other side.'

'Mmphmm?' Helen's mouth held a safety pin – she was in the process of changing the baby.

'Miss Mackay says though it's just a little cafe for working folk, she wants it run like the big restaurants.'

'I hope you'll not expect your big rest-your-ant ideas in this kitchen.' Helen laid little John down in his pram and looked proudly at the girl. 'I took John out in his pram this morning, and Mrs Norrie from number six come into the shop behind me, and she says to me, "I see you've had your bairn, Mrs Watson? What a bonnie wee thing he is." Well, he is, isn't he, Elspeth?'

After a slight pause, Elspeth murmured, 'Aye, he is.' She could not imagine what John Forrest would have said about her letting Helen carry on with her fantasy. It was as if she were denying their son, but she would never have been in this predicament if he had still been alive. Anyway, if the neighbours thought the baby was the Watsons', it would stop any gossip about her, and once Helen remembered and accepted that her own baby had died, it could all be put right.

When she persuaded her landlady to let her take the infant out in the pram herself after that, she had to bite her tongue when the kindly women of Quarry Street said, 'You're the lassie that lodges wi' Mrs Watson, aren't you? This'll be her bairnie?'

She found it hard to smile and nod, when her heart was telling her to shout, 'No, he's mine! Mine and a poor, dead soldier's.' After feeling particularly resentful one day, she went home and burst out, 'Helen, this has gone on long enough! I can't stand any more of it!'

'My goodness, lass, what's up wi' you?'

The woman's expression of concern made the girl take a deep breath. 'It's time to face facts. Everybody thinks John's your baby, and . . .'

166

'But John is my baby. Do you not mind the awful labour I had? Not that I'm complaining, for the lambie was worth it.'

'Aye, I mind the terrible time you had,' Elspeth began, 'and I mind how sorry I felt when Doctor Robb said . . .' She broke off, unable to remind her landlady what had been the outcome of that labour.

Her eyes narrowing, Helen said, a little impatiently, 'I think you're working too hard at that cafe. It's making you muddle things up in your mind. I didna like to say anything before in case you didna want to speak about it, but I suppose it's wi' me having John so quick after you lost your bairnie that's made you . . .'

'I didna lose my baby!' Elspeth shouted. 'It was you!'

Shaking her head and tutting, Helen said, sadly, 'I ken how you must feel, but you'll get over it, lass.'

Utterly defeated, Elspeth turned away. It was no use, for Helen would not be told, but it would all come back to her one of these days.

As the weeks passed, Elspeth found little time to dwell on the rights and wrongs of allowing people to believe their mistaken conclusions, and gradually put it to the back of her mind. She loved her job, and found herself parrying the teasing – even giving back as good as she got – of the bluff, hearty regulars to the cafe, with their store of witticisms. They had no counterparts in Auchlonie, where the men were more dour and serious, their few jokes lacking the snappiness of the city workers. The servicemen she had to deal with, however, were mostly single men out for a lark with any young girl, and she soon learned how to rebuff their amorous advances without causing offence, and to smilingly refuse if one of them, bolder than the rest, asked her to go out with him.

She could never keep company with anybody again, and, in any case, not one of these boys caused the slightest flutter in her heart. Nobody could ever replace her lost love.

Part Two

Chapter Fifteen

1917

David Fullerton was sitting outside on the verandah, the penetrating February wind making him shiver in spite of the sunshine. The doctor had told him this morning that he was fit enough now to go into the town, instead of just walking round the hospital grounds – but he did not feel ready yet. He could not face other people, normal people, with this terrible guilt in his gut. How could he be glad to be alive when his friends and comrades had all been killed, their bodies blown to bits and scattered over a Belgian field?

The horror of the trenches engulfed him again. The filthy, rotting stench filled his nostrils, and the ghostly rats crept round him looking for something to eat; dead human flesh – or the living, if they were not careful. Their own food had to be gulped between bombardments, and sleep also had to be snatched during the lulls. Mud-caked clothing rasped against his skin once more, and his feet ached within the confines of rock-hard, ill-fitting boots. His whole body crawled with lice, and he scratched his head in a vain effort to rid his hair of them. His mind returned to his closest friends, the three young men who had been with him through so much.

They were what had made everything bearable; they had been in it together, till death did them part, but never for one minute believing that such a time would ever come. They had been a happy-go-lucky lot, singing without a care as they marched, if the pipes weren't playing in front of the column. They had teased each other, told crude jokes, even argued and quarrelled at times, but always there had been the easy feeling of close brotherhood, the knowledge that they were facing danger together. They had helped each other to bear the sarcasm of their NCOs, to obey without question the commands of their officers. Other units were wiped out by the shelling, other men were shot, but it could never happen to them.

And his friends hadn't known about it, David thought, with some gratitude. They couldn't have had time to realize what was happening. He, himself, could only remember the terrific explosion close beside him, and being lifted off the ground by it. He discovered later that he had been thrown some feet away from where he had been crouching, and must have lain unconscious for several minutes – or several hours – but he had gradually become aware of screams and groans, the heart-rending noises of men in mortal agony. That was when he had started to search for his friends. It had meant nothing to him when he came across other comrades writhing in the throes of death – they were not his special three – and he had kept looking until he found them.

He shouldn't think about it. Every doctor he had ever seen had said he should try to forget, to blot it from his mind, but he couldn't. Even when he was asleep he could see them, the bits of them – arms, legs, broken bodies – in

172

the mud and against the sand-bagged walls of the dug-out. He vaguely remembered scrabbling in the debris then, scouring for someone else who was still alive, and going back to the wounded men he had callously passed before, but the screaming and groaning had stopped. He was the only living person left. It was then that he'd heard a low moaning sound and had lifted his head, hope rising in his breast until it came to him that the sound was issuing from his own throat.

Reliving the horror of Ypres, as he had done every night and day for months, he shivered again. They told him afterwards, those dim faceless figures who had rushed to help him over the last few yards to the base, that he had been crawling on hands and knees when they saw him. Later still, doctors said he had travelled more than five miles, but though he could hear them, he could not tell them what had happened. His mind had been blank for weeks, and he wished now that it had stayed that way, because, by the time he had begun to notice his surroundings, he was in a hospital in England and the nightmares had started. They said he was lucky, but how could he be, when he was the only one of four – the only one of a hundred – still alive? He had shut himself off from the world and wished from the depths of his still-beating heart that he had been killed along with the others.

'It'll take time, but you will forget.' He had heard the useless words from medical men – men who worked out what went on inside the human brain – in Belgium, in England and now in Aberdeen, his home town. It was easy for them to say – how would they have reacted in the same situation? – but it would remain with him for the rest of his days.

David was so deeply involved in his horrific memories that he didn't hear the nurse approaching. 'Right, Fullerton,' she said briskly. 'Doctor Menzies says you must go into town this afternoon. Walking round the grounds is all right as far as it goes, but you've got to try yourself properly.' The alarm in his eyes made her add, kindly, 'You can ask somebody to go with you this time, if you're scared to go on your own.'

'I'm not scared,' he protested automatically. He wasn't scared, he was petrified, panic-stricken, but he knew that he would have to face it one day, and it may as well be now.

They gave him a greatcoat to put over the blue suit he wore as a patient, and money for his fares to and from town, plus a little extra in case he wanted to buy something. Dr Menzies, who knew that the young man dreaded leaving the sanctuary of the hospital, asked, gently, 'Why don't you go to see your father?'

David didn't repeat his reason for not contacting his father – he had told it often enough. How could he go home when his mother's place had been taken by someone else?

During the long walk to the tram terminus, he wondered for the hundredth time how his father could have married another woman when his wife had been dead for such a short time. The letter had really upset him. They had been back off the line for a respite when he received it and had opened it eagerly. What he read was still imprinted on his mind.

Dear Son,

No doubt you will be surprised to hear I am getting married next week. I met Isabel at Willie Black's, and I think he meant this to happen, for she was a widow and we were both lonely. We started seeing each other and we get on very well together, so we think we would be happier sharing our lives.

In blind fury, David had ripped up the letter without reading any more. His friends had told him to accept it, that it was his father's life, not his, but he could never forgive his father, not even after what he had been through himself since.

He sat rigidly all the way into the city, his arms across his body, trying to force his distress out of his mind, but it was still too vivid. Coming off the tram, he walked down Market Street to the harbour where there was always some activity, but when he reached the water his legs felt weak, his head throbbed and he knew he could not go on. It would be best to step off the side of the quay and let himself be swallowed up by the filthy water in the dock . . . but someone would be sure to see him and try to save him. Turning, he went slowly back up towards Union Street, doubtful if his strength would hold out long enough for him to reach the top of the hill, but when he came to the Market, he remembered that there was a tearoom inside. A little refreshment might help him to pull himself together.

'Tea, please,' he managed to get out to the young waitress who served him, shaking his head when she asked if he wanted anything to eat, and when the cup and saucer were placed in front of him, he watched the pretty, golden-haired girl smiling and joking with people at the other tables. Maybe she had wondered why he had been so unfriendly, but he had never been good at clever repartee, and he never would be. What was more, he did not want anybody feeling sorry for him. Death was what he craved, not pity, and if the only place he was likely to get himself killed was Belgium, he would have to go back there. He returned to the hospital determined to make the doctors discharge him ready for active service again.

He spent most of the next day trying to persuade doctors and consultants that he was sound in mind and body – especially in mind – until at last he was told that he would possibly be released in two weeks' time, provided that he had no relapse. Surprisingly, although he was totally exhausted – or perhaps because of it – he had no night-mares that night.

The following morning, Wednesday, he felt better than he had done for a very long time, and when he went out in the afternoon he went directly to the People's Cafe, sitting down in the same corner and enjoying the bustle and the hum of conversation. The same waitress served him, smiling when she said, 'What can I get you?'

Making a great effort, he smiled back. 'A cup of tea and a bun, please. One spoon of sugar.'

She returned in a few minutes with his order. 'Which hospital is it?' She gestured to his blues.

'Oldmill, but I'll soon be going back to the front.'

She gave a little giggle. 'Back to the front? That sounds funny, like back to front, but I don't suppose it's funny over there.' She could see that her remark had upset him a little, but there were people waiting for attention and she had to leave him.

As he cut open his bun and spread it with butter from the little dish already on the table, David wished that he could have laughed with her, but he had felt slightly disappointed in her for making light of what he had said, although he knew that she had no idea what it was like at the front. Was he being stupid wanting to go back? Should he tell Doctor Menzies that he had changed his mind? Suddenly remembering why he had wanted to go back to Belgium, a black mood descended on him, and he rose and walked out, leaving tea and bun untasted.

On the tram journey back to Oldmill, he admitted to himself that his emotions were still far from stable. It was best that he went back to the front . . . back to front? . . . so that his useless life could be ended. What future had he like this?

That night, he awoke screaming because of the renewed nightmares, and refused point blank to go out on Thursday afternoon. Doctor Menzies, having been given a report by the ward sister, came to see him. 'What's this I'm hearing about you not wanting to go out today? What's the problem?'

'I'm just not wanting to go out,' David said, his face surly. 'I bet you don't do anything you don't want to.'

The other man smiled. 'I've to do many things I don't want to, but I thought you wanted to go back on active service, and this is a bit of a setback, you know.'

'Do you mean I won't be released?'

'Not if you go on like this.'

After considering briefly, David mumbled, 'If I do go out today, will you forget about it?'

'I might, if your progress gets back to normal.'

'All right, then, I'll go. I was feeling a bit . . . well, you likely know I had nightmares again last night?'

'Yes, and you'll probably keep having them from time to time, but they'll become less real, I promise, and there will be longer between them. It's up to you to fight them.'

David knew that he could not fight them, but in his desperation to get back to Belgium he said, 'I'll try.'

'Good lad. Now, off you go, otherwise you'll be late in getting back for tea, and Matron'll have your head on the chopping block.'

David was over an hour later than usual when he left the hospital, and had made up his mind not to go to the cafe, but he found himself drawn to the Market opening when he walked down Market Street. He told himself that he should have got off the tram at a different stop, that he should have gone to the beach, anywhere to avoid this place, but he knew that in his heart of hearts he wanted to see the little waitress again. When he went inside the People's Cafe, however, there was no sign of her, and his spirits sank when a rather busty woman came to serve him. 'What's happened to the waitress who usually serves this table?' he asked.

'Elspeth? She's on early shift this week and next, and she finishes at three.'

He ordered only a cup of tea, and left as soon as he had drunk it, but as he walked up Union Street – giving himself a little time to think before he returned to Oldmill – he wondered where the little waitress lived. Elspeth? It was a nice name for such a pretty girl. Could he possibly arrange it so that he would be in the cafe tomorrow when she was going off duty? Would she let him walk a little way with her, so that he could find out more about her? Even though he would soon be leaving Aberdeen, it would be good to have her to remember, to pretend that she was his girl. Just for the little time he had left to live?

'Do you remember me telling you on Monday about that soldier wi' the sad eyes?' Elspeth asked Helen when she went home. 'He didna come on Tuesday, he was back on Wednesday, though he went out without drinking his tea or anything, and he wasna in the day again. I wonder what's happened to him.'

'His leave's maybe finished.' Helen gave seventeen-month-old John another bounce on her leg.

'He wasn't on leave, he's a patient at Oldmill Hospital.'

'Well, maybe he's been discharged. Och, John, you'll have my leg off me. That's enough the now.'

'He'd have said yesterday if he was being discharged. He just said he'd be going back to the front soon, and I think I upset him by laughing.'

'You laughed because he was going back to the front?'

'No, I was laughing because it sounded so funny. Back to front. Oh, I hope I haven't annoyed him.'

Lying back in her chair to recover from her exertions, Helen gave the girl a searching look. 'Were you taken wi' him? Is that why you're worried?'

'No, it's nothing like that, but I felt that sorry for him on Monday, and he's a real nice lad.'

'He'll maybe come in the morrow.'

'Aye, maybe. Has John been a good boy the day?'

'He's aye a good boy, are you not, my wee lamb?' Helen

ruffled the dark curls beside her chair, and the child looked up, showing his small, even teeth in a wide grin.

Elspeth turned away to fill the kettle. She could see his father in him every time he smiled like that, and it tore at her heart to think he didn't know she was his mother, but how could she say anything after all this time? She should have made a stand from the very beginning, and Helen would have had to get over losing her own baby, but she had let the opportunity slip away because she'd been sorry for the woman. She had nearly protested the first time she heard John saying 'Mam-mam' to her landlady, but Helen had looked so proud that she hadn't the heart to disillusion her, and maybe it was best to leave things the way they were, Elspeth reflected sadly. At least she knew that John was being cared for lovingly when she was at work, and the boy himself was happy. When he grew old enough to ask about things, to wonder if she was his sister, she would tell him the truth . . . if Helen hadn't done it herself before then.

On Friday, Elspeth was rather disappointed that the sad-eyed soldier did not come in at his usual time, but was pleased to see him when he turned up at ten to three. 'You didn't come in yesterday,' she observed, when she went to his table, then turned pink as she realized that he might think she was prying.

'I did come,' David said, thinking how fetching she was when she blushed, 'but you'd gone home.'

'Aye, I go off at three this week. Is it just tea the day, or do you want a bun, as well?'

'Yes, please.'

Elspeth could feel his eyes following her as she walked

away, and a warmth stole over her when she realized that he must have asked about her yesterday, otherwise how could he have known she'd gone home? But maybe he'd just guessed she'd gone home when he didn't see her . . . and what did it matter, anyway?

When she took his order to his table, he looked up at her and smiled, which encouraged her to say, 'Was it France you were wounded?'

'No, it was Belgium.' He was too ashamed to tell her that it had been shellshock, not an actual wound.

She moved away to serve other customers, but when he stood up to leave, she turned round and called out, 'See you the morrow?' She was glad to see that his eyes brightened as he nodded, because she'd been worried by the sadness in them before. Maybe he didn't want to be cured and have to go back to Belgium, for it must be awful there.

David lay awake for some time that night, thinking about Elspeth, and wishing that he'd had the courage to ask if he could walk home with her. Instead, he'd gulped down the tea and bun and gone out about one minute before she was due to be off duty, but when she'd asked if he was going back the next day, his heart, frozen for so long, had given a tiny skip of pleasure. She wanted to see him again.

'Two nights running with no nightmares,' one of the nurses smiled on Saturday morning.

'No,' he said proudly, not daring to say that his dreams had been of the little waitress in case the nurse teased him. It was too new an experience for him to joke about it.

All forenoon, he looked forward to seeing the golden-haired girl again, but he felt embarrassed when one of the other patients remarked on his cheerfulness, and he said nothing when Doctor Menzies complimented him on the fight he was putting up.

It was ten to three again when he sat down at the table he had come to regard as his and the subject of his dreams came to take his order. When she brought it to him, she smiled and said, 'My landlady always says it's better to know folk's names if you're speaking to them. Mine's Elspeth Gray. What's yours?'

'David Fullerton.' He hesitated for a moment, then added, 'So you're in lodgings?'

'Aye, at Quarry Street. It's not far from Oldmill.'

He knew that she was probably just making conversation, but the opening was too good to miss. 'You'll be finished here in a few minutes, will you not? If . . . if you didn't object, I'd . . . I wouldn't mind going up in the tram with you . . . that's if it's the same tram and you're going straight home?' The brightness had vanished from her face, and he said hastily, 'It was only an idea, for us both to have company, but it's all right if you'd rather not.'

His eyes were so anxious that Elspeth capitulated. 'No, I don't mind, really. It is the same tram, and I'd be glad of your company.'

Left alone, David started to tremble. He should never have asked her, for he knew he couldn't sustain a conversation with her on the long journey to the terminus. He couldn't talk to anyone . . . but he'd already told her his name and a few other things. Bewildered, he nearly rose to leave, but something held him back. He was going to be killed soon – but this Elspeth was so . . . she was the kind of girl he could have fallen in love with if he had been normal.

182

At two minutes past three, she appeared with her coat on. 'Are you ready, David?'

A tramcar came almost as soon as they stood up at the stop in Union Street. Elspeth plumped down on the wooden seat with a sigh of relief, and he sat beside her, trying not to let any part of his body come in contact with hers. 'It's good to get off my feet,' she observed. 'Working in a cafe can be real tiring.'

'Aye, it must be,' he murmured, shyly.

'Where were you wounded?'

The question was natural, but unexpected, and he didn't want to talk about it, so he misunderstood deliberately. 'It was at Wipers, and there was a shell, and . . . '

His agitation made the girl change the subject. 'You've an Aberdeen tongue. Do you belong here?'

He relaxed, very slightly. 'Aye, I was born and brought up in Holburn Street.'

'Is your mother and father still there?'

He looked away. 'My mother . . . died just before the war, but my father's still there.'

'Does he bide on his own?'

He took a deep breath. This girl could really find his weak spots. 'No, he . . . took another wife.'

Elspeth stopped probing – it was none of her business – and kept up a steady recital of anecdotes about the cafe and its customers until they reached the terminus.

As they walked towards the quarry lane, David said, 'I'm not going to see my father and his wife.'

'Oh, do you not like her?' Elspeth sounded surprised.

'I've never met her.'

'Well, why . . . ?'

'I couldn't face seeing another woman in my mother's place, sitting on her chair . . .'

'But, David, if your father's happy, that's what counts. You should do the right thing and go to see them. I'm sure he'd be pleased.'

He fell silent. Elspeth had a way with her, and she'd have helped him to sort himself out if only he'd met her before. It was too late now, but maybe he should do this one thing to please her? 'You really think I should go?'

'Go the morrow, and let me ken on Monday how you got on.'

'Aye, I will.' His troubled brain cleared, but he was glad when Elspeth started telling him a little about herself.

'I come from Auchlonie, a wee place about twenty-five mile from Aberdeen – you'll likely not have heard of it. I'd a row wi' my folk near two year ago, and come to the town to work, and . . . I got lodgings in Quarry Street.'

'I've heard that lodgings can be real bad, sometimes.'

'Maybe, but I was lucky. The Watsons are good folk. I was in service wi' a doctor and his wife for a while, before I got the waitress job.'

'Meeting a lot o' folk must be interesting for you.'

'Aye, the time just flies past.' They had reached the quarry lane by this time, and she said, 'Well, here's where I'll have to leave you.' His disappointed expression made her eye him anxiously. 'Will you manage the rest yourself, David? It's not very far, but I can come right to Oldmill wi' you, if you want.'

'No, I'll manage. I'll see you on Monday . . . Elspeth.'

Standing for a moment, she watched him walking away, then ran along the lane. She didn't tell Helen anything when she went into the house – she needed time to think. Why had she agreed to come on the tram with him? She had always vowed not to give any man the chance to get too friendly with her, but it had been the lost look of him – something in his eyes. Poor lad, she hoped that he could cope tomorrow at his father's house.

She held young John in her arms for a while, then laid him back in his pram and took out the iron, becoming aware that Helen was regarding her thoughtfully. 'You're awful quiet the day, Elspeth. Did something happen at the cafe?'

'Nothing much.' She smoothed out the old blanket they used to protect the kitchen table, and laid one of her aprons on it, then her natural need to describe what she'd been doing made her say, 'Nothing bad, any road.'

'Something, though?'

The prompting was all Elspeth needed, so she told Helen about her conversation with David Fullerton. 'Something terrible must have happened to him in Wipers,' she added. 'I could see the terrified look about him when he spoke, like it was something that would haunt him for the rest o' his days, but he couldna come out wi' it. I'm pleased he's going to see his father and his step-mother, though.'

'You've fair surprised me, Elspeth. Making up to a soldier? You'll maybe fall in love wi' him, if he's a nice laddie.' Laughing at the girl's vehement denials, Helen changed the subject. 'I wish I ken't how my Donald really is. He never comes home, though he must get leave sometime, and he never tells me much in his letters, just that he's well and hopes me and Jimmy are the same. Still,

I suppose I should be thankful he writes at all, and I suppose I'd hear quick enough if anything happened to him.'

Elspeth, trying to analyse her feelings for David, nodded abstractedly. She wouldn't fall in love with him – she could never fall in love again. She was just sorry for him. He was like a wounded animal, his sad eyes pleading for him not to be hurt any more, and there was no harm in just speaking to him. After he went back to Belgium, she would never see him again. 'That's me finished.' She picked up the pile of aprons, caps and baby clothes and turned to take them through to her room.

Having some ironing of her own to do, Helen lifted the iron from the upturned enamel plate the girl had been using as a stand. 'You should ask David to come for his supper some night, Elspeth. It would be a fine change for him.'

Elspeth turned the suggestion over in her mind. It would be a friendly gesture, but he might think she was encouraging him, and he'd be hurt if she built up his hopes then let him down. She would hate to cause him any more distress. Besides, the last time she had invited a young man to supper, she had been left waiting, and she couldn't face that again. 'No, Helen,' she said, at last. 'I'm not wanting to get too friendly wi' another lad that might never come back from the war.'

On Monday, Elspeth had begun to think that David wouldn't be coming when he walked in at ten to three, with a spring in his step that hadn't been there before, and she went to him as soon as she was free. 'How did you get on? Did you like her?'

He screwed up his nose. 'She wouldn't be my choice.'

'She was your father's. Are you going back to see them?'

'I don't know. I felt real awkward wi' them, but I'm glad you made me go, Elspeth.'

'And I'm glad I made you.' She giggled as she walked away, but when she brought his tea she had to serve someone else.

They went out together when she finished work, and Elspeth looked up at him shyly when they sat down in the tram. 'Tell me more about your visit, David.'

'My father got a right shock when he saw me.'

'He'd been pleased, though?'

'Aye, he was, but his wife glowered at me like I'd no business being there. She doesna like me, and I don't like her, for she's nothing like my mother. Oh, Elspeth, can you understand how I feel?'

'Aye, it must be terrible to lose your mother.' She had lost both her mother and her father, but only through her own folly. No, not folly. She didn't regret what she'd done.

'It wasn't my home any more, for she's changed everything, but I made the effort.' He paused briefly. 'You're a good friend, Elspeth, for telling me I should go.'

'You just needed a wee push,' she laughed.

'Maybe, but now you've sorted me out, what about you? Will you not go home and make things up wi' your folk?'

'No, David.' Her face clouded over. 'I can never go home – it was a different thing altogether.'

'What was your row about? Was it over a lad?'

'Aye, it was, and I can't go back . . . ever again.' She was too ashamed to tell him why she'd had to leave home.

Having an illegitimate child was something to keep quiet about.

The next few days followed the same pattern, with David arriving at the People's Cafe in time to go back in the tram with Elspeth. She kept this from Helen, of course, as she did not want to fire her landlady's imagination any further. She liked David Fullerton, but that was all. It was good to have somebody of her own age to talk to, somebody who didn't try to pressurize her into going out at nights with him like so many of the other servicemen did. It was a comfortable relationship, friendly but not too friendly.

When he appeared on the second Thursday, she was surprised to see that he was in uniform, the kilt swinging as he went purposefully to the corner table, the flat Balmoral bonnet set at a jaunty angle on his head. He looked better than she had ever seen him, and she hurried across to him as soon as she could, exclaiming, 'Oh, David, you really suit the kilt. You've got the right build for it.'

He didn't even smile. 'It's good to feel the wind about my knees again, they get soft wearing trousers. The English lads used to torment us about our skirts, but we were proud to wear them.'

'And so you should be.' Becoming aware that there was a tension about him, she asked, 'What's wrong?' The strain on his face made her pity him after the cheerful mood he had been in for the past week. It made her more certain than ever that there was something he hadn't told her about the reason for his being in hospital.

'Nothing's wrong exactly,' he told her. 'It's just . . . this is the last time I'll see you, for I've to go back the day.'

'To Belgium, you mean?' She felt an unexpected pang

of . . . regret? She had thought he didn't mean a thing to her, only a passing acquaintance, yet she didn't want him to leave.

'I've just got time to see you on to the tram before I go to the station. I've been to the Barracks this morning, to get kitted out, and I've got all the papers I'll need to take me over there.' His eyes held hers for a moment. 'Will you write to me, Elspeth? My father was the only one that sent me letters before, and the other lads aye spoke about their lasses. Oh!' He reddened. 'I didn't mean you were to be my lass, just a friend – a letter now and then. Please?'

His look was so beseeching that her resolve not to be too friendly began to waver, but she gathered up his dirty dishes before she said, 'Well, you write to me first, and I'll think about it.'

His face lit up as she walked away, and she was glad that there was no great farewell scene when he saw her on to the tramcar later. Gripping her hand, he said, 'I'll write, Elspeth, and I'll keep hoping I get an answer.'

Feeling strangely empty when she sat down, she admitted to herself that she would miss David. Something obviously preyed on his mind, and she wished he had confided in her. She would have helped him to get over it, whatever it was, for she was drawn to him, as she'd never thought to be drawn to any man again. But she didn't love him.

Helen Watson was at a loss to understand why the girl was so wary of writing. 'He just wants a friendly letter.'

The next time Elspeth took young John down to King's Gate, Ann Robb couldn't understand it, either. 'Some young friends of mine write to dozens of soldiers and sailors, and there's nothing serious in any of it. The boys need something to keep their spirits up, you know.'

'I suppose so.' Elspeth sighed deeply. 'There's nothing binding in just a few letters, is there? I'm just worried about what he'll expect when he comes back . . . if he ever comes back.'

She was rather put out when Ann laughed at her pessimism.

Chapter Sixteen

When the all-too-well remembered buff envelope arrived a few weeks later, Elspeth was almost afraid to open it.

'It'll not bite you,' Helen teased.

Smiling, the girl tore it open then drew out a double sheet of paper covered with neat writing, the first page more than half taken up with his rank, name and number.

'Dear Elspeth,' she read aloud, 'Here is my letter to you as promised. The channel crossing was bad but we arrived safe and sound. I am in a different place with the same battalion. I think of you often, and I hope you are not too busy. We have a mascot, a scruffy little terrier that wandered in one day, half starved, and we washed him and fed him, and now he will not leave us. Some of the lads called him Pierre, just for fun, but he answers to it now. There is nothing more to write about, but I am looking forward to you answering this. From your friend, David Fullerton.'

'You see?' Helen cried, triumphantly. 'Just your friend, so you will write to him, surely?'

'Aye, I think I will.' Elspeth had been relieved by the general tone of the letter. 'He's a nice lad, and I still feel kind o' sorry for him.'

Although David did not write regularly, Elspeth wrote to him every Sunday. One morning, a few months after he had gone back, she was on the point of opening an envelope when she noticed that it was addressed to Mrs James Watson. Knowing that Helen was worried about not hearing from Donald for some time, she hurried into the kitchen and handed it over, anxiously watching the changing expressions flitting across her landlady's face.

When she came to the end, Helen looked at Elspeth, her eyes wide with surprise. 'Donald says he was angry when I tell't him I'd let you have his room, that's why he never come home when he got leave. He'd been going to Hull wi' another laddie, and he'd met this lassie, and the last time he was there, he wed her.' She stopped, swallowing before she burst out, 'My Donald a married man! You ken, I aye kind o' hoped he would take a fancy to you once he was home.'

Elspeth was taken aback at this. 'Oh, I never thought . . .'

'It wasn't meant to be, and I'm pleased he's got himself a wife – even if she is English.' Helen grinned impishly.

'You should never have given me his room – it's little wonder he was angry.'

'I thought he'd understand, but that's men for you. Any road, it's water under the brig. He says he understands now why I did it, seeing you'd no place else to go, though I never tell't him you were expecting . . . and I didna say I was, either, in case it upset him. He's bringing his wife here on his next leave, and he says not to worry about a bed, for they'll take a room in a hotel.'

Elspeth frowned. 'I should leave and let them get the room. It was Donald's, and it's only right . . .'

'It's only a single bed, lassie. No, it's best the way he says. Well, well! Who'd have thought it!' Helen clearly couldn't get over the shock.

Elspeth was on the evening shift that week and did not see Jimmy's reaction to the news, but Helen told her next day that he'd been very pleased. 'He said he hoped the English lassie would make our Donald as happy as I've made him, and that near made me break down, Elspeth, for he's never been a great one for flowery words, my Jimmy, though he's a good man, for all that.'

Over the next few weeks, the two women cleaned the small flat from top to bottom so that Donald's English wife would have nothing to criticize, and at last the great Saturday arrived, the tears and recriminations being over by the time Elspeth went home at half past three.

'This is Donald,' Helen said, proudly, 'and this is his wife, Margaret.'

Elspeth had her hand almost shaken off by the broad, round-cheeked young man in the kilt, and by the cheery, dark-haired girl who came forward smiling, and Helen laughed in delight. 'Me and Margaret's having a job understanding each other, but Donald's translating for us.'

'Margaret's beginning to know most of what I'm saying now, aren't you, dear?' Donald spoke slowly and deliberately for his wife's benefit, his eyes revealing his love for her.

'Oh, yes. It was very difficult at first – I thought he was a foreigner.' Margaret had a silvery laugh which didn't stop at her lips, but spread all over her face and crinkled her eyes and nose. She was a reasonably pretty girl, but there was an indefinable beauty about her when she laughed, as if she were illuminated from within.

Elspeth could see that both Helen and Jimmy were besotted with her, and felt a small twinge of jealousy – Margaret was a real part of the Watson family and it was Elspeth who was the outsider – but she quickly stifled it.

'It's you that's the foreigner here,' Donald teased his wife, making her gurgle with laughter again.

'No, no, don't mind him, Margaret,' Helen smiled. 'We're very pleased to have you as our daughter-in-law.'

'I wasn't the only one to be keeping secrets, though,' Donald remarked, rather more seriously. 'I got a right shock when I saw wee John here. You never told me, Mother, but it's great to have a new brother at my age. He's a real bonnie wee thing, isn't he, Elspeth?'

Elspeth shot a pleading glance at Helen in the hope that her landlady would tell her son the truth, but she was dismayed to see the woman smiling proudly. 'Aye,' the girl said, very carefully, 'he's a bonnie bairn.' She was afraid that by not correcting Donald she had irrevocably condoned a ghastly deception, but what else could she have done? She was dependent on Helen to look after John, and she would be for ever grateful to her for her kindness before and after the time of his birth. Surely it could all be put right at some time in the future couldn't it?

The young couple were blissfully unaware of Elspeth's quandary. 'Donald wanted to wait until after the war before we were married,' Margaret told them, tucking her arm through her husband's, 'but I persuaded him to change his mind. You've got to grab your happiness while you can in wartime, haven't you?'

'That's true,' agreed Elspeth, 'for you never know what's going to happen to spoil it.'

After Donald and his wife left to go to their hotel – 'It's really our honeymoon,' Margaret laughingly remarked – Elspeth went sadly to bed. She still resented the fact that, in the eyes of the world, her child belonged to the Watsons. If only their baby daughter had been born alive, nothing like this would have happened. She had been so sorry for Helen at the time that she had gone along with the charade, and she would have to be a much stronger person than she was before she could end it . . . but she must end it some day, however much it hurt Helen. In the meantime, she would have to be content to let things drift on as they were.

When he learned that his son's wife was expecting a baby in December, Jimmy grumbled, only half joking, 'I'll never hear the end o' it when folk ken I'm to be a grandfather.'

'It's worse for me being a Granny,' Helen objected, then gave a little laugh. 'I must say I'm looking forward to it, though, but it's hard to think our grandchild'll be that far away we might never see it till's the war's done. I just hope and pray Donald'll come back to Aberdeen wi' his wife and the bairn when he's out o' the Gordons. He'll surely not want to settle down in Hull? What d'you think, Jimmy?'

'He'll make up his own mind about it, lass.'

Elspeth was elated about Margaret's pregnancy. When Donald came home for good with another child for Helen to fuss over, she might be more willing to relinquish John. Her hopes seemed to be doomed, however, for in the next instant, Helen was saying, 'It just come to me. John'll be an uncle when he's only two year and three month.'

The young woman looked at Jimmy, appealing to him to

say something, but he shook his head hopelessly and she knew that he, like herself, could not hurt his wife by reminding her that John and Donald were not really brothers.

'We wouldna have room for them all here, of course,' Helen went on, happily, 'so you'll not need to worry about having to leave, Elspeth, for Donald'll get a house for his family, and he'll likely make sure it's near enough for me to see the bairnie every day.'

The two pairs of anguished eyes met again for a second, then Jimmy turned away rather shamefacedly. Elspeth did not feel angry; he was only shielding his wife, after all.

The letter Helen had been long awaiting arrived on the day before Christmas. 'Margaret had a son on the 22nd,' she told Elspeth, in great excitement, 'and she says he's to be called James, after his grandfather. That's nice, isn't it?'

'Jimmy'll be pleased,' Elspeth smiled.

'He'll be like a dog wi' two tails.'

Jimmy was indeed delighted. 'He'll be the fourth James Watson that I ken o',' he grinned, when he was told the news, 'for I was named for my father, and him for his father before him, and it could go even further back than that.'

'Now I can send on the baby jackets I've knitted,' Helen said, then added, 'I was feared to do it before, you see, in case . . . well . . . you never ken, do you?'

Elspeth held her breath. Had Helen remembered about her own dead baby at last? Was this the reminder she had needed? But Helen went on, 'I was lucky wi' John, but . . .' Breaking off, she hesitated for a moment then shook her head. 'Ach, I'm sorry, Elspeth, I shouldna have said anything about things going wrong.'

Jimmy was still too busy thinking proudly of his new namesake to notice what she was saying, and Elspeth sighed as she stood up. Margaret's baby had changed nothing . . . except, perhaps, to show that Helen's mind had exchanged her own confinement for Elspeth's and vice versa.

The first few months of 1918 passed fairly smoothly for the inhabitants of the middle floor flat, with letters at odd intervals from both Donald and David, and from Margaret regularly once a week, telling his grandparents about the progress little James was making. Elspeth, although she was interested to hear about the baby, was more interested in what David wrote. He told her little about what he was doing himself, but he always asked her to tell him what she had been doing, and she sat down every Sunday and told him any little things she thought might amuse him. In his replies, he told her how much her letters cheered him, and in his last one he had said, 'I keep seeing you in my mind in your apron and cap, your beautiful golden hair poking out.' That had made a warm glow spread through her, but she was beginning to get a little worried because she had not heard from him for some time.

'I wish David would write more often,' she said to Helen one Saturday afternoon, when she came home and was told, once again, that there was no letter, 'but he's likely too busy fighting the Huns.'

'It's the same wi' Donald,' Helen sighed.

'I'm sure they write as often as they can,' Jimmy observed, sitting down on the mat with John to play with a box of lead soldiers of Donald's that Helen had found when she was cleaning out a cupboard.

'Bang! Bang!' the little boy shouted, his deep brown eyes dancing 'Don soota Derries!'

'What things to learn the laddie.' Helen ruffled the boy's curls as she passed. 'Shooting Jerries!'

Watching her son, Elspeth laughed when he pushed the Soldiers flat to the floor and came over to her, pointing to them 'Look, Ep . . . pie! All deaded!'

'Oh, Helen!' Elspeth was overcome. 'That's the first time he's said my name, an' it's what my mother called me, for that's what I said when I was little.' She was as proud as if he had said 'Mammy', and Jimmy looked at her with pity.

A loud knock made them all jump. 'Who could that be?' Helen was already half way to the door, and when Elspeth heard the deep voice asking, 'Mrs Watson?' she jumped up and ran through to the lobby. 'David!' she exclaimed, then stopped, embarrassed. In her joy at seeing him after fifteen whole months, she had nearly thrown her arms round him.

'Aye, Elspeth, it's me.' Her welcome had made hope spring to his eyes. 'I hope you don't mind me coming here, but they said at the tearoom you'd been on the early shift.' Laying his kitbag down, he removed his bonnet and stood shyly holding it. 'I'm pleased to meet you, Mrs Watson.'

Helen beamed. 'Come away in.' Taking him into the kitchen she said, 'Jimmy, this is Elspeth's . . . friend, David.'

Rising off his knees, her husband shook the visitor's hand and said, hospitably, 'Sit down, then, lad.'

Hovering over the young soldier, Helen said, 'The supper's ready – you'll have some?' Taking his acceptance for granted, she went to the stove and lifted a lid to judge if there was enough stew for this extra mouth, while Elspeth gathered the lead soldiers off the mat. John had forsaken them the moment the kilted figure had appeared, and was standing in front of David, his dark eyes huge circles in his chubby face. 'Sodger!' he said loudly, and beamed when David picked him up and set him on his knee.

When Jimmy asked him how he had fared in Belgium, he told them something of his experiences: not the gruesome details he knew would sicken them; not about the filth and discomfort of the trenches; but tales of the camaraderie and heroism he knew they wanted to hear. They lapped it up, even Helen, who set the table and dished up the stew and dumplings as she listened to him.

When they finished eating, Elspeth stood up. 'It's time John was in his bed, Helen. I'll get him ready.'

'No, no. You sit and speak to David, and me and Jimmy'll do the dishes, then I'll see to John.'

Just before nine, David said, 'I'd best be leaving. My father doesn't know I'm coming.' He glanced at the girl with a smile. 'I've been writing to him, as well, Elspeth.'

'Oh, I'm real pleased about that, David.'

Jimmy got to his feet and clapped the young man's shoulder. 'You're welcome back any time, lad. Mind that.'

'I'll walk wi' you to the tram,' Elspeth said, and lifted her coat from the peg in the lobby as they went out.

Taking his glasses out of their case in order to read the newspaper, Jimmy observed, 'I don't know how Elspeth feels, but I can see David's real taken wi' her.'

Helen nodded. 'Aye, but she doesn't want to get serious about him, in case he gets killed, like her first lad.'

Elspeth and David walked along the lane without talking, but at last he said, 'Can I see you again, please?'

'If you like, but I just want to be a friend, remember, nothing more.'

'I'll not try to make you change your mind, Elspeth, but I'll keep on hoping. There's not another lad, is there?'

'There was once, but he was killed.'

'Oh, I see now. You're feared I'll be killed, but I'm determined to come back, lass, and you'll maybe have second thoughts once the war's finished. Can I come and take you home from the tearoom on Monday?'

'If you want, but let things bide the way they are. I'm not ready yet for anything else.'

When Elspeth returned to the house, Helen asked, 'Are you to be going steady wi' him?'

'No, I said we could just be friends, and he understands why, for I tell't him about John Forrest being killed.'

David accompanied Elspeth home from the cafe every day of the next week, but put no pressure on her. They sat and talked with Helen, or took young John for walks, and the girl realized that she had come to feel more than friendship for him. He was so good with the toddler, and got on so well with Helen and Jimmy, that she wished she could overcome her fears and let their relationship develop into something deeper.

When Sunday came round again, they decided to go to the beach, Helen insisting, when they offered to take the boy, that they go by themselves. 'You'll not want to be saddled wi' the bairn seeing it's your last day, David.'

Elspeth was fully aware that her landlady was giving her an opportunity to make up her mind – or rather, to change it – about David, but she was determined not to alter her decision. She was fond of him and would miss him a lot when he went away, but she couldn't commit herself to another soldier.

Although it was a lovely, warm May day, the beach was not seething with people like it would be during June, July and August, and Elspeth's spirits lifted at the mile-long stretch of golden sand lying invitingly before them when they alighted from the tramcar. Leaning over the railings, they watched in amusement as a small dog, barking excitedly, bounded in and out of the water to retrieve the stick his elderly master was throwing for him. Farther along, an oldish man and his wife were walking along the edge of the sea with their shoes off, giggling like children each time a wave came up to lap their ankles.

After a few minutes, Elspeth pushed herself away from the metal bars and said, 'Come on down on to the sand, David.'

They went past the red brick Bathing Station and sat down on the grass to remove their shoes and boots, then Elspeth turned away to take off her stockings and stuffed them in her coat pocket, while David did the same with his long woollen socks. 'I'll race you along the beach,' she cried, laughing at his expression of surprise.

He followed her gingerly down the granite steps and sprinted to catch up with her as she ran, strands of her golden hair streaming out behind her. She squealed and ran even faster, until they collapsed together, breathlessly, then, as they looked at each other, laughing and panting, Elspeth sensed a change in David's mood – his eyes were serious and his smile had faded. Guessing that he was contemplating kissing her, her heart sank. One kiss would lead to more, and then where would it all end?

She sat up abruptly. 'What a mess I must look.'

'You're the bonniest lassie I've ever seen.'

Embarrassed, she gazed out over the sea. 'The water looks as blue as the picture of the Mediterranean in Mrs Robb's hall. N-I-C-E it said, but she said the folk there on the Riviera pronounced it "niece".'

His eyes following a seagull, David said, 'Why did you leave the Robbs, Elspeth?'

'I . . . wanted a change,' she said quickly, for she couldn't tell him that she had been expecting an illegitimate child, 'and Jimmy heard they were looking for waitresses in the People's Cafe.'

'Oh aye.'

She relaxed. He had just been making conversation to keep his mind off other things. 'D'you ken what I'd like?' she asked, looking at him with her eyes dancing. 'I'd like to paddle in the blue waters o' the Mediterranean.'

After a pause, he said, 'Maybe some day, Elspeth, if . . . ?'

She burst out laughing. 'No, no. The blue waters here, I was meaning.' Jumping up, she skipped down to the sea, lifting her skirts almost to her knees as she went.

David, a little shocked at seeing her bare, shapely legs, stood for a moment before he ran to join her in the water, his kilt flaring around him. She threw back her head and laughed as the cold sea swirled round their feet – the sand trickling through their toes with each plodding step they took. He grabbed her elbow to save her from being swept off her feet by an extra-high wave, and she didn't protest when he kept holding it. She had never seen him looking so happy and carefree before, and wondered what terrible experience had caused him to be so withdrawn as he'd been the first day he came to the cafe, but she was glad that it was she who had wrought the change in him.

Up on the grass again, they made short work of the flask of tea and the sandwiches which Helen had provided, then, putting on their footwear again, they walked along the promenade to the wide estuary of the Don, where they sat for a long time watching the seabirds circling over the water looking for fish. Strolling back to catch the tram home, he took her hand and she didn't pull it away as she would have done even yesterday – it was comforting to know how he felt about her – but she couldn't bring herself to respond.

They talked companionably during the long journey, but when they were walking past the quarry, he said, 'Elspeth, you must ken I love you. Is there a chance you could . . . ?'

She shook her head reprovingly. 'Don't spoil things, David. Not when we've had such a lovely day.'

Sighing, he let the matter drop and the ensuing oppressive silence totally engulfed them until they went into the house. Helen could see that nothing had changed but couldn't make up her mind whether to be glad or sorry.

When David was going home, Elspeth offered to see him to the tram, but he said, 'No, you've done enough walking for one day.'

Being tired, and having to be on early shift the following morning, she gave in. 'I'll come down the stair, any road.'

On the bottom step, he said, 'You don't need to come any farther.' Hesitating for a moment, he went on, softly,

'I'll never stop loving you, Elspeth. It gives me something to live for, and I hope you'll have changed your mind about things when I come back next time.'

'I'll not say I'll never change my mind,' she whispered, 'but not yet, David. Not yet.'

He kissed her cheek lightly and walked away.

No letter came for Elspeth over the summer and autumn. She had written to David every week in the five months since he went back, but now she didn't bother, although Helen, ever the optimist, assured her that he must still be alive. 'I'm sure you'd feel it inside you if anything had happened to him,' she had repeated, over and over again.

The girl was convinced that David had been killed, but put a brave face on to fool her landlady. 'Maybe he found somebody that was willing to be more than a friend to him.'

'What chance would the laddie have for that, out there in the trenches?' Helen couldn't have been more scornful.

Elspeth was glad that the People's Cafe kept her mind fully occupied for at least eight hours every day, and Helen, feeling sorry for her, allowed her to take John out for walks more often, but even that did not lift the girl's spirits. She felt bitter, and resentful that David had been taken from her, too. 'It's not that I loved him,' she said to Ann Robb one day when she took John to visit the doctor's wife, 'but I'd grown real fond of him and I don't like to think he's been killed.'

'Perhaps he's only been wounded,' Mrs Robb suggested.

'If he'd been wounded, he could write,' Elspeth said, stubbornly. 'He would know I'd be worried about not hearing from him.'

'If he'd been killed, you'd have seen it in the newspaper. They publish lists, remember.'

'I hardly ever look at the paper.'

'But Mr Watson does, I've heard you saying, so he'd have seen it, if it had been in.'

'Aye, that's right,' Elspeth said, thoughtfully.

Mrs Robb left it at that, and turned to John. 'Goodness, you're growing a big boy.'

Elspeth smiled. 'He's three now, and his dark curly hair and big brown eyes are just like his father's.'

The big brown eyes were regarding her solemnly, but she had a shock when the boy turned to the other woman. 'My father works at the Quarry,' he told her.

'He thinks Jimmy Watson's his father,' Elspeth whispered, her face flaming.

Ann Robb laughed. 'It's only natural.'

Elspeth could have told her that Helen's attitude to the boy was most unnatural, but she was so ashamed at having let it run on for so long that she kept quiet.

It was all over on the 11th November. The Armistice came as a blessing to the world in general, but more especially to the women with husbands, sons or lovers in the forces.

When the next letter came from Margaret, full of glowing descriptions of baby James, Helen remarked, 'I can hardly wait to see my grandson, but I couldna face the journey to Hull, even if I had the fare, so I'll have to wait till Donald gets out o' the Gordons and they bring him up here.' Glancing at Elspeth's unresponsive face, she said, kindly, 'I ken you're worried about David, lass, but no news is good news and it'll likely not be long till you see him now.'

'Aye.' Elspeth did not feel inclined to discuss it.

Gradually, the men returned home – those who were fit enough, those who would return – to the long unemployment queues and soup kitchens. The promise of a 'land fit for heroes' was to be left unfulfilled.

In March, 1919, Margaret wrote, 'Donald is home for good, and he was lucky to find a job in a shipyard, so we will be looking for a house near there. Little James is growing every day. Of course, he is 15 months old now.' As if his grandmother needed to be reminded of that. 'He looks so beautiful in the little knitted suits you sent for his birthday and his Christmas, I wish you could see him.'

'That's that, then!' Helen, feeling bitterly let down, did her best to accept it – or to pretend that she accepted it. 'It's Donald's life, and he'd wanted to put his roots down where his wife and his bairn are.'

'Oh, Helen, I'm sorry,' Elspeth murmured. 'I ken how much you were looking forward to seeing James every day.'

'It's maybe just as well they'll not be here, for I'd likely spoil him. Grannies are aye blamed for that.'

Elspeth's smile was rueful. No one would ever be able to accuse John's two grannies of spoiling him. Her own mother would never acknowledge his existence now, and Mrs Forrest – his other granny – would never know that he existed at all.

Returning servicemen – ex-servicemen – thronged the cafe now, their high-spirited teasing making Elspeth feel just as exhilarated as they did . . . until they left. At the back of her mind lay the hope that David would walk in one day, but she knew that it was very unlikely.

The numbers tailed off eventually, and by November – a whole year after the Armistice – the only servicemen she served were the sailors from ships in the harbour, and the regular soldiers from the Barracks. David had not come back from the war – or if he had, he had not come back to her.

At Quarry Street, Helen and Jimmy never mentioned him, but Elspeth could sense their pity and tried to keep cheerful in front of them. Only in the privacy of her own room did she give way to tears – tears of regret for a friendship which had never had the chance to blossom into romance.

She felt ashamed now at having rebuffed his love. It would have been easy to say that she returned his feelings, to make him feel loved and wanted, but through her own fears she had let him believe that she hadn't cared for him at all. She had cared. Her present heartache was proof of that, and whether he was dead or had found someone else, she had lost him.

Chapter Seventeen

A week after the new year of 1920 had come in, Elspeth was jolted out of the cocoon she had spun for herself in her efforts to put David Fullerton out of her mind. Having just started her shift one afternoon, she went to serve a stout woman who was sitting in what had been his special place.

The customer looked up. 'I'm just wanting . . .' Her mouth stayed open. 'Mercy on us, it's Elspeth Gray!'

'Mrs Taylor!' She was completely taken aback at coming face to face again with this woman from Auchlonie, who had been the one to tell her why John Forrest had not appeared for supper that November night over five years ago.

Mrs Taylor, however, was never thrown out of her stride. 'We wondered what had become o' you, for your folk never speak about you.'

Elspeth stood motionless, miserably wishing that the floor would open up and swallow her. 'I got a better job.'

'Aye, so Miss Fraser said, but we couldna understand why your mother never said anything about it.'

Her expression showed that she did not consider working as a waitress an improvement on being a dressmaker, and the girl could well imagine the speculations that had gone on, but none of the village women could have known about her association with John Forrest. Nettie Duffus and Kirsty Tough had, of course, but they would never have disclosed her secret, and, anyway, they didn't know all of it.

'Did you have a row wi' your folk?' Mrs Taylor persisted, her skin as thick as a rhinoceros.

'Aye, and I walked out.'

Because this was not an uncommon occurrence, the woman accepted it without question. 'You're looking well enough, any road, the town air seems to be agreeing wi' you. Will I tell Lizzie I've seen you?'

'Oh, no! Don't tell anybody,' Elspeth pleaded, then caught sight of Miss Mackay looking at them over the top of her pince nez. 'I'm sorry, Mrs Taylor, but I'm not supposed to stand and speak. The manageress is glowering.'

'I see that. Well, I just want a cup o' tea, to shove in time for the train.'

When she was leaving, Mrs Taylor looked across and put a finger to her lips, indicating that she would say nothing about the meeting. She was a gossip, Elspeth knew that, but she could be trusted not to break her promise and Lizzie would never hear about her daughter from her.

The incident unsettled the girl, however, and after fretting over it all night, she told her landlady, who was quite upset for her, she looked so unhappy. 'Do you not think you should try writing to your mother again?'

'She never answered my other letters.'

'Aye, well, but she'd likely still been angry at you for leaving your auntie's. She'll have cooled down now.'

'I'm not writing to her ever again.' Elspeth had been deeply hurt by her mother's silence, and had inherited her father's obstinacy. 'I'll need to change my job, though, in case somebody else from Auchlonie comes in and sees me.'

'You can please yourself about writing', Helen said, slightly impatiently, 'but you're not to give up your job, that's just cutting off your nose to spite your face.'

Elspeth couldn't help smiling at this, but took her advice and did nothing about handing in her notice. She also pleased herself and did not write to her mother.

Nearing the end of her shift one afternoon at the beginning of June, a hand touching her elbow made Elspeth turn round, her eyes and mouth flying open the sight of the tall Gordon Highlander who was looking at her rather timidly.

'David!' She could hardly believe it. After all the long months of anxiety and despondency, it was too much for her to find that he was still alive, and she burst into tears.

'Whisht, Elspeth, folk'll be looking.' He was embarrassed, but pleased, by her reaction, and squeezed her arm before he sat down at his old table. 'I was hoping you'd be on the early shift, so I'll have a cup o' tea and wait for you.'

'I thought . . . something had happened to you when you never wrote,' she whispered.

'I ken, lass, but I'll tell you about it later on.'

For the next ten minutes, she took and served orders in a pleasant haze, looking across at David every now and then as if to make sure he was really there, but at last it was time for her to put on her coat. As soon as they were outside, she looked up at him. 'Why did you stop writing? I thought you'd found somebody else, then I thought you'd been . . . killed. Oh, I just didna ken what to think.'

210

'There'll never be anybody else for me, Elspeth.'

David's voice was quiet, and she felt herself responding to his earnestness. She had a deep affection for him – no, it was more than that. She did love him.

'I was wounded the week after I went back, and I was in a French hospital, a monastery it had been once.' He paused, unwilling to tell her that he had been delirious for weeks. 'Well, the sisters thought I might have to lose my leg, and I couldn't risk telling you. If you'd said you loved me after that, I'd never have ken't if it was true or out o' pity, and I couldna face that. But, thank God, they managed to save it, though it's shorter than the other one and I'll aye be a cripple.'

'Oh, David,' she half-sobbed, 'I'm sorry about your leg, but I'm awful glad you weren't killed. At least you've come back to me.'

He didn't tell her that he had often wished that he had been killed. It would have saved him from the excruciating pain he'd had to suffer, and the mind-twisting nightmares which had returned, worse than ever. Careful surgery and tender nursing had brought him back to sanity, however, and by the time he was transferred to a hospital in the north of England, he had been looking forward to coming home – home to this wonderful girl. Although he had contacted his father then, he still hadn't written to her. He wanted to see her face when she discovered that he was safe, and her reaction was all that he had hoped for. 'Will you marry me now?'

Her hesitation lasted for only a fraction of a second. She couldn't expect to love anyone as intensely as she had loved John Forrest, but her love for David was different. 'Aye,' she said, seriously. 'Aye, David, I will.'

His haggard face lit up as he grasped her hand tightly, and on the tram he sat with his arm round her, both of them so wrapped up in their love that they were quite oblivious of the smiles of the other passengers. When they burst in on Helen, she was delighted to see David home safely and didn't need to ask why they were so happy. They decided on a quiet wedding as soon as possible, and were still discussing it when Jimmy came home, so he joined in the jubilation, while wee John moved from one to the other, wondering what all the excitement was about.

When it was time for David to leave, Elspeth said that she would go to the end of the lane with him, and as soon as they had gone out, Helen sighed, 'Oh, I'm that pleased for her, though it's going to break my heart when she leaves us, but she deserves some happiness, the poor lassie, and David's a good man for her.'

Jimmy had stretched over to pick up the *Press and Journal* from the table, but his wife's words made him retract his hand. 'Aye,' he said, slowly, 'he's a good man, and he'll understand about John.'

His wife looked puzzled. 'What's John got to do wi' it?'

'Oh, Helen,' he said, sadly, 'John's got everything to do wi' it. Elspeth'll want to take him wi' her when she gets wed, and you'll have to give him up.'

'But why would she want to take our John?'

Shaking his head, Jimmy said, carefully, and very gently, 'I should have said something long before this, but . . . I ken't you werena yourself. You'll have to face up to it now, though. John's Elspeth's son, lass, not ours.'

Her perplexity deepening, she said, 'I don't know what

you're speaking about. What funny idea have you got in your head now?'

'I wish to God it was just a funny idea, for it's been eating at my very soul for years. John belongs to Elspeth.'

'No, no!' she burst out, her whole face crinkling. 'How can you say that, when you ken what a hard time I had when he was born?'

'Aye, you'd a terrible time, but it wasna wi' John.'

'It was, oh Jimmy, it was wi' John. He's not Elspeth's.'

'Aye, lass, he is. There's no getting away from it.'

'But, I . . . Doctor Robb was here when I had him, Jimmy, you ken that. He'll tell you himself, if you ask him.'

His heart aching for her, her husband had risen from his own chair to kneel beside her, and now he took her hand gently in his. 'I don't need to ask him, Helen. He was here attending to you, but . . . you lost your bairnie. Do you not mind, she was dead born?'

Her lips quivered. 'D . . . dead born? No, it's not true. What are you trying to do to me?'

'I'm trying to make you face the truth, lass.'

Her eyes wild now, her fingers tore at her hair. 'You're trying to drive me mad, that's what it is. How can you say things like that to me?'

He gripped the hand he was holding, even tighter. 'Helen, lass, I'd do anything not to have to say them, but they've got to be said now.'

'I'll not listen!' she screamed.

'You'll have to listen.' He let go her hand and put his arms round her. 'You were sleeping after Doctor Robb went away, and when you woke up and saw Elspeth wi' John, you thought he was your baby.'

213

Her chest heaving now, she shook her head as if she were a dog worrying a rabbit. 'John was my baby!' It was a wail, a pathetic wail that tore at her husband's heart. 'He came out of my womb, and I suckled him . . .'

'The infant that came out of your womb was dead, Helen. It had been dead for weeks, that's what Elspeth told me the doctor said, and it was after Elspeth had John. I ken you suckled him, but I should never have let that go on, and neither should Elspeth, but maybe she didna want to hurt you either, seeing it was you took wee John into the world when the midwife couldna come. And you nursed her back to health, the same as she did for you. Do you not remember?'

The sudden anguish on his wife's face made him increase the pressure of his embrace. 'I don't blame you, Helen, for you were out o' your mind at the time. You'd lost your own infant, and you couldna accept it . . . maybe you couldna even take it in, but I've been heart-sorry for Elspeth sometimes, and when Donald was here, I near tell't him myself that John wasna his brother.'

After a long silence, Helen said, 'There was aye something at the back o' my mind that bothered me, but . . .' She broke off, tears edging down her now chalk white cheeks. 'Oh God, Jimmy, what have I done?'

'You couldna help it, lass. You'd had a big shock, and you couldna believe you'd lost your own bairnie when wee John was there in front o' your eyes.'

'You say I attended to Elspeth? Was it not her bairn that was dead born?'

The hope rising again in her eyes made her husband's throat tighten. 'No, Helen, it was ours.'

Her hands were fidgeting now, as she tried to picture the

sequence of events. 'I could sometimes see that poor, wee purple infant in my mind, but I kept telling myself it was Elspeth's, and that was why I had to bind her to stop her milk coming. I can mind on that.'

'She was too weak to feed John, that was why you'd to stop her milk coming. Oh, Helen, lass, I'm sorry for bringing it all back to you, but I had to sort things out for Elspeth, though I wish to God I'd done it years ago.'

The tremor in his voice made her stroke his stubbly cheek. 'And I wish you'd done it years ago, and all, but I can see why you held back.'

Relieved that it was over, Jimmy stood up and rubbed his knees. 'That hasna helped my rheumatics,' he observed, ruefully, knowing, as he sat down, that Helen was agonizing over the terrible thing she had done.

They were sitting silently when Elspeth came back. 'I can't believe it yet,' she said, blissfully, surprised that they didn't seem eager to carry on the discussion about her forthcoming wedding.

Jimmy cleared his throat. 'Me and Helen was . . . have you tell't David about young John?'

It was like a kick in the teeth to her, and her radiance vanished as if it had been turned off at a tap, her face crumpling. She had forgotten that David didn't know the truth about John's parentage, she had almost forgotten herself that John was not Helen's son. Helen? Elspeth turned to the woman, whose tortured face told her all she needed to know. 'You've minded?' she whispered.

'It was Jimmy tell't me, but I've minded now. Oh, Elspeth, I'm sorry. It must have been awful for you to stand by and watch me . . .'

Afraid that his wife would become too emotional, Jimmy interrupted her. 'Have you tell't David?' he asked Elspeth again.

'No, I havena. I thought . . . I ken't Helen thought John was hers, and I . . . I havena had time to think . . .'

'You'll need to think about it, though,' Jimmy stated, firmly. 'John's your son, and if you want to take him wi' you when you wed David . . . it's up to you, for Helen kens where her duty lies now.'

Looking distracted, Elspeth moaned, 'Oh, Helen, what should I do?' She was pleading for her mind to be made up for her, but her landlady shook her head.

'I'm saying nothing. I've caused you enough trouble, and I'm willing to give John up if you want to take him, but you'll have to work this out for yourself.'

'David thinks John's your son, and I don't want to hurt him – he's suffered enough already.'

'You'll have to make your mind up, one way or the other.' Helen looked as miserable as the girl.

'If I tell him John's mine, and he's illegitimate, he might change his mind about marrying me, and I . . .'

Jimmy got to his feet and came over to pat Elspeth's head awkwardly. 'I'm sorry we've spoiled it for you, lass, but it had to be sorted out before the wedding. Sleep on it, and see what you think in the morning.'

The two women eyed each other uncertainly as they listened to him taking the lavatory key off its hook in the lobby and going down the stairs, then Helen said, slowly, 'It's all my fault you're in this predicament now, lass, and I'll never forgive myself for it, but Jimmy's right. Things'll not look so bad once you've had a good night's sleep.'

In her little room, Elspeth wrestled with her thoughts. The Watsons would be heartbroken if she took her child away from them, but they would respect her wishes, if that was what she decided. But what about John himself? Was it fair to spring it on him, at four years old, that Helen and Jimmy were not his real parents and to catapult him into a situation that could only confuse him? David would be a good father – if he accepted the boy. On the other hand, he might be hurt and angry with her for not telling him the truth before, and John's presence would be a permanent reminder to him of her love for another man – two pointers to his future resentment of the child.

Her torment lasted for hours, and she wept silently before she came to her decision, with the prayer that John Forrest would understand why she was giving up their son. She would be surrendering all hope of ever claiming the boy again, but it was the only thing to do in the circumstances and she would be leaving him in good hands. Helen was a fine woman, a caring woman, and, apart from the mix-up over John – which had only come about through her own tragedy – she had been a true friend, the best there could ever be.

When she told Helen in the morning what she had decided, her landlady, having also spent a night of agony, knew exactly how much it would cost Elspeth to leave her son behind, for she would have felt the same if the decision had gone the other way. 'Thank you, lassie, for what you're doing for us,' she breathed, 'and you can come to see John as often as you like. Mind now.'

That afternoon, after Elspeth finished work, David took her to meet his father and step-mother, who were both very pleased – for different reasons – that he was going to be married. His father was pleased for his son's sake, and Isabel because David would be leaving the house. She objected to having to share her husband's attention, and had begun to hate his son for upsetting her cosy little world.

David introduced his future wife proudly. 'Father, Isabel, this is Elspeth.'

The man – an older edition of David himself, with the same fair hair and fresh complexion – stepped forward and shook her hand warmly. 'I'm very pleased to meet you, Elspeth. We got a right stammiegaster last night when David said he was getting married, for he'd never said he'd a lass, but you'll do fine.'

'How do you do.' Isabel Fullerton – her silver hair styled so perfectly that it looked like a wig, and her face showing little warmth – extended a limp hand. Elspeth felt quite at ease with David's father, but his wife's aloof manner made her feel most uncomfortable. 'David said you're a waitress in the People's Cafe?' the woman carried on, haughtily. 'Before that, I believe you were just in service.' She made it sound the most menial job anyone could have.

Her patronizing tone stung Elspeth into asking, 'What did you work at yourself before you married David's father?'

'I haven't had to work since I married my first husband, but when I was single I was a typewriter in a solicitor's office.'

Stuck-up besom, Elspeth thought, vindictively, fighting back a sarcastic retort, but luckily David stepped in. 'Elspeth'll stop working when we're wed, of course.'

'Of course.' Isabel nodded condescendingly.

'You're invited to the wedding, Father . . . and you, Isabel. It's at Craigiebuckler Kirk, three weeks the day, and Elspeth's landlady's going to lay on a bit o' a spread for us after.'

His father beamed. 'We'll be there, lad.'

Isabel laid her hand on his sleeve. 'No, that's the day you promised to take me to see my friend in Banchory, remember?'

His face grim, her husband said, 'The first I've heard of it. Anyway I want to see my son being married, and you're coming with me.'

Her eyes narrowed, but she put up no further argument. Her resentment at being ordered to do something she didn't want to, however, was so obvious that they stayed for only half an hour, and once they were outside, Elspeth said, 'I see what you mean about not feeling welcome in that house. Your father's wife didn't want to be friendly.'

David tucked her arm through his. 'We'll likely not see much of them after we're wed, but we'll be happier on our own, any road, wi' no relations interfering.'

Elspeth put thoughts of her own parents out of her head, and her nearest relative, after all, was young John, but she was giving up that relationship, too.

Two days before the wedding, she went down to King's Gate, where her ex-employer was delighted to hear her good news. 'David must be a very decent fellow if he's willing to take on another man's child.'

The girl looked uncomfortable. 'He doesn't know about John, Mrs Robb, and I'm leaving him wi' the Watsons.'

'Oh, Elspeth! You should have told him.' Ann sounded rather disapproving. 'I'm sure he would have accepted John.'

'I couldn't take the chance, for he might have been angry at me for not telling him from the start.'

'Why didn't you tell him from the start?'

Elspeth sighed. 'One o' the neighbours thought he was Helen's and it just went on till they took it for granted.'

'But why didn't either of you correct them?'

The girl could pretend no longer. 'Helen thought he was hers, that was the whole trouble. She lost her own baby, remember, and . . . I suppose some women go funny after a thing like that, and I didn't want to hurt her.'

'But you could have come and told my husband. He would have dealt with it. Oh, Elspeth, you've gone through years of misery when it could have been avoided.'

'I suppose so, but she knows the truth now, for Jimmy had to tell her in case I wanted to take John.'

'I still think you should have told David and given him the chance to make up his own mind. He has the right to know, and don't forget, facts can't always be hidden. Something could happen to bring it to light some day, and it would be worse for you then. Have you thought of that?'

'I can't see what could happen, Mrs Robb, for nobody knows except the Watsons and you and the doctor.'

Ann regarded her steadily for a moment. 'It's your life, my dear, and I'll say no more about it. Has David got a job yet, and have you found somewhere to live?'

'Oh, yes. David got a job in a men's outfitter's in George Street, it's not great wages but we'll manage. And he went round the factors, and he got a house on the top floor in Printfield Walk in Woodside. Just two rooms, but that's all we need, isn't it? We got the key two weeks ago, so we've been busy cleaning it, and David's bought some furniture, just second hand but it's good stuff and it should do us a while . . . till we can afford something better, any road.'

Elspeth Gray and David Fullerton were joined in holy matrimony in July 1920, the ceremony taking place in Craigiebuckler – the rural-style church nearest to Quarry Street – with Helen and Jimmy Watson as witnesses. David's father and Isabel were also there, but the only other person present, apart from the Reverend James Cuthbert, was little John, completely unaware that this event was a milestone in his life.

When the wedding was over, Helen turned to Isabel. 'You'll be coming to our house with us now?'

'No, I'm afraid we have another engagement,' the woman said, frostily, – 'Like her mouth was full o' marbles,' as Helen said later.

David senior looked very apologetic. 'I'm really sorry, but . . . well, it's just . . .' He shrugged expressively and Jimmy said, 'Aye, well, you'd have been welcome, but if you can't come, that's it, and it can't be helped.'

The rest of the party returned to the Watsons' house where Helen had prepared a 'spread', and happy laughter filled the kitchen until it was time for the bride and groom to go to the tiny tenement flat that David had rented. Elspeth had to restrain herself then from throwing her arms round her small son and carrying him off with her.

Helen, seeing the girl's distress, took John's hand. 'Kiss Elspeth,' she instructed him, 'to wish her good luck.'

David watched fondly as his wife knelt down to receive the boy's kiss, but Jimmy distracted him by saying loudly,

'Well, good luck in your new house, David,' thus making him turn round to shake hands. The understanding older man then shepherded the groom out to the landing, talking all the time, in order to give Elspeth time to compose herself.

As they were going down the stairs, Helen called after them, 'Come back and see us as soon as you can.'

They walked arm in arm down the lane, and Elspeth took her guilty secret with her to her new home, trusting in God that her husband would never uncover it.

Chapter Eighteen

Helen Watson had set off early with John, but, having to take two trams to get to the Woodside tenement where the Fullertons lived, it was almost ten o'clock when she arrived.

'Come in, Helen. Hello, John.' Elspeth's welcome was warm, but she was perplexed by this unexpected call.

'I've took over a letter for you. It's been redirected from the cafe, and it's got an Auchlonie postmark on it.'

Elspeth looked at the envelope with some astonishment. 'It's my mother's writing. There must be something wrong.'

'Don't stand gaping, then, open it and see what she says.'

'I don't want to open it. She's ignored me for years.'

'She's maybe apologizing.'

Elspeth opened the envelope reluctantly. 'You will likely be surprised at getting this,' she read out, 'but I thought you should know your father passed away early today. The funeral is on Thursday. Elizabeth Gray.'

Helen looked keenly at her friend, but couldn't tell from her enigmatic expression whether she was sad at her father's death or glad that her mother had written at last. As far as she was concerned herself, she couldn't help thinking it was a funny way for a mother to be signing a letter to her daughter and she wished, for Elspeth's sake, that it had been more affectionate. 'I don't know what to say,' she muttered.

'There's nothing you can say.' Elspeth sat down. 'He's dead, and it must be terrible for her, but I don't feel anything. He was a wicked man, never letting her write.'

'We never ken't if that was really the way o' it.'

'I'm near sure it was. I suppose she expects me to go to the funeral . . . that's the only reason she's written.'

'It's your duty, lass. He was your father, when all's said and done.'

Elspeth laid the letter down. 'You'll bide a while now you're here, Helen? I've something to tell you.'

'Just a wee while, then. I've got to get back, for I promised Mrs Coull at number two to keep her Billy till she goes to the doctor. She thinks she's expecting.'

'I think I'm expecting, and all . . . no, I'm sure, for I'm two month already.'

Helen clapped her hands. 'That's great news, lass. What's David saying about it, or have you not tell't him yet?'

'He's fair delighted, the same as me.'

'Aye, you'll be a family then.' Helen had noticed Elspeth watching John before he sat down on the padded fender stool, and hoped that the coming baby would compensate for the sacrifice of the girl's firstborn. She still felt guilty at the way she had usurped the boy for so long, but it had been Elspeth's choice to let her have him for good. 'You've never regretted . . . ?' she ventured, then stopped.

Elspeth knew what she meant. 'No, it left David and me free to start without any complications.' Not wanting to think about it, she stood up. 'Come ben and see the bedroom. I've made new curtains and a bedspread to match.'

Taking John's hand, she led them through. 'David's going to make a crib for the baby. He's good wi' his hands though he just serves shirts and collars from behind a counter, and we'll put it here, at the foot o' the bed. What d'you think?'

Head on one side, lips pursed, Helen considered. 'Aye, it's the only place for it, and you'll still have room to open the drawers.' She patted the heavy ogee chest standing along the opposite wall from the double bed. 'You've made a real bonnie place for yourselves, though it was all second-hand furniture.'

'David picked good solid stuff, so it would last.'

'Aye, they're not making things like that nowadays.'

'Elspeth, can I have a drink?' At five, John talked quite properly now, Helen having avoided speaking to him in the rough dialect.

Helen frowned at him. 'You forgot your manners. Say please.'

'No, my wee lamb,' Elspeth smiled, 'it was me that forgot my manners. I should have offered you something. Come through and I'll give you some lemonade. We'll have a cup o' tea, eh, Helen?'

In the kitchen again, Helen remarked, 'We got in the forms for the school, and John's to start at Mile End after the New Year. He was too late for the intake this past August, for they've to be five before the first o' September, and his birthday was the eighth. Still, it'll be time enough.'

'School already? You're getting to be a big boy, John.'

He regarded her with his large brown eyes, making her heart miss a beat. 'My dad's going to buy me a real leather schoolbag.'

Elspeth was conscious of Helen's apologetic face and forced herself to smile. 'You'll like the school.'

When her visitors left, she sat down by the fire. She had imagined that she had banished John Forrest from her mind, but it had only needed a flash of his son's dark eyes to bring the memories of him flooding back – memories of that wonderful few days in November 1914 – six years ago.

But she was being daft! She loved David, and she would love their child, but she'd have to prepare herself not to be caught off guard every time she saw John Watson. For he was John Watson, not John Forrest . . . and he would certainly never be John Fullerton, for Jimmy and Helen had officially adopted him.

'You'll never guess what happened the day,' she said to David when he came home for his dinner. 'Helen took across a letter from my mother, after all this time. Read it, it's on the sideboard.'

He picked it up and scanned it, then said, 'We'll have to go to the funeral.'

'We can't afford you losing a day's wages, and you didna ken him, any road. Besides, my mother might feel awkward wi' you, so it's best I go by myself.' If he went, her mother might tell him the real reason for her leaving home, but on her own she would have just one day to get through before she could return to her uncomplicated life – uncomplicated, that is, as long as she succeeded in pushing John Forrest and his child to the back of her mind.

Walking from Auchlonie Station, Elspeth wished that the next few hours were over, and, when she reached the cottar house, she knocked at the door and waited, for she was only a visitor now. In a moment, she followed her mother silently into the dark kitchen, the curtains drawn as a mark of respect to the dead. The well-remembered smells of wax polish, blacklead and mothballs made a wave of homesickness sweep over her and set her wondering how she would cope.

'The coffin's ben there,' Lizzie said, awkwardly. 'Would you like to see him before they come to screw him down?'

Knowing that it was expected of her, Elspeth nodded and went through to the best room, where Lizzie went straight over to the trestles with their sad burden. 'He looks peaceful enough, that's one good thing, though he had a sore fight at the end.'

'How did . . . it happen?'

'He'd some awful soakings, and he wouldna see about his cough – he was aye thrawn about things like that, for he thought it was a weakness to go to the doctor – and it turned to pumonia.'

Tears came to Elspeth's eyes as she looked at her father's mortal remains, and she fumbled up her sleeve for her handkerchief.

'He was a difficult man at times,' Lizzie said, 'but he was a good man to me.' Her voice quavered a little.

Elspeth wept openly and turned blindly to her mother. 'I'm sorry for the things I did, I was so headstrong and wilful. Will you forgive me?'

With no hesitation, Lizzie gathered her daughter into her arms. 'Oh, Eppie, the whole three o' us were headstrong and wilful, your father worst o' the lot. He was angry – a bitter man – and he tell't me to burn your letters without reading them and not to write to you. I did read them, though, for I had to ken how you were, and I was pleased you got a job. Then Janet tell't us you'd said some terrible things to her and she'd put you out, and I was really angry at you for a while, thinking you'd been so ungrateful, though I got over that and I wished I hadna burned the letter wi' your address.'

Elspeth kept back the accusations she could have made against her aunt – what was the good of raking it all up again? – and they clung to each other, sharing their common grief, but weeping also for the long, wasted years.

'I wouldna have ken't where to write to you to let you ken about your father, but I let it out to Mrs Taylor when she come to say she was sorry about Geordie, and she said she'd seen you a while ago in the cafe in the Market.'

Elspeth had been so astonished by receiving the letter that it had never crossed her mind to wonder why it had been readdressed, but now she said, a little sadly, 'I might have ken't she couldna keep her mouth shut about it.'

Lizzie was off on another tack. 'Your father guessed about the bairn, Eppie, and he forced me to tell him the truth when he come back from seeing you away at the station.' She drew back abruptly. 'Was it a boy or a girl you got?'

Elspeth froze. She had forgotten, in her over-emotional state, the tangled web she had woven, which now threatened to engulf her. Should she tell the truth and give her mother a potential lever to ruin her life again? Before she took time to consider properly, she blurted out, 'It was a boy, but it was dead born.'

'Eppie, I'm sorry! I'd never have asked if I'd ken't.'

'It was God's will.' Elspeth wondered if she would be

struck dumb for this blasphemy, but went on with forced cheerfulness. 'I'm married now, though. His name's David Fullerton, and he was wounded in the war, but he's got a job in a men's shop. He kens about . . . John Forrest, but not about the bairn, so you must promise never to tell him.'

'I'd never cause trouble for you, Eppie, you've suffered enough already, but I'd like to meet your David. Why did you not bring him wi' you the day?'

'I wasna sure what kind o' reception I would get.'

This explanation satisfied Lizzie, who had also been rather unsure of the outcome of their meeting, and over a cup of tea Elspeth told her everything that had happened since she went to Aberdeen. Before they knew it, the mourners began to arrive and the hearse was waiting to load the coffin.

Neighbours and friends commented on how well Elspeth was looking, and Jimmy Bain – representing Janet, who had elected not to attend, on the pretext of being too upset – came over to speak to her. 'I'm sorry about what Janet did to you,' he whispered, as he shook her hand. 'She's aye been in her element rampaging, and she's getting worse every day – her temper, I mean, not her health, for she's as strong as a horse, no matter what she says, and I'm sure she'll see me off the face of the earth. I know the fight she had with you wasn't your fault.'

'Thank you for understanding.' Elspeth gulped.

'Where did you go? I was worried for you and you so near your time.'

'I got lodgings in Quarry Street, and my landlady looked after me.'

'Thank God for that, and you're looking fine.' Giving her hand another brief grip, he moved away.

The minister's lengthy eulogy over, the cortege set off, the mourners walking the mile and a half behind the hearse. At the graveside, Elspeth prayed that her father had forgiven her before he died. She couldn't bear to believe that he had gone to his eternal rest despising her.

'Father, I'm sorry.' For a moment, she watched the gravedigger shovelling the sods on top of the coffin, then turned to join her mother, who was surrounded by members of the farming community expressing their condolences.

'Just a minute, Elspeth.'

The woman who stood behind her was another ghost from the past, and Elspeth's stomach churned violently. 'Oh, it's Mrs Forrest!'

'I'm pleased to make your acquaintance at last, though it's in sad circumstances. I made Blairton take me wi' him, for I was sure you'd be at your father's funeral, and I've been wanting to speak to you for a long time.'

'Aye?' Elspeth was shaking all over.

'Did you ken my John had got a grandfather clock made for you? He meant to give it to you on your wedding day, but . . .'

This was totally unexpected. 'He never said anything about it – I only got the one letter.' She didn't say it had long since disintegrated and been burned.

Mrs Forrest lifted her spectacles to wipe her eyes before the tears spilled over. 'You must have been as upset as me when you learned he'd been killed?'

'I was . . . awful upset,' Elspeth murmured.

'I thought that must be why you didna come to see me, and you'd likely gone away to try to get over it? Maybe it was best, but the clock was delivered two days after we got the telegram. It was meant for you, but I didna ken where you were, so it's been in our parlour ever since, waiting for you to take it.'

'But I can't take it, Mrs Forrest, for I'm married now.'

Meg looked at her shrewdly. 'Did you not tell your man about you and my son?'

'I did tell him,' Elspeth murmured – but not everything, came the unwelcome thought.

'You were best not to keep secrets from him, so it'll be all right if I send the clock up by the carrier. What's your address, so I can tell Eck where to take it?'

Her mind a jumble of confusion, a bewildered Elspeth stammered out her address, and the woman went on, 'It's a lovely bit o' furniture, and I'd like to think John's wish had been carried out, though it's not the way he planned.'

'But, Mrs Forrest, I . . .'

'Blairton's been moaning about it taking up space, so he'll be pleased to see the back o' it.'

Her head spinning, Elspeth joined her mother. The farm men had to return to work, but most of the women went back to the cottar house, where Lizzie had prepared sandwiches, so it was almost two hours before mother and daughter were alone again.

'Was that Blairton's wife that spoke to you in the kirkyard?' Distressed as she was, Lizzie's keen eyes had not missed the little episode. 'What did she have to say?'

'It was the queerest thing out. She said her John had got a clock made for me, and it come after they ken't he'd been killed, but she didna ken where I was, and she asked my address, and she's sending it up by the carrier.'

'That's good, it'll be a reminder to you.'

'Oh, Mother, David'll maybe not be pleased to have a reminder o' John Forrest in his house.'

'He'd surely not be jealous o' a dead man?'

Elspeth wasn't so sure. A month or so earlier, she had been awakened one night by David's moans, and when she roused him from his nightmare, he had told her about the deaths of his comrades and how his mind had been affected by shell-shock. She was afraid that being faced with this situation would hurt him at a time when he was still feeling vulnerable. 'John bought it to give me on our wedding day,' she muttered, 'and what'll David say about that?'

'He'll want you to have it, if he's as good a man as you say, Eppie.' Lizzie glanced hopefully at her daughter. 'Can I come and meet him and judge for myself?'

Torn between rekindled love for her mother and fear that Lizzie might inadvertently make some reference to the 'dead born' child in front of David, Elspeth said, rather half-heartedly, that she'd be welcome to visit them the following Wednesday, that being his half day.

When Elspeth went home, David was glad that she had made up with her mother, but he couldn't understand why she was so upset about the clock. 'It was meant for you, so take it and be grateful, for I'm not jealous o' your first lad.'

When Lizzie paid her promised visit, Elspeth showed her into the bedroom first, to leave her coat on the bed, and was proud when her mother admired the room. 'David's making a crib, and it'll stand at the foot o' the bed there.'

It was out before she thought, because she hadn't made up her mind if she should tell her mother about the expected child.

'A crib?' Lizzie's head swivelled round. 'Are you . . . ?'

'Aye, but not till June.'

'I'm right pleased about it, Eppie, for it means I'll have a grandchild at last. Is your David happy about it?'

'We're both happy about it, Mother.'

When Lizzie went through to the kitchen, she was amazed to find the grandfather clock already at the side of Elspeth's fireside. 'Oh, Eppie,' she burst out, after studying it for a moment, 'it's the very marrow o' the one your father gave me. John Forrest must have had a good memory.'

'I got a shock about that, and all, and he even got our initials put on the pendulum.' When she had first seen the flowing JF–EG so lovingly intertwined, Elspeth had sat down and wept for the boy she had loved so much, the father of the child she had left behind. This was tangible proof, everlasting proof, of how much he had loved her, and every time she looked at it she would remember him. When she recovered, she had worried that the initials would upset David, and had been a little worried about the flatness of his voice when he said, 'It's a beautiful clock.'

Over a cup of tea, Lizzie brought her daughter up to date with the happenings in Auchlonie, Elspeth expressing surprise, amusement, disbelief or pleasure as was expected of her, and when she finally got the chance, she asked, 'Are Nettie Duffus and Kirsty Tough still wi' Miss Fraser?'

Annoyed at herself for forgetting them, Lizzie said, 'No, and you'll not ken the lassies that's there now. Nettie got wed to Johnny Low about three year ago, do you mind him?'

'Aye, I mind him,' Elspeth laughed, recalling what Nettie had said about Johnny kissing all the girls when he was drunk one Hogmanay. 'She aye fancied him.'

'Well, he got a job down about Fife, some place, and they seem to be doing well, from what I've heard.'

'I'm pleased to hear that, but what about Kirsty?'

Lizzie shook her head, sadly. 'Poor Kirsty didna do so well for herself. She had to get wed – you'll not ken him, either, for he didna come to work at Denseat till four year ago. He was a bit o' a lad, and he didn't bide very long – long enough to put Kirsty in the family way, though. I heard he's working near Peterhead, and they say he ill-uses her.'

Poor wee Kirsty, Elspeth reflected; so romantic and wanting to know about love, and she lands with a brute of a husband.

When David came home at quarter past one, having finished work for the day, Lizzie took to him straight away, remarking to Elspeth, 'You picked a good man, any road. Oh, I near forgot,' she continued, in almost the same breath, 'I'm getting to bide on in the cottar house. I was feared I'd be put out, for it went wi' the grieve's job, but Ferguson himself come to tell me he's building another house for the new man, wi' an inside lavatory. Young folk nowadays need all the conveniences, they'll not put up wi' what the older generation had to put up wi'. We'd a dry lavvy for years, till they laid pipes for water. Any road, he just wants me to pay a token rent, seeing Geordie was wi' him so long.'

At David's insistence – he thought very highly of his mother-in-law – Lizzie visited at least once a month and followed her daughter's pregnancy with interest, often bringing small items she had knitted, in spite of Elspeth's protestations that she shouldn't.

Helen Watson and Ann Robb had both been pleased about the reconciliation, but Elspeth had been too ashamed to let them know that she had told Lizzie her first child had died. The lie had been uttered on the spur of the moment, and now she could never risk asking the Watsons over when her mother was there, in case she said something about the 'dead' child and let the whole terrible secret come out in front of David.

Elspeth couldn't fully explain to her husband why she wanted to call their daughter Laura, but she felt that, in some way, she was repaying the debt she owed to the Robbs. Both before and after John's birth, the doctor and his wife had pulled her through when she was very low – in spirits and in health – and the only way she could think of to show her gratitude was to name her daughter after theirs.

Helen, of course, understood, and thought that it was a nice gesture. 'Neither me or you would be here the day if it hadna been for Doctor Robb,' she said, when she went to see the new infant. 'Did you have him this time, and all?'

'Aye, he's very good, though I wasna near as bad as I was wi' John.' Remembering that it was Helen who had delivered John, Elspeth thought, with belated comprehension, that her friend had had every right to think of him as her own. When she herself had given up her son, it had almost torn her apart, but she had done the right thing.

Ann was delighted about the name when Elspeth went to show her daughter off. 'You've done us a great honour, Elspeth, and she's an absolute darling. I think we could have a wee glass of sherry to celebrate, don't you?'

Elspeth felt that this baby almost compensated for her past sacrifice, and swore to herself, as she sipped from the dainty glass, that she would never allow anything to happen to spoil Laura's life.

Chapter Nineteen

1925

David Fullerton, loving his mother-in-law as much as he had his mother, could not understand why Elspeth was relieved each time Lizzie went home. When her visits first began, he had suggested they ask her to stay for a week at the time of Elspeth's confinement, but his wife had retorted angrily that she didn't want her, and that Mrs Flynn next door had promised to look in during the days and he would be there in the evenings. A few months later, he had made a proposal that they should ask Lizzie to come for a week's holiday, but Elspeth had said, 'There's not a bed for her.'

'She could sleep wi' you, and I'd manage fine on the easy chairs,' he had protested, but her agitated displeasure had kept him from pursuing it, and he had never brought up the subject again.

Laura was four years old when he saw, in the window of a Building Society, an advertisement which made him think – it could solve the problem of the sleeping accommodation.

'ONLY £20 DOWN, AND THE HOUSE OF YOUR DREAMS COULD BE YOURS,' it proclaimed, in large letters.

Since being promoted to head salesman, he had managed to save a bit – he had planned to take his wife and daughter for a holiday – so he had more than enough for the deposit. Going in to make enquiries, he was pleasantly surprised at the monthly amount to be repaid, but, afraid of being too rash, he said he would like time to consider before he committed himself.

He put forward his proposition to Elspeth the next morning. 'Laura needs a room to herself, and your mother should really be where you could keep an eye on her,' he began, tentatively.

His wife looked wary. 'I don't know what you're getting at, David. I've tell't you before, there's no room for her to bide here.'

'I could buy a bungalow with three bedrooms, big enough for us all. I've been finding out about it.'

'Buy a house? We could never afford that.'

'After the deposit, it would just cost us about the same as we're paying for rent here, and it would belong to us in sixteen years.' David sounded triumphant. 'Read the pamphlet they gave me, and you'll see it's the best thing for us.'

Elspeth felt trapped when he went out. It would be good to have a house of their own, but taking her mother to live with them was a different thing. It would be tempting fate, and she had found to her cost that fate had a way of retaliating. After reading the pamphlet, she understood why David was so keen, but tried to dissuade him from the move when he came home.

'It would be an awful millstone round our necks for the next sixteen year, David. Just suppose you took ill and couldn't work? We'd not be able to keep up the payments, and they'd likely take the house away from us.'

His laugh held a hint of irritation. 'You're always worrying, Elspeth. If everybody was the same as you, nobody would ever buy houses, and Building Societies would be out of business. I'm quite sure they make allowances for that – different terms.'

Elspeth felt annoyed at him for using his 'shop voice'. She was quite aware that he had to talk like that to his customers, but she wished that he would be his old couthy self with her, especially now when she was at her wits' end to know what to do. She waited fearfully when he told her mother about his plan on her next visit, and sagged with with relief when Lizzie said, 'No, no, I'm not giving up my independence, but you go ahead and buy your bungalow, David, for Laura needs a room to herself now.'

David went ahead. The bungalow was to be in Woodlands Avenue, a new street off King's Gate. Development had already begun in the area – houses having been built on King's Gate itself to within a short distance of Quarry Street – and Elspeth was very pleased with the location of her new home, because it meant that she would be nearer Helen . . . and John.

Over the next few months, they monitored the progress of the builders every Sunday, then the joiners, electricians and plumbers, the plasterers and decorators, but eventually the bungalow was ready for them.

Elspeth spent the first few weeks making curtains for the large picture windows, then devoted herself to re-arranging the furniture. It amused David at first to come home to find everything shifted round, but when he saw the bed sitting in a different place from where it had been in the morning, he said, flatly, 'I can't sleep unless my head's to the north.'

Giggling, she helped him to move it, as quietly as they could so they wouldn't disturb Laura, and when it was back in its original place they both collapsed on it, helpless with mirth.

At last the house was as she wanted it, or nearly, because they couldn't afford to buy everything she would have liked. The living room sported a brand new, oak dining suite – a sideboard with mirror, square table with slide-out extensions, and four chairs to match. On either side of the low tiled fireplace stood a sturdy leather armchair, which David had picked up in a saleroom along with the two chairs padded in brown plush. The floor had a cheap jute square, floral-patterned in muted autumn tones, the surrounds being stained with oak varnish to match the suite, and although the curtains were only cheap cotton, they were in the same colours as the carpet.

The three bedrooms were furnished with dressing tables with mirrors, and wardrobes with full-length mirrors – also found in salerooms – and had congoleum on the floors, with rugs at the sides of the beds. The scullery was painted in eau-de-nil, a delicate green which Elspeth found restful and relaxing, and the pink bathroom had gingham curtains at the frosted windows.

In the spacious hallway, her grandfather clock bestowed an air of grandeur on their modest 'castle'; it was the last thing Elspeth saw when she went out, and the first thing to welcome her when she returned. Her marriage to David was happy and satisfying, but the clock was a reminder of the ecstasy – and sorrow – of her association with John Forrest, who, by his untimely death, was glorified for ever in her mind.

In order to earn higher wages, David had moved to the men's department of a rather elite store in Union Street, which closed on Saturdays instead of Wednesdays like the ordinary shops, and now that they lived nearer it became the custom for the Fullertons to visit the Watsons every Saturday afternoon. While the two men went for a walk, the women exchanged recipes and discussed husbands and children. Laura, who had always looked up to the tall, curly-haired boy as a kind of hero, was delighted when she was allowed to go out to play with John and his pals, but the six-year-gap between them manifested itself from the start.

'Why do I have to take her with me,' John complained. 'She's too little to play our kind of games.'

'I am not, John Watson.' Laura tossed her auburn tresses, her face pink with indignation.

'John, take her with you and stop arguing.' Helen laughed at the boy's outraged expression, and making a face, he pushed the small girl out in front of him.

About an hour later, Laura came back with her knees scraped and her dress ripped, and John, slinking in behind her, tried to absolve himself from any blame. 'We told her not to climb the tree, but you know what she's like, she never takes a telling, and she fell off a branch.'

Helen sponged the raw knees and daubed on Germolene, while Elspeth deftly stitched the torn cotton dress. John stood miserably in the background, well aware that he would receive his chastisement after the visitors left. He was twelve now and growing daily – or so it seemed to Helen, who constantly had to let down the legs of his shorts.

On another visit, some weeks later, the little girl came home wailing and bedraggled, and John explained sheepishly, 'She fell in the burn. We were fishing for bandies and we told her to keep away but she didn't, and she slipped off the bank.' He watched the dripping clothes being whipped off and replaced by a large towel.

'Hush, my little pet,' Helen crooned, rubbing vigorously to dry the still howling Laura.

Elspeth felt angry with her daughter. 'You've been told time and time again not to go near that burn.'

'Don't blame the bairn.' Helen turned to John. 'It's your fault, you should have been watching her.'

Laura sprang to his defence, forgetting to cry in her concern for him. 'It was my own fault for not listening.'

John continued to protest vehemently every Saturday. 'Not again! She's just a pest.'

'I am not! I am not!' Laura would shout.

John's treatment did not diminish Laura's hero-worship, and she loved going to Quarry Street, although the other boys took their lead from him and did everything they could to put her off joining them in their exploits. She wasn't so happy on the occasional visits to King's Gate with her mother. Her namesake allowed her to play with the beautiful dolls in the playroom, and all the other expensive toys, but the eight years between them prevented them from being true companions. Moreover, Laura Robb attended a private girls' school, while Laura Fullerton went to Mile End, where John had gone before he passed the qualifying examination and moved to Rosemount Intermediate.

Elspeth and Ann laughed every time they heard the plaintive, piping cry floating downstairs, 'I want to be the teacher this time,' because the more modulated voice always answered, 'You're too small to be the teacher.' Of course, Laura Fullerton always had the final retort. 'Well, I'm not playing schools at all, then.'

The girl's enjoyment at Quarry Street was marred only when Donald and his family came for a week's holiday, Helen having bought a bed settee for the best room to accommodate them, and making James share the single bed in the small room which had been his father's before it had been Elspeth's and was now John's. Only a little over two years younger than John, he was welcomed by the other children, and enjoyed the novelty of the burn at the foot of the street, with the mature, graceful trees on its banks. He and his 'uncle' became inseparable, and both ordered Laura around, and she was annoyed that her beloved John devoted all his time to showing James the best trees to climb. She was always glad when Donald took his family back to Hull.

David had thought, when he bought the bungalow, that he would put his jealousy of John Forrest behind him when the clock was no longer standing at his elbow when he sat down at the fire, but it had only intensified. When he came home at nights, tired and resentful at being told by the manager that he could push sales further if he put his mind to it, what was the first thing he saw when he let himself into his own house? That damned grandfather clock! It galled him to think that Elspeth seemed to have made it a shrine to her first love, keeping it highly polished and flicking imaginary specks of dust off it each time she went past it. She paid more attention to it than she did to him.

Although Elspeth was content to be a housewife, her marriage was not as peaceful as it had been. David seemed to be drawing farther and farther away from her, and she felt hurt that he had stopped kissing her before he went to work in the mornings.

'Is anything wrong?' she asked one evening, after he had been sitting silently reading for some time. 'You hardly speak to me at all now.'

'What is there to speak about?'

His abruptness dismayed her. He had never spoken to her like that before. 'Is anything worrying you at your work?' she persevered. 'You'll maybe feel better for telling me, though I'll likely not be able to help you.'

'Nothing's worrying me, and I wish you'd stop harping on about things.'

Tears pricked her eyes. 'I'm sorry, David, I didn't mean to nag at you.'

That night, she lay beside him worrying about the change in his manner, and when she did eventually fall asleep, she was soon catapulted out of it by his flailing arms. He'd had no nightmares for some time, and she was actually relieved that he was having one now. It must have been building up in him, which would explain his earlier brusque behaviour. As she usually did at such times, she stroked his brow and tried to soothe him, but he would not be pacified. It was fully thirty minutes before he quietened down, then he opened his eyes and looked at her accusingly.

'You're all right now, David,' she crooned.

'I'm not all right when I know my wife spends all her time thinking about another man,' he snapped.

Recoiling in shock, she said, 'I never think about another man. I've never thought about anybody else except you.'

'You can't tell me you don't think about your precious John Forrest every time you look at that clock,' he sneered.

'Oh, David,' she gasped, 'I knew fine you'd be jealous.'

'I'm not jealous, but no man wants to have his wife's first lover's gift to her staring him in the face every time he comes home.'

'He wasn't my . . .' The words stuck in her throat.

'Ha! You can't deny it, can you? He was your lover!'

Steeling herself, she muttered, 'He wasn't my lover, we were just . . . friends, and it was long before I met you, David, so you can't hold that against me, surely?'

Letting out a shuddering sigh, he gasped her hand. 'No, you're right, I can't hold it against you. I'm sorry, Elspeth, it's just the damned nightmares that get at me, so I can't think straight.'

'Do you want me to get rid of the clock?'

'No, no! I just said the first thing that came into my head. Oh, Elspeth, Elspeth, I love you.'

Turning towards him, she submitted to his lovemaking but got no pleasure from it because of the hurtful things he had said . . . and she had to admit they were true. She did think of John Forrest, not every time she looked at the clock, but every time she polished it or wound it up, and he had been her lover, but only for a brief moment in her life. How could David understand? Her love for him was not the same, perhaps not quite deep enough, but it was still a satisfying love, and he had no need to be jealous.

David's nightmares became more frequent over the next

few months, and were usually followed by veiled accusations, but Elspeth was prepared for them now and was glad that they were not as specific as the first time. The trouble was that they made her think more and more of John Forrest, and she was afraid that, if her husband asked her again if the dead soldier had been her lover, she wouldn't be able to deny it.

On her visits, Lizzie did notice that her daughter seemed to be worrying about something, but Elspeth wouldn't tell her what it was. She even denied that there was anything wrong, though her mother was positive that it had something to do with David, who seemed to have grown dour lately.

In October, 1927, David was promoted to manager, his tormentor having retired, and because he no longer had the aggravation, his mind eased. Elspeth believed that the fits of depression he had suffered before had been due to worry about his work, because he had fewer nightmares now, and he seemed to have got over his jealousy, too. Their love life was not as exciting as it had once been, but they had been married for over seven years now and the bloom would have worn off anybody's marriage in that time.

Elspeth's first purchase with her extra housekeeping allowance was heavier curtains for the living room, but she had set her sights on replacing all her furniture, which was beginning to look shabby. Her life was running smoothly again, her happiness being evident from the bloom on her cheeks and her ever-ready smile.

Lizzie was pleased that her daughter was looking so well, because her own health was beginning to deteriorate, with rheumatics and pains in her chest, but she never mentioned them to anyone. She sometimes wished that she had accepted David's offer of a home three years earlier, but she had known that two women in one kitchen always spelt trouble.

Even when she had let David persuade her to stay for a few days a year or so back, Elspeth had been kind of short with her. She was happiest in her own little house, which she kept clean and tidy, though she wasn't able to do as much as she used to do.

One afternoon at the end of August, 1928, Elspeth was surprised by a visit from Mrs Wallace, who had occupied the cottar house next to Lizzie for the past four years.

'Your mother's had a heart attack,' the woman said, as soon as the door was opened. 'I come in the ambulance wi' her, for they took her to Woolmanhill.'

Elspeth's face had blanched. 'Will she be all right?'

'I waited will they said she was a wee bit better, but I think she's real bad.'

'Oh, God, I'll have to go to her.' Elspeth turned to get her coat from the bedroom, then hesitated and said, 'I'm sorry, I should have asked you in and offered you a cup o' tea. It was good o' you to come and tell me.'

'They gave me tea at the hospital the time I was waiting, thanks just the same, and I was pleased I could be doing something for Lizzie, she's been a good neighbour to me.'

'I'll come back wi' you on the bus, for I'm anxious to ken how she is.' Elspeth disappeared and returned slipping her arms into her coat sleeves. 'I'd best leave a note to let David ken where I am, in case I'm not back by teatime.

Laura'll go next door when she comes home from the school, for she kens Mrs Sangster'll take her in if I'm not here.'

Elspeth was so worried that she hardly spoke on the journey into town, and ran along the streets to the Infirmary when she came off the bus, stopping in shock as she entered the ward and saw her mother. The effects of the passing years had not been evident before, but this frail figure in the bed looked very old – very old and very ill.

'Mother, I'm here, and you're going to be fine.'

Lizzie smiled weakly. 'It's good to see you, Eppie, but I'm feared I'll not get better. My time has come.'

'No, no! Don't speak daft! You'll be up and about in no time.' Elspeth ruined her confident statement by starting to weep softly.

'Don't upset yourself, Eppie. I've lived my life, and I'm not sorry to be slipping away.'

A nurse motioning to Elspeth to leave then, she bent to kiss the bluish lips before she went, and did her best to hold back her feelings on the journey home, but when she let herself into the bungalow, she held on to the side of the grandfather clock and burst into noisy sobs. She had composed herself before her daughter came home from school, and was able to tell David quite calmly what had happened.

'Let me go in to see her tonight,' he said. 'You're too upset to go back so soon.'

'No, I want to go myself, so you'll have to stay with Laura.'

Having had time to think, Elspeth sought out the ward sister when she went to the hospital. 'I'm Mrs Gray's daughter. Is she going to get better?'

'There's always hope,' the woman said, 'but it was quite a bad attack, and another one may prove fatal . . .' Her manner became brisker. 'You never know, she may fool us all and be back on her feet in a week or two.'

Lizzie's dull eyes brightened a little when Elspeth went into the ward. 'You were here the day already, there's no need for you to come twice a day.'

'I wanted to come, Mother, and I'm sure you'll just be in here for a wee while, then I'll take you to bide wi' me.'

'It's good o' you to offer, Eppie lass, but I can't see myself ever being happy in the town.'

'You can't bide on your own now, though, so just make up your mind you're coming to me.'

Lizzie closed her eyes, and Elspeth prayed that she would indeed 'fool them all' and recover, and was relieved when her mother looked up at her. 'I'm right pleased things have worked out wi' you and David.' She smoothed the counterpane with a transparent hand. 'I often worried myself in case he found out about the bairn that died. You should have tell't him, Eppie, for there shouldna be secrets between a woman and her man.'

Elspeth felt sick. Why did her mother have to bring that up? It was bad enough that she believed the child to be dead, but John, a gangling thirteen-year-old, was the living image of his father, as Lizzie would see the second she set eyes on him, and a meeting with the Watsons would be inevitable if she came to live at the bungalow. It was all bound to come out.

Her mother was regarding her curiously, so she said, 'It's long past and forgotten, and David'll never find out, for the Watsons and the Robbs would never tell him.'

249

'No more would I, Eppie, but skeletons have a habit o' coming out o' the cupboard when you least expect it. They'll not bide hidden for ever, you ken.' Lizzie lifted her thin, wasted hand and studied her fingernails carefully. 'Eppie, I've left written instructions wi' Mr Reid, the solicitor, to sell up my things when I've passed on, and to put the . . .'

'Don't speak about passing on, Mother, for you'll get over this turn, and live for years yet.'

Lizzie ignored the interruption. 'I've tell't him to put the money in a trust for you. I ken you're not needing it the now, but there might come a time when you will.'

Elspeth returned home tired and depressed. Her mother had been trying to remind her that, if David ever found out about her first child, he might cast her off without a shilling, as the saying went. She was very quiet all evening, and David, presuming that she was upset by her mother's condition, was extra loving and caring towards her, which made her feel more guilty and more worried than ever. She didn't deserve his love and trust. She had told so many lies in her life that she was bound to be punished for them some day.

Lizzie had another, massive, heart attack the next day, and died just before Elspeth went in to see her in the afternoon. The sister offered to telephone David's shop, and he arrived within ten minutes to comfort his wife.

'She was hardly sixty,' she sobbed, 'and when I think o' the worry I caused her, I can hardly bear it.'

'Most children give their parents cause to worry some time,' he soothed. 'Stop blaming yourself and just try to remember she's with your father again.' He waited until

250

she calmed down, then took her home, remaining with her for some time before he went out to make the necessary arrangements.

Left on her own, Elspeth wept once more, reproaching herself for the things she had done, and for the things she hadn't done, as is usual when a loved one dies.

They left Laura with Helen when they went to Auchlonie for the funeral. Elspeth had been afraid that Mrs Forrest would be there, but only Blairton himself attended, coming over to shake hands with her at the graveside.

Mr Ferguson of Mains of Denseat came up to her next. 'It's not a very good time to be asking, Elspeth, but I'd be obliged if you'd clear out the house as quick as you can. You see, one o' my men's getting wed, so he'll be moving out o' the bothy once I get a lavatory put in to the house.'

She smiled faintly. 'I was meaning to clear things out the day, any road, for I'm not wanting to have to come back.'

'That's fine, then. Eh . . . I'm sorry about your mother.'

Harry Bain – again without his wife – patted Elspeth's back. 'I'm pleased to see you again, though it's a sad occasion.' He glanced at David, standing awkwardly by her side. 'You'll be Elspeth's man? See and look after her, then, for she's had a hard life.'

Elspeth's heart almost stopped. She had forgotten that Harry was another person who knew about her first child and was extremely thankful when he, too, moved away.

Under the circumstances, no one expected to be asked back to the little house, so Elspeth and David went there alone, and, while she sorted through her mother's belongings – packing all the personal things into a box for Mrs

251

Wallace to dispose of, and checking that the furniture was in a fit state to be sold – he went out to the back garden.

At the end of three hours, her task over, Elspeth looked sadly at the grandfather clock and wished that it didn't have to be sold. If Laura had been of marriageable age, it could have been given to her, but there was no room in the bungalow to store it for that eventuality. It occurred to Elspeth that the identical one in Aberdeen should rightfully go to John Watson after she died, having been bought by his father, but he didn't know that he was her son, and, God willing, he never would. Even if he ever needed to produce his birth certificate for anything, it was in a shortened form since the Watsons had adopted him legally, and there would be no mention of his being illegitimate.

David came in carrying a wooden box filled to the brim with vegetables. 'We may as well take the good of them,' he told her. 'Are you ready? I know it's been a difficult day for you, but it's all over now.'

When they went outside, Elspeth turned the heavy key in the lock, handed it in to Mrs Wallace, then left her childhood home forever.

Part Three

Chapter Twenty

1938

In Laird and Company's office, the conversation between the men centred on the precarious situation in Europe, but the three young clerkesses weren't bothered that the Germans had invaded Austria – they were more interested in the latest fashions in clothes and hair styles or the private lives of the glamorous Hollywood filmstars.

Mr Steele, the chief clerk, was on his favourite hobby horse. 'Hitler's after supremacy in Europe.'

The head cashier, Mr McDonald, nodded gravely. 'Yes, he'll likely have a go at some other countries before Britain, but there's going to be a second world war shortly, unless I'm very much mistaken.'

One of the younger clerks laughed. 'Hitler would never be so stupid as to risk a war with us.'

His superior frowned. 'Don't be too sure, sonny boy.'

Laura Fullerton was glad to be handed a docket to take to the warehouse, but because there were some really nice boys there, she went into the cloakroom first to make sure that she was presentable. Her reflection pleased her. Her heart-shaped face was free of ink stains and smuts, the eyes that looked back at her were a clear blue and her rich auburn hair was still as curly as it had been when she was a child, shining like satin in the electric light. Her lips – softer and more natural looking than the cupid's bow some girls painted on – might be better with a touch more colour, but her lipstick was in her handbag in a drawer of her desk.

Before she left the tiny room, she smoothed her tartan skirt over her hips where it had wrinkled from sitting, and pulled her jumper down. Her bust was the only thing that she wasn't happy with, but, hopefully, it would develop a bit more.

She often wished that one of the store boys would ask her out – she was an ardent film fan and couldn't afford to go as often as she wanted. After giving her mother five shillings for her board, and paying her bus fares, she was left with less than a shilling a week, and that had to cover make-up, toiletries and entertainment. She didn't care for the sixpenny seats in the cinema – they were too near the screen and gave her a crick in the neck – so her visits were limited to the ninepennies, once every few weeks with her two female colleagues, who were in the same financial straits as she was.

Only one boy was in the warehouse when she went in, not one of the good-looking ones, unfortunately, but she smiled sweetly anyway, and his reaction was gratifying. 'Hiya, gorgeous! How about you and me getting together?'

Assuming that he was only joking, she retorted, 'No thank you, I've other fish to fry.'

'We could go to the flicks.' He sounded less flippant now.

She didn't really fancy going out with him, but the lure of seeing a film was too great to refuse. 'Tomorrow?'

'See you at the Monkey House at seven. OK?'

'OK.' She returned to the office quite pleased, if a little apprehensive of what her parents would say if she told them she was going to the cinema with a boy. She would soon be seventeen, but they were so old-fashioned it might be best to let them believe she was going with Bunty and Ella as usual.

When she set off the following evening, she hoped that she wouldn't be first – the Monkey House was a popular meeting place and she didn't want to have to wait. She wondered idly how it had got its name. Perhaps it was the stone pillars in front of the insurance offices that gave the impression of bars on a cage.

Her escort was there before her, and handed her a paper bag. 'Chocolate cubes,' he said, off-handedly. 'Is the Queen's OK with you?'

The Queen's Cinema was cheaper than the big theatres, but it was showing 'King Kong' and she felt very grown up waiting in the foyer while he bought their tickets. 'Your name's Laura, isn't it?' he asked, as they walked through into the auditorium. 'Mine's Gordon.'

She was uneasy when he led her into the back row, but lost her fears when they were watching the cartoon. They ate some of the chocolates while the B film, a Hopalong Cassidy, was showing, and had some more during the advertisements and the newsreel, because neither of them wanted to watch Hitler's storm-troopers strutting into Austria, the country they had newly annexed. About five minutes into the main feature, she was conscious of Gordon's hand sliding along the back of her seat but she gave all her attention to the picture, until a close-up of the huge gorilla made her move closer to the boy in terror.

257

Encouraged, he put his arm round her shoulders, and it felt so comforting that she let it remain there. Once, his hand slid down and touched her breast – by accident, she innocently believed, and didn't like to say anything – but she moved and offered him a chocolate and, although he took more care after that, the National Anthem came as quite a relief to her. She had enjoyed the show, but sitting close to this sweaty, spotty youth in a stuffy cinema was not her idea of pleasure, and she breathed the fresh air in deeply when they emerged on to the street.

Fortunately, Gordon had no idea how she felt. 'I'll see you home – where do you live?'

She couldn't think of a way to put him off without making it obvious that he didn't appeal to her, and he had taken her to the cinema, after all. 'Woodlands Avenue. It's on the eleven bus route, off King's Gate.'

At the bus stop, they giggled at the antics of several men who were still staggering drunkenly all over the pavement an hour after the public houses had closed at half past nine, but their laughter was brought to an abrupt halt when one man advanced towards them with his hands raised menacingly. Their bus arriving, they jumped aboard thankfully and left him mouthing obscenities on the kerb.

Laura was quite glad after all that someone was seeing her home, even if it was only a drip like Gordon, because she felt a bit nervous after seeing 'King Kong'. When they were walking past a small clump of trees – all that was left of the original wood which had given her street its name – Gordon steered her off the pavement and pushed her against one of the silver birches. Her heart pounded with fear. She had seen films where young girls were strangled in woods and left lying dead. Was this . . . ?

Her eyes closed in panic as his hands moved from her waist to her neck, and she wondered if anyone would hear her if she screamed, but before she drew in enough breath to make the effort, his hot, clammy lips came down hard on her mouth and she tried to twist her head away.

'You've never been kissed before, that's for sure,' Gordon said, as he forced her lips to meet his again.

Pushing him away with all her strength, she was amazed when he stepped back and laughed. 'I'll let you go the rest of the way yourself, for I don't want to be accused of kidnapping. It'll be a while yet before you're ready for picking, but you'll be a real plum some day.'

She ran along the street, puzzled as to what he had meant by his last remark, and her mother regarded her suspiciously when she went in. 'You're all flushed, Laura, what's wrong?'

'I ran all the way from the bus, that's all.'

'Where were you till this time of night, and who were you with?' Elspeth persisted.

The girl heaved a sigh. 'Oh, Mum! Must you always give me the third degree? I was with Bunty and Ella and we went to see "King Kong", but it was kind of scarey.'

Looking up from his newspaper, David laughed. 'You young things like to be scared, though, don't you?'

'You and Mum had been the same when you were my age.'

'I never saw any pictures when I was your age,' Elspeth said, sadly. 'There was nothing like that in Auchlonie.'

Laura went to bed, reflecting as she undressed how easy it was to deceive her parents. She could guarantee that neither

259

of them had ever kept secrets from the other – straight as a die, both of them. Anyway, she wouldn't have to tell any more fibs, because she didn't intend to go out with another boy for a long time. Tonight was enough. If it had been a boy she'd fancied, somebody nice, it might have been different. Clark Gable or Tyrone Power, for instance, wouldn't have made her flesh creep in disgust. A kiss should be thrilling and pleasurable to both sides, and she hadn't met anyone yet that she'd be happy to allow that privilege.

One of her childish fantasies had been John Watson kissing her, but she hadn't seen him since he began to work at Henderson's, the engineering firm – he had been an errand boy until he was sixteen and was now an apprentice plumber and electrician – but she could remember how hurt she had been when he started going down town every Saturday afternoon to meet some of his workmates. She had carried on going out to play with the other children in Quarry Street to show him that she didn't care, and the boys of her own age hadn't teased her like John and his pals had.

Even James Watson had been much friendlier when he came on holidays. He'd sat by the side of the burn with her and told her of his ambition to join the Navy, but when he had left school Margaret and Donald had been against it, so he was working in the store of some pharmaceutical firm now. Yes, James had been quite nice, but he was too far away. Still, Laura thought, turning over to settle for sleep, there must be someone who would make her heart beat faster, but maybe she wasn't ready for love yet. That was probably what the obnoxious Gordon had meant.

At the end of September, when the newreels showed Neville Chamberlain waving a piece of paper and saying

'Peace in our time', the older men in Laura's office were sceptical. 'He shouldn't trust Hitler,' Mr Steele announced. 'Even his Youth Movement's just a front to teach boys to fight – a back-up to his army.'

Mr McDonald added his twopence-worth. 'He's power mad.'

Their doubts were intensified in a few months. 'I see Schickelgruber's done it again.' Mr Steele's deep voice was doom-laden.

'Schickelgruber?' Laura asked, never having heard the name before. 'Who's he?'

'Hitler, you dope,' sneered the fourteen-year-old office boy. 'That's his real name.'

Ignoring them, the chief clerk continued. 'It said on the wireless this morning he's invaded Czechoslovakia now, after that agreement with Chamberlain. I can bet my boots it'll be Britain next.'

The office boy grinned. 'If there is a war, I'm going to join up as soon as I'm old enough.'

Mr McDonald, an old soldier himself, turned on him. 'If you ever do have to go into the army, laddie, you won't think it's so bloody marvellous.'

Fred, a young clerk, snorted. 'You and Mr Steele are just a couple of scare-mongers. There'll never be another war.'

This completely dispelled Laura's growing uneasiness. Fred was more up-to-date, and had a good grasp of current affairs. What did these old fogeys know, for goodness' sake?

The murmurings of war reminded David of the things he had tried to forget. The horror of Ypres and the later battle in the fields near Moeuvres, in which he had been so badly

261

wounded that he had almost lost a leg, came back to haunt his dreams. With his mind in such a state of instability, the presence of the grandfather clock in the hall revived his old jealousy and he began to taunt Elspeth again; just small, snide remarks at first, but enough to alarm her. She had thought he had got over it, but now she realized that his obsession about her first love had merely been lying in abeyance. At first the sneers had followed his nightmares, but now they occurred at any time and she dreaded him coming home each night, spending her Sundays in constant fear of another direct accusation.

It came one evening, as he stormed into the living room. 'I see you've been polishing John Forrest's clock again?'

'It has to be polished sometimes,' she said, praying that would be the end of it.

'And you just love doing it, don't you?' His top lip had curled. 'I suppose you imagine you're stroking his body.'

'Don't be stupid.' Although she was angry, she kept her voice down to avoid annoying him further.

'It's not stupid. I know how your mind works.'

'My mind was just on keeping the clock looking nice, for it would soon look neglected if I didn't polish it.'

'He didn't neglect you, though, did he? I'm sure he kept you satisfied, not like me.'

The last little barb incensed her, for his lovemaking had deteriorated into a quick five minutes once a month, if that, and she burst out, 'No, he didn't neglect me though we didn't have long enough together before he was killed, but the time I was with him was the best I ever had in my . . .' Stricken with remorse, she whispered, 'I'm sorry,

David. I shouldn't have said that, but you got me so riled, I couldn't help it.'

'So we've got at the truth at last?' His eyes had narrowed to slits. 'You've always been comparing me with him, haven't you, and it seems I fell short of your expectations.'

'No!' she exclaimed, in dismay. 'You're all wrong, David! I never compared you . . . I never thought about him at all . . . not when we were . . . um . . . making love.'

'So you did think about him at other times?'

'Oh, you're getting me so muddled, I don't know what I'm saying. I did love John Forrest . . . I never kept it a secret from you . . . but it's you I love now, it's you I've loved for nearly twenty years. I swear that's the truth, David. I never think about him at all except when you fling him in my face. Can't you understand that?'

He had cooled down now. 'I suppose I do keep reminding you. I don't mean to hurt you, but thinking about him touching you makes me . . . oh, God, I'm sorry, Elspeth. That's why I can't bring myself to . . . I keep wondering if you're thinking of him when I'm . . .' He gave his head a violent shake. 'I know I'm silly, but I can't help it.'

Going to him, she slid her arms round his neck. 'Put it out of your head, David, for it's not true. When you're . . . loving me, it's you I think of, nobody else. I want you to love me, and I'm satisfied with you . . . I'm more than satisfied with you, my dear.'

Giving a choking sob, he buried his head in her hair. 'I'm sorry, Elspeth. It's this mind of mine, it gets so twisted I can't think straight.'

'I know,' she whispered, then after a minute, she said, 'I'll sell the clock, if that's what bothers you.'

'No, I don't want you to sell it. It's not really the clock at all, it's just . . . it's just me.'

That night, he fulfilled her as he had not done for some time, and she lay back happily after it was over, reflecting that he couldn't help being the way he was. As he had said himself, his mind got twisted, and was it any wonder, after what he had gone through in the last war? It was hard for her to put up with his moods, but she still loved him, in spite of them. Maybe she should sell the clock, but it would likely make no difference, and could easily make him more annoyed at his own shortcomings. Thank God he didn't know about young John, for if he ever found out, he might go over the edge altogether.

But there was no likelihood of his ever finding out . . . not after all this time.

Chapter Twenty-one

After the invasion of Poland, the Fullertons, like most families in Britain on Sunday, 3rd September 1939, gathered round their wireless set at 11 a.m. to listen to the Prime Minister's special broadcast, and at the concluding words David and Elspeth looked at each other in anguish. It was excitement, however, that surged up in Laura at knowing she was living through history. Even the King himself would be listening to the same thing.

'You'd think they'd have learned something from the last war,' David said, quietly, recalling the slaughter he had seen on the battlefields, 'but now there'll be more bloody carnage.'

'It won't be so bad this time.' Elspeth tried to take his mind off the event that still haunted his dreams. 'We're more prepared, so it should be over a lot quicker than the last one. Four years was a long time.'

Her initial thrill past, Laura kept silent, wondering how a war would affect her, and she came to the conclusion that it could make little difference. Her father's bad leg would stop him from having to fight again and, anyway, he was too old for the army now. Nothing would change.

At Quarry Street, Jimmy Watson muttered, 'We should never have settled for an armistice in 1918, we should have finished the bloody Jerries properly when we'd the chance. I only hope the Americans'll come in a bit earlier than they did the last time.'

John shook his head. 'Look, Dad, the British Forces are the best in the world. It might take a few months – even a year or two – but we'll win, with or without the Yanks.'

Helen added a pinch of salt to the flour in her baking bowl. 'Thank God you're too old to go, Jimmy, and they'll start making munitions at Henderson's again, and you'll be needed there, John, so you'll not be called up.'

John looked at her defiantly. 'I'm volunteering.'

'No, John, you can't.' Helen's eyes filled with tears as she mixed the pastry for the steak and kidney pie. 'There's the regular army and the Territorials. They don't need you.'

'I'm not going into the army, Mum. This war's going to be won from the air.' John stood up, frowning. 'I'm going out.'

'The dinner'll be ready at one, mind.'

'I'll be back.' He closed the door with a bang.

Helen turned to her husband. 'Jimmy, could you not have said something? He might have listened to you.'

Jimmy was on his feet now, taking the box of shoe brushes and polish from under the sink. 'He's twenty-four now, and he'll do what he wants. I'd have went myself the last time, if it hadn't been for you, though I was near forty when it started. A man wants to prove himself, you see, but . . . ach, well, Donald went instead.' Dabbing a brush into the small tin, he applied Cherry Blossom to his working boots so that they would be black first thing on

Monday though they would be whitish-grey again in about five minutes.

When John made no further reference to volunteering over the next three weeks, Helen believed that he had changed his mind, but he came home one night and said, quietly, 'I signed on for the Royal Air Force at dinner time. They said it shouldn't be long before I get a medical then I'll be notified where and when I've to report.'

'Oh, no, John!' Remembering Jimmy's caution, Helen said no more – she would have to let him go. She had borne the worry of Donald during the last war, and no doubt she would come through this one, too, however anxious she was for John . . . but the Air Force would be much worse than the Gordon Highlanders.

Jimmy tried a little reasoning. 'Have you thought about this enough, John? It's all very well doing things on the spur o' the minute, but you need to think about the dangers, and all. It's not a piece o' cake, you know.'

'It's up to all able-bodied men to fight for our country's freedom – we can't let the Nazis dictate to us.'

'Well, lad, I only hope you'll not live to regret it.'

Helen's only hope was that the young man would live, to regret it or not, but she served up the toad-in-the-hole and set his plate down in front of him with no comment.

After tea, John said that he was going to see the Fullertons. 'I bet David'll be pleased about me going into the RAF.'

His assumption was to be proved incorrect. Elspeth was appalled – was John destined to be killed in a war like his father? – but she couldn't voice her fears. John must never know how much he meant to her . . . and neither must her husband.

David tried to make him change his mind. 'You can say your parents wouldn't let you go, it's not too late.'

'I'm over twenty-one, I don't need permission.'

'You've no idea what it's like, John. I still have nightmares about the trenches.'

With all the confidence of youth, John laughed derisively. 'It's modern warfare now, David, and it's the Air Force I've joined, not the Army, so I'll never be in any trenches.'

The only encouragement he received was from Laura, who was filled with admiration for his bravery. 'You'll make a good pilot, John,' she breathed.

'That's what I'd like to be, but I'll have to wait and see what they tell me when I get to wherever I've to go.'

'I think I'll volunteer, too. They'll likely need girls to do all sorts of things.'

'No,' David snapped. 'You're not going, that's final.'

He had not reckoned with his eighteen-year-old daughter's determination, however, and within weeks both John and Laura were in airforce blue – John doing his six weeks' training at Padgate, and Laura at Lytham St Anne's.

'It'll not be long till John gets home,' Helen said, one afternoon. 'It seems a lot longer than six weeks since he went away.' She couldn't hide the pride she felt.

Elspeth, too, was proud of him, and of her daughter, also doing her bit to help win the war. 'Laura'll be coming home shortly, as well. She went away the week after John.'

Helen looked thoughtful. 'You ken, Elspeth, I was thinking last night about the first time we met – on the train, mind, during the last war? Little did we think that near a quarter o' a century on my son and your daughter would both be in the Royal Air Force fighting another war.'

Elspeth knew for certain now, having suspected it for some considerable time, that Helen's mind had blotted out for the second time the fact that John was not her real son, but it was better to leave well alone, for she had enough worries at the moment without upsetting Helen. David's nightmares had been recurring more frequently of late, and not only that, his jealousy was getting worse, though he denied that that was what it was. His health was beginning to suffer, too. He was only forty-six, but his hair was completely grey, his forehead gouged by deep furrows. His job, of course, carried much more responsibility since he'd been made manager of the whole shop, and she hoped that he wasn't overdoing things.

When John Watson came home on his first leave, he was quite happy to satisfy Jimmy's curiosity. 'You should have seen us, Dad, doing our square-bashing in civvies. They hadn't uniforms to give us for a start, and I don't think they knew what to do with us. Then we were issued with our kits and they ticked off our names and numbers as we got them, like this.' Standing stiffly to attention, he barked out a staccato imitation of the sergeant in charge of stores. 'Two shirts, tunic – airmen for the use of.'

Jimmy chuckled at the mimicry and the forces' jargon. 'Oh, John, what a laddie you are.'

Helen looked puzzled. 'Tunic shirts? What's that?'

'They're tunic style,' John said, patiently. 'They don't open all the way down the front, and we pull them on over

269

our heads. We got collars and studs, though, and I think we all looked very smart on our first parade after that.'

'Well, you look real smart now, any road,' Helen smiled, her pride in him making a tightness come in her throat.

'So what happens to you now?' Jimmy asked.

John's eyes clouded. 'I'm a bit disappointed I wasn't accepted for pilot's training, but I've applied to train as a wireless operator. I'll have to pass tests, and if I fail, I'll just have to be a Sparkie, I suppose.'

'It's what you should be – you're a time served plumber and electrician.' Jimmy couldn't understand why John was so reluctant to go in for his own trade.

'But I want to be part of an air crew, doing something definite against the Jerries.'

'The lads on the ground do something against the Jerries, and all,' Jimmy reminded him. 'They've to keep all the aeroplanes checked and repaired, so they're running smooth. Every single tradesman has his part to play.'

'I know that, but I want to fly.'

Just days later, Laura was horrifying her mother with tales of the deprivations she'd had to suffer. 'Fancy having to eat off a tin plate,' Elspeth moaned, when she learned of the crude arrangements in the Mess. 'Do you want me to give you a cup and plate to take back with you?'

'God, no. They'd all laugh their heads off at me.'

David saw that his wife and daughter could easily get irritated at each other. 'John Watson's home just now, too,' he observed, in order to lighten the atmosphere.

'That's right, Laura, you'll likely see him on Saturday. I think Helen said he didn't have to go back till Sunday.'

Laura hoped that her uniform would make John take notice of her, because the wolf whistles she often received proved that it suited her. She had even gone out with several of the young airmen, and she could now fend off even the most amorous flirts. God, how naive she had been with that stupid oaf Gordon before the war.

On Saturday, when the Fullerton family visited the Watsons, John was out with some of his ex-workmates, and Laura felt angry and hurt. If he couldn't be bothered to stay in when he knew she'd be visiting, he'd had his chance. But she hid her feelings, and kept Helen and Jimmy laughing with humorous anecdotes of the tribulations of service life.

Most of her leave was spent just lazing around the bungalow. 'It's nice to be idle,' she told her mother one day, 'but I wouldn't like it all the time. I love being a WAAF, and the social life's great – concerts, dances, dozens of boys. We forget there's a war on, sometimes.'

Shortly after going back, Laura wrote that she had been posted to Turnhouse, in Edinburgh. 'I'm training to be a plotter, and I've passed all my tests so far, so your daughter will soon be an LACW (Leading Aircraft Woman). What do you think of that?'

Elspeth could hardly wait to tell Helen this good news, but Helen had some of her own to pass on. 'John's been posted to Lincolnshire to train as a wireless operator, and he says he's not an AC Plonk any longer, though I've no idea what that means.'

In addition to worrying about her son's determination to fly, Elspeth was now concerned about her daughter. With all these young men taking her out, would Laura get serious with one of them and end up being left like her mother had been – with an illegitimate child?

In the dark days of May 1940, David Fullerton became gloomy about the outcome of the war, studying all the reports in the newspapers and listening to the bulletins on the wireless. 'That's the finish!' he exclaimed on the 26th. 'Our boys have had to retreat to Dunkirk, and they're being picked up off the beaches. What a terrible defeat.'

Elspeth tried to cheer him up. 'But the evacuation's still going on, and they think they'll get most of the men off.'

'It's still a German victory,' he said, mournfully.

Her husband was a defeatist, Elspeth thought, but she had to believe that things were not as hopeless as they seemed to be. 'There's always dark before the dawn.'

By the 3rd June, David was jubilant. 'The paper says it was a glorious defeat, not a real defeat, and ordinary folk in little boats helped to ferry the men across the Channel. Only the British could make an effort like that, and we'll win this war, I'm sure of it now.'

At Turnhouse, each aircraft's position near the coast was plotted, and the approach of enemy planes was tracked, but Laura's letters home told only about the dances she attended and the various airmen who took her, which made Elspeth worry even more. She had heard rumours of how those RAF boys could charm their way into any girl's heart, and her daughter would be easily led astray.

David was more concerned about German activity in the air over Britain, especially after a daylight raid on Aberdeen on July 12th. 'It was only one bomber,' he said, that night, 'and it was shot down, but think of the destruction it caused. They're saying it had lost its way and shouldn't have been anywhere near Aberdeen, but I have my doubts.'

A couple of weeks later, he looked up from the *Evening Express*. 'It says here that our losses aren't as heavy as theirs, but Lord Haw-Haw said on the wireless last night that hundreds of British planes had been destroyed and no German aircraft was lost, and they're bombing London now.'

'You shouldn't listen to that traitor.' Elspeth hated to see him crouched in front of the wireless, lapping up every word uttered by the grating, nasal voice. 'It's propaganda and doesn't mean a thing. If things were as bad as he makes out, we'd have had to surrender ages ago.'

'We'll have to surrender soon, no doubt about it.'

David was more hopeful by the middle of May 1941. 'London survived the Blitz and our boys won the Battle of Britain, so the Luftwaffe's had a slap in the face, and Hitler'll never dare to invade us now.'

'What did I tell you?' Elspeth's prayers had been for John, but she had consoled herself by thinking that he couldn't have been involved in the dog-fights over southern England, not being a pilot. Nevertheless, she was always relieved when Helen got a letter from him, and passed the good news on to Laura, whose letters often asked about him.

When her daughter came on leave, Elspeth took the chance to enquire, 'Have you a steady boyfriend yet?'

Laura smiled and shook her head. 'Nobody serious. They're all nice boys, and I go out with them if they ask me – we all need some relief from the war. If we don't see some of them for a while, we think they've been posted, and it's only when we remember that they'd been on the plane that didn't come back on such-and-such a night that we realize what's happened. We can't afford to brood over it, of course, but that's why I don't let myself get involved.'

Elspeth marvelled at her daughter's calm acceptance of the tragedies that were taking place around her, and felt, sadly, that Laura was growing away from her. What would happen when the war came to an end? She wouldn't want to come back and settle in a dull office job.

Laura sometimes wondered about this herself. How could she bear her old humdrum existence after the thrills, sorrow and danger of service life? Apart from the reason she had given her mother, the boys she met were too immature to be serious about, but she was only twenty and could wait for romance, if she ever felt like it. She might try for an interesting career in England after the war, or go abroad – Canada, South Africa, anywhere. The world would be her oyster.

Flight Sergeant Wireless Operator John Watson was glad he had been posted to dear old Scotland for a while – Scampton had been pretty hectic lately. Bombing German munition barges in Antwerp Basin had been bad enough, but the raids on Bremen and Wilhelmshaven had been worse, and he had often been surprised that he wasn't scared out of his wits during these missions. Instead, he had felt a kind of exhilarated fascination as the flak burst round them. Even seeing aircraft from his own squadron bursting into flames and plunging down hadn't made him lose concentration on the job he had to do. It was only after he returned to base that the fear had come, and the realization that they had been fortunate to get back in one piece, but now the crews of the old Hampdens were being 'rested' as a reward for all the hours of danger.

Shutting his ears to the noise in the Sergeants' Mess, he remembered that his mother had told him Laura Fullerton was still at Turnhouse, and, although he wasn't long back off leave, it would be good to see a face from home, even if it was only the girl who had pestered the life out of him when she was a kid. He had hated her then, but she had tamed down a bit when she grew older – still a pest, but not quite so annoying. She would have changed, of course, since he'd seen her last, just after war was declared, and she would likely be involved with some officer-type with a big handlebar moustache by this time. Not to worry. He was looking for a more sophisticated girl than Laura Fullerton and he intended to play the field.

Taking a stroll to the YMCA canteen the following afternoon, he was surprised to find Laura there with two other WAAFs. She was prettier than he remembered, her hair darkened to a rich auburn and cut short so that it curled appealingly round her heart-shaped face. Funny, he hadn't noticed the shape of her face before. He walked over to their table, smiling.

'Wonders will never cease!' Laura jumped to her feet. 'Girls, let me introduce Flight Sergeant John Watson, an old friend of mine from Aberdeen. John – Trish, Wendy.'

The two girls shook hands then stood up, Wendy saying, 'We'll leave you two to talk over old times,' and Trish winking mischievously as she went out.

John was amazed at how Laura had changed, but he joked as he sat down, to cover a sudden feeling of shyness. 'You've got them well trained, leaving us alone so tactfully.'

She gave a wicked chuckle. 'At one time you wouldn't have been pleased at being alone with me. You used to moan like billy-o every time I went to Quarry Street.'

'That was when we were kids, and my pals laughed at me for having to play nursemaid to you.'

'You didn't make a very good job of it, did you? Remember the day I fell out of the tree?'

He laughed at the memory of Laura howling all the way back to his house. 'You were showing off as usual. I was kept in for a couple of days after that, you know, and I hated you.'

'You don't have to tell me that, but I got a ticking off from my mum and dad, too.'

Thinking that the age gap had narrowed considerably now that she was twenty to John's twenty-six, Laura spent the next half hour reminiscing with him about the things he had done to get rid of her, until they sensed that their hearty laughter had made them the focus of attention.

John turned serious. 'I'd willingly play nursemaid to you any time now, Laura,' he said, softly.

She blushed, but her embarrassment was covered by the arrival of some more WAAFs, one saying, 'Your shift's gone back on, Fullerton.'

'Oh, blast!' She picked up her cap and respirator. 'I'll have to run, John, but I'll likely see you around.'

'Wait, Laura. Can't we meet properly? We could go to the pictures in Edinburgh, or something.'

'Wizard! I'm off at nineteen hundred hours tomorrow, if

that's OK . . . ? Meet me at the main gate.' She waved her hand as she ran through the door.

When they met the next night, John found it impossible to treat Laura like the other girls he had taken out – it seemed unnatural to flirt with her or to make passes at her. She had been a tomboy as a child, but she had metamorphosed into a beautiful slim young woman, self-assured and, most surprising, sophisticated. Unable to bring himself to take her arm when they were walking, he wondered if she felt as awkward with him.

Two days later, at a dance in a local hall, he found that she was very popular and didn't think twice about leaving him on his own. In the old days, he had complained that she stuck to him like glue, but now he felt like kicking her other partners for taking her away.

Afterwards, they walked back to the aerodrome in silence for most of the way. 'John,' Laura said, at last, 'are you mad at me for dancing with those other guys?'

'Not at all,' he said, stiffly. 'I'm only the poor sap who took you to the dance. An old man like me shouldn't try to compete with youngsters.'

'I couldn't refuse, I'd danced with them all before, and anyway, what right have you to be so possessive, John Watson? I bet you've danced with hundreds of girls yourself.'

'Yes, but they didn't go waltzing off with other men. At least they had the good sense to remember their manners.'

'Thank you very much, Sir Galahad,' Laura said icily, and stalked off in front of him.

'Don't mention it,' was his equally cold reply.

Angrily, she kept ahead of him until a motor cycle

whizzed past, flinging up gravel from the side of the road. 'Ouch!' she yelped, as a piece of grit lodged in her eye.

John ran to her, anxiously, but, when he saw her holding her hand up to her eye and screwing up her face, he realized what had happened and took out his handkerchief. 'Let me try to get it out for you.'

The pain in her watering eye made her swallow her outraged pride and hold her head up in the pale moonlight, her heart acting strangely when he placed a hand under her chin with his face close to hers. 'That's it!' he said, in a moment, looking carefully into her eye to check that no grit remained, and in the next moment, his arms were round her, and his kiss was all that she had ever longed for in her girlish dreams.

'Oh, Laura, I've been wanting to do that all evening,' he murmured. 'I'm sorry I was so touchy before, but I was jealous, and I've just understood why. I love you, my darling little pest.'

Between kisses, she managed to tell him that she felt the same way about him. 'But I've always loved you,' she added, somewhat ruefully, 'for as long as I can remember.'

'I suppose I knew that, but I resented having to look after you. You weren't the easiest of kids to handle.'

Laura giggled with delight. 'I bet this is the last thing our mums and dads'll be expecting.'

'Oh, I don't know. They were always pushing us together, so my guess is, they'll be delighted. It's funny, I couldn't stand the sight of you once – I dreaded Saturday afternoons when I'd have you tagging along after me – and it's taken a war to bring me to my senses.'

'I shouldn't really say this, I suppose,' she made a face

278

about it, 'but thank God for the war. We might have gone on all our lives without knowing how we felt about each other.'

'We've wasted enough time as it is, we can't waste any more.' With this in mind, he kissed her again . . . and again.

John lay happily wakeful that night. He knew he'd feel like a washed-out rag in the morning, but he didn't care. Laura! Laura! His heart sang with her name. Of course their parents would be pleased. Elspeth and his mother had likely planned it from the day Laura was born, wonderful, wonderful mothers that they were, and it was the most natural thing in the world for two close families to be united like this.

A chilling thought assailed him suddenly. It didn't seem fitting, in the middle of a war, to be so ecstatically happy – would something happen to spoil it? Would he be . . . ? No, no! Taking a long, deep breath he pushed the repulsive idea aside. He was being morbid because his love for Laura had blossomed so quickly; nothing – repeat, nothing – could ever come between them, and nobody could ever drive them apart.

End of message! Over and out!

Chapter Twenty-two

'It's good to see you, Laura.'

'It's good to be home, Mum, but I hope you haven't planned any visits for me this time.' Laura hadn't been too happy at having to go to King's Gate the last time she was home. She had never liked going there.

'You'll have to visit Helen. She always asks about you.'

'I was going to, anyway. She'll want to know all the gen on John, he's at Turnhouse now, too.' Laura was confident that her mother would give her blessing on their love, but she didn't intend to tell her just yet. It was a secret she wanted to hug for a little longer before sharing it.

A slight frown crossing her face, Elspeth carried a large, circular, chromium-plated tray through from the scullery. 'You never said in your letters that John was at Turnhouse.'

'I thought Helen would have told you. He's been there for about three weeks.' Three glorious weeks and two heavenly days, Laura thought, then felt that it might be better to give her mother some inkling of what was to come. 'We've been going to the pictures, and dances, and that sort of thing, so you see he doesn't object to me any longer.'

She laughed – an excited, trilly laugh which made Elspeth pause in the act of pouring out tea. 'He's a wizard dancer, and it feels like we were always meant to dance together. He's good company, too.' That should be enough to pave the way, Laura thought, then noticed that her mother's face had paled and tightened. It couldn't be possible that she wouldn't be pleased about it? 'How's Dad?'

'His leg plays him up now and again, but you know your father, he never complains.'

Laura was puzzled by her mother's expression. She had seen it before, a look of sadness . . . fear? She had once asked her father about it, but he had just said, 'She worries a lot, and sometimes makes mountains out of molehills.'

Elspeth certainly seemed to be worried now. 'I see Helen every week, and she's never said John was at Turnhouse.' If she had only known, her friend had been in a quandary about whether or not to tell her.

'John's been posted to Turnhouse,' Helen had told Jimmy after the letter came, 'and he's been going out wi' Laura Fullerton. Well, they've been playmates all their lives – more like brother and sister, really.' Jimmy's grunt had stopped her flow.

'They are brother and sister, half brother and sister, any road. I'm surprised at you forgetting, after what happened before Elspeth wed David.'

Helen's face had fallen. 'I didn't really forget, I just put it out o' my mind, for I'm that used to thinking John's ours. But surely Laura and him can't be . . . ?'

Jimmy had shaken his head. 'He's just taking her out, what he'd do wi' any lassie he'd ken't all her life.'

This did nothing to assuage Helen's fears. 'I'd best warn Elspeth in case they get serious about each other.'

'There's no sense in meeting trouble half way, and you'll just upset her, you ken what a worrier she is. And there's nothing to tell, really. They're in a strange place, among strangers, and they'll be fine company for each other.'

Feeling most uneasy about it, Helen had decided not to tell Elspeth. Jimmy must be right, they were just two young people enjoying each other's company.

Fear that her cosy little world was about to come crashing round her was gnawing at Elspeth now, but she told herself that she was imagining things. Laura had always been fond of John, but he'd never had any time for her. He'd had a few girlfriends before he joined up, and he'd likely had a lot more since . . . he wouldn't get seriously involved with Laura. Elspeth started talking, telling her daughter how hard it was to manage on the food rations, how she used the dried eggs – anything, to forget her doubts.

The girl stopped listening and let her mind drift back to the happiest night of her life. Instant Love. The memory of John's first kiss still made her go weak at the knees, though it had been repeated countless times since. They had spent every available minute together, until she had longed for him to make love to her properly. She had never allowed any of the other boys to go that far, but John was more than just another boy. He was the boy she had loved all her life. Her mother's voice, raised in complaint about her butcher, penetrated her thoughts.

'When I told him I wasn't going to give up my meat coupons for lumps of fat and gristle, he said, "Take it or leave it, it's all the same to me." So I'd just to take it, but what a nerve he has, selling stuff that's only fit for pigs.'

Laura was laughing as her father came in, his tired, haggard face lighting up when he saw her. 'It's great to see you again and I hope you'll be here longer than forty-eight hours this time.'

'Yes, I've got ten days, Dad,' she said, brightly. 'I've just been telling Mum that John Watson's at Turnhouse now, and we've been going out together quite a lot.'

'That's good news! It would be a turn-up for the books if you had Helen and Jimmy for in-laws.' Both he and the girl failed to see the look of horror on Elspeth's face as she rose to serve the tea.

'You wouldn't mind, then, Dad?' Laura was glad that he had brought up the subject. It was sooner than she had meant, but what difference did it make? 'We haven't made any definite plans yet, but we're going to get married.'

'We're delighted, aren't we?' David glanced confidently at his wife, but she was standing in the doorway, with a plate in each hand, as though transfixed, her bobbed hair, now faded to a sandy colour, framing her ashen face, and tears brimming in her eyes – the perfect picture of abject misery. He jumped to his feet to take the plates from her before she dropped them. 'What's wrong?'

Pulling herself together, Elspeth muttered, 'I just felt a bit dizzy. I must have turned too quickly.'

David sat down again, but Laura said, 'Are you sure that's all it is, Mum?'

'I'm fine, stop fussing.' Elspeth, in great distraction, knew that she would have to stop what was going on between Laura and John, but she couldn't get peace to think. In any case, she couldn't cope with it on her own.

Her behaviour had effectively put a stop to the discussion, and it wasn't until the next morning that Laura had a chance to tackle her about her health. 'Are you sure there's nothing seriously wrong with you, Mum? You look really ghastly. You would tell me, wouldn't you? I'll only worry more if I don't know.'

Elspeth drew in a deep breath. 'I'm not ill. I told you, I must have turned too quickly. I'm all right now.'

'Well, I promised one of the other WAAFs that I'd go to see her mother in Stonehaven. She hasn't been well, and Trish is really worried about her, but I won't go today if you'd rather I stayed with you.'

'No, off you go. Will you be back for your dinner?'

'I'll get a snack somewhere, but I'll be home for tea.'

After Laura left, Elspeth hurried to Quarry Street. Jimmy, due to retire shortly, would be at work, so she and Helen could talk confidentially.

'Elspeth! What brings you here at this time o' the day?' Helen Watson had never known her friend to go visiting in the morning before; she was always too busy with her housework.

Elspeth sat down on Jimmy's leather chair without taking her coat off and came straight to the point. 'Did you ken about Laura and John?'

'I ken they've been going to dances and things.' Helen was glad that the other woman knew about it. 'Jimmy says there's nothing to bother about.'

'They're speaking about getting married.'

Helen's hand flew to her chest. 'But they . . .'

'I couldna sleep for worrying. I can't tell her the truth, for she'd be broken-hearted, and what would David say?'

Helen's normally cheery face was agonized. 'We can't let it go on any longer. They can't get wed, you ken that.'

'Oh, Helen, I'm sure this is a judgement on me for what I did wi' John Forrest, and for the lies I tell't David.'

'You never really tell't him a lie, for it was . . . oh, what a muddle!' Helen wrung her hands in agitation and Elspeth twisted her handkerchief almost to shreds, both of them searching feverishly for a solution.

After a few minutes, Helen said, 'There's nothing for it but to tell her the truth, whatever way we look at it.'

Elspeth had known deep down that there was no other way out. 'What'll she think o' me, Helen? And David's aye been jealous o' John Forrest, but I'm sure he's never for one minute suspected young John was mine.'

The older woman looked contrite. 'It was me that never put folk right from the very start. If I'd only had my senses at the time, we wouldna be in this predicament now.'

'I didn't need much persuading to let folk think the wrong thing, though, to save my good name. And it was just the way it happened. You losing your baby, and thinking . . . and . . . everybody round about taking it for granted that John was yours . . . and I thought if I gave him up it would let David and me start wi' a clean slate. I should have tell't him, for it's a lot worse coming out like this.'

'We'll both need to face up to it, Elspeth. What's done's done, and it's no good greeting over spilt milk.' Helen's sigh showed how despondent she was.

Elspeth pulled herself to her feet wearily. 'I'd best get home, but God kens how I'll tell them.'

At teatime, Elspeth's brooding silence convinced Laura that there was more to the 'dizzy turn' than her mother had admitted, but she tried to hide her alarm by chattering all through the meal. When the dishes were washed and put away, she and her mother joined David at the fireside, Elspeth sitting tensely upright on one of the uncut moquette chairs of the Chesterfield suite which had been bought years before to replace the old, second-hand seats, Laura sprawled out on the settee.

'Now, Laura, tell us more about your romance.' David's eyes were twinkling as he laid down his newspaper. 'How did this wonderful love affair start? I know you always liked John, but I thought he couldn't stand the sight of you.'

He unwittingly set the ball rolling, and Laura was glad of the opening. 'We went to the flicks the first time he asked me out, but we felt a bit awkward with each other. The second time, we went to a dance, and on the way back we discovered we loved each other. It was as simple as that. John says we shouldn't get married till the war's finished, but I can't see any point in wasting our lives – it might last for years yet.' She gave a throaty chuckle. 'Don't worry, Dad, we haven't slept together – he's too much of a gentleman to do anything like that – but I wouldn't have said no if he'd asked me.'

David was too shocked to speak, but Elspeth – relieved that there would be no possibility of a pregnancy to complicate matters further – said, 'Laura, David, I've something to tell you.'

'I knew there was something seriously wrong with you.' Laura was concerned, and David sat up in alarm.

'Let me tell you this in my own way, and don't interrupt. It's going to be difficult enough for me as it is.'

Mystified, David nodded his head gravely, and the girl,

to cover her apprehension, said, facetiously, 'You'd better get it over quickly before the suspense kills us.'

Fixing her eyes on a picture above her husband's head, she began, 'John's not Helen's and Jimmy's real son.' Shaking her head in warning at Laura's involuntary exclamation, she told them as much as was necessary, coming finally to her decision to leave John with the Watsons. 'So you see,' – her voice, which had been quite steady before, began to waver tremulously – 'he's your half brother, Laura, and you can't marry him.'

David was staring in disbelief, but Laura shouted, 'For God's sake! And you've kept that a secret all these years, even from your own husband? How could you deceive us like that? You're a . . .' She searched for words strong enough to convey her contempt, then spat them out. 'You're a cruel bitch! A cruel, selfish bitch! You've ruined my whole life . . . and John's!'

Bursting into tears, she ran out, slamming the door viciously behind her. The noise reverberated in the still room and was followed by the sound of hysterical sobbing, which wrenched at Elspeth's heart. 'Oh, God!' she moaned, holding her hands out in appeal to her shocked husband. 'David? Please say something!'

His eyes refused to meet hers. 'I always knew that man had been your lover,' he muttered, 'but . . . Christ! I never dreamt he'd left you with a bastard.' His head swivelled round and his eyes were filled with such smouldering fury that her whole body shook with fear.

'I'm sorry I didn't tell you, David,' she muttered through chattering teeth, 'but I was feared you wouldn't marry me if you knew about . . .'

287

'But you kept it from me for over twenty years!' he shouted, springing to his feet and towering above her as she cringed before him. 'How do you think I feel now? If you'd told me John was yours when I first went to Quarry Street to see you, I'd have accepted it, but . . .'

'I couldn't, David, for like I told you, Helen thought he was hers, and it wasn't till I'd said I'd marry you that Jimmy made her see he wasn't.'

'But you didn't even tell me then! God almighty, Elspeth! You've been deceiving me all these years.'

'I didn't want to deceive you, but . . .' She tried to stand up, but he shoved her roughly back into her chair.

'You didn't try very hard not to. Even when I tackled you about . . . that man, you swore for years that he hadn't been your lover . . . till I forced it out of you.'

He stopped, a distant look in his eyes, and she knew that he was remembering his own fears that she had been thinking of John Forrest every time they made love. She moved forward a little in her seat, and meeting no opposition this time, she stood up beside him. 'You don't know how sorry I am about this, David,' she whispered. 'I should have told you after you came back from the war, but I thought what I was doing was the right thing.'

Flinging off the hand she had tried to place on his arm, he sneered, 'So you thought lying was the right thing?'

'I didn't tell you a lie,' she muttered, 'I just didn't tell you the truth.'

'It comes to the same thing in the end. Christ, Elspeth, I thought I knew you, but obviously I didn't. What you did to me was a wicked thing, but how will you ever square your conscience for what you've done to Laura and John?'

288

'I never thought they'd fall in love.'

'That's the trouble! You never thought of anybody but yourself. And I don't suppose you'd have told me at all if they hadn't . . .' His hands jerked up to his head. 'Oh, God, I can't stand any more!' Shaking off her detaining hand, he went out, his limp more pronounced than ever.

Elspeth sank weakly into her chair, her mind too confused to think properly, and did not move until Laura appeared again about ten minutes later, her face streaked with tears, her breath coming in short hiccups. Her respirator and haversack were slung over her shoulder and she stood with her cap in her hand looking at her mother as if at a stranger. 'I'm leaving,' she said, flatly, 'and I'll never come back. You've ruined my life, and I despise you.'

'You can't leave, Laura!' Elspeth's voice was high with desperation, in contrast to the girl's calmness. 'Things'll look better after a while. You'll get over this, and you'll meet somebody else, and . . .' Appalled by the sheer hatred in her daughter's eyes, she stopped.

Losing her grip on herself at last, Laura cried, 'How can you have the effrontery to say that? You, with your supposed eternal love for that John Forrest? You should understand how I feel, if anyone should. I'll never be able to love another man now, thanks to you, and I'll never forgive you. Never! Never! Never!'

The crash of the front door echoed through Elspeth's head, and, as once before when her life had disintegrated around her, she found that she couldn't weep.

Coming to the open doorway, David said, 'Laura told me she was leaving, and I thought of doing the same, for your lies and deceit . . .'

'I didn't tell you any lies, David!' She had to defend herself, although he was regarding her with disgust. 'Ask Helen if you don't believe me.'

'You both knew what I thought, and you didn't correct me.'

Elspeth, fighting for her marriage, her very existence, burst out wildly. 'Don't leave me, David!'

'I only said I was thinking about it,' he said, harshly, 'but I'm not going to. I worked hard to pay the mortgage on this house, but it's mine now and I mean to keep it. You're the one that's leaving, first thing in the morning, and I'll sleep in the spare-room tonight.'

Flowing now, her tears gave no relief. 'Please don't put me out, David, I've been punished enough. You're upset the now, but you'll get over it.'

He pushed her aside as she stood up, and when the spare-room door clicked shut, she collapsed once more into her chair. When would this nightmare end? The sword of Damocles had fallen at last, the retribution she had dreaded over the years had overtaken her, more severe than she had ever imagined. She had sacrificed her love-child twenty-one years ago, and now she had lost both her husband and her daughter.

As Laura stumbled blindly towards Quarry Street, she tried to convince herself that it wasn't true. She needed corroboration, explanation or, better still, denial . . . but, if it wasn't true, why would her mother have incriminated herself like that?

Taking one look at the girl's anguished face, Helen Watson knew that the fatal moment had come, that

290

Elspeth had told her daughter the truth, and that she, Helen, must own up to her part in the deception. 'Come in, Laura,' she said, as cheerfully as she could with her lips frozen and her heart somersaulting in panic. 'Jimmy's working late the night, so we'll have the house to ourselves.'

Laura laid her haversack on the floor. 'I've left home.' It came out calmly, in spite of the boiling anger in her heart, in spite of the sickening agony in her innards, in spite of the scream waiting in her throat – the scream which, once released, might carry on for ever. 'My . . . I've been told why John and I can't marry, but I want to hear your side of the story.'

'Laura, I'm heart-sorry for you and John, but I'm sure your mother's tell't you the truth.'

'A bit late, wouldn't you say?' The girl couldn't help the bitter sarcasm. 'And I still want to hear it from you.'

'If that's what you want.' Helen sat down, gesturing to the girl to do likewise, but Laura shook her head, and after a brief pause, the older woman began. 'Your mother was a pathetic wee creature the first time I met her . . .' Her version differed from Elspeth's only by beginning a few months later – in the train instead of on the road to the cottar house in a snowstorm. Strangely enough, neither of them mentioned the time she had spent at Rosemount Viaduct, letting their listeners conclude that Elspeth had gone to Quarry Street as soon as she arrived in Aberdeen.

The girl said nothing until she heard why the confusion over whose child it was hadn't been corrected. 'So it all stemmed from not wanting her character blackened?'

'That meant a lot in those days,' Helen reminded her. 'It was a real disgrace for a single lassie to have a bairn.'

'She'd have got over it,' Laura said, sarcastically. 'It would have blown over and been forgotten.'

'It might have, if I hadn't lost my baby and my wits. I'd come to believe John was mine, and your mother didn't want to hurt me by claiming him, and it was just before she married your father that Jimmy brought me to my senses.'

'I can't excuse her for not telling Dad right from the start, but even if she'd only owned up when they were married, John and I would never have . . .'

The girl's bitterness and the naked torture in her eyes were like stakes being driven into Helen's heart. 'It was my blame at the start, and it wasn't easy for her to give her bairn up when she was wed. She wasna thinking o' herself, it was your father she was thinking o', and me and Jimmy, and John. It near broke her heart to leave him. Can you not understand how she was placed, lassie, and have some pity for her?'

Picking up her haversack, Laura said, stonily, 'It's you two living a lie all these years that I can't stomach. I'll never forgive her for what's she's done, nor you, either.'

The tears came again when Laura was walking down the lane, and she was at the edge of the quarry before she realized that she had walked up the grassy bank. Bewildered, she looked at the opposite side, and could see the observation platform which had been built to give sightseers a safe view of the awe-inspiring hole. A cable, slung between two pylons, spanned the chasm, and she remembered Jimmy once saying that this was known as the Blondin, although the famous tightrope walker had never attempted to walk across it. Suspended from the cable were the wire cages used to transport stone and men from the quarry floor. Shifting her gaze, she could see, just below the edge, flights of wooden steps fixed against the sheer side, and found her eyes following them down, down, down, hundreds of feet to the bottom, where the idle pieces of equipment looked like toys.

To her left, the machinery of the crusher was grinding slowly – the mills of God? – yet the whole place had an air of unreality about it in the semi-darkness, a sense of doom, and as she stood on the brink looking down, she wondered if she was being given a sign of what to do. Was this what fate had decided for her? Was this to be the end? Jimmy had also told her once that several suicides had taken place here over the years, but even as she contemplated it she knew she hadn't the courage to jump. There could be no easy way out for her. She must face the excruciating ordeal of telling John the whole distasteful story, to explain why they could never marry.

Turning, she went down the bank again and continued on her way to the tram stop at the end of the lane, the lines having been extended, years ago, to Hazlehead, not far from Oldmill Hospital where her father had been a patient in the first war. This route was one of the most beautiful in Aberdeen, but she saw nothing of the graceful trees and colourful gardens on her journey, and was still in a state of limbo when she reached Union Street. Forcing herself to think, she booked into a rather second-rate hotel near the railway station, and spent most of the night going over her mother's terrible revelation, positive that this evening would remain for ever in her mind as the worst in her life.

When Jimmy arrived home – about fifteen minutes after Laura had left – his wife led up to the ghastly confrontation by telling him about her other visitor first. 'Elspeth was here this morning and it's gone a lot further between Laura and John than you tried to make out, for they meant to get wed.'

'Oh, surely no'. That wouldna be possible.' Jimmy, a week short of his sixty-fifth birthday, felt too tired, after a full day's work and two hours' overtime, to contend with a situation like this, but he knew that his wife wouldn't let it rest.

'Me and Elspeth both ken't that,' she was saying, 'and we racked our brains trying to think how to stop it, but the only thing was for her to tell the lassie the truth, and Laura come here a wee while ago to get my side o' the story. She's left home, Jimmy, and she says she'll never forgive her mother, or me either.'

'Poor Laura, but it's better to be out in the open at last.' Jimmy bent down to remove his boots. 'She's young, though, and she'll get over it – it's Elspeth I'm sorriest for. Fate aye has something up its sleeve to knock her down wi'. It's a great pity the lassie walked out, but David'll understand what his wife went through, for he's a good man.'

'That's right,' Helen said, in some relief. 'He'll not let Elspeth down. He'll stand by her.'

Chapter Twenty-three

After a gruelling night, and an equally gruelling train journey the following forenoon, Laura telephoned to Turnhouse Aerodrome from a kiosk in Princes Street. 'John, I must see you,' she said, when the operator eventually located him. 'I've something awful to tell you.'

Her voice sounded strained, but he knew how prone she was to exaggeration. 'I can't come to Aberdeen just now.'

'I'm not in Aberdeen, I'm in Edinburgh.'

'But I can't drop everything and run, we're going up on a recce tonight.' A vague foreboding had stolen over him. 'What's up? You're not due back for more than a week.'

'John, it's vitally important, but I can't tell you over the phone. Can you meet me outside the 'drome?'

Sensing her urgency, he said, 'OK, make it fifteen hundred at the main gate.'

Laura booked into a small hotel off Leith Walk, and lay on the bed to rehearse what she would say, but after half an hour she decided that it was impossible to cushion the lethal blow. It would have to be short and simple. Plain facts. She washed her face before going to catch the bus to Turnhouse, and had just arrived when John appeared.

'What's all the mystery, Laura? You sounded so serious.'

She brushed off his arm when he tried to link it with hers, and burst out, forgetting, in her misery, to make it plain and simple, 'Oh John . . . my mother's your mother . . . your mother and father knew about it . . . but my father didn't.'

Her incoherency alarmed him, but he could see that she was nearly out of her mind and tried to calm her down. 'I don't know what you're getting at, my dearest dear, but whatever it is, you've got it all wrong. I thought you knew the story by this time. Your mother lodged with my mother during the first war, that's all.'

'She'd an illegitimate baby and . . . oh, God, it's all a bloody, bloody mix-up!'

He shook his head in bewilderment. 'I can't understand what you're saying, Laura. You're not making sense.'

'I'm too upset to think straight.' Her voice held a sob.

'Would tea help? There's a wee place along the road.'

The tearoom was empty, but they chose a secluded corner, and John waited until two steaming cups were set in front of them before saying, 'Now, Laura, tell me slowly.'

Trying to be rational, she spoke deliberately as if to a child. 'I was telling Mum and Dad about us, then Mum told us to listen without interrupting.' She repeated Elspeth's tale as fully as she could, and ended by asking, 'Now do you understand? We're half brother and sister.'

John's face had drained of all colour. 'But why did . . . what . . . ?' He straightened up suddenly. 'No, it's not true.'

'I wish to God it wasn't, but Helen told me exactly the same. Her baby was stillborn, and all the neighbours thought you were hers . . . and losing her own baby made her think you were hers, too.' John's stupefied expression made her wonder if her reaction had been the same, until she recalled her angry outburst at her mother. At least John was quiet. 'They let my father think you were Helen's, and he only learned the truth last night along with me, and when I said I was leaving for good, he said he would, too.'

After a pause, John muttered, 'I can't believe it.'

'That's what I said, at first, but it's true. We have the same mother, so we can never marry. It's against the law.'

She started to weep quietly, but John thumped his fist on the table, making the girl at the counter look at them in surprise. 'It's like the end of the world,' he moaned, trying to keep his voice low. 'How can I go on seeing you every day without . . . oh, God, Laura, I can't believe you're my sister. It's unthinkable.'

They didn't speak for some time, then John glanced at his watch. 'I'm sorry, I'll have to go back, darl . . . er . . . Laura. Laura, oh, Laura!'

He buried his face in his hands, and she stroked his head. 'I know, I've been through it all myself a dozen times. I'm going to apply for a posting and I won't let you know where they send me. I'm never going back to Aberdeen, so there won't be any chance of meeting accidentally there, either. It must be a clean break, it's the only way.'

When he could bring himself to speak, John said, brokenly, 'I hope you won't be angry, but I can't forsake my parents, no matter how much they were involved in the deception. They brought me up, and had to make sacrifices to put me through my apprenticeship. I know they were disappointed when I gave up my job to join the RAF, but they didn't try to stop me. I'll always consider them as my mum and dad.'

'Of course you will.'

He walked her back to the bus stop. 'Let me kiss you one last time, Laura,' he pleaded as the bus approached.

Her anger at her mother and Helen for causing so much trouble was dispelled by a rising flood of nausea. 'Oh, no! We can't even kiss each other goodbye – it's a sin between brother and sister.'

Jumping aboard the vehicle, she wept quietly for the entire journey, but in her hotel room she flung herself face down on the bed, great sobs breaking from her in wave after wave. At last, sapped, she walked across to the wash-basin in the corner, and, catching sight of her reflection in the mirror, she thought that even John wouldn't find her attractive now, but what did it matter? What did anything matter any more?

Suddenly, inexplicably, she was standing by the quarry again, and could feel herself drawing back from the brink. She had been unable – unwilling? – to end her life when she was given the opportunity, and she would have to make the best of it.

Elspeth had sat in her chair all night, weeping in self-pity and regretting the past by turns. She had heard her husband pacing the floor of the spare room and had pitied him for the torment he must be going through. When she heard him coming out of the spare room, she sat up in the hope that he would come and tell her that he didn't want her to leave, after all, but he went straight into the bathroom. As soon as she heard the door opening again, she ran into the hall, determined to make him talk to her. 'David,' she began, 'I'm really sorry for what I did . . .'

His eyes were like flint as he looked at her. 'There's no point in saying anything else. I haven't changed my mind, and I don't want to find you here when I get home tonight.'

'Oh, please, David, listen to me. I thought you wouldn't want to marry me if you knew I'd had an illegitimate child, that's why I didn't tell you. I should have known you were too good a man to . . .'

'I was too gullible,' he snapped. 'I suppose you married me because you were sorry for me.'

'I married you because I loved you, and I didn't want to hurt you after what you'd been through. That's why I let Helen and Jimmy keep John.'

His expression had softened a little, but unfortunately his eyes fell on the grandfather clock. 'And you were quite happy to take that thing into my house so you could remember your lover?' he said, coldly.

'I didn't want to take it, my mother could have told you that it was Mrs Forrest that made me.'

'Your mother had known about your bastard, of course. She must have taken me for a proper fool.'

'I told her the baby died.'

'What an accomplished liar you were, and did the other woman know . . . his mother?'

'No, Mrs Forrest never knew about it. Oh, David, all the lies I told were to save you being hurt.'

'But you ended up crucifying me, and I could never trust you again. Get out of my way, I have to get dressed.'

She stood aside then, her shoulders drooping, her senses numb, but she knew that the pain would come later. Meantime, she had to make one last effort, but as soon as David came out of the bedroom she could tell by his face that it would be useless. Nevertheless, she tried. 'Please . . . ?'

'Take whatever you want,' he frowned, 'because you'll never get back.'

She stood for some minutes after he went out, but at last she went to wash and change her clothes. If she had to leave, it would be best to go as quickly as possible. After packing some things into a suitcase, she went into the scullery to make herself a cup of tea, and just over ten minutes later she walked into the hall again. Half past nine on her beloved grandfather clock, which had been the cause of David's well-founded jealousy, and which he would likely get rid of once she had gone. Opening the door, she took one last look at the pendulum with its entwined initials JF–EG. This was her only legacy of John Forrest's love . . . no, that wasn't altogether true. He had also left her with something far more precious than this – his son . . . the son she had deserted and cruelly wounded, though John wouldn't know yet about what she had done to him, not unless Laura had gone straight to Edinburgh after she walked out last night.

Elspeth gulped. This was the end of more than twenty-one years of marriage, the end of David, of Laura, of John. She would have to start from scratch again, but she had made one fresh start in her life carrying only a Gladstone bag – though look how that had ended – and this time she had a suitcase. Where would she go from here? Not to Helen Watson this time, for she had inflicted enough trouble on her already. Without planning it, Elspeth found herself walking down King's Gate. Ann Robb would advise her what to do.

The doctor's wife was surprised when her young maid showed Elspeth in, and alarmed when she saw the case. 'Where are you going? I hope nothing's wrong?'

'Oh, Mrs Robb, David knows about John and there's been an awful row.'

'How on earth did he find out, Elspeth? Who could have told him? Surely not Mr or Mrs Watson?'

'Laura and John fell in love and they were going to get married, so I had to tell her and David myself, and she said she'd never forgive me and just walked out.'

'Oh, Elspeth, I'm so sorry, but what about David?'

'He's put me out. He said he couldn't trust me again after the lies I told.'

Ann felt like reminding her that she'd been advised at the time to be honest with her bridegroom, but Elspeth was in no fit state for that. 'Have you anywhere to go?'

'That's why I came to you . . . oh!' Elspeth stopped, and added hastily, 'I wasn't asking you to take me in. I just thought you'd tell me what I could do.'

'Look, my dear, you're quite welcome to stay, for as long as you want. Alex won't mind, and the children are away.'

Elspeth knew that Alexander was an officer in the Seaforth Highlanders, and that Laura was married to a captain in the Merchant Navy and living in Portsmouth, but she couldn't accept Mrs Robb's offer. 'I'd be too near David here. I'll have to go right away, but I can't think where.'

Correctly interpreting her problem, Mrs Robb said, 'If you're worried about money, you'll have to find yourself a job wherever you go.'

'But I haven't worked since I was married, and . . .'

'Wait!' Ann's head shot up. 'Didn't you tell me once that your mother had told her solicitor to put the money he got from the sale of her belongings in a trust for you?'

A rather uncertain, tremulous smile hovered on Elspeth's lips for a moment. 'I'd forgotten that. She must have had second sight, for she said there could come a time when I'd need it. There wouldn't be much, but it would see me through for a wee while. Oh, Mrs Robb, I knew I could count on you.'

'I haven't done anything. You'd have remembered yourself when you were calmer. Do you have enough money for your fare to Auchlonie to see the solicitor?'

'I've a few pounds in my purse.'

'Well, if you run into any problems over the trust, come back here and we'll see what we can work out. As my mother used to say, "There's light at the end of every tunnel."'

Elspeth left King's Gate more confident about the future. At forty-four, she surely wasn't too old to begin anew.

When she arrived in the village of her birth, not much over an hour later, she went directly to Mr Reid's office. He had been a friend of the family, besides being Lizzie's solicitor, and welcomed her warmly. 'It's a long time since I've seen you, Elspeth. It must have been at your mother's funeral, I suppose.'

'It must be, I haven't been back since.'

Her obvious tension made him stop making small talk. 'What can I do for you, Elspeth?'

'Well, my marriage is finished, Mr Reid, and I . . .'

His cheery smile faded. 'I'm sorry to hear that. Have you come to instigate divorce proceedings?'

She was horrified. 'It's nothing like that. I've come to ask about the money you've been holding in trust for me. My mother said I could get it when I needed it.'

'Certainly.' Lifting his pen, he twirled it idly in his fingers. 'You'll be wondering how much is involved?'

'It'll not be much, for she'd a hard struggle to make ends meet all her life, but even ten pounds would be a blessing.'

Mr Reid beamed. 'You'll be blessed two-hundred-fold, then. There's over two thousand pounds. Perhaps I should have written to tell you, but I gathered that your mother did not want you to find out the amount of her estate until you needed it, not that she would have had any idea how large it would be. All her effects were sold, and the grandfather clock brought in more than all the rest put together.'

'Father aye said it was worth a lot, but I never . . .'

'An American friend of mine, a dealer in antiques, was here on holiday at the time, and recognized it as being the work of a famous clock-maker of the eighteenth century. He was astonished that such a valuable clock had come from a cottar house. Have you any idea how your father came by it?'

'He said he'd got it at a sale in Findhavon House when old Lord Hay died.'

'Ah! It must have belonged to the Hay family for many generations – an heirloom, in fact. Lord Hay, of course, died with no near relatives, and the cousin who inherited lived in Australia and gave instructions to sell the lot. Anyway, my friend was fascinated with the clock, especially the initials on the pendulum.'

'My father had them put on . . . his and my mother's.'

Mr Reid's eyebrows rose. Geordie Gray had never struck him as being a sentimental type, but it just showed how little one knew of people. 'It was over a hundred and fifty years old, a true antique. He paid fifteen hundred pounds for the clock and bought the dresser as well.'

'What would he want with an old dresser? It wasn't an antique, for Jockie Paul, the cabinet-maker, made it for my father when I was born.'

The solicitor shrugged his shoulders. 'He said his fellow countrymen go mad over good solid furniture like that. Do you want all the money just now, because I could write you a cheque to cash at . . .'

Elspeth's head was reeling. 'I'd be terrified to have all that at one time. If you just give me enough to see me through for a few weeks, I'd be grateful.'

'Shall we say one hundred pounds, then? That's a nice, round figure.' He buzzed for his secretary and asked her to get it from the safe, then said, 'Are you to be living with relatives, Elspeth, now that you no longer have a home?'

'I've nobody left.' The only blood relative she had now, apart from those she had just left, was her mother's sister Janet, and hell would have to freeze over before she would go back there.

While they were waiting for the money to be taken through, Mr Reid said, conversationally, 'John Forrest of Blairton died a few days ago. Would you remember him?'

Her heart had leapt at the name, but it was her John's father he was speaking about. 'I never knew Mr Forrest to speak to, just to see in the kirk.'

'He died last week – the funeral was yesterday – and I had his widow in here earlier this morning asking me to sell the farm for her. She is a very nice, capable woman, but her eyesight is failing badly, unfortunately.'

'Oh, the poor woman!' Elspeth's involuntary exclamation made her mind return to the time of John's death, when she had said exactly the same thing about his mother. The entrance of the secretary broke into her thoughts, and she accepted the twenty crisp five-pound notes the solicitor counted into her hand.

'Now remember,' he said, kindly, rising to see her to the door, 'just let me know when you need any more.'

In a daze, she walked through the outer office on to the High Street. One hundred pounds would take her anywhere she wanted to go, but where did she want to go? With Mrs Forrest fresh in her mind, she remembered the invitation to Blairton which had once been issued, but would John's mother welcome her after all this time? Elspeth felt a compulsion now to confess to this woman, the only one connected with it who didn't yet know the truth. Taking no more time to think, she stepped back inside. 'Could I leave my case here, please? I've a call to make, and I don't want to have to carry it with me.'

The girl behind the glass partition smiled pleasantly. 'We don't close until half past five.'

Blairton Farm was two miles from the village and it wasn't until she neared it that Elspeth's resolution wavered. What would she do if Mrs Forrest was angry at what she had to say and threw her out? She smiled wryly as the answer came to her – she would be no worse off than she was now.

Striding determinedly up to the farmhouse, she rapped on the back door, but her mouth went dry when she came face to face with the plump, rather tired-looking woman who peered at her through thick-lensed spectacles. 'Mrs Forrest, it's Elspeth Full . . . Gray. I don't know if you remember me, but . . .'

Meg brightened as she clapped her hand up to her cheek. 'Well I never! Come in, come in.'

In the kitchen, she went over to the stove. 'You look fair done in, I'm sure you could do wi' a cup o' tea. Now, what brings you to Blairton?'

Recalling the day she had secretly spent in this house, Elspeth found it more difficult than she had thought to speak to this woman from whom she had fled so shamefully. 'I've a confession to make, Mrs Forrest, and I hope you'll not think badly of me when you hear it.'

The old lady smiled. 'I'm sure I'll not think badly of you, m'dear, whatever you tell me.'

'I was . . . expecting John's child when he was killed.'

The pupils of Meg's eyes dilated, but they remained friendly. 'I should have ken't that was why you went away, but it never . . . you were just a young lassie, and . . .'

'You didn't think I'd do things like that? We hadn't long together, but we loved each other, truly we did.'

Meg leaned over and patted her hand. 'There's no need to make excuses, m'dear, I'm not condemning you, but I can see you've got more than that on your mind, so, when we've had our cuppie, we'll go ben to the parlour, and you'd best tell me the whole story.'

In the room where she and John had made love so madly for a whole day, Elspeth told his mother only of the short time at the fireside in the cottar house and of its dramatic consequences up to the time of her son's birth, ending by saying, 'Are you shocked at me now?'

'Not me. I once spent a whole afternoon wi' Blairton in my father's barn, the sweetest hours I ever spent, as Rabbie Burns would say. I was lucky, though, for I didna fall wi' John till a year after I was wed. So you'd a boy, and all?'

Elspeth gave a long sigh. 'I havena finished yet.' She went on to tell the rest, her voice quivering when she revealed the anguish she had gone through before making her decision to leave John with the Watsons.

'Don't blame yourself for that, lass,' Meg said, softly, 'you couldna have done anything else without telling your man he was your bairn.' Pursing her lips for a second, she added, 'Mind you, it would have been best if you had tell't him.'

Elspeth drew a deep breath. 'I wish I had – I wouldn't be in this trouble the day.' Resuming her account, she explained why she had been forced to tell the truth the evening before. 'And Laura walked out, and David said I'd to leave this morning.'

'So now you're out on the street, penniless?'

When Elspeth told her what had transpired in the solicitor's office, the old woman exclaimed, 'Well, well! Just fancy a clock being worth all that. You'll have something at your back, any road – you'll never need to worry where your next meal's coming from.' She looked at Elspeth wistfully. 'Why did you not come and tell me about John's bairn at the time? I'd have seen that you and the laddie never went short o' anything. It would have helped to make up to me and Blairton for . . . if only you'd done that, you'd not be in this predicament now.'

If only. There were so many 'if onlys' in Elspeth's mind that she burst out, 'If only John hadn't been killed. If only Helen's baby had lived . . .'

'And if only you and my son hadn't taken advantage o' an empty house,' Meg said, quietly and without reproach.

Elspeth was stunned. She had thoughtlessly blamed others when it had all stemmed from her own sin, and not just in one empty house, but in two, though she was not going to tell Mrs Forrest about the day she had spent here.

'What are you to be doing, now your man's put you out?'

'I don't know yet, but the money'll not last for ever and I'll need to get a job and some place to bide.'

'Was that the reason you come to me, lass?'

'Oh, no!' Elspeth was flustered. 'I don't know what made me come. It was maybe Mr Reid telling me your man had died. . .' She broke off, appalled. 'Oh, I forgot. I was awful sorry to hear about Blairton, Mrs Forrest, but I thought you deserved to ken about . . . your grandson.'

'Aye, my heart's that full, I can't . . . to think I've had a grandson . . . my John's son . . . if Blairton had still been . . .' She broke off and took a second to compose herself. 'You'd come to clear your conscience, maybe?'

'I'll never clear my conscience, but something made me come. I can't explain it.'

Meg looked pensive. 'It was fate took you to my door the day, Elspeth, I'm sure o' it. I'd made up my mind to sell up here and go to Edinburgh to bide, for I used to go on holidays there when I was young and I've aye liked it.'

Admiring the old lady's courage in moving to a strange city when she must be over seventy, it occurred to Elspeth

308

that perhaps Mrs Forrest was telling her, in a roundabout way, to stop feeling sorry for herself, so she was totally unprepared for what came next.

'Would you consider coming wi' me, Elspeth? We'd be doing each other a favour – you'd be company for me, and I'd be providing a roof over your head.' She went on in spite of the look of amazement on Elspeth's face. 'You could bide here till I get things settled, and I'll buy a house in Edinburgh, and you can look for a job there if you want. What d'you say?'

Elspeth had been taken aback at its being sprung on her so quickly, but she had nowhere else to go and Edinburgh would be as good a place as any. 'If you're sure, Mrs Forrest, I'd be very grateful. Oh, I've just minded. I left my suitcase at Mr Reid's office, and it shuts at half past five.'

'We can get it in the morning. You ken, pulling up my roots was a hard decision, for I came here as a bride, and Blairton meant to hand it on to John, but . . . och well, that's in the past. I was worried how I'd manage in Edinburgh on my own wi' my eyes getting worse every day, but I'll be fine wi' you there.'

Elspeth was relieved that Mrs Forrest was so confident, because she wasn't so sure herself. Two helpless women in a strange city – how would they cope?

Now that things had been arranged to Meg's satisfaction, she told Elspeth about her husband's death. 'I found him lying lifeless in the bed beside me, and the doctor said it was a heart attack, but I ken he never recovered from losing John. His heart was broken that day, and he only existed after that. It wasna so bad for me, for I was able to let my grief out. There was days I thought I'd never be able to stop greeting, but he just gave way for a minute or two after we got the telegram, and then bottled it up. Any road, after the funeral yesterday, I sat down to think. I couldna run this place on my own, and honest men are hard to find, and nobody would want to work day and night like Blairton did, so that's the reason I'm selling.'

'Mr Reid said you'd been to see him this morning.'

'I didna want to put it off.'

Meg sat silently for a moment, then suddenly started to reminisce about John's childhood – his youth, his quarrel with his father about going to Canada – and while the quiet voice carried on, Elspeth realized, to her amazement, that although she was quite interested in hearing about him, she didn't feel the burning sorrow that she would once have felt. She was sorry that John been killed, but she had known him for so short a time that she had discovered nothing about him: his likes and dislikes; if he had a quick temper or was slow to take offence; if he would have been a good husband. Apart from David's nightmares and outbursts of jealousy – and he really couldn't help that when the clock was there to remind him every day of her first lad – he had been a very good husband . . . but she must forget about David.

If John had loved her as much as he said he did, he wouldn't have blindly followed the wishes of his friends to go drinking that Saturday forenoon. It was the first time this thought had ever entered her head, and she glanced at his mother guiltily.

Meg noticed the look, but misconstrued its meaning. 'I'm sorry, lass. I've been going on and on, and your

310

mind's got enough to contend wi'. We'll have something to eat, then you can tell me about your man.'

Not having had anything except two cups of tea since she rose, Elspeth was glad of the ham sandwiches which Mrs Forrest produced. 'They're left over from the funeral tea,' she smiled, 'but I had them in a tin, and my pantry's that cold they're still as fresh as when they were made.'

Afterwards, when Elspeth started to speak about David, she became so engrossed in recalling his nightmares, his pride in their daughter, his dear habits and sayings, that she hardly noticed the old woman rising to switch on the light, but at last the ache in her heart grew so overpowering that she had to stop.

Mrs Forrest regarded her compassionately. 'I can see you still love him, and it's a shame the way things turned out.'

On the verge of tears, Elspeth thought that it was ironic how things had happened. Only twenty-four hours earlier, she had split four lives asunder with her disclosure about her love for John Forrest and the bearing of his child, yet here she was, sitting with his mother and pouring out her love for David Fullerton. What must the woman think of her? She felt a hand being laid gently over hers and looked up into eyes misty behind the spectacles.

'I'm pleased you found such a good man after what you'd been through, m'dear. Now, you likely didna sleep much last night, and I think you should get some rest. You can have one o' my nightgowns, seeing your case is at Mr Reid's.'

She led Elspeth upstairs to a room containing a single bed covered by a patchwork quilt, a chest of drawers and an old straight-backed wooden chair with a cushion on it;

311

the room from which, although she did not know it, her visitor had withdrawn in embarrassment the first time she had been here.

'This is John's room,' Meg said, looking sheepish. 'Oh, I ken it's more than twenty-six year, but it's aye been John's room to me, and I've lit a fire in here every week to air it. Now, get a good night's sleep, lass, and we can speak about things in the morning, when you're rested.'

'Thank you, Mrs Forrest . . . for everything.'

Exhaustion caught up on Elspeth as she lay down – in a single bed for the first time since her marriage. The events of this astonishing day whirled round and round in her head when she closed her eyes, flashing into her subconscious and changing constantly like a kaleidoscope.

David hadn't changed his mind in the morning . . . What a blessing Mrs Robb remembered about the trust money . . . Mr Reid . . . One thousand five hundred pounds for the grandfather clock . . . Blairton . . . What a kind woman Mrs Forrest is . . . Sandwiches left over from a funeral tea . . . John Forrest's bed . . . But she didn't love him any longer, she loved David . . . She had always loved David, and she would never see him again.

Chapter Twenty-four

Meg, as she insisted on being called, was not as helpless as Elspeth had imagined. One of the farm workers drove her to the village the following morning, where she asked Mr Reid to make enquiries about houses in Edinburgh. 'Not too dear, though,' she warned him, 'for what I get for Blairton'll need to last me the rest o' my days.'

'That's set things moving,' she said, when she return to the farmhouse, 'and I minded to collect your case as well.'

Over the next two weeks, the two women sorted the contents of cupboards and drawers into two piles – what was to be kept and what was to be thrown out – Meg being ruthless in the disposal of all inessential items. 'I'm just taking what I'll need, though there's years o' memories in some o' this stuff I'm leaving.' She looked sadly at Elspeth, who couldn't help thinking that her 'years of memories' were still lying in Aberdeen.

Mr Reid called while they were still thus occupied. 'Most of the houses were quite expensive, Mrs Forrest,' he said, 'so in view of your instructions, I've listed several flats in tenements, too, but you don't need to . . .'

'I've no objection to a tenement,' Meg said, brightly, 'it would be good to have some close neighbours for a change.'

She and Elspeth set off for Edinburgh the following day, but the first three flats they inspected held no appeal for Meg. 'We'll just take a look at the one in Leston Road,' she observed, as they came down four flights of stairs, 'and that'll be enough for one day. If it's not suitable, we'll have to come back another time.'

Elspeth wondered where the old lady got her energy, but by the time they reached the second floor of their last call, even Meg was out of breath. She had, however, been impressed by the well-kept entrance and staircase. The flat itself had large airy rooms, and the kitchen window looked out towards the rear of the Castle. She smiled as she looked round. 'The rooms are a decent size, any road, and they'll not need papering or painting. I'd be quite happy here, Elspeth, how about you?'

Tired and miserable, Elspeth felt that she would never be happy again, no matter where she was, but she said, 'Aye, Meg, this place looks fine.' It didn't matter, anyway, as long as she had somewhere to lay her head at nights.

'I'll let Mr Reid ken we've settled on this.' Meg beamed happily. 'I'm getting real excited about it.'

The removal came three weeks later. The farm equipment was to be auctioned the day after they left, but the excess furniture went to a saleroom in Aberdeen because Meg had said, 'I'm not wanting all the folk in Auchlonie gawking at my bits o' things and belittling them.'

At long last they were in their new home, in the midst of chaos, the removal men having left the furniture and tea chests wherever had been handiest for themselves. 'It'll take us a while to sort this lot out.' Meg stretched her stockinged feet to relieve her throbbing bunions while she relaxed with a cup of tea. 'It's a good thing you thought to take the teapot and things in your bag, Elspeth, for we'd have died o' thirst before we found them in the boxes.'

Elspeth, also without shoes, was having second thoughts about coming to Edinburgh. She had nothing of her own except the few clothes in the suitcase, and she was already feeling like a waif brought in off the streets.

'Well, lass.' Meg heaved herself out of the chair. 'We'll need to make a start, or there'll be no beds ready for us to sleep on this night.'

They made up the double bed in one room and the single bed in the other, and when they were stacking the last of the pans and dishes in the kitchen cupboard, Meg said, 'Will we have a fish supper? I noticed a chip shop down the street.'

'Whatever you think.' Elspeth's spirits were very low.

'You can get them, lass, your legs are younger than mine.' Taking a ten-shilling note out of her purse, Meg held it out to Elspeth, who turned her back on it.

'I can manage to pay for the suppers,' she said, curtly, as she went out. 'I'm not destitute . . . yet.'

Meg shook her head as she laid her handbag down again. It was understandable that Elspeth was touchy about money in the present set-up, but she would have to face up to reality and not take offence at the least little thing.

Next morning, Meg suggested that they should take a walk round the neighbourhood, and going down the hill they passed several shops – a grocer, butcher, newsagent, ironmonger, an empty shop and the chip shop. 'There's near everything we need right on our doorstep,' she exclaimed in delight, then added, 'We've come far enough the now. It's uphill going back.' She made some purchases in the butcher's shop first, then went into the grocer, ignoring Elspeth's plea to let her pay for something.

Home again, Meg looked at her companion. 'We'll have to make some arrangement about money, for I can see you're not happy the way things are. Maybe I should pay for everything and just charge you your keep?'

Elspeth was not too happy with this proposal, either – it meant that she would just be a lodger again. 'What were you thinking of charging me?'

'Oh . . . say . . . ten shillings a week? Is that too much?'

'It's not enough,' Elspeth snapped, angrily. 'I don't want charity.'

'It's not charity, for goodness' sake.' Meg's patience was wearing thin. 'You can help me in the house, if that'll make you feel any better.'

The disapproval in her voice convinced Elspeth that this wasn't going to work. Her hundred pounds would soon dwindle away, and she didn't want to touch the rest of the money. 'All right,' she muttered. 'Ten shillings a week.' She would have to remain beholden to Meg for a while yet, so no good would come of antagonizing her.

Elspeth thought furiously while they were having lunch, and when they had cleared up, she said, 'I'm going out to look for a job. One o' the shops is bound to be needing an assistant or something, but if they're not, I saw cards up in the grocer's door wi' folk needing cleaners.'

Meg frowned. 'Take your time and get something a bit more suitable than that. You trained as a dressmaker, and you've been a waitress – look for that kind o' thing.'

There were no vacancies in the Leston Road shops, Elspeth discovered, so she carried on to Princes Street and into the first large store she came to, but her courage failed her at the sight of all the efficient sales ladies in their smart black dresses. What chance would a dowdy, middle-aged woman have of getting a job here? Walking back dejectedly, she bought a newspaper before she went into the tenement.

'How did you get on?'

Meg's cheery voice annoyed her. 'I didna!' she said, a little too sharply, and instantly regretted it, for the old lady was only trying to be kind. 'I've bought a paper, so I'll look and see if there's any jobs in it.'

She sat down with a pencil and skimmed over the Situations Vacant section, marking three items which she thought might be worth a try – two shops in Princes Street and one in Shandwick Place. The others were mainly for clerkesses and domestics. If she couldn't get in as a shop assistant, she thought, it would be no disgrace if she had to go back into service.

'I met an awful nice woman when you were out, Elspeth,' Meg said as she set the tea. 'I went down to see which was our coal cellar, and she spoke to me out of her window. She's on the ground floor, and she's a widow like me.'

'Oh aye?' Elspeth wasn't really interested.

'Her name's Milne, and she asked if I'd like to go to the pictures wi' her for company the night. I haven't been to the pictures for years, being so far from the town at Blairton, but I thought it would be a fine change for us. It would pass the time, and it would maybe cheer you up.'

'Me?' Elspeth looked surprised. 'I'm not going – the woman didn't ask me. Besides, I'm tired wi' trailing about,

317

and I'd rather bide in and listen to the wireless. You go, though, she'll be better company than me.'

'I think I will.' Meg regarded her anxiously. 'Are you sure you'll not mind being left on your own?'

'No, I'll be glad o' a rest – honest.'

When Meg left the house at half past six, Elspeth turned on the large, wet-battery wireless, but after she had been listening to some pleasant, light music for about five minutes, the news came on. When the announcer gave the sad information that the British naval tanker *Darkdale* had been sunk by a U-boat in the Atlantic, she switched off. She did not want to be reminded of how badly the war was going. She had enough to contend with without that. She couldn't let Meg subsidize her for ever, and the money she'd got from Mr Reid wouldn't last long, even if she was only paying ten shillings a week for her keep. And if today was anything to go by, the two of them would get on each other's nerves stuck up here day in, day out.

Her agonized mind wandering, she wondered what had happened between Laura and John. Would her son hate her now, like her husband and daughter? It wouldn't be surprising if he did. What a mess she had made of her own life, and of so many others. She was no good to anyone – she'd be better off dead. It wouldn't take long, and it would be all over by the time Meg came back from the pictures.

She stood up, laid the cushions behind the door, checked that the window was closed then took Meg's writing pad and pen from the dresser and sat down at the table to write.

318

Dear Meg,

I'm sorry, but I can't go on. Tell David and Laura I love them, and try to make them understand. John and Helen, as well. Thank you for what you tried to do for me, but it wouldn't work.

Your friend,
Elspeth

Having propped the note against the clock, she walked over to the gas cooker, turned on the oven and lay down on the mat with her head inside.

Chapter Twenty-five

A sandwich would do him, David thought, with the bit of corned beef left over from yesterday. He couldn't be bothered cooking and he'd have to clean the bathroom later because he'd taken a bath that morning. Lifting the lid of the bread bin, he was dismayed to find only two heels of bread. It would have to be a 'doorstep' sandwich, and he'd have to remember to buy a loaf tomorrow. In three weeks, he still hadn't learned to plan ahead, but when he forgot to buy something for his supper, there was always a packet of dried eggs to fall back on, though he did get fed up of them.

He never bothered with breakfasts, but he wasn't starving himself; he went to the cafe in the Market at lunchtimes for a decent meal – the new one at the top of the steps to the fish market, not the People's Cafe where he had first met Elspeth, which was no longer there. His heart turned over as he remembered those distant happy days. She had been so bonnie, so kind to him, and he'd never suspected that she . . . if she had told him, he would happily have taken the child along with the girl he loved so much.

Spreading margarine on the two ends of bread, he reminded himself that she hadn't been the kind of girl he thought she was and she'd probably laughed at him for being so gullible. Yet, they'd been happy. Yes, they had been happy, and Laura was the outcome of their love.

He lifted the saucer covering the plate in front of him and placed the small piece of meat nestling on it between the crusts of bread, wondering, as he gaped his mouth to eat, if his daughter had overcome the outrage and anger he'd seen on her face on that last, terrible night. And why had Laura stayed away? *He* hadn't caused her heartbreak; his heartache was every bit as deep as hers could have been. He had lost his wife and daughter at one fell swoop, and she had only lost that man's son. Her mother, too, of course, and himself, her father, but that was only because she chose not to come home. If anything happened to him, she would be sorry she had ignored him.

He wished now that he had been closer to his own father. They had kept in touch until his death, but they hadn't seen each other very often. Isabel had never let her husband go out on his own, and she had refused to visit Woodlands Avenue – she'd likely been jealous of the bungalow. But he and his father had met occasionally after work, and had a quick drink together – maybe once every six months or so. He had gone to the funeral, two years ago, but he hadn't told Elspeth that he'd wept at the graveside. He'd been afraid that she might think he was going off his head altogether.

David's wandering thoughts returned to Laura. He supposed he could contact her by writing to Turnhouse, but it was she who had walked out, and it was up to her to make the first move. He wouldn't demean himself by pleading with her. Sitting up, he took another bite of his sandwich. It was stupid to brood. Once upon a time, he'd had a wife and daughter, and now he was completely alone. That was the sum and substance of it, and he would have to face up to it.

Oh, God! How could he face up to losing Elspeth? At the time he had told her to get out, he was so angry that he could have killed her, but the weeks had blunted that anger, and it was his wife who filled his dreams in the little sleep he had – there had been no nightmares about the trenches since she went. What had happened to his comrades was as nothing compared to the agony he had inflicted on her. Poor Elspeth, he could understand why she had guarded her secret so closely; she had been so ashamed of what she had done that she would have died rather than tell anybody. But exactly what had she done? Loving John Forrest was no sin; having a child out of wedlock was no sin when the father had promised to marry her. Her sin lay in not telling her husband about her child before they married, but in view of all the circumstances, he could even excuse her for that.

She must have been in torment when she gave up her son. It must have gnawed at her soul each time she saw him, watching him grow to manhood without knowing he was her son, worrying herself sick about him after he joined the air force, and he, David, had tortured her further by carrying on about the grandfather clock. He'd been a brute to her – how had she borne it all?

It was some weeks after John was told about his parentage before Helen saw him. He had written, stressing that he still thought of her as his mother, but his subsequent letters had not referred to it at all.

322

'I'll make a cup of tea when the kettle boils,' she said, the questions crowding her mind making her awkward with him for the very first time, 'and we'll have our supper when your father comes in.'

Dreading having to think about that horrendous afternoon, he was acutely conscious of her anxious curiosity. 'I know you want to find out,' he muttered, 'so I'll tell you now and get it over.' He took a deep breath. 'Laura was very upset when she told me, babbling things I couldn't take in, and when I did, I couldn't believe it. It was terrible, learning that the only girl I've ever loved was my sister.'

'Half sister,' Helen corrected automatically.

'It's just as bad. I was demented at first and I even hoped our kite would be shot down that night, so I'd be killed.'

'Oh, John, it surely wasn't as bad as that, was it?'

He regarded her sadly. 'You'll never know how bad it was, Mum. Luckily, our squadron was sent back to Scampton the next week, so I haven't had much time to brood about it.' Only when he was trying to snatch some sleep, he thought, wryly, then it returned vividly and painfully – Laura's strained face, more concerned for him than for herself.

Helen's eyes filled with tears. 'Oh, John, I'm sorry for what I did to you, and I wish I'd the time over again. I'd make sure everybody knew you weren't my son.'

'I am your son,' he said, vehemently. He paused for a moment, then went on thoughtfully. 'I blamed Elspeth for a while, for I couldn't understand how any mother could abandon her child.'

323

'She didn't abandon you. She knew you thought I was your mother, and she was doing what she considered was best for you . . . and me. It was all my fault.'

'I can understand about that since I've had time to think. I feel quite sorry for Elspeth now, especially after you wrote and told me David had put her out. Have you ever found out where she is?'

Helen shook her head. 'No. Like I said in my letter, I went to see her the next forenoon, but the house was empty. I was that worried about her, I went back at teatime, and that's when David said he'd made her leave. I went back in a week to see if he'd heard from her, but he said no and he didn't want to. He was awful bitter, and he didn't want to speak about it.'

'I can understand that.' John thought that David must have felt as badly as he himself had felt.

Falling silent, he slumped in his chair, his chin resting on his chest, his eyes hooded, but within minutes he straightened up.

'That's it,' he said, firmly. 'It's like a knife twisting in my gut every time I think about it.'

Nodding sympathetically, Helen asked, 'Would you like a wee dram, John, rather than a cup of tea?' She would not normally have encouraged him to drink, but his agonized face told her that he needed it.

'Thanks, I could do with one.'

Sipping the whisky slowly, he described the bombing raids over Antwerp and Kiel, the missions right into the heart of Germany itself to smash the war industries, 'The flak's pretty bad, but we always get back.'

Helen was fascinated, in spite of her horror at the

thought of the poor people at the receiving end, in spite of knowing he was dicing with death every day. 'I've worried about you. I'm near scared to answer the door, in case . . .'

John gave a barking laugh. 'It'll take more than a few Jerries to kill me.' The whisky was taking effect and making him feel alive again. 'How's Dad enjoying his retirement? I suppose he's getting under your feet?'

Her face clearing, Helen laughed. 'No, he joined the Home Guard, and he's fair interested in the bowling he took up, and all. He's hardly ever in . . . oh, speak o' the devil.'

John turned as Jimmy came in smiling.

'How's things, Dad? You're looking better than the last time I saw you.'

'Aye, I feel a lot better since I stopped working.' Jimmy took his woods out of their bag and polished them reverently with a duster. 'Helen, you'll not believe this, but I beat Willie McIntyre the day.'

'A real old hand now, eh, Dad?' John teased.

'You can come an' watch me the morrow afternoon, if you like, for we're playing in the Westburn Park.'

Setting the table, Helen listened to the men discussing the setbacks the Allies were facing at the hands of Rommel in Egypt, Jimmy expounding what his strategy would be if he were Montgomery, John winking at her every now and then. She hoped that Laura had survived as well as he had. David and Elspeth would have been worse affected, being older, though David had been managing quite well the last time she went to see him – bitter, of course, which was only natural. But what about poor Elspeth, God knows where? She would likely be accepting her lot as the retribution she'd always feared for her one fall from grace. Why hadn't she come to Quarry Street, instead of just disappearing like that? There was no need for her to be suffering on her own.

When John went to bed that night, Helen knew why Jimmy looked at her expectantly. 'He hasn't got over Laura yet.'

Her husband nodded. 'It'll take a while.'

'He tell't me he wished his aeroplane would be shot down . . . what a thing for a young man to be thinking, and what would Laura have been feeling . . . and Elspeth?'

Chapter Twenty-six

Meg Forrest left Mrs Milne in the lobby and went on up the stairs. She had thoroughly enjoyed the film, though it was an old one, and had laughed and cried all the way through it – mostly cried. Elspeth would have liked it if she'd only come with them, the old woman thought. That Clark Gable was a right lady's man, but thank goodness he'd found Jeanette MacDonald after the earthquake. It must be terrible for the folk living in San Francisco, never knowing when another one would come. Her favourite was Spencer Tracy, though. He was her kind of man, not all that handsome, but kind of cuddly. He put her in mind of Blairton a bit.

Stopping for breath on the first floor landing, Meg detected a whiff of gas. A dangerous thing gas, if it was leaking, she thought, then a chilling fear gripped her. Elspeth had been in such a funny mood at teatime, surely she wouldn't have . . . ?

The old lady hurried up the next flight as fast as she could, the smell growing worse with each step, her mouth even feeling the taste of it. In her panic, she fumbled with the knob of the door, then, heart thumping madly, lungs almost bursting with the effort she had made, she flung herself into the kitchen and clutched at the doorpost in relief. 'Oh, Elspeth, I smelt gas and I thought . . .' Meg stopped when she saw the tear-stained face and swollen eyes. Elspeth had been having a good cry, that's why she'd wanted to be on her own, and no wonder, after what she'd been through. 'I should have ken't you'd more sense. I'll have to report that gas leak in the morning.'

Elspeth's eyes met hers squarely. 'There's not a leak. I did mean to gas myself, but I hadn't the courage.'

'Thank God! Oh, what in heaven's name come over you, lass? I thought you'd be happy here, but if you want to look for another place to bide . . .' Feeling that she had let Elspeth down in some way, Meg patted the bent head gently. 'It's just reaction. You'd lost everything, and I took you to a strange place and left you here on your own before you'd a chance to come to yourself.'

'It wasna your fault, Meg.'

'It was so. I should have understood what you were feeling and not traipsed off to the pictures. You would never have tried anything so silly if I'd been here.'

Lifting her head, Elspeth grimaced. 'Aye, it was silly. I've had a good greet, though, and I feel a bit better. I was tired, and depressed about not getting the kind o' job I was looking for, but there's plenty jobs in the paper.'

'Not the kind you're looking for. I was telling Mrs Milne you'd been a dressmaker, and she said there was a lot o' women round here were saying they wished they ken't somebody to do alterations for them. Would you consider that? It maybe wouldna bring in much, but it would be better than nothing. Just till you found a job you'd be happy at?'

After considering for a moment, Elspeth nodded. 'I suppose I could. I'd have to sew everything by hand, but it would be something for me to do.'

'I'll tell Mrs Milne the morrow, and she can pass the word round. Now, what about a cup o' tea before we go to bed?'

'I'll make it.'

While Elspeth was engaged in this important task, Meg sat down. She had still not quite recovered from the shock she'd had when she came in, and was glad to have time to think.

They had almost finished their tea when the old lady burst out. 'I've got it! The very dab!'

Wondering what Meg was going to spring on her this time, Elspeth said, 'What's the very dab?'

'There's an empty shop down the street next the chip shop, mind? Well, you could buy it and start a dressmaker's shop.'

'But I could never afford to buy a shop.'

'Aye could you. There's all that money you tell't me about, just waiting to be put to a good use.'

'I was wanting to keep that for my old age.'

'What next?' Meg couldn't help laughing. 'Any road, you can sew till you're a hundred unless your sight goes, and yours is better than mine ever was. Folk havena the coupons to buy the things they'd like, and some women are no use at make do and mend like the papers tell us. We'll go and see about it the morrow . . . and I've just thought – maybe it's for renting and you could easy manage to pay a rent out of what you take in.'

The shop was not for renting, as they discovered the following morning, Elspeth's heart sinking when she saw the small notice on the door: 'FOR SALE. APPLY TO LINDSAY & FERGUSON, SOLICITORS, GRASS-MARKET, FOR FURTHER PARTICULARS'.

They made their way to the Grassmarket and were shown through to Mr Lindsay – small and dapper, his black hair slicked back – who drove them back to Leston Road and took them into the three-roomed ground floor flat which had been converted, many years before, into a front shop with a small room off it, and a room at the back with a sink and a gas ring. Looking at her keenly, he asked, 'What type of business were you intending to start, Mrs Fullerton?'

'Just a little dressmaker's – alterations and mending, and that sort of thing.'

The solicitor smiled approvingly. 'The premises are good value for the money – quite bright, and the decoration seems in fairly good order.'

Sensing that Elspeth was dithering, Meg said, 'It's just fine. The wee room could be a fitting room, and a lick o' paint on the doors is all the place needs.'

After a few token protests – swept airily aside by Meg – Elspeth agreed to buy the shop, and in the solicitor's office, in the act of signing the necessary documents, an unexpected little thrill shot through her at what she was accomplishing. 'I suppose I'd better go and see about the things I'll have to buy before I can start.'

Mr Lindsay beamed. 'I can give you the address of a firm of wholesalers who could supply practically everything you would need, or tell you where to get them if they did not have certain items in stock themselves.'

Outside, Meg said, 'I think we should get something to eat first, and that'll give you time to write out a list.'

When they finally went home, Elspeth had bought an old sewing machine and as many of the required goods as were available, all to be delivered when requested. She had even asked a signwriter to paint her name and the nature of her business above the door.

That evening, she wrote to Mr Reid in Auchlonie, asking him to transfer the balance of her money to a bank in Edinburgh to pay for the shop she had bought, then she drafted a notice to place in her window to let people know the date she would open.

Too excited to sleep, her thoughts turned to David and Laura. What would they have said about her starting a dressmaker's shop? But it was best not to think about them. They belonged in the past, and it was the future she had to concentrate on now. The present was taking care of itself – once Meg had shown her the way.

When Elspeth received the key to 29 Leston Road, Meg gave her a hand to paint the doors and clean up generally, then the wholesalers were instructed to deliver the goods she had ordered. All that remained to be done was to organize the layout to her own satisfaction, Meg being amused at first, then slightly irritated, by her indecisions. On Saturday they worked until fairly late, because Meg put her foot down about going in on Sunday. 'You're not wanting to open your door on Monday looking like something the tide's washed in,' she said, in her droll manner, 'and working on the Sabbath would maybe bring bad luck.'

Elspeth was secretly glad of the rest, and it was with great pride that she slid the key into the lock on Monday morning and entered her own shop. The long wooden counter with its brass yard measure was gleaming from Saturday's polishing, but she gave it another rub with a duster to make sure that there were no fingermarks on the calibrated strip. Next, she twitched at the roll of cotton material she had been able to get with her own clothing coupons combined with Meg's and Mrs Milne's, in case she might be asked to make a few blouses or summer skirts. She held her breath as two women stopped to look at the material in the window, artistically draped over cardboard boxes, but they walked on after a few moments.

Just after eleven, when she had come to the conclusion that it had all been a waste of money and effort, a young mother, with a small boy in tow, came in to ask how much it would cost to let down a pair of his trousers. Having had the foresight to work out a scale of charges, Elspeth replied, with a smile, 'It should really be a shilling, but I'll do it for nothing seeing you're my first customer.'

The woman was delighted. 'I'll take them in after dinner.'

At twelve o'clock, Meg brought in sandwiches and a flask of soup, but Elspeth said, her voice a little flat, 'I'm not hungry. You didn't need to bother.'

Meg gathered that the morning had not gone well. 'You need to eat something, though. It'll take time to establish yourself, but things'll pick up.'

'I hope so.' Elspeth had imagined a queue waiting for the shop to open and a steady flow all day, so her one potential customer was something of a let-down.

About ten past one, the young mother returned with two pairs of trousers and a girl's skirt, so Elspeth had something to occupy her at last. A few assorted items were taken in that afternoon and the following day, to be shortened or let down, so she was kept busy, and at the end of the first week there was just over three pounds in her till. But there were the rates to pay, the electricity and gas, and she would have to replace all the threads and tape she had used. Three pounds was not enough to cover all that and leave her enough to live on, she thought sadly.

Business picked up in a few weeks, as Meg had foretold, and so did Elspeth's spirits. She had quite a few 'regulars' now, all of them just asking alterations to be done, so she changed her window display to several large placards, and felt much happier and more optimistic than she had done since leaving Aberdeen. She had even gone out several times with Mrs Farquharson, a widow who lived round the corner from the shop, and who often came in for a chat. Elspeth had refused her first two invitations, having enjoyed the peace when Meg was out, but she had realized that it would do her good to take an interest in something other than her shop.

If anyone had told her when she came to Edinburgh first, she thought one night, that she could pick up the pieces and remodel her existence like this, she would never have believed it. Yet after only a few weeks, she owned a prospering business and was free to do what she liked, when she liked and with whoever she liked. And it was all because of the grandfather clock her father had picked up at a country sale before she was even born.

Chapter Twenty-seven

Watching the brawny corporal making his way towards her with a purposeful glint in his eyes, Laura felt amused. He was new at Wick, and if he thought she was a pushover, he was in for a rude awakening. 'Hey, good looking, whatcha got cooking?' he said, brashly, in the words of a popular song.

'Nothing you'd fancy,' she replied, tartly.

His smile was broad and confident. 'You're wrong, baby. I do fancy you. How about this dance?'

Shrugging, she went into his arms and he led her expertly round the floor as the three-piece band played 'We're Going to Hang Out Our Washing On the Siegfried Line', but after a minute or two his hold tightened, and she said, her voice dripping with sarcasm, 'I'd like to be able to breathe, if you don't mind?'

He relaxed his grip. 'Sorry, most girls like it. The name's Tony, by the way. The one and only Tony Sharp.'

She smiled slightly, it was so appropriate – they didn't come much sharper than this one. 'I'm Laura Fullerton.'

'Hi, Laura. Are you always so prickly?'

She couldn't help laughing now. 'I didn't realize I was being prickly. Please accept my humblest apologies.'

Tony looked pleased that he was getting through to her. 'You should laugh more often, it makes you look human, beautiful even.'

Laura laughed again. He was obviously an accomplished flirt looking for a few laughs and she felt easier with him. 'Thank you, kind sir.'

'That's better. Have you been at Wick long?'

'Three months, one week and two days, to be exact.'

He looked surprised by her precision. 'Do you always keep count of the time like that?'

'I've a reason for remembering how long I've been here.'

'You're Scottish, aren't you? Ock aye the noo, and all that sort of thing?'

'Oh, God, I've never heard anybody saying that, not even the most dyed-in-the-wool Scotsman. It's as bad as thinking all the Welsh say "Indeed to goodness" all the time.'

'Prickle, prickle,' Tony murmured, his eyes twinkling.

She grinned. 'I'm at it again, am I? Sorry.'

'My fault for teasing you.' He whirled her round and round as the music came to an end. 'Thanks, I enjoyed that.'

'Even with an old prickle like me?'

'Especially with you.' He held her hand when she tried to pull it away. 'No, you're mine for the rest of the night.'

She gave in. There was no sense in depriving herself of an entertaining partner and she could brush him off later. His gaiety was so infectious that the evening passed so quickly that she was dismayed when the last waltz was announced. She had meant to ditch him long before that.

When the lights dimmed, he rested his chin on her head as they moved slowly round the small hall. 'I couldn't believe my luck when I saw you first, and I'm not letting you go now I've found you. I'll see you back to camp and . . .'

'I prefer going on my own, if you don't mind.'

'I do mind. Nobody's ever refused me before.'

'There's always a first time.' Laura realized that Tony wouldn't be so easy to squash as she had thought. 'I never let anybody see me back.'

'You don't know what you're missing,' he smiled, then gripped her as she tried to pull away. 'No, my prickly little friend, you won't get off like that.'

Not wanting to make a spectacle of herself in the middle of the floor, she let him take her outside, where he steered her roughly round a corner into the shadows. 'No,' she gasped, struggling to get out of his hold, 'I don't want you to kiss me.'

'Don't you, though?' Covering her lips with his mouth, he pressed against her, breathing heavily, and when he tried to lift her skirt, she lashed out wildly with her foot.

'You teasing little bitch! They said you were a dead loss and I didn't believe them.' He bent down to rub his tender shin, and seizing her chance, she dodged him and ran off as fast as her shaking legs would carry her.

'You'll meet your match,' he shouted after her. 'One day you'll fall in love and it'll all go wrong, I guarantee it.'

His prediction was more than three months too late, Laura thought, wryly, as she sprinted along, her heart racing and a stitch starting in her side. Bursting into the hut, she ran to her bed, out of breath and still trembling.

The girl lying on the next bed looked up. 'What's wrong?'

'I'll tell you later, Pat,' Laura said, then, to her chagrin, burst into tears.

Pat Haggarty rose and sat on the edge of the other WAAF's bed. 'I think you'd better tell me now.'

Laura swallowed. 'This corporal said he'd see me back, and then . . . he tried to . . .'

'Oh.' Pat came from Glasgow and was a quiet, reserved girl who took no interest in the opposite sex. 'That shouldn't have surprised you.'

'I've never let it get as far as that before,' Laura said, rather forlornly. 'He was good fun in the hall, and I thought I'd be able to handle him, but I couldn't.'

'If you play with fire, you must expect to be burned.'

She sounded so motherly that Laura smiled briefly. 'I'd to kick him before I could get away from him.'

Pat swung her dangling feet for a moment. 'Your leave starts the same day as mine, doesn't it? Are you going home to Aberdeen?'

Laura, who never spoke about her family, knew that Pat had placed her by her accent. 'I'm never going home again.'

Gathering that she didn't want to be questioned about it, Pat didn't press her. 'Where will you be going?'

'God knows,' Laura said, morosely. 'I've nothing planned, but no doubt I'll think of somewhere.'

Pat raised her blonde eyebrows. 'You can come to Glasgow with me, if you like. My Mum won't mind, but I'd better write her first to let her know you're coming.'

Laura's last leave, apart from two nights in hotels in Aberdeen and Edinburgh, had been spent crying her eyes out in a YWCA hostel, and Pat's offer was very tempting. 'Are you sure it'll be OK?'

'I'll write tomorrow.' The other girl moved back to her own bed and picked up her book, ending the conversation.

She was a pretty girl, Laura thought, as she studied her. She had very blonde hair, almost silvery, but her lashes were dark, her skin creamy, and she always wore dark lipstick. She kept herself to herself and didn't even go dancing, so she must have a serious boyfriend somewhere. They were about the same age, and it would be good to have a close friend. They could steer clear of boys altogether, because there were always those who wouldn't take no for an answer – like Tony. It wasn't fair, she'd begun to like him before he did what he did. John had never tried to . . . no, she mustn't think about John.

Pat's mother was a small, cheery person, widowed for more than ten years, who ran a boarding house for commercial travellers. She welcomed Laura warmly, then looked at her apologetically. 'You'll have to share Pat's room, if that's all right? There are two single beds.'

'They're all single beds in this house,' Pat smiled.

While they were dressing on the first morning, Pat said, 'I give Mum a hand with the beds and things while I'm here, but there's no need for you to hang around all fore-noon.'

'No, I'll help you, and your mum can do something else.'

Mrs Haggarty, delighted with this arrangement, cleaned each room as the girls made the beds, keeping Laura giggling with her pawky Glaswegian humour, for she was a complete extrovert, not like her daughter. Pat showed Laura round Glasgow in the afternoons, and in the

338

evenings they went to the cinema or just sat in the lounge with the boarders, playing cards with them or listening to their fund of somewhat risqué jokes. Their ten days passed in a flash.

'Haste ye back,' Mrs Haggarty said, as they were leaving.

'How much do I owe you,' Laura asked, hastily. 'I wasn't expecting you to keep me for nothing.'

The woman roared with laughter. 'How much do I owe you, would be more like it. You've worked like a slave since you came, so I'll call it quits, and remember, even if you're not on leave at the same time as Pat again, you'll be welcome any time.'

As they walked away, Pat said, 'She really meant that.'

Very grateful to them for not having tried out to find out why she didn't go home, Laura realized that there had been no mention, either, of Pat having a steady boyfriend.

Their next leaves not coinciding, Laura went to Glasgow by herself. Mrs Haggarty, thankful for her help in the mornings, insisted that she took a break in the afternoons, so the girl sometimes wandered round the larger stores in Sauchiehall Street and Buchanan Street; sometimes she went to the Broomielaw to watch the ships on the Clyde; once to Kelvingrove Park, where she spent a very pleasant hour in the Art Gallery. But she was happiest just pottering about with Mrs Haggarty, who treated her like a daughter and made her promise to regard Glasgow as her home.

Jenny Porter, another WAAF, joined her at Inverness on the last lap of her return journey. 'Thank goodness I've met you, Fullerton. I hate travelling on my own, don't you?'

339

'I don't really mind. Have you been on leave, too?'

Jenny beamed. 'Yes, and I'd a super time. I went out every night with a boy I met, and he's going to write to me, so it might be the start of something big. How was yours?'

Laura shrugged. 'Nothing so exciting, but I enjoyed it.'

'I heard you were going to Glasgow?'

'Yes. I went with Pat Haggarty last time, and her mother invited me back.'

After a quick, sideways glance, Jenny murmured, 'We were all amazed at you going away with Haggarty, you know.'

'Oh? Why was that?' Laura was mystified.

Looking uncomfortable, Jenny said, 'You know.'

'No, I don't. Why shouldn't I go home with Pat?'

'She's not like the rest of us. She's . . . er . . .'

With a sinking stomach, it dawned on Laura what was being implied. 'Are you saying she's . . . one of those?'

'We thought you knew, and with you not bothering with any boys either, we wondered if you . . .' Jenny's voice tailed off at the other girl's expression. 'We didn't really think you were.'

'I'm bloody not!' Laura was indignant. 'And Pat never did anything to make me think she was either.'

'Oh, well, you probably had a lucky escape.' Jenny took a paper bag out of her respirator. 'My Mum saves up her sweet coupons until I go home,' she explained, and offered the bag to Laura, who took one absentmindedly.

They chewed the caramels in silence. It could only happen to her, Laura thought, dismally. Why could her life not be straightforward like other girls'? She understood now about Pat, but it gave her no satisfaction. What a fool she'd been, but such a thing had never entered her head.

Trying to atone for the shock she had sprung, Jenny chattered about her boyfriend for the remainder of the journey, but Laura was not listening. What could she say when she was alone with Pat, knowing what she did about her? She could hardly come straight out and say, 'Are you a lesbian?' It was a word she had only read, never heard actually spoken, and this was going to be another drama-fraught situation.

Her problem was solved when Pat approached her next day as they left the Mess. 'I believe you travelled part of the way back last night with Jenny Porter? Did she tell you what they all say about me?'

'Yes, Pat, she did.'

'I'm glad you know.'

Laura could detect something odd about the other girl's manner. 'It's not true, though, is it?'

'No, it's not.'

'Why don't you set the daft bitches straight, then?'

'I don't care what they say. It doesn't hurt now.'

Laura felt sorry for her, but suspected that there was more to it than Pat was saying. 'There's something else behind it, isn't there? The real reason you don't go out with any boys?'

The silence was so long that Laura wished she hadn't tried to find out, but at last Pat said, 'There is a reason, but I can't speak about it.'

'That's all right. There's something I can't tell anybody, either, so now we understand, we won't ask each other any awkward questions.' Laura paused, then said, 'Are we going to the pictures tonight?'

341

Pat gripped her hand gratefully. 'OK, Laura.'

They carried on as they had done before Jenny Porter's cruel insinuation, but Laura was annoyed when the other girls avoided her too. It was a few weeks before she became accustomed to it, but eventually she could laugh when she saw them change direction when she and Pat went anywhere near them.

Chapter Twenty-eight

1943

When the last two passengers left their carriage at Newcastle, John Watson wasted no time in kissing his wife. Agnes smiled at him uncertainly, her green eyes, set in long dark fringes, making him want to kiss her over and over again. 'I'm really scared, darling,' she murmured.

'There's no need. Mum and Dad are going to love you, so stop worrying and look forward to our honeymoon. We'd only forty-eight hours when we got married, so it didn't count.'

A twinkle appeared in the twin green pools. 'It counted for me.'

Blushing boyishly, he grinned. 'You know what I meant. All that matters is I love you, isn't it?'

'Yes, I suppose so.' Agnes settled back into the padded seat and looked out of the window.

John's mind returned to the day they had met. He had been going home on leave, with no interest in life, but as soon as she had hovered in the doorway of his carriage, his spirits had soared and his heart, dead for over a year, had played a loud tattoo against his ribs. He had squeezed up to make room for her and when she sat down, they had begun to talk.

'I work in a munitions factory in Dagenham,' she had told him, 'but I'm going to see my Aunt Dolly. Her husband's stationed at Dyce Aerodrome, and my dad said it would be safer up there. I didn't want to leave Mum and him, not with the bombing, but they persuaded me to go – just for a week, though I nearly changed my mind when I saw how full the train was.'

He glanced at her now, but she was still gazing pensively out at the countryside. 'Penny for 'em, darling,' he joked.

'I was remembering the last time we made this journey.'

'Two minds with but a single thought. We were old friends by the time we got off the train.'

She giggled delightedly. 'Before we reached Edinburgh, you'd made me promise to meet you in Aberdeen.'

'I didn't want to lose contact with you, for I've loved you since I saw you in the corridor looking lost.'

'Me, too. Are you glad now I made you marry me?'

'You know I am, but I still think we should have waited. For your sake, I mean – in case anything happens to me.'

The light went out of her eyes. 'Nothing's going to happen to you, darling, so don't be so pessimistic.'

Before he could kiss her again, a passing soldier peered into their compartment and shouted behind him, 'There's some empty seats here.' Immediately, another three Seaforth Highlanders appeared and bundled in beside Agnes and John.

'We've been standing since York,' one of them remarked as they sat down. 'How long have these seats been free?'

'Just since Newcastle. Sorry, I didn't realize anybody was still standing.' John was even more sorry that he would no longer be alone with his wife, but it couldn't be helped.

'That's OK, mate. Are we intruding on young love?'

'You are,' laughed John, 'but we're married.'

The soldier pulled out a battered packet of cigarettes and held it towards John. 'Fag?'

'No thanks.'

Good-natured ribbing between the four soldiers – on the way to Aberdeen to change trains for Forres – gave Agnes and John no further chance to talk privately, and when the train pulled into the Joint Station, they said goodbye to their travelling companions and made their way out.

'Just as well they didn't know we've only been married for a couple of months and this is our honeymoon. They'd have made a meal of that.' He tucked her arm through his and looked at her solicitously. 'Not long now, darling.'

Helen and Jimmy were also anxious about this meeting. As she had said when John had written that he was bringing his wife to see them, 'We've been blessed with one wonderful daughter-in-law, we can't expect Providence to provide us with another one as good as Margaret.' Their worries were forgotten as soon as John ushered in the tall, raven-haired girl, her green eyes friendly and her pleasant face breaking into an attractive smile, and Helen put up a silent prayer of thanks that he had got over Laura Fullerton.

While Jimmy was questioning Agnes about the London bombing, Helen took the opportunity to have a quiet word with John. 'Have you told her about . . . ?'

'Yes, Mum, I have. She knows everything, so don't worry.'

'Thank goodness for that.' Helen's cup of happiness would have been full if it hadn't been that she still did not know what had become of Laura and Elspeth. She supposed that the girl had fallen in love with somebody else by now, like John, but her mother . . .

Over the past two years, Laura had stoically endured her self-imposed withdrawal from social contact with the opposite sex, but eventually the lure of the dance hall proved too strong to ignore. She longed for the music, the lights, the atmosphere the excitement of being held in a man's arms – any man's arms. Towards the middle of December, she raised the subject with her friend. 'Did you never go to any dances at all?'

Pat Haggarty smiled sadly. 'At one time, I went dancing every week. It was at a dance that I met . . .' Biting her lip, she broke off, her eyes revealing a deep sorrow.

Guessing that it must have been someone very special, Laura wondered what had gone wrong, but if Pat had enjoyed dancing before, it was time she gave it another try. 'Would it upset you to go to the do tonight? We'd go together and come back together, and you don't have to dance with anybody if you don't want to.'

'In that case, there's not much point in me going,' Pat said, drily, then saw how disappointed Laura was. 'You really want to go, don't you? Why don't you go by yourself?'

'I'm not going unless you come, too.'

'Well, you've been very understanding with me so far . . . OK, I'll go with you – just this once.'

Laura's face lit up. 'Wizard! But remember, if you feel you can't take it, say the word and we'll leave right away.'

After tea, they applied their make-up, swapping lipsticks for a change, and Laura, whose short curls needed little attention, waited until Pat pinned up her side hair and brushed the back into a pageboy roll. When they were ready, each gave the other an approving 'thumbs-up'.

Laura's excitement reached fever pitch when she entered the hall and picked up the familiar smell – a conglomeration of cheap perfume, perspiration and Slipperene. They sat down at the side, but after a quickstep and a Lambeth Walk with no one asking them to dance, Laura pulled Pat reluctantly to her feet. She soon mastered the art of leading, and noticed that several boys looked at them but turned away, red-faced, after their partners whispered to them. Pat and she were going to be ostracized, she realized, and held her head high to show that she didn't care, but when she glanced at her friend, she saw from her set mouth that she, too, had tumbled to what was going on, and that she did care.

When the MC announced a Paul Jones, Laura said, 'Come on. This is the only way we'll get partners.'

Hesitating for a moment, Pat followed her into the circle of girls, and they skipped round with the others until the music stopped. Laura found herself opposite a stout, florid sergeant, who swung her into the tango, and she saw that a tall blonde boy was dancing with Pat. She gave herself up to the gliding and dipping then joined the circle until the music stopped again. The tempo changed to three-four time, her partner a corporal who whirled her round energetically, so she did not see Pat again until they were back in the circle, and was relieved that she looked quite happy.

During the slow foxtrot, Laura spotted her friend with the tall blonde boy again, and wasn't surprised when she brought him over when the Paul Jones ended. 'He's another Pat,' she laughed, breathlessly. 'Pat Sandison, this is Laura Fullerton.'

The two Pats danced together for the rest of the evening, and Laura was never left on her own either. Only one of her partners asked if he could see her back to camp, but she said she was going with her friend and he didn't persist.

Just before the last dance began, Pat came over, holding the other Pat's hand. 'I hope you don't mind, Laura, but Pat and I are going now.'

'That's OK. See you later.' Laura's brightness hid her dismay. Pat Haggarty was attracted to Pat Sandison, that was obvious, and she, herself, would have to spend her evenings on her own in future, but it was her own fault for making it possible for them to meet. She watched them leaving, then turned forlornly to go to the cloakroom.

'I see your friend's gone. Well, my offer still holds.'

It was the boy she had previously refused, an LAC, but she let him lead her on to the dance floor. To hell with Pat, she thought rebelliously, to hell with the two Pats, to hell with everybody. She'd come here to enjoy herself and by God she would.

The boy smiled shyly. 'I'm Doug Phillips.'

'Laura Fullerton.'

'It's my last night in this country,' he observed. 'We're off to warmer climes tomorrow. Well, we've been issued with light clothing and the rumour is we'll be spending Christmas in Malta, or the Med somewhere.'

'Are you looking forward to it?'

'Yes and no. Yes, because it's an adventure, if you like – and no, because I've just met you.'

'Don't start having ideas about me,' Laura said, quietly. 'I don't want to be involved, serious or otherwise.'

Looking quite surprised at first, Doug's features slowly relaxed in a smile. 'Getting over an unhappy love affair? Oh, well, it's the luck of the draw, I suppose, but you'll surely let me walk you back?'

'As long as you remember to keep your hands to yourself.'

After the dance ended, they walked along the road side by side, talking companionably, and Laura felt good – it had been so long since she had allowed herself the pleasure of talking to a boy. Just before they reached the camp gates, Doug said, 'This is it, then. Aren't you going to wish me luck, Laura?'

'Oh, yes. Good luck, and . . . I enjoyed dancing with you.'

'Me, too.' He planted a light kiss on her forehead, then, without warning, his mouth found hers. Realizing why, she didn't protest – anyway, it was rather nice.

'Thank you, Laura,' he murmured, as he drew away. 'That's something for me to remember. I'll maybe run into you again, some day – who knows?' Saluting, he walked off, and she went into the hut, thankful that he hadn't wanted to keep in touch with her.

When Pat came in, a short time later, she announced joyfully, 'It was love at first sight for Pat and me.'

Laura pulled a resigned face. 'I thought as much.'

'He's being posted overseas tomorrow, but he's going to write. He's not part of an air crew, so there won't be any chance of him being shot down and killed, like . . .' Pat's eyes clouded.

Her friend's reason for not having anything to do with boys was now explained to Laura, but it was best not to ask questions. 'He seemed a decent sort.'

The other girl's face brightened. 'He is, Laura, and I'm glad you made me go to the dance tonight.'

When Laura went to Glasgow again – two weeks after Pat came back – Mrs Haggarty gave her a hug. 'It's good to see you, my dear, and thanks for what you've done for Pat. She withdrew into a shell after her fiancé was killed, two and a half years ago, but now she's back to being the girl she used to be.'

'Poor Pat. I gathered that a boy she'd been very fond of had been shot down, but I didn't know they'd been engaged.'

'I thought she'd never get over it, but life has to go on, even if you lose the man you love. I speak from experience.'

'Yes, life has to go on.' Laura could also vouch for that.

On her solitary afternoon outings, she found herself drawn to the warm-hearted Glaswegians, and was sorry when the time came for her to leave. Kissing her cheek at the door, Mrs Haggarty said, 'I've enjoyed having you, and now that my Pat's found another boy, I hope I'll soon be hearing that you've fallen in love too.'

'Pigs'll fly,' Laura joked. She was tempted to pour out her own sad experience, but even after all this time, she still hadn't recovered enough to take any commiserations.

On the train, she couldn't concentrate to read because of a niggle of apprehension that had started deep down inside her. Something dreadful had happened or was just about to happen. She tried to tell herself that it was

350

imagination, but the feeling only intensified and by the time she reached Wick Station she was in a cold sweat. Running all the way to the airfield, she burst into the hut and looked for Pat, hoping that she'd been worrying needlessly, but her friend's bed was empty.

Jenny Porter jumped to her feet when she saw who had come in. 'Oh, thank goodness you're back. Haggarty's gone.'

Laura licked her dry lips and tried to control her heaving stomach. 'Gone? Where?'

'She went out last night and never came back.'

'But what . . . ?' Throwing her kitbag and respirator on her bed, Laura made for the door again. 'I'm going to see the CO. There must be something you don't know, Jenny.'

The officer's face was grave when she admitted the girl to her quarters. 'Ah, it's you, Fullerton. I was going to speak to you in the morning. Pat Haggarty's missing, and I believe you and she were good friends?'

'I've just found out about it, Ma'am, but what . . .'

'We don't know what's happened. All I've been able to find out is that she received a letter yesterday, but whether it had any connection . . .'

'She's been writing to a boy overseas.' Laura's voice sounded strangled. 'Maybe he wrote to tell her he'd found somebody else. Oh God, Ma'am, that would have finished her.'

'I assumed she was sick when she didn't come on duty this morning, and it wasn't until lunchtime that I discovered no one had seen her since last night. Do you have any idea where she might be?'

'She hasn't gone home to Glasgow, because I've just come from her mother's house. It must have been something in that letter that . . . can I do anything to help?'

'See if you can find it in her locker.'

Laura was rummaging through Pat's belongings before she even realized what she was doing, and when she found the letter under a pile of underclothes she read it with no compunction.

Dear Pat Haggarty,

I'm very sorry to have to tell you that Pat Sandison was killed when enemy planes strafed our camp yesterday. I found some letters from you amongst his things and I thought you should know. I can only say again how sorry I am, and if it's any comfort, he was always speaking about you, and I'm sure he loved you very much.

Sincerely, Bill Davis.
PS I'm going to miss him, too.
We were good buddies.

Sinking down on her own bed, Laura stared into space, her heart filling with black anger.

'Was it bad news?' Jenny Porter was standing beside her.

Laura nodded miserably. 'Her boyfriend's been killed.' Her feelings overpowering her, she said, viciously, 'And the boy she was engaged to before was killed, too, so you see how bloody wrong you were about her?'

Jenny looked contrite. 'Oh, God, I'm sorry for what I said before. I hope she's OK, wherever she is.'

'So do I!' Laura rose and went back to the CO.

The woman looked up sympathetically from the letter. 'Poor child, this must have been quite a blow to her.'

'Her fiancé was killed about two and a half years ago.'

'Oh, no! She must have been out of her mind at getting this, then. I'd better contact her mother to see if she's gone home now, but I'll have a search party sent out in the morning. I think you should go on duty as usual tomorrow, Fullerton. It will be worse for you if you brood about it.'

'Yes, Ma'am.' Laura returned to the hut, wishing fervently that she had been there when that letter arrived. Pat might not have taken it so badly if there had been a shoulder to cry on.

At eleven o'clock the following morning, she was called to the CO's office, and knew, even before she went in, what she was going to hear. 'Sit down, Fullerton.' The officer's voice was serious, her expression compassionate. 'They found your friend's body at the bottom of the gorge beside the old Castle. We'll never know if she went with the intention of throwing herself over, or if it was an accident, and I know it won't help, but I'm very, very sorry. Your sergeant has already identified her, so there's no need for you to see her. In fact, it would be better if you remembered her the way you saw her last. I have already notified her mother.'

'Oh, poor Mrs Haggarty.' Laura's throat constricted. 'It'll be a terrible shock to her – they were very close.'

'It's a great tragedy. It's the people who are left behind who have the burden to bear.' Showing how upset she was, the CO fiddled briefly with some papers on her desk, then said, 'You are excused duty today, and you will be allowed to attend your friend's funeral – even if Mrs Haggarty wants it to be in Glasgow.'

'May I have permission to leave the camp, Ma'am, just for a short time? I . . . I'd like to be on my own.' Noticing the narrowing of her officer's eyes, Laura said, hastily, 'I'm not going to do anything stupid, I just want to have some time to think.'

When she went through the gates, she turned towards the open countryside. She had often walked this way with Pat, and the memory released the tears – welcome, welcome tears.

Old Wick Castle was grim and forbidding, the gorge was dark and deep. Laura was certain that Pat had jumped and could understand why. Even with only sadness and pity in her heart, the chasm drew her like a magnet, and Pat Haggarty had felt much more than sadness, much more than pity, at Pat Sandison's death. She had likely been trying to come to terms with the second tragedy to strike her, and the depressing atmosphere of this fearsome place had made her take her own life.

After taking a step nearer the brink, Laura drew back in horror. It would be so easy to go over – much easier than it had been at Rubislaw Quarry. Well, she had survived the parting from the man she loved, she would survive the death of her friend, she could survive anything that fate held in store – nothing could be worse than what had befallen her already. And this had taught her a lesson. It was best to live life to the full while you could, and she would do exactly that in future. She would dance with as many boys as she could, laugh with them, flirt with them, but never, never, would she let herself fall in love.

Over the next few days, there seemed to be a damper over the whole camp, and Laura had to brace herself to accept the sympathy of the other WAAFs when she felt like shouting that she hoped they were ashamed of how they had treated Pat.

A much more harrowing experience for her came when she had to travel to Glasgow on the same train as the coffin, and it took all her will power not to break down at Inverness station, where she watched it being transferred to the Glasgow train. She had always hoped that she and Pat would return to Glasgow together some time, but not like this.

The ordeal of facing Mrs Haggarty was not as traumatic as Laura had feared. The woman held out her arms and they wept together for a few moments before she patted the girl's cheek and steered her into the darkened house. The priest had known Pat all her life, and spoke of her naturally and without sorrow, as if a new life had opened up for her, something which had not occurred to Laura and which gave her great comfort.

Mrs Haggarty, pale and drawn, clasped her hand as they stood in the hallway when she left. 'Thank you for coming, Laura,' she whispered, brokenly, 'and thank you for being such a good friend to Pat.' Hesitating, she said, softly, 'I'm giving up the house. My sister's asked me to live with her in Coatbridge. She's a widow, too, so we'll be company for each other and she won't let me brood. The only thing is, you won't have anywhere to come on leave.'

'Don't worry about me.' Laura's voice had a catch in it. 'You've been very kind to me and I'm glad you won't be lonely. I'll never forget you . . . or Pat.'

'Thank you.' Mrs Haggarty kissed her cheek. 'Goodbye, my dear, and may God be with you.'

Making her way towards the station, Laura wondered why Pat's mother hadn't asked her to write, but perhaps she was afraid that it would bring back painful memories, which was quite understandable. It was probably better this way, the girl reflected, then an icy shiver ran through her as she realized that another door had been closed to her.

Chapter Twenty-nine

1944

Arms linked and laughing hilariously, the three WAAFs made their way through Porthills back to their billet, and an old fisherman shuffling in the opposite direction could not help but smile at their gaiety, although many of the older locals resented the influx of so many young people to their area.

'Wonder what old Mother Adams is concocting tonight?' The tallest of the trio led the way into a small close. Betty Fry was five feet seven and well built, but neither fat nor flabby. Her straight dark hair was cropped short like a man's, and her grey eyes were dancing.

'I hope it's not her fish pie.' Louise Wilson, smallest and quietest, had an elfin face and green eyes, hence her friends' nickname for her – 'Lep', short for leprechaun.

Laura Fullerton gave a skip, her auburn curls swinging round her ears. 'What's the bets it's fish again? What else could they give you in a fishing community?' She was always ready for a laugh, and it was her imitation of one of their officers which had caused their previous hilarity.

In spite of their disparagement of her, they thought the world of Mrs Adams, a little round ball of a woman, who did have a tendency to mother them. 'Where are you bound for tonight?' she asked when they went in, producing, to their relief, a meat roll made from what the butcher cheerfully called sausage meat, although it consisted mainly of bread.

Betty laughed. 'I think we'll mosey along and see who we can pick up at the dance.'

The old lady reacted as the girl had expected. 'You WAAFs and your slang. In my days, we'd to wait till we were asked to any dances, and we'd to stay the whole night with the same lad.'

Laura winked to her friends. 'I'd gladly stay the whole night with any lad,' she said, obviously meaning to shock, and they all laughed, including Mrs Adams.

When they reached the hall, it was already packed, a sea of Air Force blue moving in smooth waves, flecked with the bright colours worn by the local girls who flirted with all the young airmen, for Porthills had been a quiet backwater until the RAF came to Bonachy Aerodrome. The three WAAFs were intrigued by being stamped on the back of their hands with a purple star as soon as they went through the door.

'What's that for?' Betty asked.

The organizer of the dance, a local man, said, 'It's so people can leave the hall and come back in without paying again. Some of the young lads here used to pretend they'd paid when they hadn't.'

'I felt like a cow being branded.' Betty observed, as they went inside.

'You're the one that said it.' Laura and Lep howled with unrestrained laughter.

On the dance floor, they surveyed the seething, swaying

mass, and Laura's eye was caught by a scraggy, sandy-haired sergeant, who made a bee line towards her when the quickstep came to an end. She nodded when he raised his eyebrows, and while they were foxtrotting, he told her that his name was Bill Darbourne, and that he came from London.

'Oh, a Cockney?' she teased.

'No, I'm not a Cockney,' he replied, earnestly. 'I wasn't born within the sound of Bow Bells, it was Barnet, actually, in north London. What's your name and where do you belong?'

'Laura Fullerton, and I belong . . . anywhere I happen to be.' Smiling at his puzzled expression, and aping his accent, she added, 'It's Aberdeen, actually.'

'You're not so very far from home, then.' Bill guided her through a complicated pattern of small scissors steps to fit in with the slow rhythm. 'It's a helluva journey from London to Banffshire. You should thank your lucky stars you don't have to contend with that when you go on leave.'

Having been so affected by Pat's tragic death, Laura had asked to be posted away from Wick, and now that Mrs Haggarty had given up her boarding house, she had nowhere to go, but who cared? She couldn't let herself worry about things like that when she was enjoying herself. Dancing was almost an obsession with her these days and she gladly went up with Bill Darbourne to the next dance, a tango. Glancing round, she saw Betty gliding past in the arms of a small, owlish-looking aircraftman with glasses, and smiled at the odd picture they made – the long and short of it. Then Louise, all four feet eleven of her, was swept past by a strapping six-footer, and Laura burst out laughing – the short and long of it this time.

Bill frowned. 'What's the joke?'

Laura pointed out the other two couples and told him what had passed through her mind, and he laughed, too. 'I'd say we were pretty well matched, though, wouldn't you?'

He was looking at her admiringly, so Laura made another joke to avoid any sentimentality developing. The tango finishing, the MC announced a Paul Jones, so she ran into the middle of the floor and contrived to miss Bill each time the music changed. She flirted mildly for the rest of the evening, but Bill claimed her for another dance near the end. 'I think you've been avoiding me, Laura,' he scolded.

It had taken some very careful manoeuvring on her part to avoid him every time he'd come towards her, but she grinned. 'I can't help being popular.' She didn't want to offend him, but she had to keep things on a manageable level. As soon as the Lambeth Walk was over, she dashed away from him. 'Time to go, before the last waltz,' she told Louise and Betty. Bill was looking for her and she didn't want to give him the chance of asking to take her back to her billet, so she hustled the other two through the door.

'What's the rush?' Betty sounded peevish when they were outside. 'I was hoping to get a decent partner for the last dance. That shrimp of an AC2 was determined to walk me back, but I felt like a beanpole beside him.'

'I'm quite happy to leave,' remarked Lep. 'I don't feel easy trying to flirt like you two.'

Betty sighed. 'Two against one – outvoted, poor me.'

Giggling, Laura began to waltz along the road, singing the song that had been playing when they left. 'Who's taking you home tonight, after the dance is through . . . oo . . . oo? Who's going to hold you tight, and . . .'

360

'Why didn't you want to dance with that sergeant?' Betty interrupted. 'I could see he was keen on you.'

'Who, Bill?' Laura laughed airily. 'He was OK, but little old Laura doesn't want any commitments, thank you. It's more fun not being tied to any one boy.'

'I guess it is more fun that way,' Betty agreed, 'and we can't break up the Three Musketeers, can we?'

'It's not that I don't want a boyfriend,' Louise remarked, 'but nobody looks at me when you two are around.'

'Oh, you poor little Lep.' Laura smiled to show she was teasing. 'But I bet you'll be the first one of us to get serious about a boy. Come on, girls. Race you to the house, and last one there's a hairy witch.'

Louise, with her short legs, was last inside, but when Laura went to the bathroom, she said, 'You know, Betty, I think she must have had a disappointment over a boy at some time. She never wants to be serious with any of the fellows she dances with, and some of them have been really nice.'

Betty smiled. 'You're very profound tonight, Lep, but I know what you mean. The flirting and joking do seem a bit forced at times, and it makes me wonder, too. It must have been pretty bad, because she never talks about it.'

Their tête-à-tête was stopped abruptly when Laura came into the room again.

Just over three months later, Louise astonished her friends one evening by saying, shyly, 'I'm going out with one of the fitters tonight. He asked me at lunchtime in the Mess, and I thought, why not?'

'Why not, indeed, my little leprechaun?' Laura cried. 'I can't wait to see you married and having babies.'

'We're only going to see the film,' Louise protested, her face colouring.

'But it's what could happen afterwards that you've got to watch.' Betty poked her in the ribs. 'Are you strong enough to fight off his immoral advances?'

'Oh, you two!' Louise rubbed some Pond's Vanishing Cream into her face and patted on some powder, then took a tube of Max Factor lipstick and a bottle of Californian Poppy out of her bag.

'Oho, we're really out to make a kill.' Laura winked at Betty as Lep dabbed the perfume behind her ears.

'Be careful, Lep,' Betty warned, when her friend went out. 'That scent might go to his head.' She lay back on her bed, her arm under her head. 'Laura, don't you ever fancy having a steady boyfriend? I know I do, sometimes.'

Laura hesitated. 'No, not really. I'm having a whale of a time as it is.'

Giving up, Betty warbled, 'Whale meat again, don't know where, don't know when, but we'll have whale meat again some sunny day,' and they dissolved into giggles.

When they simmered down, Laura said, 'I don't fancy the film, it's one of those dreary gangster things, and I wouldn't want to embarrass Lep by going anyway, but I don't feel like staying in. How about going for a walk?'

Calling in at the local hotel on their way back, they struck up a conversation with two young civilians. 'We're due to register next week,' one of them said.

'I'm going to say I'm a conchie,' said the other. 'I don't want to have to salute all the time like the Brylcreem boys.

Their hands go up and down like yo-yos when they meet an officer, even when they're off duty. And the air crews – boy, they don't half fancy themselves.'

'They've something to be proud of,' Laura snapped, quite unexpectedly. 'They're fighting to keep the likes of you free, and they're risking their lives every time they go up. Anyway, they'll put you in prison if you say you're a conscientious objector, and it'll serve you bloody well right. Come on, Betty, we shouldn't waste our time speaking to this idiot.' She jumped to her feet and marched out.

Hurrying to catch up with her, Betty puffed, 'That wasn't like you, Laura – what got into you? Where's your sense of humour? He was only a kid.' She had been rather shocked by her friend's outburst.

'He made me so blasted mad criticizing the air crews like that.' Laura was cooling down now, and laughed suddenly. 'Did you see his face, though? If his mouth had fallen open any more, his chin would have hit his chest.'

Betty smiled momentarily, then said, 'Are you jealous of Lep having a boyfriend? Is that why you're so touchy?'

'I'm not jealous, honestly, but I sometimes wish I could let myself be serious about somebody.'

'Why can't you? It's not a crime. It's only natural for a girl to fall in love and get married.'

'I won't let it happen to me! I just won't!'

Her vehemence astonished Betty. 'I don't know if someone you loved was killed, or what it was that's making you like this, but whatever it was, surely you can tell me about it? That's what friends are for, you know.'

Sighing, Laura slowed her pace, but kept her eyes to the

front. 'It was nearly three years ago, at Turnhouse. We fell in love, but marriage was out of the question.'

'Why? Was he married already?'

'Yes.' It seemed the simplest explanation.

'Wouldn't his wife divorce him?'

'No.' Feeling that she was getting in deep water, Laura said, 'I asked for a posting and was sent to Wick, then I came here. Do you mind if we don't discuss it any more?'

Betty walked a few steps before saying, 'Your leave starts next week, doesn't it? I heard you telling that sergeant you came from Aberdeen, are you going home?'

Realizing that Betty probably thought it strange that she never mentioned her family, Laura said, carefully, 'There's nobody in Aberdeen for me to visit now.'

'Have your Mum and Dad moved?'

'They're . . . both dead.' It was all she could think of to stop the questions, but it didn't work.

'Oh, I'm sorry. How did it happen? Was it a bomb?'

Laura was aware that Betty was only showing concern, and decided that it might be best to tell her the truth – so much of it, at any rate. To continue with this deception would make her as bad as her . . . 'That wasn't true. They're not dead, as far as I know. We'd a flaming row in 1941 and I walked out. Don't ask about it, because I can't tell you.'

'Don't you ever feel like going home and apologizing?'

'No, and you'd never understand. Can't we just let it drop now – please?'

Louise came in at eleven o'clock, enthusing about the film she had seen, and raving about Ernie Partington, the fitter who had escorted her. 'I'm going out with him again on Friday. I really like him, girls, and I think he likes me, but I'm keeping my fingers crossed to make sure.'

'You'd better cross your legs, too,' Betty said, wickedly, making the girl blush with embarrassment.

'I hope it's the real thing, Lep,' Laura said, seriously. 'You deserve it.' She also hoped that her friend would never have to undergo the trauma of losing a boy she loved.

They said nothing to spoil Louise's obvious bliss when she returned on Friday night; they were fond of their little 'leprechaun' and were only too pleased that she was happy.

That weekend, her second leave from Bonachy due in a few days, Laura felt depressed. She had gone to Glasgow in May, but the boarding house she had found had felt alien to her, and, although she had seen a lot more of the city, she had been glad when it was time to return to Banffshire. Then Operation Overlord had started in June, and the pressure on the Ops Room had put everything else out of her head, but it had eased off now. She would have been quite happy to carry on without a break, but knew that it would not be allowed. Where would she go, that was the problem.

On an impulse, when the time came, she took her warrant out to London – perhaps to disprove Bill Darbourne's remark that it was a 'helluva journey'; perhaps to be somewhere that held no unpleasant memories, where she would be lost in anonymity.

When she set off, the challenge of breaking new ground buoyed up her spirits, but, waiting in Aberdeen Joint Station for a train, she remembered that the last time she had been there was on her way to Edinburgh to say goodbye to John Watson for ever. The same sickness clutched at the pit of her stomach, the same ache gnawed at her heart, and for several minutes she wallowed in misery. It was only three years ago, but it seemed like another life, another world, and so much had happened in between.

At last she stood up and walked over to the kiosk to buy something to read on her journey, and by the time she was served the gates were open and she joined the queue, showing her travel documents to the ticket collector on her way to the correct platform. Finding an empty carriage, she slung her bag up on the luggage rack and settled down next the window. Most of the other travellers going past were in the services, but there was a sprinkling of civilians, and Laura wondered where and why they were travelling, because there were huge posters everywhere demanding, 'Is your journey really necessary?' Was hers, for that matter?

Before long, her carriage was filling up. Two REME boys, a sailor and a Wren had crushed into the opposite side, and two women, one young and the other middle-aged, were facing the engine like herself. Then a tall Norwegian sailor popped his head round the door and sighed with relief when he saw the small space next to Laura. The rack was full, but he sat down with his kitbag between his feet.

Noticing that people were standing in the corridor now, Laura supposed that Bill Darbourne must have had to stand all the way at some time, but the sudden vibration of the carriage and the hiss of the engine building up steam made everything else go out of her head. She was on her way to London, where anything could happen . . . but she shouldn't expect too much, otherwise she might be disappointed.

After they left the station, she read her newspaper then

lay back, trying to shut her ears to the conversations around her, but she couldn't help hearing the woman telling the girl that she was on her way to see her son, injured in an air raid and now in hospital in London, and the girl responding by saying that she was on her way to meet her husband in Rosyth, where his ship was in for repairs after having been hit by a torpedo. Laura picked up her magazine, reflecting that it was odd how total strangers could talk on trains as though they had known each other all their lives.

'Excuse?' The Norwegian sailor had turned towards her and was pointing to her newspaper with his eyebrows raised in question. 'You read . . . yes?'

'I've finished with it.' Handing it over, she looked at him properly for the first time. The wide collar set off his broad shoulders; his dimpled smile sat rather impudently in a longish face; his blonde hair nestled against the tips of his ears; his eyes – not deep blue, more the colour of the sky in summer – were regarding her with some amusement. In great confusion, she looked away, but he said, 'Go . . . *hjem*?'

The last word, so like the Scots 'hame', made Laura smile. 'No, I'm not going home. I'm going to London on leave.'

'I go London. I see you, yes?'

'I wouldn't think so. London's a big place.' Her heart was fluttering as she bent her head to read. She had imagined that no man would have this effect on her again, but she hoped that she would run into him in London. It would help to fill the days which were looming emptily ahead. She laid down her magazine, aware that he was still watching her, and smiled to him. 'Is your ship based in Aberdeen?'

He seemed to understand. 'Aberdeen . . . *tre dag.*' He held up three fingers. 'I go hospital.' He shrugged, the English word eluding him, then said, '*Blindtarmbetendalse.*' Laying his hand low down on his right side, he grimaced to mime pain then drew his finger quickly across and pretended to pull something out.

Puzzling for a moment, Laura said, 'Appendicitis?'

He nodded eagerly. 'A . . . pen . . . dee . . . site . . . iss.'

'That was bad luck for you in a strange place.'

'Bad? No.' A mischievous glint came into his eyes now. 'Nurses good.'

'I bet they were.' Laura could picture them falling over each other to look after this gorgeous creature.

'I no spik English good. No read. Nurse get *Norske bøker.*' He shrugged again.

'One of the nurses got Norwegian books for you? Oh yes, I believe someone told me that Aberdeen had set up a Reading Room for Norwegians. But wait a minute, if you can't read English, why did you ask for my newspaper?'

Smiling broadly and winking, he pointed to himself then to her, implying that he had only wanted to talk to her. Laura laughed, but she was flattered by the compliment. 'Are you all right now?'

'All right?' He looked mystified.

'Better? Recovered? Well?' Laura tried to think of a word he could understand.

'Well?' The blue eyes cleared instantly. 'I well. *Bøt seile,* I no. Hull . . . two? . . . weeks?'

'You've to join your ship in Hull in two weeks, is that it? And you're going to London to pass the time?'

He nodded, delighted that she had understood so quickly,

but Laura had become conscious that the other people in the carriage were looking at them and smiling, so she picked up her magazine again. It was one thing to enter into a little conversation with a foreign sailor, but quite a different matter when the eyes and ears of the world were on them.

The other girl left the train at Edinburgh, presumably to catch a bus to Rosyth, and a lanky Australian took over the vacant seat. He sank down in it wearily, a sure sign that he had been standing for some time, then leaned back and closed his eyes.

As they were borne swiftly through the night, Laura and her fellow passengers dozed, waking fitfully each time the train stopped. There was a large exodus at York, where the young sailor and Wren got out, but their seats were filled immediately, and when the train restarted, Laura went to the toilet. She discovered that the corridor was still packed. Servicemen and women were sitting on the floor, on kitbags, even standing, and, picking her way over luggage and feet, she half regretted ever having set out on the crazy journey.

When she returned to her seat, the Norwegian placed his hand on his chest and said, '*Jeg heter* . . . Fridjof Hougland.'

Guessing that he was telling her his name, she smiled. 'I'm Laura Fullerton.'

'Laura? Good. *Møte* London, yes?'

'Meet you in London? Why not? We could go and see the sights together.'

'Sights?'

'The important places, the Tower, Buckingham Palace, that sort of thing.'

'Buckingham Palace? Yes!'

'OK, we'll go exploring.' It would probably be great fun taking this blonde Adonis around London even if she had never been there herself, and it wasn't too difficult to understand what he was saying, many of his words sounded similar to the dialect she had once despised.

'*Min alder* . . .' Using his fingers, he indicated twenty-four, which she took to be his age.

'I'm twenty-three.' Also using her fingers, she laughed.

'Excuse.' He looked hurt by her amusement.

'No, I'm sorry. I wasn't laughing at you. I don't speak any Norwegian at all, and I admire you for knowing as much English as you do. I just love the way you speak.'

He seemed pleased at this, and they talked quietly and companionably, if a little disjointedly, until the train steamed into King's Cross a little before seven. Allowing the other passengers to go first, Fridjof took her haversack down from the rack and held her arm until she jumped on to the platform, then, as they walked towards the barriers, he asked, '*Hvor skal du hen?*' and pointed forward.

From his gesture, Laura gathered that he was asking where she was going. 'I'll have to find a room in a hotel.'

'I komme?'

'You want to stay at the same place as me?' She had not foreseen this, but thought she may as well be hung for a sheep as a lamb. She had frittered away three years of her life and she was only young once. 'OK, if we're lucky.'

They went out into the grey light of the London dawn and found a hotel round the corner, where Laura asked if there were any vacancies. 'One room, dear?' The receptionist seemed to be quite accustomed to British girls taking a room with foreign servicemen.

Laura blushed. 'No, no. Two separate rooms.'

The painted eyebrows rose a fraction. 'We do have two small rooms vacant on the top floor. Would that suit?'

'That'll be fine.'

'One night, dear, or two?'

'I'm intending staying for nine nights, but I don't know about the gentleman. How many nights do you want to book for, Fridjof? Until you go to Hull?'

Before the sailor could reply, the woman said, 'Sorry, dear, but they're only free for six nights, then they're booked for two Yanks.'

'Well, that's it. We'll take them for the six nights.'

After they signed the register, the receptionist handed Laura two keys. 'Thirty-two and thirty-three, on the top floor. Breakfast's at half past eight, if you'd like some.'

'Yes, please. We've been travelling all night.'

When they reached the top floor, Laura said, 'I'll take thirty-two and you can have thirty-three. Now, I'm going to lie down for an hour, but I'll give you a knock at oh-eight-two-five.'

'Excuse?'

'Wait a minute.' Rummaging in her pocket, she produced a pencil and a piece of paper, then drew a clock face with the hands at twenty-five past eight. 'Do you understand?'

'You komme.' He pointed to her sketch and then to his own watch.

'That's it. See you later.'

Laura flopped on the bed when she went into her room. What on earth had she let herself in for? Betty and Lep were never going to believe this.

Chapter Thirty

They went sightseeing every day – Buckingham Palace and the Tower, as Laura had suggested, Trafalgar Square, St Paul's Cathedral, Hampton Court, Westminster Abbey – but the rubble and destruction they saw everywhere had far more impact on them than any of the historic buildings.

Britain's capital city had been subjected to tremendous bombardments, but the people were still cheery, still openly confident about winning the war. Cheeky signs were pasted over the boarded-up windows, or pithy slogans daubed on with paint, and Laura explained them as well as she could to the curious Fridjof, the humour, unfortunately, being somewhat lost in the retelling.

The weather was good, and they returned to the hotel each evening tired out. On the first night, the Norwegian bought a bottle of wine, which they drank in Laura's room, using the two tumblers from their wash basins and sitting together on her bed. As they discussed the places they had seen, he placed his arm round her shoulders, but she froze at the contact, holding herself rigid until his gentle, reassuring pressure made her relax a little – not too much, because she was aware that the situation could easily get out of hand.

He looked at her sadly. 'No like?'

How could she get out of this? 'I do like you,' she said, cautiously, 'but I don't want to get involved with anybody.'

'Involved?'

'I don't want to . . .' She couldn't say 'fall in love', that would be taking things too far. 'I don't want to like anybody too much.'

'I like too much.'

Perversely, Laura was a little disappointed that he did not even try to kiss her when he left soon afterwards, but she had only herself to blame.

They had a few drinks in a bar on the second night, but an alert sounded as they came out, and two air-raid wardens shepherded them through the piled sandbags into an Underground Station. Laura and Fridjof went down with the crowd, feeling quite safe amongst the devil-may-care, cocky Londoners, who appeared to be figuratively thumbing their noses at the Luftwaffe. The singing and joking passed the time so quickly that it didn't seem long until the All Clear sounded, although the warning had lasted for the best part of an hour.

'Not much doing tonight yet,' remarked a lively, white-haired woman as they moved to leave. 'It's them ruddy V2s that's the worst. Scare the pants off us old folk, they do.'

Her cackling laughter followed them as they made their way through the blanketed figures lying on the platform. Laura considered suggesting that they ought to remain there – it was only just after eleven and the guided missiles might still be to come – but Fridjof propelled her up the stairs. Thrusting aside her fears, she let herself be swept up into the open air.

In the street, a warden said, 'Mind how you go.' Winking lewdly, he added, 'And if you can't be good, be careful.'

Embarrassed, Laura did not attempt to explain this to her escort, and they carried on to their hotel. In her room, the Norwegian drew her towards him tentatively, and being in his arms felt so right to her that she let him kiss her . . . but only to satisfy him that she did like him.

There being only one chair, they sat down on her bed, and after they had been talking for a short time, Fridjof stood up and pulled her to her feet. This kiss, although longer, was no more demanding than the first, but it demolished the barriers which Laura had built around her heart. Stepping back, he saluted and said, softly, 'Godnatt, Laura.'

'Goodnight, Fridjof,' she whispered as he went out.

Lying down, she realized that his second kiss had done something to her, and try as she would she could not call up John Watson's image. It was three years since she had seen him, and she had burned the only photograph she had, but . . . could she be falling in love again? She certainly hoped that he had found someone else, too. She fell asleep thinking about the tall Norwegian with the dancing eyes and adorable accent.

Fridjof took her hand as they walked the following day. He was so considerate, such good company, that Laura had to admit to herself that she was falling in love. Correction – she had fallen in love.

Dancing in a Services Club that evening, she felt like a girl in her teens again, and had no inclination to mourn the wasted years. Fridjof had been worth waiting for. They had very little to drink, but returned to the hotel laughing at everything, and their love-making followed quite naturally.

'*Min kjaereste* Laura, *jeg elsker,*' Fridjof whispered against her hair, 'I much happy.'

She could tell that his first words were words of love, but smiled at his fractured English. 'I love you, my darling,' she murmured, and room thirty-three was left unused that night and for the rest of their time in the hotel.

On their last morning, Laura said, 'Will we look for somewhere else to stay? I've still got three days, and it's a week before you've to join your ship.'

He nodded, then grinned. 'Komme Hull?'

His pleading eyes were enough without the kiss he gave her to make sure she would agree, and when they arrived in Hull, Laura booked them into a hotel as Mr and Mrs Hougland. She got the impression that the receptionist guessed the truth, but she was passionately, recklessly, in love, and nothing was going to spoil it.

Walking about later, they saw dozens of foreign sailors, Fridjof shouting greetings to his own countrymen and saluting the Free French with the distinctive red pom-poms on their caps. Farther out of the town, a familiar name on a side street set Laura puzzling. Summergangs Road? Where had she heard that before? They were well past it before she remembered. It was where Donald Watson lived, the person she had always thought of as John's much older brother until that evening of revelation, which, surprisingly, did not seem nearly so bad now.

In her euphoric state, Laura took no time to think. 'I know some people who live in that street back there. Would you mind if we pay them a quick call since we're here?'

Fridjof could understand, or make a guess at, most of what she said now, and they turned and went hand in hand into Summergangs Road, but, walking up the Watsons' path, Laura wondered if this was a wise move. She had seen Margaret and Donald only once or twice a year before the war, but they were still links in the chain she had snapped in 1941.

Before she could walk off, Donald – now a rather stocky man in his late forties – opened the door. 'Laura Fullerton! I saw you from the window, and you haven't changed a bit.'

He ushered them into a small sitting room, where a petite woman rose to greet them. 'What a pleasant surprise, Laura.' Margaret kissed Laura's cheek then turned to the sailor.

'Our son, James, is in the Navy, too . . . the Royal Navy.'

'This is Fridjof Hougland, he's Norwegian.' Laura guessed that Donald and his wife knew of her previous troubles, but they were talking now to Fridjof, and she sat down, pleased that he seemed to be coping, even enjoying himself.

The Watsons made their unexpected callers very welcome, and after some time, Margaret said, 'You'll stay for tea, of course. Come through and help me get things ready, Laura, and we can have a chat at the same time.'

The girl followed her into the kitchen rather reluctantly, knowing that this was a ruse to get her alone, and dreading what might be said. Margaret closed the door. 'Grandma Watson wrote and told us everything, Laura, and we were truly sorry for you and John, though we could pity the two mothers just as much. It must have been a terrible ordeal for them.'

'They don't deserve your pity,' Laura muttered. 'They carried on a horrible deception for years and years.'

'They only did what they thought was best at the time,

my dear, don't forget that. I know you walked out, but did you know that your father made your mother leave, too? Grandma has never heard from her and still worries about her.'

Laura didn't know what to say or think about this; it was difficult hearing about people she had once loved when she had shut them out of her life. This visit had definitely been a mistake, and she wished she had never given in to the stupid impulse. 'I didn't know about . . . my mother,' she said, at last, 'and I do feel sorry for her if Dad put her out, but, to be quite honest, I feel more sorry for him.'

Noticing that the tears were not far off, Margaret opened the door and said, 'Donald, why don't you take Fridjof out for a walk? Take him in for a pint when the pubs open, if you like. Tea won't be ready until after six.'

She made a sign to her husband to let him know that she wanted to be rid of them, and when they went out, she led the girl back into the sitting room. 'I know it's been a long time,' she said, as they sat down, 'and you've probably pushed it right to the back of your mind, but it would be much better to give it an airing and get it out of your system completely. Life's too short to harbour bitterness.'

After a brief pause, Laura began, hesitantly at first, but gaining confidence as she went on, describing her feelings as well as the facts and letting everything come out just as she remembered it, while the woman listened silently. 'I swore I'd never forgive Mum, or Helen,' she gulped at last, twisting her now sodden handkerchief.

'How do you feel about them now?' Margaret asked, gently. 'Have you exorcized the evil spirit you've been nurturing all these years?'

'I do feel better now I've told somebody,' Laura admitted in some surprise. 'I suppose I'd been letting it fester in my mind, instead of trying to understand how it happened.' She gratefully accepted the clean handkerchief Margaret handed her.

'You condemned them too quickly, that was the trouble. It's easy to blame, but when you take time to think clearly, you can usually find a good reason for someone's behaviour.'

'I see that now. Helen must have felt awful when her own baby died, and it's not surprising she came to believe John was hers. Mum had been hurt at not being able to acknowledge her son, and I can understand now why she gave him up. It must have been hard for her, and she couldn't foresee . . .' Laura took a deep breath. 'Oh, Margaret, you're a clever woman. I honestly do feel different about it now.'

Margaret smiled. 'Good. I'm glad we got that sorted out, and we'd better start getting this tea ready now.'

'I'll write to Dad when I get back,' Laura said, when they returned to the kitchen. 'I feel awful about him being on his own for so long, but I didn't know. Anyway, now that I do, I can help him to trace Mum . . . if he's forgiven her too and wants to get her back.'

'If he doesn't, you'll have to persuade him.' Margaret knew that her counselling had been successful so far, but she still had something to say, the real test. 'John was married a few months ago.' She half expected another flood of tears and hurried on. 'Agnes is from London and she's a really nice girl. They're very happy.'

'Oh, I'm glad to hear that.' Laura's spontaneous reply

378

banished all Margaret's doubts as to the cure being complete. 'I hoped he'd found somebody else, too.'

'Oh, have you . . . ?'

'I thought you'd have realized I'm in love with Fridjof. Thank God I've got that other business out of my system. I'll tell him about it, though – I don't mean to keep any secrets from him.'

'I'm glad I've helped you to lay your ghosts.' Margaret pulled a basket of vegetables out of the cupboard, and set about peeling and slicing.

Laura told her then about Pat Haggarty, another part of her life which she had been unable to talk about before, and Margaret was vehement in her condemnation of all wars, and more sympathetic than ever towards her young visitor.

After a short silence, Laura said, 'Let's get off sad things. I'm going to look forward from now on, not back.'

'That's the best way.'

By the time the men returned, the meal was ready, the two women were laughing at something Laura had said, and Donald, who hadn't known what to expect, was greatly relieved.

At ten past ten, after a very pleasant evening, Laura said they would have to go and was pleased that they were not asked to stay the night. She knew that Margaret would not approve of them sharing a room.

'You must come to see us again.' Donald held up Laura's jacket for her. 'How long are you to be here?'

'I've to leave on Saturday, unfortunately, but Fridjof's here until his shop docks, four days after I go back.'

Slapping the Norwegian on the back, Donald said, 'You

can have a bed here when Laura's away. It's not much fun being in a hotel on your own, and I'd be glad to have some male company for a change. This woman henpecks me.'

Fridjof looked bewildered, but once he understood that it was an invitation, he grinned. 'Laura go, I komme.'

'Have a good journey back, Laura,' Donald went on, 'and I'm very glad you came to see us.'

'So am I,' Laura breathed, 'you don't know how glad. And thank you again, Margaret, for setting me straight.'

'Let me know what happens.'

In bed, Laura told Fridjof the whole story of her living nightmare of three years earlier, having to make double explanations when he couldn't understand. She was grateful to Margaret Watson for purging her of the bitternesss which had consumed her for so long. She could talk about it to her lover, calmly and dispassionately. Their life together – and she was sure that they would have a life together – would be frank and open right from the start, with no secrets to foul things up. After she stopped speaking, her emotions clearly exhausted, Fridjof cradled her in his arms all night.

Awake first in the morning, Laura glanced idly round the room. A dressing table with mirror, a wardrobe with mirror, a mirror over the tiny wash basin, one rickety chair. This place must be meant for couples who were interested only in the big double bed, she thought, before her eyes moved on again. A window shaded by heavy black-out curtains, an ancient radiator, a small cabinet at – she looked round to check – each side of the bed. One was bound to contain the obligatory chamber pot, but what would be in the other? In the London hotel there had been a pile of sexy American magazines which had shocked her when she found them, but they wouldn't shock her now, not after what she and Fridjof had been doing for the past week.

Need for him rising within her, she sat up to kiss him, resting on one elbow and letting her free hand run over his downy chest. His blue eyes flew open, and his hand guided hers down until she could feel the rise of his need for her.

'*Min kjaereste,*' he whispered, lifting his hand to her breast, then adding thickly, 'He ready.'

'I know,' she murmured. 'Me, too.'

His mouth covered hers while his hand removed hers from his beating manhood. 'He much ready.'

By the time he entered her, she was also near the stage where she would be 'much ready', but he took his time, bringing her slowly to a point where she pleaded with him frantically to hurry. 'Good?' he asked, a few moments later.

'Oh, yes, very good. I love you, Fridjof.'

'*Jeg elsker,* Laura.'

She knew now that he was using his own language to tell her he loved her, and her heart swelled as she watched him reaching for his cigarettes. It was the first time he had ever smoked in their bedroom, but she did not reprove him, saying only, 'If we don't hurry, we're going to be late for breakfast.'

Swinging his feet to the floor, Fridjof stood up, eyeing her naked body with pleasure as she jumped out at the other side of the bed. She no longer felt embarrassed by this, it gave her a chance to study him, too – the broad chest, the firm flat stomach, the narrow hips, the . . .

He gave a soft laugh as he followed her gaze and said, ruefully, 'He sleep . . . for night.'

She flushed, not really having been conscious of letting her eyes rest on the pathetic little thing which, only a short time before, had been a throbbing monster. She was aware that he was not inexperienced as a lover, but he was twenty-four, after all, and she could not expect him to have led a life of celibacy. She was content that she was the one he loved now.

On their last full day, they walked along the coast until they felt tired and sat down to eat the fruit they had bought in a little shop they had passed. Then they lay back, side by side on the grass, and, as she watched the gulls swooping and screeching above them, Laura thought that this was something else to remember. Her entire leave had been spent carving memories with this loving, lovable man, memories she would cherish till the day she died.

'Fridjof,' she said, softly, 'will you remember all this when you're back on your ship?'

Rolling over, he stroked her cheek. 'I ever remember.' He took her in his arms then, kissing her again and again to prove it, but suddenly drawing away and pulling her roughly to her feet. 'Komme, Laura, hotel, eat, bed.' Looking down at his straining trousers, he chuckled. 'He no sleep. He ready.'

'Oh, you.' She gave him a small push, but her heart was racing in anticipation of their last night.

In the hotel dining room after their meal, he grabbed her hand urgently and led her upstairs to their room, and although it was not quite half past eight, they undressed and went to bed. Fridjof's need for her by this time was so obvious that she couldn't help giggling somewhat nervously, but he said, solemnly, 'Jeg elsker. I love you, Laura. He love you.'

'I love you, and him too,' she managed to say before his

382

body enveloped hers and she was transported into a world and time where nothing mattered except their passion.

They were asleep before eleven, exhausted by their love-making as much as by their outing, and it seemed no time until they received the early morning call they had requested.

When they were ready to leave the hotel, Fridjof put his hands on her shoulders and looked at her seriously. 'Laura, you be my wife, yes?'

'I should hope so, after all this.' She laughed, but his puzzled, disappointed expression made her kiss him. 'Yes, my darling, I'll be honoured to be your wife. We don't have time now to discuss it, so we'll have to do it by letters.' She wrote her address on a sheet of hotel note-paper, then looked enquiringly at him. 'What about you? Aren't you going to tell me where I can write to you?'

He shrugged sadly. 'I no . . . *skrive Engelsk*. Captain *skrive* . . . I *laere*.'

Walking to the station, arms round waists, their happiness was blunted by the imminent parting. Fridjof clung to Laura on the platform, as if he were afraid to let her go in case she would be lost to him for good, and she had to struggle out of his embrace to board the train.

'Goodbye, my darling,' she called, stretching as far as she could out of the window.

'Goodbye, Laura, wife,' he replied, tears edging out of his eyes.

She blew a kiss, waved until the forlorn figure waving back had dwindled away and disappeared, then sat down to relive the most outstanding, most wonderful, most marvel-lous ten days of her whole life.

Chapter Thirty-one

Her two room-mates were out when Laura arrived back at Mrs Adams' house. Her journey had been tiring, but she did not want to go to sleep until she had told Betty and Louise what had happened. Lying out on top of the quilt, she recalled Fridjof's tender passion of the evening before and knew that her love for him, although it had blossomed so quickly, was deeper, more exciting, more satisfying, than her feelings for John Watson had ever been.

She had dozed off before her friends came in, and woke as Betty stormed into the room. 'That was a lousy evening, Lep. I'll never go out with you on a blind date again. That Bob, wherever you dug him up, was a first-class creep. Oh, hi, Laura,' she added, noticing her for the first time.

'Hello, Laura.' Louise took off her jacket and hung it up. 'I'm really sorry about it, Betty, but Bob was the only one Ernie could find who didn't have a date for tonight.'

'That doesn't surprise me.' Betty rolled her eyes. 'I didn't say anything at first when his hands started to wander, I just shoved them away when they got to where they shouldn't be, but when he tried to give me a slobbery great kiss, that was the end! I thought I was being sucked in by a vacuum cleaner.'

'He wasn't that bad,' Louise protested. 'His ears maybe stuck out a bit and his nose was reddish, but I thought he'd quite nice eyes.'

'Nice eyes?' Betty exploded. 'I hadn't time to look at his eyes for keeping track of his hands. It was like wrestling with an octopus, but you were too taken up with your Ernie to notice. I'd to slap his face eventually, and I told him I'd gone out to see a film, not to be manhandled by an ape. Yeuck! I feel sick just thinking about it.'

'I wondered why you suddenly marched out of the hall.'

'That's why, Lep, but you didn't need to come with me, I'd have managed on my own. Thank God you're back, Laura. At least I'll have you for company again.'

'Sorry I ignored you, Laura,' Louise said, 'but as you'll have gathered there's been a crisis. How was your leave?'

'I thought you'd never ask.' Laura smiled broadly as she sat up. She had been itching to spring her surprise on them, and at last the moment had come. 'Hold on to your hats, this is going to make your hair stand on end.'

Louise waited expectantly, but Betty said, 'I'd prefer a good laugh after what I've just been through.'

'I don't think it's funny, but maybe you will. Are you ready? Well, I've been living in sin with a Norwegian sailor.' Laura savoured their astonishment to the full.

'You've been what?' Betty gasped. 'Oh, come off it, Laura. You're handing us some duff gen.'

Rather shocked, Louise said, 'Are you pulling our legs?'

'No, it's the truth. We met on the train going down and he's tall and blonde, with gorgeous blue eyes and an accent that makes me go all shivery.'

385

'Well, go on,' Betty urged, impatiently. 'How did this living in sin bit start?'

'He wanted to stay in the same hotel as me, so we took two rooms . . . just for six nights, because . . .'

Betty's face dropped. 'Two rooms? I might have known.'

'He only used his room for two nights, then . . . well, it just sort of happened, and we only used one after that. Then I went to Hull with him, and we booked in as husband and wife.'

'My God, Laura, you're a dark horse! You always said you wouldn't get involved with anybody, and now . . .' For once, Betty Fry was lost for words.

'Love makes a girl do things she'd never have dreamt of before, isn't that right, Lep?' Laura winked mischievously.

Louise looked flustered. 'Ernie and I have never . . .'

'I was only teasing you. But Fridjof and I had . . .'

'Freejoff?' Betty screwed her nose up in puzzlement.

'Fridjof Hougland, and don't ask me how it's spelt.'

'Freejoff Hoogland?' Betty repeated, then grinned. 'What a mouthful, and it really exercises your lips, doesn't it?'

'Wait, that's not all.' Laura told them about her visit to the Watsons. 'Margaret gave me a lecture . . . so I'm going to write to Dad tomorrow. You'll be pleased about that, Betty.'

'Yes, I am.'

'But you ain't heard nothing yet. Before I left, Fridjof asked me to be his wife, and I said yes.'

Grabbing her hands, Betty danced round the room with her. 'You've slept with a man and you're going to marry him – all in ten days? That's pretty good going.'

386

'It's usually done the other way round,' Louise pointed out, in her usual prim manner.

The other two collapsed on Laura's bed. 'Oh, Lep, trust you,' Betty giggled. 'But do you know anything about him, Laura? What sort of work he does in civvy street, etcetera.'

'He told me about his family one afternoon we were out walking. His father owns a sawmill somewhere near Trondheim, and Fridjof and his two brothers worked there before the Nazis invaded Norway. They'd got away by the skin of their teeth, apparently. Their mother died when the youngest one was just a toddler, but their aunt, the father's sister, brought them up. She's getting old, though, and Fridjof says she'll welcome me with open arms. He can't express himself in English very well yet, but that's what he meant.'

Betty's eyes had widened again. 'So you'll be going to Norway after the war? But you'll get married before that, of course, so when's the wedding going to be?'

'We hadn't time to discuss it, but he's going to write . . . well, get his Captain to write for him.'

'Can I be bridesmaid? Can't you just see me carrying a posy and looking like the fairy on a Christmas tree?' Betty placed her finger under her chin and made a small curtsey.

The idea of Betty, so tall and well-built, sitting on a tree and looking like a fairy doll, was so incongruous that it sent her two friends into near hysterics, and they were still shrieking with laughter when the door was flung open by an apparition in a thick flannel dressing gown, head bristling with metal curlers. 'What's going on in here? You're making enough noise to waken the dead.'

'Sit down, Mrs Adams,' Betty soothed, guiding her to a chair. 'Laura's going to marry a Norwegian sailor she met.'

'Oh, that's different.' A huge smile replaced the frown. 'Congratulations, Laura, m'dear, and . . . wait a minute! I've a bottle of whisky downstairs.'

She hurried out and returned carrying a bottle and four glasses. 'I've been keeping this for a celebration some time, but there's been nothing to celebrate for years.'

After her third glass, she became nostalgic about her own wedding day. 'My Aleckie was a trawl skipper and we'd a right big do – all our relations were there.'

'They're nearly all related here,' Betty whispered to Laura, 'so it must have been some affair.'

Chuckling, Laura whispered back, 'I can just imagine them hooching and skirling all night.'

Refilling her glass, Mrs Adams continued, her eyes misty. 'It went on till six in the morning, and it might have carried on if the men hadna had to sail with the tide. The good Lord only knows how they got their boats out, they were that drunk.' She let out a loud cackle.

Betty winked at Laura and Louise. 'So you hadn't had your first night until your husband came back, then?'

Mrs Adams laid her finger on the side of her nose. 'We werena daft. We had it the night before, for we knew what the wedding night would be like.'

She spluttered, and the other three howled with mirth, then Betty told a few bawdy jokes about newly-weds, so it was quite some time before the household settled down.

Laura wrote to her father the following day. She had been trying to think how to word the letter, but finally settled on simplicity and truth, and just told him that

Margaret Watson had made her see sense and asked if she could visit him on Saturday of the following week. His reply came in two days, rather guarded, but agreeing to the visit, so she went to Aberdeen on her next twenty-four-hour pass. She had made up her mind to be calm and sensible, but as soon as she went into the bungalow her father gathered her in his arms and she burst into happy tears.

David spoke first. 'Why didn't you write before, Laura? I'd nothing to do with the mess things were in.'

Wiping her eyes, she defended herself. 'You told me you were leaving home too, Dad, remember?'

'I changed my mind.' His eyes dropped. 'I . . . I made your mother leave instead.'

'I didn't know about that till Margaret Watson told me. I thought Mum would be here, that's why I never wrote, but I've forgiven her now.' Assuming that it would take a little diplomacy to make him do likewise, she said gently, 'She'd been left to bring a child into the world on her own, and when people took it for granted that John was Helen's baby, it saved any scandal about Mum, and then after Helen . . . oh, Dad, can't you see why Mum did what she did?'

'I do see, Laura,' he muttered, 'but I was hurt that night because she hadn't trusted me enough to confide in me.'

'It wasn't like that. She was in agony over having to give up her child, and she was frightened she would lose you. She had to live with her guilt for more than twenty years, not able to share the burden with anybody. Can't you forgive her, too? You must have loved her once.'

David's anguish showed in his eyes. 'I still love her, Laura, and I forgave her long ago. I've missed her more

389

than you'll ever know, and I wish I knew where she was so I could tell her I need her.'

'I mean to find her, for both of us. First, I'm going to ask Helen Watson if she's any idea . . .'

'She hadn't, the last time I saw her.' A faint ray of hope had appeared on his face. 'But that was ages ago, and maybe she's heard by this time.' He eased his leg out and massaged it, excusing himself, when he saw his daughter watching, by saying, 'It gives a wee twinge now and then.'

She tried to cheer him. 'If all else fails, we can get the police to issue a wanted poster.' His look of alarm made her hurry on. 'Something along the lines of . . . Elspeth Fullerton, née Gray, five feet one inch tall, light brown hair greying in parts, wanted by husband and daughter.' Her laugh was a trifle unsteady.

David smiled crookedly. 'Her hair used to be golden, and she's desperately wanted by her husband.'

'Me, too.' Laura hesitated. 'I haven't told you yet how I came to be speaking to Margaret.'

'I thought you must have been stationed near Hull before you went to Banffshire.'

'I was stationed at Wick before, but I went to London on my last leave, and ended up in Hull.' Her eyes softened.

Observing this, David said, 'It's something to do with a lad, I take it?'

'It's everything to do with a lad, a Norwegian lad and his name's Fridjof Hougland. He's a sailor I got speaking to on the train and we booked into the same hotel.' Seeing her father's eyebrows lift, she said, 'I know what you're thinking, and you're absolutely right. We slept in separate rooms for two nights, but after that we only used one.' Pulling a face, she added, 'Does that shock you?'

'Nothing shocks me nowadays.'

'It's OK, he's asked me to marry him. We'd to leave after six days – the rooms had been booked – and he'd to join his ship at Hull, so I went there with him. You see, he'd had his appendix out in Aberdeen, and he'd missed one trip.'

'And when you were in Hull, you met Margaret Watson?'

'Not actually met. We passed their street and I went in without thinking. She made me see how stupid and selfish I'd been – that's why I wrote to you – and I must find Mum because I want her to be at my wedding.'

Clasping his hands together, David said hopefully, 'It's going to be like it was before, isn't it? All three of us together again?'

'Plus a new son-in-law, don't forget.' Laura got to her feet. 'I'll have a quick wash then go over to Quarry Street.' She glanced round approvingly. 'You've kept things looking quite nice, Dad.'

'I've done my best. I've even polished your mother's clock every week. I used to resent it being here, you know, because I was sure it reminded her of him. I made her life a misery at times with my jealousy, but it hasn't bothered me for a long time. In fact, not long after she left – no, I'd better call a spade a spade, she didn't leave of her own free will, I put her out. Anyway, she'd only been gone a week or so when I came to my senses about it. John Forrest meant to give her the clock on their wedding day, but . . .'

His pause made his daughter grip his shoulder in sympathy, but he went on, '. . . but he was killed. Your mother had made no secret of having loved him, and it was natural enough that he'd . . . made love to her before he went to France. I'd have done the same myself before I went back to Belgium, if she'd given me the chance, but she still hadn't got over him at that time. So you see, I'm not jealous now, and I love the clock as much as she did, for it just tells me that another man had loved her as much as I did . . . as I do, and I'm grateful for that. Oh, I'm not explaining it very well, but can you understand what I mean?'

'Yes, Dad, I think I can, and I'm glad you got over it.'

'I'll have to make your mother understand as well, once she comes home . . . maybe you'll help?'

'I'll try, if we find her. I'd better go and see Helen, that's the first step.'

'Laura Fullerton! What a grand surprise.' In spite of the welcome, there was a hint of wariness in Helen Watson's tired eyes.

'Helen, I'm here for two reasons. First, to apologize for what I said to you the last time I was here, but as you'll understand, I was so upset I didn't know what I was saying.'

'Lassie, I understood only too well. There's no need to apologize, we'll let bygones be bygones and just forget all about it.'

'Thanks, Helen, but the other thing is, I want to find Mum. Did she ever write to tell you where she was?'

'Never,' Helen said, sadly. 'I've been worried sick, and I'm glad you want to find her.'

'Could she have gone back to Auchlonie?'

'I doubt it, for she'd nobody left there.' After thinking for a moment, Helen snapped her fingers. 'I've just minded, what about Mrs Robb? They were aye awful friendly.'

Laura's face lit up. 'I'd forgotten about Mrs Robb.'

'And there's your mother's Auntie Janet.'

'I didn't know Mum had an aunt in Aberdeen.'

'She was a nasty besom, and she put Elspeth out, so I wouldn't think she'd go back there.' Becoming aware that the girl was looking somewhat uneasy, Helen asked, 'Is something bothering you, lass?'

'No, there's nothing.'

'Aye, there is so something. You'd best tell me, so I can sort it out, whatever it is.'

'Well, I never knew she had an aunt, and why did the woman put her out? Is this something else she was hiding?'

'No, no, Laura. She bade wi' her auntie for a while when she came to the town first, but they'd a terrible row, and she never went near the woman after that.' Helen paused, wrinkling her nose. 'She'd have been desperate, of course, so you never ken, and if I mind right, this Janet bade near the Co-opie baker in Rosemount Viaduct. She was the kind that aye made out she was real poorly, and her poor man did everything for her. Elspeth liked him, so I suppose it's just possible she . . . his first name was Harry – I mind that, for it was the same as my sister's man's – but his last name . . . began wi' a B, I'm near sure.'

'Baxter? Beattie? Burnett? Bremner?' Laura suggested, helpfully. 'Bruce? Buchan? Bisset?'

'No, it wasn't any o' them, and I'll mind myself, if you'll just let me be.'

'It should be easy to find them, once I know their name.'

393

'Aye, you'd just need to look at the nameplates on the street doors . . . Bain! That's it. Harry Bain – I knew it would come back to me.'

'Thanks, Helen, at least that's something. I'll try Mrs Robb before I go home to Dad, and if I've no luck, I'll go to see the Bains on my way to the country bus.'

'Let me know if you find your mother, Laura, for she's been on my conscience these years past. But I'm forgetting, how's your father?'

'He's wonderful, considering. By the way, I may as well tell you – I'm going to marry a Norwegian sailor.'

'I some thought that would happen, after Margaret said they'd had a visit from you. Her and Donald think a lot o' your lad, and she said she'd had a long talk wi' you.'

'Yes, it was Margaret who set me straight. You've got a very good daughter-in-law, Helen.'

The woman smiled. 'It's two good daughter-in-laws I've got, for John's married now, and all.'

'I was really happy to hear about John. We both seem to have survived things pretty well, haven't we. Well, I'd better go.' Laura walked into the small lobby, and Helen breathed a sigh of relief when she closed the door.

Ann Robb shook her head. 'No, I haven't heard from your mother since she came here the morning she left home.'

Laura pounced. 'She did come here? What did she say? Did she give you any idea of where she was going?'

'No, I . . . wait.' Ann jerked up. 'I reminded her about the money that was left in trust for her.'

Laura looked perplexed. 'Money in trust?'

'I suppose you were too young to remember, but when

your grandmother died, her belongings were sold and the money put in trust for your mother, so she was going to Auchlonie when she left here, to see the solicitor. I don't recall his name, but there would only be one in a place that size.'

Jumping up, Laura exclaimed, 'Thank you, Mrs Robb, that's the first lead I've got so far.'

'Good luck, my dear, and I'd love to see her again, if you succeed in tracing her.'

'I'll succeed,' Laura assured her.

When she told her father what Mrs Robb had said, he was delighted. 'I'd forgotten about that money. It's the first piece of the jig-saw, isn't it?'

'Don't build your hopes up too high, Dad,' she cautioned him. 'It might be a dead end.'

David's eager face fell. 'Do you think the solicitor won't tell you where your mother went?'

'It's not a case of not telling me, he probably won't know where she went after she'd seen him.'

'Did Helen know anything about her?'

'No, but she did say that Mum had an aunt in Rosemount Viaduct, though it's unlikely she went there.' She told him why, because he was just as surprised as she had been that his wife had any relatives in the city. 'I may as well go and ask the Bains if they know anything about Mum,' she went on, 'if I can find them. Helen didn't know their number. If I get nothing from them, I'll go to Auchlonie on my next pass. I haven't time to go today.'

'You'll come home again soon, won't you?'

A pang of guilt coursed through her at not having been in touch with her father for so long. 'I've forty-eight hours coming up shortly. Now, what about something to eat?'

'I'd nearly forgotten, I made a casserole. I hardly ever use up my meat coupons, so I was able to get a nice bit of steak down town yesterday for you.'

'Are you a good cook, Dad?'

He gave a self-conscious smile. 'I manage.'

Chatting over their meal, they gradually slipped back into the old loving father/daughter relationship, and by the time they were finished, she felt easy enough to tease him as she pushed her plate away. 'That wasn't too bad, Dad. It's a bit better than I expected, anyway.'

David pretended to cuff her ear. 'I thought it was cordon bleu standard, myself.'

Swivelling round, Laura stood up. I'm going to need all my time if I'm to stop off at Rosemount Viaduct. Do you mind if I don't help with the dishes?'

'No, that's all right.' He looked somewhat ashamed. 'I'm sorry I'm leaving it all to you, Laura, but I couldn't meet your mother again in a public place. I hope you understand.'

'Of course I do, and I'm quite happy to act the detective. I've always fancied myself as a Miss Marple.'

His face holding a gleam of hope, David said, 'Couldn't we write to the solicitor? It would save time.'

'It would, but we don't know his name and address. Mrs Robb said there was likely only one in Auchlonie, but . . .'

'Whatever you think, then.' He sounded disappointed.

Twirling her cap in her hands, Laura considered for a moment. 'I think the personal touch would be best, and I want to see Mum's reaction when she knows we want her home.'

'I suppose you're right. Well, good luck at your first port of call.'

Laura smiled wryly. 'I'll likely need all the luck I can get having to face the notorious Auntie Janet.' Making a face, she slapped her cap on her head and picked up her respirator and haversack. 'Cheerio, Dad. See you soon.'

'As soon as you can,' David murmured, 'and don't forget to write to let me know what this Janet says.'

To save fuel for the duration of the war, there was only a shuttle bus service to Mile End, so while Laura waited for the connecting tram, she crossed her fingers that she could find the people she was looking for, but she had to scan three sets of nameplates near the Co-operative bakery before she saw 'H. Bain'. A pulse beat in her throat as she walked through the dark lobby and climbed the stairs to the first floor, and her hand trembled as she pushed the bell button.

A thin-faced, sharp-eyed woman opened the door a crack, her expression deeply suspicious. 'Yes?' she barked.

'You won't know me . . .' Laura began, hesitantly.

'No, I don't know you. Who are you and what do you want?'

'I'm Laura Fullerton, Elspeth Gray's daughter, and I . . .'

'Elspeth Gray?' Her voice sneered now. 'Lizzie wrote me years ago that she'd a grand-daughter, but you're not the baby Elspeth was expecting when she was here.'

'Look, Auntie Janet . . .'

'I'm not your auntie, and I don't even consider myself your mother's auntie – that was finished when . . .'

'Can I come in, Mrs Bain?' Laura interrupted. 'I don't want to discuss this where your neighbours can hear.'

'Whatever you've got to say, you can say it right there.'

'If that's what you want.' The girl returned the frosty glare. 'Do you know where my mother is?'

'She's walked out on you, has she? That doesn't surprise me – she always took her own way without a thought to anybody else. I've no idea where she is, and what's more, I don't care.'

The girl's hopes had plunged as soon as she saw the unpleasant face, but, thinking that Harry Bain couldn't be as bad as his wife – nobody could – she made one last attempt. 'Is your husband at home, please?'

'My husband died two years ago.' The steely eyes narrowed in self-pity. 'I've had to do everything for myself ever since, and me so ill some days, I was hardly able to lift a finger.'

'I'm sure it didn't do you any harm.' Laura couldn't resist the jibe, and when the door slammed in her face, she stuck out her tongue. 'Twisted old bitch!'

Too early for her bus, she sat for a good half hour in the Union Terrace Gardens, seething with anger at the reception she had received, and despondent because she was no nearer tracing her mother. But she still had to contact the solicitor in Auchlonie. He must know something – he was her only hope.

Chapter Thirty-two

Before she received Fridjof's letter, Laura had fluctuated between imagining that something terrible had happened to him, and doubting if he had actually proposed at all.

'Maybe he's got a wife and kids in Norway,' she had said to Betty Fry one day when she was feeling particularly low.

Betty, who had been thinking along the same lines, had nevertheless hastened to console her. 'I'm sure he'd have told you if he had. Have patience.'

Laura tore open the envelope anxiously when it came. 'It's OK,' she said, in great relief. 'He's still speaking about marriage, though he didn't write himself. But this puts my mind at ease, because his captain would know if there was any reason why Fridjof and I shouldn't be married.'

'If any person present knows of any just cause,' Betty intoned, 'let him speak now or forever hold his . . .'

'When's the wedding to be, Laura?' Louise interrupted.

'His ship's coming to Aberdeen for a few days in January, and we can fix it up, then. Oh, God, that's months yet.'

Betty looked sympathetic. 'It'll soon pass.'

Laura was looking longingly at the signature, the only thing her lover had written – a large scrawled 'Fridjof'. Oh my darling, I love you, she thought, or as he himself would say it, *Min kjaereste, jeg elsker.* 'This bloody war!' she burst out, suddenly. 'Keeping people apart like this.'

'If it hadn't been for the bloody war, you wouldn't have met him in the first place,' Betty reminded her, 'but it's bound to be over soon. I'd say the Germans are coming to the end of their tether.'

Cheering a little, Laura said, 'Maybe it'll be finished by the time we're married.'

'It's going to be funny being back in civvy street,' Betty remarked. 'I'll be five years older than I was when I joined up, and it won't be the same. No excitement, no nothing except trying to find a decent job, or preferably a decent husband, to keep me in the luxury to which I have never been accustomed . . . ho, ho! But you won't have to worry about that, Laura, you lucky thing.'

'Neither will I,' remarked Louise. 'Ernie proposed last night, and I accepted.'

'Lep Wilson! Why didn't you tell us when you came back?' Betty couldn't understand how any girl could have kept such exciting information to herself until the next morning.

'I wanted to get used to the idea first.' Louise smiled shyly. 'Could we arrange a double wedding, Laura? That's why I wanted to know if your Norwegian had set the date.'

'What?' Betty pretended to be horrified. 'And do me out of a second chance to shine as bridesmaid?'

'I'd quite like a double wedding, Lep,' Laura said, 'but I don't know when or where ours will be. When depends on us both being available at the same time, and where depends on where Fridjof's boat happens to dock.'

'Oh, well, I suppose we'll have to wait and see.' Louise seemed rather disappointed.

Laura, who had been looking forward to penning her first love letter, felt depressed at being denied that pleasure, and it would be a long time before she saw Fridjof again. Could she survive months of worrying about him? And she still had to find her mother – that was a big enough worry in itself.

As soon as she was given the date of her forty-eight-hour pass, Laura wrote to David. 'I'm off Saturday and Sunday, but I'll go to Auchlonie before I come home, to save time. If I find out anything from the solicitor, I'll go to wherever Mum is, but I'll definitely be home that night, whatever happens, though it might be fairly late – or fairly early, if I've no luck. So keep your fingers crossed that Mum'll be with me.'

On the Friday, she asked several RAF drivers if they were going anywhere near Auchlonie the following morning, but the nearest she could get was a lift from one who had to collect a senior officer from Keith railway station. It wasn't ideal, but at least she could get a train there to take her the rest of the way, otherwise she would have to travel to Aberdeen and back, which would take much longer.

When she arrived in Auchlonie on Saturday, she approached the stationmaster first. 'Excuse me, I'm trying to find a solicitor here, but I don't know his name.'

The man looked surprised, but answered readily. 'It's Mr Reid you'll be wanting. Turn left when you go out, carry on to the High Street and turn right. He's a few doors along.'

'Thank you very much.'

Walking purposefully to the exit, Laura's mind was in a whirl. Was it left then right, or the other way round? No, it was the first way – left, right, like marching. She found the office with no difficulty, and asked the young girl at the desk if she could see Mr Reid.

'Have you an appointment, Miss . . . ?'

'Fullerton,' Laura supplied. 'No, I'm afraid I don't have an appointment, but it's very important.' She tried to remain calm – or to give the appearance of being calm – but it was very difficult.

'I'll find out if he can see you.' The girl disappeared through a door marked 'Private' and came back in a few seconds. 'Go straight in, Miss Fullerton.'

'Thank you.' Laura's legs were shaking as she walked into the solicitor's private office, but she was immediately struck by the drabness of the room. Everything in it was some shade of brown, except the filing cabinet which was dark grey. The walls were wood-panelled halfway up and had been painted a fawny colour above that, but time and smoke had left their mark; the linoleum was brown, with several bare patches from the traffic of many feet; the huge desk was made of oak; the chairs were upholstered in dark brown leather. The only relief was provided by Mr Reid himself, a stout little figure with a bush of pure white hair. Above rosy cheeks, his bright blue eyes gave the same welcome as his smile. 'You wish to consult me, Miss Fullerton?'

'Yes . . . no . . . well . . . not exactly consult,' Laura stammered, not sure of what to say now that she was face to face with him at last. He was regarding her with some curiosity, so she tried to explain. 'You see . . .'

'Are you Elspeth Gray's daughter?' he asked suddenly, and when she nodded in astonishment, he added, 'You're very like her. The spit and image of her when she was younger.'

'It was my mother I wanted to ask about. Did she, by any chance, come to see you about three years ago?'

'She did, and it was your name being Fullerton that first put me on to you, then the resemblance . . . but that's not what you wanted to know. She came to ask about the money that had been held in trust for her since her mother died.'

'So I was led to believe. Was there enough to . . . ?'

'There was over two thousand pounds, but she just took one hundred with her.'

At a normal time, Laura would have been more impressed by the total amount, but she was intent on her quest. 'Do you know where she was going when she left here?'

'I didn't know at the time, but I received a letter from her a few weeks later asking me to transfer the balance to a bank in Edinburgh.'

'Have you still got that letter, please? I need to know her address – it's a matter of . . . life and death.'

The old man heaved himself up and walked round his desk, cluttered with overflowing wire trays, and crossed to the tall metal filing cabinet. Sliding out the second drawer, he fingered through it then extracted one folder and leafed over the papers inside. In a minute, he looked up in triumph. 'Yes, here it is. I'm afraid it's the address of the shop she was in the process of buying at the time, at twenty-nine Leston Road, but no doubt that will suffice.'

Laura's brain could scarcely digest this latest piece of information. The money must have gone to her mother's head. What could have possessed her to buy a shop, and what kind of shop could she possibly run?

Mr Reid handed her the letter. 'There's a pad and pencil beside the phone there, if you want to make a note of it.'

'Yes . . . thank you.' Hastily scribbling down the address, she tore off the sheet of paper and placed it in her pocket. 'Can you tell me when I'll get a train to Aberdeen?' Her spirits were so high that, if she'd had wings, she would have flown all the way to Edinburgh.

Miraculously producing a dog-eared timetable from the confusion of other items on his desk, the solicitor pored over it for a moment, then grunted and glanced at the clock on the wall. 'You'd come on the ten eight, and there's not another one until after two, but I know there's a bus at five past eleven, and you'll catch that easily. The stop's along the High Street, to the right as you go out.'

Laura jumped to her feet. 'Thank you very much, Mr Reid.'

He smiled indulgently. 'I hope you find your mother.'

'So do I.'

As she walked along the uneven pavement, Laura's thoughts jumped ahead to Edinburgh, where she had gone through such a harrowing experience and had imagined her life to be finished. What a coincidence that she was returning to it, full of hope, to find her mother. Coming to a side road, she looked up idly at the signpost. 'BLAIRTON 2, MOSSMOUNT 5', it said. Blairton? That name rang a bell . . . yes, of course. It was the name of the farm her mother had said belonged to her lover's parents.

Laura had almost forgotten that this was the village in which her mother had grown up, and took more interest in it now. The street had a charming higgledy-piggledy appeal to it, a mixture of low cottages and larger houses, some having gardens and some where the pavement went right up to the windows, which were discreetly screened by snow-white lace.

She looked inside as she passed a grocer's shop, and saw an elderly man, the proprietor presumably, in shirt sleeves and a long white apron, cheerfully serving his customers. Farther along, an empty shop had a placard in the window, 'CLEARANCE SALE. OWNER RETIRING.' Wondering idly what kind of business had been carried on there, she glanced up at the sign above the door. 'G. Fraser. Dressmaker.' So this was where her mother had once worked. How long had it been closed? Seeing a yellowing card lying on the inside window sill, Laura twisted her head to read it. 'Final Day of Sale Saturday 21st'. Very informative, she thought, in some amusement. Twenty-first of which month? Which year?

When she reached the bus stop, she consulted her watch, found that she had ten minutes to wait and a little jingle came into her head. 'Ten minutes to wait, so mine's a Minor', the slogan used on the posters advertising De Reske Minors, which showed a healthy, smiling girl holding a cigarette with the smoke spiralling up. Well, smoking was one vice she didn't have. She did enjoy a little drink occasionally, but never more than that.

It wouldn't bother her if all the pubs and hotels were to close their doors tomorrow. Ah, but wait! Hotels were used for other purposes besides drinking. She had hit on her one vice – sex. She could easily become addicted to sex – quite easily. Oh, Fridjof, min kjaereste.

'It's a fine day now.'

Not having realized that anyone was near, she looked up in surprise at two young mothers who were passing with their prams. 'Yes, it is,' she replied, noticing for the first time that the clouds had disappeared and that the sun was shining. Taking a glance inside the prams, she wondered what her babies would look like when they made their appearance. With her auburn colouring and Fridjof's blondeness, they certainly wouldn't be dark, but blonde or auburn, she wouldn't give a damn as long as they were healthy.

'The bus shouldna be long.' A man was standing beside her.

'Good.' Laura hoped that she wouldn't have to wait long for a train when she reached Aberdeen. All this waiting about was putting years on her.

After hurrying all the way from the bus terminus to the Joint Station, she asked a porter when the next London train would be leaving, and had to sprint to catch it, the guard holding a door open for her.

'That was close.' The soldier who had risen to help her in made sure that the carriage door was closed properly before he sat down himself.

'I'll say,' she puffed. 'Too close for comfort.'

She sank back and took a few deep breaths, then shut her eyes. Was this to be the last lap of her search, or would it bring disillusionment and despair? No, no. If her mother had bought a shop, she must have intended to stay in

Edinburgh for some time, so she was bound to be there still.

Laura's body grew stiff with sitting in the same position pretending to be asleep so that no one would talk to her, and her one-track brain was repeating over and over to the train's rhythm, 'twenty-nine-Leston-Road, twenty-nine-Leston-Road, twenty-nine-Leston Road'. The journey seemed never-ending.

When, at long last, she reached her destination, she went to the newspaper stall to ask how to get to Leston Road and as she walked along Princes Street, she remembered once thinking that the towering Castle to her left, on a pedestal of volcanic rock, made a magnificent backdrop to the lovely gardens running alongside the railway line at a lower level than the street, in the same mould as the Union Terrace Gardens in Aberdeen, but much larger and more impressive. Passing the Scott Monument, she recalled climbing all two hundred and eighty-seven steps to the top with some other WAAFs, and how tired they had been when they reached the ground again. But finding her mother, her reason for being here now, was far more important than the Castle, the Gardens, the Scott Monument and even the large shops to her right, which she had browsed through when she was stationed at Turnhouse.

At the end of the famous street she turned left, coming eventually to Leston Road and finding that number twenty-nine wasn't far up, but her hopes faded when she saw the closed shutters. A sign above the window, 'E. Fullerton, Dressmaker', showed that it was definitely her mother's. Of course, what else would it be but a dressmaker's shop? A card on the door announced, 'Hours 9 to 6. Saturdays 9 to 1', and although she knew that it was long past one, Laura looked at her watch – five to four. Her frustration almost made her weep – to be so close, yet no nearer her goal. She would have to make the journey again another day. Turning to walk back down the hill, she kicked viciously at a small stone, her eyes following it until it ricocheted against a wall.

Noticing a chip shop, she was assailed by a sudden pang of hunger and made to go in, but this door was also locked. She had taken a few more steps before it struck her that the owner, or one of the assistants, might know where her mother lived. She turned back to see if the opening hours were displayed, and her heart lifted when she saw the scribbled chalking on the window, 'Frying tonight – 4.30 to 11'. Only just over half an hour to go, less probably, because the fish and chips would have to be cooked before they opened for business. It had been like a slap in the face when she found her mother's shop closed, and she hadn't been able to think, but somebody here would be able to tell her what she was so desperate to know.

All the travelling she had done, and the see-sawing her spirits had suffered, caught up on Laura then, and she leaned wearily against the door to wait. There was no one in sight except two small girls sitting on a doorstep on the opposite pavement swapping paper scraps, and a scruffy mongrel sniffing in the gutter. After a moment, the dog went over to the girls, obviously hoping for a tidbit, but given nothing he moved to a drainpipe and lifted his leg. The children sniggered and Laura gave a little smile as she shifted her feet to ease them.

At that moment, a very fat old lady waddled out of a door farther up, so Laura hurried to meet her. 'Excuse me, can you tell me where Mrs Fullerton, the dressmaker, lives? I have to find her and her shop's shut.'

The woman studied her doubtfully, then, probably deciding that Laura was not a German spy in disguise, she said, 'Just a few doors up. I'm no' sure of the number, I think it's maybe fifty-nine, but it's the only one with a green door.'

'Oh, thank you. Thank you very much.'

Walking quickly towards number fifty-nine, or the green door whichever number it was, Laura passed more shops, all open. Why hadn't she thought of that? Still, it didn't matter now. Here was the green door – it was number fifty-nine – but her mother's name did not appear on any of the nameplates. By good luck, as she stood wondering what to do, the door opened and a young woman came out holding a small boy by the hand. 'Excuse me,' Laura said hopefully, 'does a Mrs Fullerton live here?'

'Second floor, right.'

Her blood coursing wildly through her veins, her weariness evaporating like a puff of smoke, Laura raced up the stairs, praying that her mother would be at home.

Chapter Thirty-three

When Meg went out, Elspeth cleared up the dinner things then settled down in her armchair, glad of some peace and quiet. She'd had a very busy morning – her feet were hot, her head ached, her body felt as if it didn't belong to her. She sympathized with her customers that they couldn't buy new clothes with coupons so limited, but some of them expected miracles of her. It was impossible to let a bust thirty-six out to fit a forty, even a thirty-eight, or to add four inches round the hips, no matter how she tried.

Sighing, she picked up her latest *People's Friend,* but the fortunes of the heroines grew less and less interesting to her, and she came to the conclusion that she was more tired than she had thought. Laying the magazine down on the floor, she pulled the pouffe towards her with her feet and lay back, closing her eyes to ease the strain of sewing so much. Not that she should complain about that – if she had no sewing to do, she would go bankrupt. As it was, her trade was flourishing, and David would be astonished if he knew how good a businesswoman she had turned out to be.

David. Why couldn't she just forget him? It would make her nights much easier, for she often lay awake thinking about him and wondering what he had been doing during the day. She loved him as much as ever . . . more than ever. How was he coping, having to look after himself? Of course, Laura would be going home on her times off duty – she had no quarrel with her father – and she would make sure he was eating properly.

Elspeth had hoped, when she first came to Edinburgh, that she might run into her daughter some day, but it was such a big city, and Turnhouse was so far out, that there was little likelihood of their ever meeting by chance. She had no worries about Laura, in any case. The girl's head was screwed on firmly, and once she recovered from the initial shock she would have bounced back from the despair and anger that had consumed her that fateful evening.

If only she knew how they were. She longed to see them again, and hear their dear voices, even if it was only Laura's reprimanding 'Mum'. She could almost hear it now.

'Mum, it's Laura!' She knew she was imagining it, but it was so real. 'Wake up, Mum!' The hand shaking her shoulder made her struggle to open her eyes, but they were still glazed with sleep as she looked up at the WAAF with auburn curls framing an anxious face. 'Laura? I'm not dreaming?'

'It's really me. Oh, Mum!' Laura sank to her knees and flung her arms round her mother's legs, sobbing with happiness, and Elspeth, also weeping, touched her daughter's forehead as if to make certain that she was actually flesh and bone.

After a while, Laura looked up and said, shakily, 'I rang the bell, then I tried the door and it wasn't locked, so . . . oh, I'm glad I found you. How are you, Mum?'

Elspeth swung her feet to the floor. 'I'm fine. I'm so happy, I don't know if I'm on my head or my heels.'

'You're on your bottom.'

Laughter verging on the hysterical, they clung to each other, cheeks together, tears mingling, until Laura sobered and sat down on the pouffe. 'I want you to know how sorry I am for the horrible things I said to you that night, and I'm ashamed it's taken me so long to . . .'

'Don't say anything else, I'm just glad you're here. I can still hardly believe it.'

'But I have to explain, Mum. I was angry at you for three years, and it took Margaret Watson to sort me out.'

'Donald's wife? But how did . . . ?'

'It's a long story. On my last leave . . .' She went over it meticulously, leaving nothing out, '. . . and the night Fridjof and I discovered we loved each other, we slept together.' She glanced up, expecting to see a frown of disapproval, but Elspeth was smiling sadly. 'I'm not angry or shocked. What right have I to sit in judgement on you after what I did?'

'When you're young and in love, it just happens, doesn't it?' Laura carried on to tell how she had come to visit the Watsons in Hull.

'They'd been surprised to see you.'

'They were, but Margaret made me understand about a lot of things, especially how unfair I'd been to you, and I wrote to Dad when I went back, asking if I could go to see him.'

'Had you never been home before that?'

'No, I hadn't. He told me he was going to walk out too, you see, and I didn't know he'd . . . I didn't know he was on his own till Margaret told me.'

'How is your father?'

'He's quite well, and dying to see you again.'

'After what he said, I didn't think he'd ever want to see me again.'

'Dad and I both said things we didn't mean. I'll take you to him tonight, and everything'll be all right again.'

Elspeth's joy faded after a few seconds. It was all too incredible to take in and she needed time. She couldn't make up her mind about this at the drop of a hat. She wanted to see David again – she was desperate to see him again – but how could they live together as they'd done before when the repugnant memory of their quarrel would always be between them? 'I can't leave Meg.' It was the only thing she could think of to give her breathing space.

'Who's Meg?'

'John Forrest's mother. She took me in after . . .'

'Oh, Mum!' Laura looked accusing. 'You didn't go to her? Couldn't you have got help from somebody else?'

'I didn't go to her for help.' Elspeth was saddened by her daughter's impetuous reproof. 'I thought she should know about . . . her grandson.' Her eyes pleaded with her daughter for understanding.

Laura's face became thoughtful. 'What did you mean to do after that? Where had you planned to go?'

'I hadn't planned anything. I was living from minute to minute, and praying I'd find a way out of the mess . . . wishing I was dead, sometimes.'

'I can understand that – I was the same myself.'

Elspeth nodded. 'Anyway, Meg took it out of my hands. Her man had died a few days before, and she was going to sell up Blairton and come to Edinburgh. She asked me to go with her, and I'd nowhere else to go, so I said I would.'

413

'But she won't expect you to stay here now?'

'There's the shop to consider, as well.'

'Give it up.' Laura felt quite irritated. 'Good God, I thought Dad would have been more important to you.'

'He is, but . . .' Elspeth knew that the problem didn't really lie with the shop, nor with Meg, though she didn't relish the idea of leaving her. 'I've got to have time.'

Her face showing deep disappointment, Laura said, 'Well, that's that, I suppose, and I'll have to go soon, because Dad's expecting me back tonight. What'll I tell him?'

'Just tell him I have to think things over. You'll surely have time for a cup of tea?'

'Yes, please, and maybe a sandwich? I've had nothing to eat since I left Porthills early this morning.'

Grilling the bacon ration meant for Sunday's breakfast, and spreading margarine on four slices of bread, Elspeth listened while Laura told her more about her Norwegian. 'He asked me to marry him, and we'll be arranging the wedding when he comes to Aberdeen in January,' the girl said, as her mother handed her the plate of sandwiches. 'I hope you're happy for me, Mum?'

'Of course I'm happy for you.' Elspeth didn't know how she felt about having a foreigner as a son-in-law, but she was very pleased that her daughter had got over her love for John Watson. 'Will Fridjof look for a job in Aberdeen after the war?'

'Oh no, I'll be going to Norway with him.' She explained about his father's sawmill, then added something which she hadn't said to her friends, nor to her father. 'Of course, he doesn't know if his father's still alive, or if the sawmill's been burned down by the Nazis, but he wants to go home, and I'd go to the ends of the earth with him, I love him so much.'

'Yes,' Elspeth smiled, 'I can see you've got it bad . . . no, I didn't mean to laugh about it. I can see how deeply you love him, and I hope you'll always be happy.'

'Oh, I will,' Laura breathed. 'I just know I will.'

Elspeth would have liked to find out how her son was, but couldn't bring herself to ask, in case it upset the girl. 'I wish you could have met Meg, she's been a really good friend to me.'

'I could invite her to the wedding,' Laura offered.

'Oh, she'd like that.'

When the plate was empty, Laura stood up. 'Thanks for the sandwiches, Mum, but I'll have to run now. I'm very disappointed that you won't come with me, but just remember what I've told you. Dad loves you and wants you back, so please, please, don't hurt him any more.'

After seeing her daughter out, Elspeth sat down to think, but Meg came in about five minutes later and had to be told about Laura's visit.

'And you didna go back wi' her?' Meg exclaimed in great amazement. 'I thought you loved David.'

'I do love him,' Elspeth protested, 'but . . .'

'You surely can't love him enough when you're digging your heels in like this.'

'I'm not being awkward, I said I needed time.'

'Well, the poor man'll think you're not wanting to . . . are you trying to punish him for what he did to you?'

'No,' Elspeth said, indignantly. 'I just feel . . .'

The argument went on all evening, Meg tutting and shaking her head in displeasure as she went to her own

415

room, unable to fathom her friend's reasoning, and Elspeth going to bed resentful that neither Laura nor Meg could see the position she was in. She didn't want to crawl back to David like a dog that had misbehaved. She had misbehaved, worse than that, she had sinned, but he should never have put her out. He hadn't let her explain about the pressures she had been under right from the night she had met John Forrest in the snowstorm. She had been forced to leave Auchlonie, Janet had thrown her out for sticking up for herself, Helen had taken possession of her son, David hadn't written for so long that she'd thought he'd been killed, and after he had come back, she had been terrified that he wouldn't marry her if he knew about her child. Even after they married, she'd always been on tenterhooks in case he found out . . . and then there had been his constant harping on about the grandfather clock. Oh, she should have asked Laura if it was still there. If it was, it would mean that David had got over his jealousy, and maybe things would work out, after all.

But he should have come to her himself, not sent Laura. How could she be sure that he had truly forgiven her? If she could have seen his eyes, she'd have known straight away . . . oh, David! Was she subconsciously trying to punish him? Was she cutting off her nose to spite her face, as Helen would likely say. Why couldn't she just go home and forget the past? It was only pride that kept her here, but where would she be if she let go of her self-respect?

Elspeth had hardly slept at all, and one look at her haggard face was enough for Meg. 'I think I'll go to the kirk this morning, and I'll maybe go in and see Phemmy for a while when I come back.'

Relieved that the old lady was taking herself out of the way, Elspeth said, 'When do you want the dinner ready?'

'Oh . . . about half past one.'

The church service due to begin at eleven, Meg left the house at twenty to, and Elspeth decided to have a seat for an hour. That would leave her plenty of time to prepare the vegetables and cook the small piece of mutton, not that she felt like eating, but Meg would.

Only half an hour later, the doorbell rang, and Elspeth hoisted herself wearily out of her chair to answer it, thinking that it was young Mrs McRae from across the landing wanting to borrow something, but when she saw the caller, her legs almost gave way. 'Oh, my God, it's John!'

Grinning from ear to ear, the young man brought forward a dark-haired girl. 'And this is my wife, Agnes.'

'I'm pleased to meet you,' Elspeth gasped, automatically shaking the hand held out to her.

'May we come in?' John asked.

'Oh . . . yes, I should have said, but I got such a shock.'

In the kitchen, John said, very deliberately, 'Agnes, I've told you about Elspeth. She's my real mother.'

This proved too much for Elspeth. Her legs buckling under her, she thumped heavily down on a chair, tears trickling down her cheeks. 'I never thought I'd ever hear you saying that.' Struggling to gain control of herself, she murmured, 'How did you know where I was?'

'You look as if you need a cup of tea, but Agnes can make it.' When his wife went to the sink to fill the kettle, he leaned towards Elspeth and whispered, 'She's a wonderful girl, I'm a lucky man.'

Still too overcome at being openly acknowledged as his mother, she nodded, and he went on, 'If you tell her where the tea and everything is . . . ?'

'They're in the press,' she mumbled, and nothing more was said until they each had a cup in their hands.

John took one sip, then started his explanations. 'I bought an old Austin last week, and I splurged all my petrol ration on going to see Mum and Dad . . .' He stopped, looking at Elspeth uncertainly.

'Yes, they are your Mum and Dad,' she assured him.

'We went to see them yesterday – I'm stationed at Leuchars, and we rented a house there, so it's not too far from Aberdeen. Anyway, when Mum knew I was off duty till Monday night, she asked us to stay the weekend, and we were all sitting talking late on – it must have been eleven or after – when Laura came to tell Mum she'd traced you here. She'd come straight from the train because she was worried about what David would say when she told him you wouldn't go back with her. Mum told me to drive her home and to go in with her for support.'

Elspeth's anxious glance at her made Agnes say, 'John told me all about Laura before he married me. He said he didn't want any secrets between us.'

Giving a self-conscious smile, John carried on. 'Laura and I did feel a bit strange at seeing each other again, but it didn't take long for the awkwardness to wear off and we were just old friends again. Well, as you can imagine, my turning up came as a surprise to David, but he said he was glad he knew I was your son. When Laura told him she'd traced you, he was absolutely delighted, but he was pretty cut up when she told him what you'd said. He just sat there, wringing his hands and wishing that he'd come to see you himself.'

Elspeth sat up with a sigh. 'That's what I wished too. I was sure it was just Laura that had forgiven me, not David.'

'David has forgiven you. He even showed me the initials on the grandfather clock. I was very touched, seeing it was my father who had got them engraved for you.'

'So he didn't sell it,' Elspeth murmured. 'I thought he would as soon as he got the chance.'

'Oh, I don't think he would ever think of selling it,' John said, looking quite puzzled. 'He told me . . .'

'I think we should go now, John,' Agnes interrupted.

'Oh, will you not wait and see Meg? She's at the kirk just now, and she said she was going to see her friend downstairs when she came back, but I could go and tell her you're here. She'd like to meet you, John . . . she's your grandmother.'

'I'll come back to see her, but . . . we've something else to do right now.'

They all stood up then, and John kissed Elspeth's cheek before going to the door. 'I'm glad I know the truth,' he whispered.

She had just been sitting down again for a minute or two, her heart full because John had called her his real mother, when she heard more footsteps on the stairs. Meg hadn't gone to Phemmy's after all, she thought, but what a pity she hadn't come home before John left. The ring of the bell made her jump up quickly. He must have changed his mind and was going to wait after all.

When she opened the door, she had hardly time to take in that it wasn't John before she was enveloped in a strong pair of arms. 'Oh, Elspeth, my dear, dear Elspeth.'

'David!' she gasped, sure that her brain was turned with all that had happened.

'I had to come,' he said simply.

'We'd better go inside.' Drawing away from him in some embarrassment, she led him into the kitchen. 'It's funny, John Watson's just this minute gone.'

'I know. I asked him last night if he'd take me to see you this morning. We set off very early, but he thought it would be a good idea if he came up to speak to you first. I've been sitting in his car waiting to see you, biting my nails with impatience.' With something like a sob, he took her in his arms again. 'Why won't you come back to me, Elspeth?'

His eyes had told her all that she needed to know, and she let her pride go without a thought, nestling against him as he kissed her, over and over again, as he hadn't done for many years. Unfortunately, something else came into her mind, something that she had never told a living soul, but, if her life with David was to be free of secrets, she must tell him now. Pushing him away, she muttered, 'Sit down, we have to talk.'

'What is there to say? I want you back, and . . . oh, Elspeth, you will come home now, won't you?'

'I must tell you something first, and you'll maybe not want me back after that. It wasn't . . . just once with John Forrest . . . I spent a whole day with him when his mother and father were away in Aberdeen.' She watched his face, but there seemed to be no shock or disgust. 'We were alone for hours,' she went on, to make quite sure that he knew what she meant, 'so it was a lot more than once.'

There was no hesitation. 'Once, twice, a hundred times, I don't care. It was so long ago, and you were just a young girl. I've got every particle of my jealousy out of me, and we'll never speak about it again. It's forgiven, forgotten.'

There was still something on her mind, however. 'What about your nightmares? That was when you always . . .'

'I haven't had a nightmare since you left. It was you I dreamt about, you I thought about all the time. I know I made you leave, but when I went home to the empty house that night, I regretted losing my temper.' He paused for a moment. 'I'll be quite honest, though. For the first few weeks, the black days, I loved you one minute and was angry at you the next . . . I was very bitter. Then, gradually, I began to see things in perspective. I was so cruel to you, Elspeth, and it's you who'll have to forgive me.'

'You'd every right to be angry and bitter, I don't hold that against you, but I can't leave Edinburgh till I've sold the shop and . . . there's Meg, too.'

'Laura told me how good she had been to you.'

'I can't go off and leave her just like that. She's going blind, and she'll soon not be able to manage by herself.'

'We could take her to live with us. We'd have room.'

'But she's John Forrest's mother, remember?'

'That wouldn't bother me.'

Elspeth sighed. 'You think that now, but having her there all the time, and the clock . . .'

'Maybe you won't believe this, Elspeth, but I love the clock now. It's like a friend waiting to greet me when I come home at nights. I polish it every week, and John

421

Forrest's initials made me realize that he was only another man who had loved you as much as I love you. I'm changed, my dear, and having his mother there wouldn't make a whit of difference to me.'

At that moment, Meg herself came bustling in. 'There's a young couple sitting outside in a car. . . I wonder what they're up to? . . . I didna bide long wi' Phemmy, for . . .' Coming to an abrupt halt, she peered at David. 'I'm sorry, Elspeth, I didna realize you'd a visitor.'

'Meet David, Meg.'

The old lady's face broke into a smile. 'So everything's all right now, I suppose?'

Elspeth turned to David again. 'Is it John and his wife in the car?' When he nodded, she said, 'Go down and bring them up.'

As soon as he went out, Meg said, 'I didna bide wi' Phemmy because . . . I was telling her about you and David, and she wondered if it was me that was keeping you here.'

'It wasn't you, though I didn't really like the idea of leaving you on your own.'

'But I'll not be on my own,' Meg said, looking a little smug. 'Phemmy said I should sell up and move in wi' her.'

'Would you not mind selling the house?'

'Not a bit, and Phemmy and me have always got on well. When I go to see Mr Lindsay, I could tell him to sell your shop, and all.'

'I believe Jane Farquharson might buy it. She used to be a tailoress at one time, and she's often helped me out if I was busy. She did once say she envied me the shop, so she'd likely jump at the chance . . .'

'Well then, that's everything arranged.'

Smiling, Elspeth said, 'Meg, do you not realize who it is that David'll be taking in?'

'Aye, the young couple in the . . . oh!' As comprehension dawned, the old lady's hand jumped to her heart. 'It's never . . . ? You said John, but it didna click.'

When the door opened again, Elspeth said, 'David, I think I know a buyer for the shop, but I'll have to go and ask her. Will you come with me?'

Leaving Meg alone with her grandson and his wife, they went to see Jane Farquharson, who did jump at the chance of buying the shop, and walking back, Elspeth said blissfully, 'That's it all settled now.'

David gripped her arm more tightly. 'What about Meg?'

'She's going to move in with Mrs Milne, down the stairs.'

'So you'll come home with me?'

'If there's room in John's car,' she joked.

'I would make sure there was room, supposing I'd to make Agnes get out and walk, but John hasn't enough petrol to make another journey to Aberdeen and back to Leuchars. We'll have to take a train. There's one just after six.'

'That's good. It'll give me time to pack.'

Meg was also glad that they were not to be leaving right away. 'You'll all have time for something to eat. There's not a lot of mutton, but the veggies will eke it out.'

Leaving Agnes to help the old lady to prepare the meal, and John and David to talk, Elspeth went through to her room, and as she folded her clothes and put them in her suitcase, her mind was on other things. She had no feelings for John Forrest now, just a sadness that he had died so

423

young. It was David who meant everything to her . . . had always meant everything to her, although she had once thought that her love for him was not deep enough. Their future would be much better than their past, for there were no secrets left to come out. It was strange, though, she reflected, how two grandfather clocks had figured so largely in her life. The one that she had grown up loving had made it possible for her to buy her shop – the shop that had kept her sane at a time she might have become deranged altogether – and its twin, apart from the different initials, had been the means of David finally coming to terms with her first love, despite his previous hatred of it.

Her father had often said, 'Time shall reap', meaning that people would be punished for the wicked things they did, and she had certainly been punished, over and over, for all the wicked things she had done when she was younger, but she had survived everything that God or the Devil had sent. The slate was wiped clean, and she could begin afresh. Giving a satisfied grunt, she laid the last item into her case and closed the lid, having to press her full weight on it before she could get the catch to engage.

At half past five, John offered to drive them to Waverley Station, and David, knowing that parting from Meg would be a wrench for his wife, said that they would wait in the car for her. She held out her hand to the old lady as soon as the others went out. 'This is goodbye, then, Meg, but I'll always be grateful for what you did for me.'

Sniffling, the old lady ignored the hand and hugged her old friend. 'And I'll always be grateful to you for giving me a grandson. They said they'd come and see me sometimes, for Leuchars is just up the road a bit . . . oh, Elspeth, I can see my John in him.' She stopped with a sob, then said, 'I'm going to miss you.'

'I'm going to miss you, and all.' Elspeth could feel the tears welling up as they clung to each other. 'I'll write to you, and I'll come back some time wi' David, to see how you're getting on wi' Phemmy.'

'I'll be pleased to see you any time. You'd better hurry though, and not keep the folk waiting. God bless you, lass.'

'God bless you, Meg.' Kissing the wrinkled cheek, Elspeth hurried out, but as she went downstairs she shed her sadness like a snake sloughs its skin. What had she to be sad about, after all? She was going to be with her husband again, Meg would be in good hands and Phemmy wouldn't let her mope, Laura would be married soon, and although her mother would rather it was to a Scotsman – even an Englishman or a Welshman – the Norwegian was the girl's choice, and no one could interfere.

John was waiting at the outside door to put her case in the boot of his car, and in another seven minutes he was pulling up at the station. 'It won't be long till we see you again,' he remarked cheerfully, 'as soon as I get my next month's ration of petrol.'

David gripped his hand for a moment. 'Thanks for taking me to Edinburgh. It meant an awful lot to me, for I don't know if I'd have had the courage to come on my own.' Picking up the case, he made to walk away, but Elspeth slipped her arm through his as the car moved off.

'I've been thinking,' she murmured. 'Would you mind if I gave the grandfather clock to John?'

He seemed surprised. 'I don't mind, if that's what you want to do, but I can assure you I'm not jeal . . .'

'I know, but I still think it would be best. It would be something of his father's for him to keep . . . to let him see that . . .' She broke off, looking at him apprehensively, then went on with what she had been about to say, '. . . to let him see that he was conceived in love, not lust.'

He squeezed her hand. 'I do understand that, and I'd think he'd be proud to have it, as long as you're sure?'

'I never really wanted it . . . it was Meg who made me take it, if you remember? All I want now is to be with you, and there'll just be the two of us when Laura goes to Norway. Maybe we could go to see her sometimes, though? Once the sale of the shop's all settled, we'll have plenty money. Oh, David, I can hardly believe I'm really going home again.'

Laying down the suitcase, he took her in his arms, kissing her as he had done on their wedding night, as a lover would kiss, and when he let her go, a cheer went up from several groups of servicemen and women standing nearby. 'Oh, David,' she gasped, flushing with embarrassment. 'What must they think of us? We're too old to be kissing like that.'

'We'll never be too old for that,' he smiled, kissing her again to the accompaniment of wild applause and shouts of 'Encore! Encore!'